The right of Gloria Sync to be identified as the author of this work has been asserted by her in accordance with the Copyright, Designs and Patents act of 1988.

This book is in copyright. Subject to statutory exception no part may be reproduced without written permission from the publisher.

This edition 2024

This book is a work of fiction. Any reference to historical events, real people or real places are used fictitiously. Any resemblance to actual persons, living or dead, is co-incidental.

Published by Dirty Sexy Words 2024.

Cover art by Arrival of Birds.

Graphic design by Gloria Sync.

SOUNDTRACK

Full playlists of the soundtrack to *Swinella* can be found by following the links to Spotify and YouTube at: www.hamdentown.com

Bauhaus- *Bela Lugosi's Dead.*
The Cure- *One Hundred Years.*
The Clash- *London Calling.*
Diamanda Galas- *The Litanies of Satan.*
The Jam- *Going Underground.*
UB40- *One In Ten.*
Echo and The Bunnymen- *The Cutter.*
Hawkwind- *Born To Go.*
Mat Mathews- *As Time Goes By.*
Soft Cell- *Memorabilia.*
Nina Hagen- *Cosma Shiva Legendada.*
Suicide- *Ghost Rider.*
Donna Summer- *I Feel Love.*
Patti Smith- *Gloria.*
Patti Smith- *Kimberly.*
Swans- *Power For Power.*
Danielle Dax- *Bed Caves.*
Stray Cats- *Rock This Town.*
The Ruts- *In A Rut.*
Siouxie and The Banshees- *Cascade.*

Siouxie and The Banshees- *Melt*.

Sham 69- *Angels With Dirty Faces*.

Susan Cadogan- *Hurt So Good*.

Bauhaus- *Stigmata Martyr*.

Blondie- *The Tide is High*.*

Bad Manners- *Special Brew*.*

Dennis Waterman- *I Could Be So Good For You*.*

Diana Ross- *I'm Coming Out*.*

The Sisters of Mercy- *Temple of Love*.

Siouxie and The Banshees- *Dear Prudence*.

Southern Death Cult- *Moya*.

Specimen- *Kiss Kiss Bang Bang*.

Joy Division- *Shadowplay*.

Symarip- *Skinhead Girl*.

The Specials- *Gangsters*.

The Bodysnatchers- *Do The Rocksteady*.

Sonic Youth- *I Dreamed I Dream*.

Shirley Bassey- *Diamonds Are Forever*.

Specimen- *Hex*.

The Cure-*A Forest*.

*These are the first four tracks on the 1983 'Top of The Pops' album.

Please do not read this book if you are easily offended by extremely graphic depictions of sodomy and the free exchange of bodily fluids.

Don't say we didn't warn you.

Seriously.

SWINELLA

A HAMDEN TOWN TALE

By

Gloria Sync

PROLOGUE

I am reclining on a vintage gynaecological examination chair. My tail is squished beneath my bum and my ankles are raised and firmly strapped onto two padded footrests; my feet are held high and my legs wide apart. My wrists are bound to the arms of the chair with padded leather restraints. I am naked, of course. The room is dim and a mix tape that I made, featuring Bauhaus, Siouxie and The Banshees, Television and The Velvet Underground, plays tinny and distant on a beat-up ghetto blaster in the corner of the dusty, sepia-toned cellar, deep beneath Hamden Town.

The room itself is spartan, exposed brickwork and concrete floor. There is a beaten-up brown leather Chesterfield pushed up against one of the walls. An old table stands in the corner, stacked with the equipment Dave the photographer will need for the shoot. I look at my feet and wiggle my toes. I am wearing some new electric blue nail varnish that I bought from Boots on the high street this afternoon. It looks good. Somewhere nearby a train rumbles past, but I cannot tell if it is down below in the tube line beneath us, or up above on the railway bridge that runs east to west above the dark and labyrinthine market. The dim, bare lightbulb overhead flickers and shivers slightly as the train grumbles past on its journey to who knows where. The air is damp and a bit chilly, but not too cold.

I try to relax, but I'm excited all the same. So many things are triggering my arousal: the two beautiful cats in their leather and heels, the presence of the photographer feeding into my exhibitionist tendencies, but most of all the anticipation of what is to come. I breathe deeply, in through my snout and out through my mouth, the way Lucretia showed me when she tried to teach me to meditate. I can smell the dry, earthy odour of old bricks and mortar and crumbling plaster. I smell the perfume of the cats, the bergamot and blackcurrant fragrance of Anais Anais perfume, the sweat of the photographer, the open tub of Trex vegetable fat on the table and, underscoring it all, the scent of my own arousal. I rock my hips from side to side in time to the music. Bela Lugosi is, indeed, dead.

"Shall we begin?" Felina purrs, not to me, but to the photographer rummaging through the box of equipment on the table in the corner.

"I'm ready when you are," he replies, straightening up, lifting the camera to his face and looking around the cellar through the viewfinder.

Felina takes a handful of Trex from the tub on the table nearby and smears it onto her right hand and forearm. She is wearing shiny black latex opera gloves that go almost all the way to her armpits. Her arms are slender and graceful, just like the rest of her lithe body. The camera clicks and flashes. Felina poses, looking into the lens as she slowly coats the black glove with greasy white fat. She opens her mouth in a kind of mock surprise, adopting a look of wide-eyed wonder, as if she can't believe what she is about to do, her drawn-on Marlene Dietrich eyebrows raised above her green cat's eyes in two perfectly symmetrical arches. She is overly dramatic, as always. She shakes out her black bobbed hair with a toss of her head, and opens her eyes wide to show off her vertical slit pupils. A lot of the blokes who buy the Danish magazine where the photos will eventually be published are going to have a cat fetish, so Felina knows to flaunt her cattishness to the max, snarling and showing off her delicately-pointed canine teeth. She looks killer in her black leather mini dress, fishnets and shit-kicking, twenty-hole, steel toe-capped boots. Her snakelike tail curls seductively around the top of her slender, leather-clad thigh.

I remind myself that a sizeable number of the men who buy the magazine will have pig fetishes. There will be anonymous blokes furiously wanking over my upturned snout and curly tail, and that's before I'm stretched out and gaping for the goddess.

The warm feeling of longing inside my pelvis grows in intensity. The idea of strange, distant men gazing at my image, at my naked body and wide-open arsehole, turns me on even more. My arse-cunt begins to shiver and twitch in anticipation.

Dave takes a few shots of the other cat, Gatita, presenting her massive strap-on, brown-skinned crimson clawed fingers wrapped around the base of the huge, veiny prosthetic cock. She snarls for the camera, bearing her pointed teeth. Her long red hair, amber cat's eyes, spike-heeled boots and eye-watering corset making her look every inch the sadistic cat-girl mistress that she is. She turns her bum towards the photographer so he can get a few shots of her tail, with its smooth red fur and serpentine grace.

And then it's my turn. I'm wearing far too much makeup. Too

much mascara clogging my long lashes, my lips slathered in the sluttiest red lipstick money can buy. I'm wearing naff blue eyeshadow like one of the women from Abba, and my cheeks have got so much blush on them I look like Aunt Sally from Worzel Gummidge.

I try my best to look terrified in an overblown, comic book way. I open my pale blue eyes wide and look to the side, emphasising the whites, making myself look panicky and trapped, as if I have been tied to a railway track by the wild-eyed and extravagantly-mustachioed villain in a black and white silent movie. I gently pull against my restraints and open my mouth into a red-lipped sex doll 'O'. I'm really enjoying myself. As Felina told me, when I started all this: 'if you're not having fun, you're doing it wrong'.

The photographer snaps me from every angle, and pays special attention to my small piggy tits, nipples hard and erect like chapel hatpegs. He takes some shots of my tiny, hairless cock and soft, empty scrotum, leaning in close and snapping away. I feel his breath, hot on my skin, as he takes the pictures, and I grow impatient; I want filling. Dave steps back and Felina moves to stand between my legs, making a fist with her shiny latex-gloved hand. She pouts and winks at the camera.

The camera clicks and the flash flashes. My pretty feet look good either side of Felina's beautiful cat face, with its pale, luminescent skin, her thin lips like a crimson knife wound. She reaches under my bum, takes my tail in her left hand and gives it a gentle tug, lifting my pelvis slightly from the leather seat, before reaching down and placing her oily fingertips onto my sensitive bumhole. I tremble with barely contained excitement and open my pigussy with that relaxed pushing motion that I know so well. She tickles my arsehole with the tips of her fingers and smiles a Cheshire-Cat grin.

But how did I get here? Just a small-town punk rock piglette, adrift in an uncaring world. How did I find myself in 'that London', strapped to a medical examination chair in a cellar in Hamden Town, about to be fisted and fucked by two of the most delectable creatures on the face of the earth? Well, I suppose I should go back to the beginning…

CHAPTER ONE

ROOTS

I had aways known, of course. We all do. I had felt it before I could define it and long before I could name it. I just didn't feel like anyone else, even though I obviously had no idea how anyone else felt. Early on it was just a kind of vague hunger, something I felt, but didn't understand, a longing to be validated in a very specific way. The attraction to girly things was part of it, I suppose, and I never really felt like a boy, but I didn't feel like a girl, either. I think 'girl-adjacent' would've been the best way I could've described myself, if I'd had the language to do so back then. I always felt like something between a girl and a boy. My body leant towards the masculine, of course, but my soul felt feminine. This feeling can make people like me extroverted and dramatic, or quiet and withdrawn. I was a solitary, introverted little boy and I fell squarely into the second category, but eventually I realised that one day the person I was would become clearly apparent, as clear as the nose on my face, as it were.

I found my outlet through punk rock, which all kicked off when I was around eleven or twelve years old. I was especially attracted to bands with female singers. Stylish and aloof punk girls who raged against the world and its varied injustices with passion and eloquence, albeit an eloquence that would escape the casual observer, which I suppose was the point and the appeal to an outsider like myself. I retreated into the world of punk rock soon after puberty, when my snout was starting to make its presence known and when my tail was just a nub at the base of my spine, nothing more than a fleshy fingertip. By the age of thirteen my nose had grown wider and had turned up at the tip, and everyone knew what I was. Along with the changes in my appearance I gained an incredibly sensitive and finely-tuned sense of smell. I could pick out one odour in a room full of different smells, which was amazing. I can still vaguely remember when I became aware of my new sense of smell, it was one of the most incredible things I've ever experienced, like the world had suddenly changed from black and white to technicolor.

My parents were kind of cool about it, but the other kids at school were sometimes mean. It would've been worse, but a pig-girl called Caroline, who was in the year above me, took me under her wing and was able to prevent most of the bullying. We hung out a lot and tried to figure out what it all meant.

"We are what we are," Caroline would say, fixing her peroxide hair and wiggling her upturned snout in the mirror. "And you know what? I'm into it. I'm glad I'm a pig. I want nothing more than to be a pig."

I knew exactly what she meant, but it was still difficult. Of course I WANTED to be a pig - that's what being a pig is all about- but we know that people will judge us and, for some reason, we believe that their judgement means something.

Living in my small town in the East Midlands, all I wanted to do was get away, to find the others.

I had been practicing on my own for a while, in the privacy of my bedroom, late at night, and I was enjoying it, but I wanted to make contact with someone who appreciated me, who appreciated my piggishness and my very specific piggy desires.

I attended a large comprehensive school of around a thousand pupils, and there were maybe fifty pigs, rabbits, goats, cats and dogs in attendance at any one time. Overall, we make up about five percent of the population, spread evenly across all races, religions, nationalities and ethnicities. Collectively we are known as 'bestiamorphs' which, in everyday speech, is often shortened to 'morphs.

We always refer to the animal versions of our types with the prefix 'four-legged', although non-'morphs, who we call apes, often don't do this. So I'll call an animal pig a 'four-legged pig' and call myself simply a 'pig'. I'll call a cat-girl a 'cat', and an animal cat a 'four-legged cat'.

You'd think it'd be fairly easy for apes to do the same, but a lot of them don't. I don't know why but, for some reason, they don't want to use the language that makes us happy and comfortable, even though it wouldn't cost them anything. I feel sorry for them, really. It just makes me think they must be pretty sad inside of themselves. When someone calls a four-legged pig a pig around me, I don't mention it. They know we don't like it, but at the end of the day, the fact they do it says nothing at all about us, but it says a lot about them. I don't make a fuss when I hear one of them do it; that'd just start a pointless fight. In a way I'm grateful for the heads up. I know who I am, regardless of the language that apes use around me.

Looking back, I guess the dogs, who are all boys, had it the worst at school, always being picked on, but maybe they liked it? I don't know. I'm not a dog, but I do know that dogs like being dominated, being told what to do, pushed around.

The goats, also all boys, were admired by the other lads, envied even. Goats are super well-endowed and have an insatiable sexual appetite, and I can see how that might've made them a threat to the rest of the boys, but all bestiamorphs are infertile, and I think that might have been a leveller. Goats might be sex gods, but they can never get a lass pregnant, so in some way, despite their obvious advantages, they could never be 'real men'.

Cat-girls were feared, and played up to that by acting arrogant and cold, although I suppose it wasn't really an act, it was who they were. No regular girl would ever pick a fight with a cat. The word in the playground was that they'd have your eyes out with those long claws of theirs before you even knew what had hit you. Cats are renowned for taking pleasure in sexual sadism, for enjoying the suffering of others. And of course, everybody secretly thought the cat-girls at school were cool as fuck. They were, after all, cats.

All the straight lads wanted to fuck a rabbit, and, of course, the rabbits wanted to fuck all the lads. The rabbit-girls were all put in the same class, regardless of their age. They were small classes with female teachers, and the rabbittes were always escorted to and from school by a parent or other responsible adult. They were essentially prisoners, never left alone once, around the age of eleven or twelve, their upper lips began to show signs of splitting into a philtrum, revealing the larger-than-average buck teeth that had been a clue to their true nature all along. Their eyes grew larger, they developed cute, pointed pixie ears, and their little furry bobtails announced themselves around the age of fourteen. Rabbits and goats produced a pheromone that made people want to fuck them and, while this was not considered a problem for the young goat, just something that girls were warned about, it was considered a problem for the rabbits.

I had been friends with a rabbit-girl called Gail since primary school and, after puberty had kicked in and revealed who we really were, we would talk for hours on the phone. Her mum and dad weren't short of money, and tolerated the exorbitant phone bills, no doubt seeing it as penance for their having spawned such a problematic child. There were locks on her bedroom window, and there was no way she could leave the house without alerting her parents. Chatting on the phone was the only way she could have a social life.

"They wanted to put me on the pill," she said with a tired sigh, one day when we would've been around sixteen. "When I started showing, the doctor gave them that NHS booklet on how to deal with a 'morph child. It explains in the first paragraph that we're sterile, for god's sake, that we can't get pregnant even if we wanted to. I don't think they even read it."

"They just want to do something, to feel in control of the situation, I suppose," I said.

"Have your parents done anything like that to you?" she asked.

"Like trying to put me on the pill? There's even less point in doing that to me than there is in doing it to you," I replied, laughing. "My parents did read the booklet, though, and I think they went to one of those support groups for 'morph parents once or twice."

"I don't mean have they put you on the pill," she said. "I mean, did they start treating you differently when they found out?"

"Well, not really. They look at my snout funny sometimes. I keep my tail under my clothes, even though that's not so comfortable. And, y'know, I have a drawer with Vaseline, johnnies and my rolling pin. I don't know if Mum has found it, or looked in it or whatever, but they've not mentioned it. I mean, what's the point, anyway? Taking away my stuff wouldn't change who I am."

"I'm fucking gagging, though. I'm literally wanking all the time, and it doesn't satisfy me at all." She declared. "I think it's easier for all the other 'morphs. None of the rest of you are prisoners."

It annoyed me that Gail thought it was easier for a piglette than for a rabbitte, but I held my tongue. She might've been right, anyway. I wasn't locked up, but I wasn't as free as an ape. I was cautious about going out on my own. A lot of ignorant men think pigs are the same as rabbits, that we'll fuck anyone, but that's not the case. I wished I was more like Caroline. She was a big girl from a tough family, who took no shit from anyone and wore her piggishness as a badge of honour. I wasn't there yet.

"Well," I said, hoping to offer some kind of comfort for my sexually-frustrated rodent friend. "It's nineteen eighty now, it's not like the old days, when they would've just killed us or cut off our tails... Or locked us in an attic and forgotten about us."

"I suppose so... What are you going to do after school?" Gail asked, changing the subject.

"I haven't given it much thought," I said, noticing that her breathing had grown heavier and faster. "Gail... Are you actually wanking now?"

"Yeah, sorry," she admitted, suddenly coy. "It was when you mentioned your rolling pin, I couldn't help myself. I started picturing what you get up to. Can we do the thing again?"

"OK." I sighed, closed my eyes, and responded in a deep voice. "You're a very pretty little rabbit, aren't you? I've got a little something for you..."

I really hadn't given much thought as to what I was going to do after school. I wasn't doing well in lessons. I just wasn't interested in what they were trying to teach me, and I couldn't respect the teachers. They'd been to university and ended up teaching in a giant, underfunded comprehensive school in a shit-hole town. In my eyes they were all failures: every art teacher was a failed artist, every science teacher was a failed scientist, every English teacher a failed writer. The only thing they could teach us was what not to do. If they told me to read something in English class, I'd go out of my way to read something else. I lost myself in the works of Stephen King, Angela Carter and Shirley Jackson, windows into worlds of fantasy and magic.

It seemed to me, from my bedroom in its row of identical red brick terrace houses, that the world was something that happened somewhere else. I felt that there was no one like me anywhere around where I lived, and not just because I was a pig - there were other pigs, of course, but I felt different, even from the other pigs. I felt like I'd been born in the wrong place. I'd read the music papers: the NME and Sounds and Melody Maker, and I knew that there was a place for me, somewhere out there, that there were people like me. I just had to find them, but I wouldn't find them in the place I was born. I'd listen to Siouxsie, Patti and Debbie, and knew that I wasn't alone, but I still had no clue as to what I was going to do with my life. I would have to make it my mission to find out.

I entered the fifth and final year of school as Caroline left. Suddenly I was the big pig, and I took on the role of mentor to a couple of pig girls in the years below me. We formed our own little piglette gang and we would walk to and from school together and hang out at break time. Sometimes ape-girls would try and pick on us, but we'd put on a united front, and any nearby cat-girls would back us up, so we were pretty safe. Caroline had taught me a very important lesson before she left school. They fear us, and that fear could protect us. Of course, their fear was also at the root of their hatred for us; I understood what the phobia part of the word 'bestiaphobia' meant.

"Never go to a chip shop at chucking out time on a Friday or Saturday night," Caroline had said to me once. "That's when they come for us, when they're pissed up and pissed off. Think ahead when choosing pubs and nightclubs. Get the bus into Nottingham and try going to gay bars or student pubs, they're a bit more tolerant there, it's not perfect, but it's less dangerous than townie pubs. Always be in a group, if you can, stuff like that. The bigger the group the better. If there's a dozen of you, then nobody will fuck with you. If you're getting a bus alone at night sit near the front on the right-hand side behind the driver and turn your head to the window. You don't want a bunch of bladdered lads to see your snout."

"But how do I use their fear to protect me?" I asked.

"You just have to be confident, walk with your chin up and your shoulders back, like you own the street. That's all, really. Never look like a victim and the world won't treat you like one. Smile and be pleasant, but not weak… That confuses them. Don't be all uppity or act shy, both of them attitudes make you more vulnerable, just be confident. Fake it till ya make it, girl.

Caroline was quite amazing, but she never left town. She got a job in some factory and married a local lad. He was a few years older, a mechanic or something, and Caroline was his second wife. He'd already had a couple of kids with his first missus, so it didn't bother him that Caroline couldn't have babies. That's often how it goes with us. Because we can't get pregnant, apes will often look for a bestiamorph partner after they've already had kids. Eventually Caroline and I lost touch, but I will always be grateful to her for looking after me in school.

After I moved to London, I always walked like I owned the street, the way Caroline had taught me. If I had to walk by a group of lads or lasses who I thought might give me grief I would tell myself that I was a hitman for the Russian mafia, I'd repeat it in my head as I walked past, with my snout in the air thinking 'Don't fuck with me, you don't know who I am, you don't know who I know'. Amazingly, nobody ever did fuck with me. The last thing you should do when walking down the street is try to be invisible. That makes you more noticeable and actually draws more attention. Don't hide, chin up, shoulders back, smile. That's the way, but choose solid ground to do this. Don't put yourself in the wrong place at the wrong time.

But I'm getting ahead of myself. Before my piggishness became apparent, I'd dressed like any other boy at school but, once my body started to change, I began feminising myself. Almost all pigs do. I knew that some pigs stayed boyish and presented as male, and I'd even seen the odd man pig out and about, but I'd never had a conversation with one.

The bottom line was that I felt that I had no choice but to express myself as a girl. At first, I just painted my nails and wore a little mascara. All pigs have long, lustrous eyelashes, which to this day I think of as one of my best features, so my mascara looked really good. I plucked my eyebrows into thin curves that made my eyes seem bigger. Thick, heavy eyebrows were the order of the day, but not for us punk girls. Pigs don't grow body hair at all, so at least I never had to think about shaving my legs or anything.

For regular ape-boys, the way I started to dress would've broken school uniform rules, but for bestiamorphs the rules were a bit looser. It was in the summer holidays between the third and fourth year, when I would've been thirteen, that I fully transformed my appearance. I left the third year a feminine boy, and returned a girl. I wore short skirts and black tights, I had a couple of large hoops in each ear, and I'd dyed my boring, mousy hair a washed-out, pinkish-red. I was average height for a boy, which made me tall for a girl, so I never had any desire to wear heels. I usually wore Doc Martens with white ankle socks, which looked really good with black tights. Mum was pretty cool with replacing my boy clothes with girl's. She wasn't stupid.

I continued to use the lads' toilets. I suppose I'd gotten used to it and did it out of habit, but the truth is it actually felt safer. Lads don't really care who uses their toilets, they're much more relaxed about it. Just look at urinals, for fuck's sake, they don't give a fuck. Boys will literally get their knobs out and piss standing between two strangers. I'd have been more worried walking into the girls' toilets alone and finding myself confronted by a couple of hard-faced older girls from some rough council estate.

My penis never grew after puberty, and by the time I was sixteen it looked very small indeed, about an inch and a half long and quite thin, but I was never going to use it and, in some way, I got off on having such a tiny, useless appendage. It wasn't the focus of my arousal anyway. My balls shrank away to nothing, and I don't ever remember having an erection. Again, it's not something that I think about.

The focus of my sexual arousal, of course, was my bumhole, my pigussy, my arse-cunt, my funcentre, my gash, my bacon sandwich, my hot pocket, my ham hole. This is what makes us pigs, not our snouts and curly tails, but our insatiable hunger for anal validation. From the first stirrings of my sexual awareness, all I wanted was to be penetrated, stretched, filled, fucked. It began with tentative fingers, but it soon escalated.

I think I should address the common misconception, often thrown as an insult, that pigs love shit. While I don't judge those that are, I'm not a fan of poo. Some pigs are, of course, but in my experience a scatological fixation does not seem limited to any specific type of person. Getting my funhole squeaky clean before having a rummage around my sensitive inner domain was a necessary skill that I had to acquire early on. Initially I would just go to the toilet and try to shit out everything I could, before setting about myself with gusto and aplomb. I'd use Vaseline as lube (how very primitive!), and utilise any household implement that seemed suited to the task of opening the gateway to my pleasure principle.

I remember being quite attached to the handle of a hairbrush for a while. It was made of smooth plastic and was tapered at the end, bulging out in the middle and narrowing where the bristles started. It really was buttplug-shaped, and it was the perfect tool for where I was at the time, although I soon outgrew it. It all seems very crude to me now, but you have to start somewhere.

Once the hairbrush became too small to satisfy me, I stole a large rolling pin from the home economics classroom at school.

It was about fifteen inches long and as thick as my wrist. It had rounded ends, no handles, and was perfect for fucking my arsehole. The wood was very smooth, but I liked to put a condom on it, to make it easier to insert and less likely to dry out.

There was this one pub near where I lived that had its toilets positioned by the main entrance, and you could get into them without having to go into the barroom itself. I'd sneak in through the door, head straight into the men's toilet (there weren't any condom vending machines in women's toilets, for some reason), put my fifty pence in the slot, and leave quick smart with three Durex Featherlite johnnies in my pocket. In and out in about two minutes. Once I got home and was safely ensconced in my room, post-bowel evacuation and clean-up, I'd slip the condom on one end of the rolling pin and tie it in a knot at the other end, and that worked just fine.

Eventually I figured out for myself that I needed some kind of douche, so I just got one of those pink rubber shower attachments from Wilko's, the ones that you fix to the taps for washing your hair in the sink. I took the sprinkler off the end and it rinsed out my pigussy pretty good. Later, as I got more into depth play, I discovered that I'd need a longer shower attachment.

CHAPTER TWO

VIRGIN ON THE RIDICULOUS

School had failed me. For a long time, I thought I had failed school, but as a fully-grown pig I now understand that the blame for a poor education can never fall on the child. The blame lies with their parents and the educational institution that they had attended. Working-class people also suffer from an ingrained culture of lowered expectations which, for some reason, nobody seems to ever talk about.

I left school at sixteen with no idea what I was going to do. I felt as if I was running towards nothing. My dad had already taken me to the job centre to look at the cards pinned to the boards along the walls, but I had no desire to work in a factory. It would've made sense for me to go to technical college and train to be a hairdresser or something, but I just wasn't feeling it.

I think, in some ways. I got an easier ride from my parents because they didn't know what to do with me. They focused on my younger brother, Jason. He was a regular boy, an ape, and he was doing well at school. He was good-looking and popular and loved football (ugh!). I think they viewed him as compensation for having brought me into the world, and they pretty much left me to my own devices.

Eventually I got a part-time job in a newsagents, through a friend of my mum's. It was easy work, and I actually quite enjoyed it. I had to tone down my appearance for work, but at least I had a bit of money and it got me out of the house. I'd spend my wages on records and clothes, of course, and I gave mum ten pounds a week for food and board. I would tie my faded pink hair into a ponytail, limit my makeup, and, underneath the green tabard that was my work uniform, I'd wear a plain black jumper, long black skirt and tights, and my old school shoes. I'd have looked almost respectable, were it not for the huge pig's snout in the centre of my face announcing to the world that, actually, I'd rather be someplace else getting fucked up the arse, thank you very much.

I ended up working there for nearly two years, which strikes me as mad when I look back, but it's easy to get stuck in a rut. I knew I had to get out of it, though.

After I turned eighteen, I decided that I simply had to get laid. Most of the people I'd been to school with were already fucking like rabbits, except for the rabbits, who were fucking like bonobos. I didn't want a relationship, I just wanted to pop my brown cherry. I'd had my eye on a boy back when we were in school. He was a bit of an arse, to be honest, and I thought he might be gay, but I decided he was the one, not THE ONE, you understand, just the one to go where no-one had gone before.

His name was Daniel, and he was one of those heavy metal, comic-reading, Dungeons-and-Dragons types, but I definitely preferred him to all the basic football lads in the local area. He was tall and not too bad-looking, with collar-length brown hair and grey eyes. He had failed at school, just like me, but was obviously not thick: just another small-town misfit.

The newsagent's I worked at in town stocked paperback books. One day, when I was working the till, Daniel came in and began looking through them. 'This is it', I thought, as he approached me with a book in his hand.

"Just this, ta," he said.

"Oh," I ventured. "I've seen that one. I thought about getting it myself."

"Did you?" he said, brightening, and looking down at the book. "It says on the back it's like *The Hobbit* meets *The Hitchhiker's Guide To The Galaxy*. Have you read them?"

"No... but I saw the *Hitchhiker's* TV show," I said, trying to seem interested.

"Yeah, it was all right... The radio play was better, though," he said.

"Maybe you could, y'know, lend me it... When you've done reading it?"

Daniel looked at me, looked at the book, looked out through the newsagent's window, and then looked back at me with a shy smile.

"I will, if you want, yeah," he said, becoming bashful. "I'm a pretty fast reader, I'll bring it in."

I never did read the book.

The door slammed behind my parents and we were alone. I had decided that that would be the night. Daniel had come around to listen to records, and we had retreated to my room soon after he had arrived. He smelled of Hai Karate aftershave, Pear's soap, Aquafresh toothpaste and piss. Most people smell of piss. It's no big deal, pigs and dogs get used to it, and we don't mind so much. I couldn't detect any shit on him, which meant he had showered since his last bowel movement. That's right, you all smell slightly of shit, as well, no matter how well you think you've wiped. If apes had as good a sense of smell as pigs and dogs, every bathroom would have a bidet fitted as standard.

We bestiamorphs don't actually talk about our enhanced senses very much with apes. We don't want to make them jealous. That'd just give them another reason to hate us. As I've said, both pigs and dogs have an amazing sense of smell; cats can see in the dark; rabbits have incredible hearing, and goats have a much wider field of vision thanks to those cool rectangular pupils of theirs.

My parents were surprisingly relaxed about my having a boy in my room. On the one hand, they knew that I couldn't get pregnant, and on the other, I genuinely believed that they didn't think a nice boy like Daniel would want to get involved with a pig like me. They probably thought he was gay as well.

I had showered and douched prior to Daniel's arrival. I have to admit, I was a bit nervous, but also quite excited.

"Y'know," Daniel said as we sat side by side on my single bed, while some atrocious heavy rock he had bought with him played in the background. "I can remember you at school."

"Oh yeah?" I answered, unsure of where this was going.

"Yeah. You knocked around with that other... That other...

Y'know?"

"You can say it. You can call me a pig, Dan," I said, taking his hand and smiling in what I hoped was a reassuring manner. "It's ok."

"Ok," he said. "That other... Pig. The older one, Caroline. She was the hardest girl in school."

"Yeah," I laughed. "She's well hard."

"I like your nose," he suddenly said, surprising me. "I think it looks wicked, like an orc, but a, y'know, a sexy orc... And not green."

I had no idea what an orc was, even less a sexy orc, but it was actually the first time in my life a boy had paid me a compliment, and I liked it.

"You think I'm sexy? Really?" I fished, batting my superb eyelashes.

"Yeah, I do," he said, leaning in for a kiss.

I leaned back out of his way, placing my hand delicately, but firmly, on his chest and gently pushing him back. I was not about to lose my virginity listening to fucking Mötley Crüe.

"Do you mind if I put something else on?" I asked.

"Put whatever you want on," he said.

I stood and headed over to the record player. As I got there, I looked back over my shoulder at Daniel.

"Do you want to see my tail?" I asked.

Daniel nodded, wide-eyed. I undid my elasticated snake belt and pulled the back of my jeans down over my bum. My tail sprang out over my waistband and I made a little involuntary grunt. I let my curly tail hang out over my jeans while I bent over and took *Shout At The Devil* off the turntable. I wiggled my arse a little, sending my tail spinning back and forth.

"What does it feel like?" Daniel asked.

"It feels like my tail," I said with a shrug. "Do you want to touch it?"

"Can I?" the boy said, enthusiastically.

I placed *Pornography* by The Cure on the turntable and put the needle on the black vinyl.

Robert Smith began to sing in his adorable whiny voice, a heartfelt prayer for the lost; that was I wanted to hear before I crossed the anal Rubicon.

I sidled over to Daniel and presented my rump. I felt his fingers touch my tail, stroking it.

"You can pull it quite hard," I said. "It doesn't hurt."

Daniel tugged my tail, not hard enough to make me fall back onto his lap, but that's exactly what I did anyway. We wrestled and laughed a little bit, and I ended up lying on my back across his thighs. I could feel his erection beneath me. He leaned in and we started to kiss. I opened my mouth and his wet tongue slid in. He was a surprisingly good kisser. He really got into it, but wasn't too sloppy or anything. He grabbed my tits through my shirt and began squeezing them. My nipples are actually super-sensitive. I'm fairly sure that a pig's nipples are way more sensitive than anyone else's, and I can easily achieve orgasm by pulling and tugging on my little piggy teats. Occasionally when I do this I lactate, tiny, volcanic spurts of salty milk leaving my body in lieu of the spunk that I'll never produce.

I had approached the whole losing-my-virginity thing in quite a scientific way. It was just something that I wanted to do, to get it over with, but I ended up getting really into it. I was totally getting off on what I was doing to him, not what he was doing to me. Never having had an erection myself, I was fascinated by the bulge in his jeans. He groped my sensitive, bee-sting tits through my Siouxie and The Banshees T-shirt and pushed me down onto the bed, climbing on top of me. I dragged my T-shirt up and over my head, and he did the same. I pulled my training bra over my head. I don't know what I was training for, my tits never grew past an A cup, but I guess I wore the bra to make me feel more like a girl.

Suddenly I knew that I had to suck his cock, but I was happy to make out topless for a bit first. I wrapped my legs around his waist and we snogged while he ground his pelvis into mine, his hard cock pressing into my flaccid dicklette through the taut fabric of his jeans. He sat back and looked at me, smiling. I coquettishly covered my hard nipples with my fingertips and smiled back.

"Do you want me to suck you off?" I said coyly, or as coyly as one can deliver a line like that. "I want to suck your cock."

Without a moment's hesitation he undid his belt and pulled down his tight black jeans and orange and white Y-fronts, releasing his rock-hard cock. His dick looked massive to me then, but with hindsight it was probably average-sized. At that point the only cock I'd had any experience of was my own, and pretty much every cock looked massive compared to that useless inch.

I sat up and took him in my hand. It was so hard! I guess it's quite difficult to describe what it's like to take hold of a hard cock for the first time when you have a penis yourself, but have never had a hard-on. It was both simultaneously alien and kind of familiar. I kept giving it little squeezes, just to feel how hard it was beneath its soft, velvety, paper-thin skin. He lay back on the bed, raising himself on his elbows so he could watch, and I went to work. I took as much in my mouth as I could, gagging slightly as his bell-end hit the back of my throat. I inhaled deeply when my snout came into contact with his wiry black pubes. He'd obviously added a squirt of Hai Karate to his crotch. I appreciated the attention to detail.

I tried to remember everything Caroline had told me about sucking cock. I pulled back until just the tip was in my mouth. I closed my eyes, pouted and moved my lips back and forth over his throbbing, purple-pink helmet. I licked the tip, tongued his slit, and cupped his balls in my hand. I was surprised to feel his testicles move inside his scrotum the way they did. My own testicles had atrophied and shrunk away to nothing during puberty, and I'd actually forgotten what it was like to have them. All I could remember was that it really hurt to get hit in them, so I didn't miss them at all. I had only been at it a minute or so when his heavy breathing made me realise he was not far off from shooting his muck.

"Sit up," I said. "Sit on the edge of the bed."

Daniel complied and did as I said. I slipped onto the floor, knelt between his legs and went back to work. I really wanted to stick my finger up his arse, but I knew I was just projecting my own desires onto him.

It was still early, and my parents wouldn't be back from the pub for hours and, if what Caroline had told me was true, Daniel would be good for another go that evening, maybe more.

He got more and more excited, and I knew that he was about to pop. I fucking loved it, the power! I had him, I really had him. In that moment I owned his soul. He was going to come when and how I wanted. I stopped slurping his twitching nob and sat back on my knees, licking my lips.

"Do you like my tits?" I asked, slowly wanking his slick foreskin back and forth.

"Yeah, fuck…" he said, gasping and nodding rapidly. "They're fucking great."

"They're not too small?" I began to squeeze my perky little left tit with my left hand while simultaneously wanking him off with my right. I spat on the end of his dick for a little more lubrication.

"No," he gasped. "They're ace."

I looked him in the eye, and licked my lips. This normy, this ape-boy, he wanted me, more than he'd ever wanted anything. He was looking from my firm little pig tits and back at his own cock again and again, lost in wonder.

"Look at my face," I said. "Look at my fucking face. Look me in the eye."

He did as he was told, wide-eyed and gasping. He was twitching like mad in my hand. I stopped wanking him off and rested my hand at the base of his cock, on top of his wiry pubes, loosely holding his shaft between my thumb and forefinger. I held his gaze for a few seconds.

"I'm a pig," I whispered.

"W-what?" He stammered, confused.

"I'm a fucking pig," I repeated, louder, beginning to move my hand slowly up and down his glistening shaft, slick with pre-cum and spit. "I'm a pig."

I started moving my right hand faster and faster up and down his twitching pole, while with my other hand I pinched and pulled at my nipple. Daniel began to breathe faster, almost hyperventilating.

"Fuck. God. Fuck. God," he moaned.

"Do you want to cum on my piggy tits? Do you? You dirty little pig-fucking ape!" I said in a harsh whisper, impressed by my own skills of improvisation. "Do you?"

Daniel never got a chance to answer, or rather his dick answered for him. His spunk shot out like an intercontinental ballistic missile made out of sticky grey wallpaper paste. The first jet smacked into my chin. I leaned back a little and pointed his dick at my tits. He let fly maybe five or six spurts in diminishing returns, twitching and swearing as he did. When he had finished spurting and convulsing, I let go of the base of his dick and began to rub his spunk onto my tiny tits, the cum on my chin dripping onto my chest. I circled my hard nipples with my fingertips. The jism changed colour and consistency as I rubbed it in, getting whiter and stickier. I lifted the fingers of one hand to my snout and sniffed. It had a very distinctive smell, with undertones of ammonia, which was only to be expected. Caroline had told me it smelled exactly the same as a particular tree we'd walked by one summer, and she was right. Nature is weird! I licked my fingertips. It wasn't the worst thing I'd tasted, but it definitely wasn't the best. I laughed. Daniel let out a long, drawn-out sigh.

"Fucking hell," he finally said. "That was a bit good."

"Do you want a cup of tea?" I asked, getting to my feet. "You better have a rest and get your strength back... you're not done yet."

I wiped my chest with a dirty sock from the laundry basket. I pulled the sock inside out, threw it back in the basket, and put my T-shirt back on. I slipped into a pair of knickers and went downstairs to the kitchen. I made two cups of milky tea. Two sugars for him, no sugar for me. I grabbed the biscuit tin and headed back to my room. I inhaled as I climbed the stairs, enjoying the smell of cum rising up from my chest. Daniel had slipped under the sheets.

"You'd better eat some custard creams," I said, placing the biscuit tin beside him on the bed. "You've got to get your strength back... you're going to be giving me some more of your own custard cream in a bit."

He dutifully did as I said, cramming biscuit after biscuit into his mouth. He was getting crumbs all in my bed, but I decided not to mention it. I flipped the vinyl, got undressed and squeezed into bed next to him. We drank our tea, and he began to clumsily caress me. We began to make out again. The energy began to build, but slower than before and in a slightly different way. Things were less desperate. I stroked his cock, and it slowly grew hard beneath my touch, not as eager as before, but still willing and able.

"Do you mind if I put Def Leppard on?" Dan asked, the Cure album having ended.

"I really fucking do," I said. "If you think you're going to fuck me while that shite's playing you can think again."

"Well, what do you want to listen to?"

This was a big thing for me. I felt that the song you lost your virginity to could dictate the future of your entire life, like magic. I slipped from under the duvet and walked over to the record player, wiggling my arse as I crossed the room. I wasn't a fan of The Clash, and I don't really know why I chose that record, but someone had lent me *London Calling* and I still had it somewhere amongst my records. I dug it out and stuck it on. The opening bars of the first song had a yearning, urgent quality to them that I thought suited the situation quite well.

"You can fuck me to this."

I pulled down my knickers and let them fall to the floor. I opened my secret drawer and took out my greasy plastic jar of Vaseline. As casually as I could I scooped out a finger-full of jelly, pulled my arse-cheeks apart with my free hand, and rubbed it into and around my pigussy. I darted over to the bed, flung the duvet to one side, lay on my back, grabbed the back of my knees, and opened my legs. Daniel seemed slightly stunned. He stared at my little hairless cock like a rabbit in the headlights, and for a second I thought he was having doubts about the whole thing.

"Um… If it's going to be up the bum," he said. "Don't we have to, like… Do it from behind or something?"

"Don't be stupid, you can get it in like this," I raised my pelvis a little. "Then we can snog while we're doing it."

I gobbed onto the fingertips of my right hand and smeared the spit onto my arsehole for a bit of extra lubrication, sticking a couple of fingers knuckle-deep into my pig-cunt, just to make sure everything was ready. Daniel moved into position, on his knees between my open legs. He took his hard cock in his hand and began clumsily poking around in the general area of my arsehole, before confidently pressing the end of his dick into my perineum and pushing.

"Fuck's sake!" I exclaimed. "Come here!"

I reached down, took hold of his dick and placed the tip onto my twitching cunt, rapidly approaching the event horizon of my becoming the anal pig I was born to be. So long, virginity!

"Now," I said, looking into his confused eyes. "Fuck me."

I pushed and relaxed. Daniel slid in and I gasped. His dick was smaller than my rolling pin, but for some reason it really hit the target. He began to fuck me. 'I'm being fucked', I thought, wanting to be fully present. I got into it as best I could, closing my eyes, throwing my head back and grunting in what I hoped was a sexy way. His dick fit my arse-cunt pretty well, and I could feel his helmet making contact with my P-spot. It wasn't half bad, actually, for a first go. I took hold of his wrists and pulled his hands onto my tits. He took the hint and began to squeeze, not hard enough, but it was good.

"Kiss me," I whispered, looking into his baffled grey eyes.

We snogged while he fucked my arsehole, and I didn't mind that he forgot to keep kneading my tits when we started kissing. I guess it's too much to expect a boy to do three things at once. I could feel his excitement building, and I was actually surprised at how much force and speed he could get out of those skinny hips of his. He was hammering me hard, my bed was creaking and the headboard was banging rhythmically against the wall. I was beginning to suspect that I might actually cum, when he started moaning and groaning.

"Fucking hell. Fucking hell," he wheezed, breaking off our kissing. "I'm going to fucking cum. Fucking hell."

I wrapped my legs around his arse and crossed my ankles, pulling him into me. He began to pound harder and harder in short desperate thrusts, his hands sinking into the mattress either side of my body as he arched his back and raised himself up, the bed making all kinds of thumps and squeaks as we buckled and writhed. His cock slid out of me, but he hurriedly grabbed hold of it and stuck it back in. He had absolutely no problem finding my sloppy arsehole the second time. Almost immediately after pushing his cock back into my guts he began to cum. His eyes rolled back in his head, and he stopped fucking me and just pushed his cock as deep as it could go. Every muscle and fibre of his body was stretched tight as a bowstring as his mess flobbed into my pighole.

"Fuuuuuuuck," he moaned.

He held himself inside me for a few seconds and then clambered from between my legs and flopped down beside me on the bed. I could feel his mess dribbling out of my newly-deflowered arsehole and onto the sheet. We lay in each other's arms for a while. It was nice, I guess. I don't know how long we fucked for, but the music was still playing, so less than twenty minutes. He might've managed fifteen, but it was definitely over too fast for my liking. I didn't orgasm in the end, but it hadn't been half bad.

We chilled out for a bit and talked. He told me he wanted to be a writer. That he was planning on writing some fantasy or science fiction novels or something. I didn't really listen. We had another cup of tea, and I kicked him out before mum and dad got back from the pub. I closed the door behind him and headed back to my bedroom. I looked at myself in the mirror, trying to discern some kind of difference between the new me and the virgin I had until very recently been, but there was none.

"Now you're a real pig," I said to myself with a smile.

I saw Daniel a few more times after that, and we fucked quite a bit, but he wasn't going to satisfy me. I needed more, not just from him, but from life. I like to imagine him, still sat in his bedroom at his mum's house, writing his novel about sexy orcs or whatever. He wasn't a bad lad, but he's only relevant because he was the first. A bit like Notts County, really.

CHAPTER THREE

HAMDEN TOWN

One lunchtime in early January, as I was sitting in the stockroom of the newsagents casually looking at some shitty tabloid newspaper between mouthfuls of pickled onion Monster Munch, an article caught my eye. 'HAMDEN TOWN - A HAVEN FOR THE TEENAGE TRIBES,' the headline ran. Apparently there was a neighbourhood in London that was a hotbed of pubs, gigs, shops and market stalls that catered for all of the various countercultural youth movements that were thriving in Britain at that time. The thing that caught my attention the most was not the article itself, interesting as it was. It was the grainy black and white picture that accompanied the story. It showed a trio of girls, punk as fuck, in ripped fishnets, boots, and leather jackets. Their hair was spiked, and they were loitering on a bridge or something, laughing and sticking two fingers up at the photographer. And one of them was a pig. She was wearing a studded leather jacket, white-framed vintage-looking sunglasses and had a short, blonde mohawk, about two inches long and perfectly fixed, like a fin. She was sneering at the camera, head held high, feet apart. I instantly fell in love with her. She just looked like she was one hundred percent being herself; she looked like she didn't give a fuck about what anybody thought of her.

I stole the copy of the newspaper, sticking it in my bag without paying for it (it seemed the punk rock thing to do), and that night in my bedroom I read and reread the article, a dozen times or more. While I knew I could never attain the heights of a Patti or a Siouxie, I felt that I could aspire to be like the piglette in the picture. That night I looked over at her, entranced, while sliding my greased rolling pin in and out of my no-longer-virgin pig-cunt bumhole. I fell asleep dreaming about Hamden Town.

I was turning nineteen that February and, for my birthday, I asked for money, which I added to the small amount I had saved from my wages. It turned out that Hamden Town was just north of King's Cross. The train that I would get down to London from Nottingham arrived at the cavernous, pigeon-infested gothic shell of St Pancras station, which, as luck would have it, was in King's Cross, and was just a short walk from Hamden Town itself.

I booked the Saturday after my birthday off from work and headed out from my hometown to Nottingham on the first bus at six thirty in the morning. I arrived into the city at half past seven and headed for the train station. I'd made as early a start as I could because I wanted to spend as much time as possible in London. I bought a ticket at the station and got the eight o'clock train, which arrived at St Pancras just before ten. The weather was cold, but clear; a perfect bright winter's morning.

On the journey down I read a book I'd recently got from the library. It was called *Plague* and was written by an American author called William Burrows. Burrows was a rabbit who presented as male, which was pretty cool. The book told of a dystopian world, not dissimilar to our own, but where people caught diseases by having sex. It focused on the outbreak of a new sex virus that was initially spread by gay men and bestiamorphs and, later, by prostitutes and drug addicts. Because the people getting the disease were considered undesirable by the authorities, nothing was done to stop the spread. It was quite grim, but it made me glad I don't live in a world where you can get a disease just by having sex. That would be terrible. I don't know what kind of god would create a world like that: some kind of blind, idiot god, I guess. It was a good book though.

Once I arrived in London I asked directions from a downbeat dog-man selling the *Evening Standard* outside of the station, and, after a twenty-five-minute walk, found myself standing in the dead centre of Hamden Town, at the crossroads of Porkway and Hamden High Street.

Hamden was fairly busy, and there were plenty of people wandering in and out of the shops that lined the high street. Straight away, I spotted the difference between the day-trippers and tourists, and the people who lived there. Hamden people were cocky and sure of themselves; they walked along unfazed by the colours and wild fashions, the outlandish hairstyles, clothes and makeup. I worked out, almost immediately, that to fit in in Hamden you had to look a bit bored, like you'd seen it all before. The tourists were wide-eyed and enthusiastic, pointing at this shop front, staring at that person, asking to take a photo of this punk or that goth, nervously eyeing the skinheads as they stomped past in their boots and braces. I realised immediately that Hamden was a circus, that the residents, the shop workers and bar tenders, the market traders and restaurant staff, and the people who just seemed to hang around doing nothing, were like the clowns and acrobats of this carnival, and that the tourists were the suckers who'd be leaving with empty pockets and stupid grins. They'd go back to wherever they came from, and kid themselves that they'd had the Hamden Town experience, but they'd never really know what it was like to live in the circus. I wanted to know. It was like a magical, alternative reality. It was England's dreaming, and I knew immediately that I had to find a future in it.

I had passed the tube station on my right, and was walking past a parade of shops that led to a bridge that crossed over a canal, when I came to a clothes shop that caught my eye. The painted sign outside read 'The Black Violet'. It seemed to stock the kind of things I liked to wear, so I headed in and began to browse. I flicked through the rails: coat-hanger after coat-hanger of fishnet and PVC and leather, T-shirts and bondage trousers.

Some kind of awful, screeching music was playing in the shop, thankfully not too loudly. I would later learn that it was Diamanda Galas's *Litanies of Satan*, and eventually I learned to appreciate its charms, but I wasn't ready for it at that point in my musical evolution. A pair of nervous-looking tourists followed me in and began looking at the selection of footwear on offer: pointy-toed winkle-picker boots with skull and crossbones buckles, and brothel-creepers with thick, two-inch soles.

"Can I help you?" a coolly indifferent voice asked.

I looked up to see a slim cat-girl goth looking down her perfect little nose at me. She had a heart-shaped face that reminded me of Debbie Harry, but with a black fringed bob, rather than Debbie's blonde tresses. Her outfit was spot-on. She was wearing tight PVC trousers, shit-kicking black patent leather boots with a shiny external steel toe cap, a tight black polo-necked woollen jumper with a cool silver pendant on a chain over the top, and a cropped leather jacket. I glanced at the pendant. It seemed to be a seven-pointed star, a septagram, with two concentric circles, one in the middle and one halfway down the triangles that made up the points of the star. I felt that I'd seen the same symbol somewhere before, and I kind of wanted one of my own.

The cat-girl smelt of coffee and cigarettes and Goya Black Rose, with an undertone of fish (it's a cliche, but apparently cats really do love fish). Her makeup was perfect; flawless pale foundation, dark red lips, no eyebrows at all, smoky eyeshadow framing her emerald-green cat eyes, with their otherworldly, vertical-slit pupils. Her slender fingers were tipped with wicked dark red claws, and she wore a large oval onyx statement ring on the middle finger of her right hand. Her sleek, black furry tail snaked around her leg as she looked me up and down, hard-faced and obviously judging me in the harshest possible way. For a moment I was on the back foot, about to shrink away from her withering gaze, but then I remembered everything Caroline had told me. I stood up straight (I was several inches taller than her, which helped), fixed my gaze on the centre of her forehead, relaxed and smiled. This was another one of Caroline's tips; whenever you find yourself in a status struggle, whenever anybody tries to look down on you or belittle you, don't look them directly in the eye, look at the middle of their forehead. This discombobulates people: they know you're looking at them, but they can't lock eyes with you. Caroline told me that a psycho who'd been in loads of fights had taught her this technique, and I didn't doubt it.

"I'm just browsing, thanks." I said with a weary sigh and a half smile, like I'd seen it all before.

"I like your look," the cat suddenly said after a moment's silence. "It's well put together."

I looked down at myself. I was wearing a black and red striped woollen jumper (Mum called it my Dennis The Menace jumper), my shortest black denim mini-skirt, ripped fishnets, Docs, red socks, and my leather jacket. The leather was far too big for me and buried me somewhat. I'd wear it hanging off one of my shoulders and let it gather at my elbow. The neck of my jumper was super wide, revealing my black bra strap and the delicate curve of my collar-bone. I was wearing a red, studded leather dog collar that I'd found in a pet shop back home. I had on a black woollen beret and fingerless black gloves with black nail varnish. I always keep my fingernails nicely painted and in good condition, but short. For the fingering of the bumhole, of course. At that time I had taken to using an old khaki haversack covered in patches as a handbag. I was wearing a black lip and winged eyeliner, and I had my biggest, heaviest earrings in. The cat was right; my look was well put together. Best of all, it had cost me next to nothing. Where I came from there were no shops selling custom-made punk stuff. You had to improvise.

"Thank you," I said, looking her in the eye now and smiling. "You look amazing. I love your boots."

We were equal now, and all was well with the world. I turned my attention back to the clothes rail.

"You people like it in the bum, don't you?" She abruptly said, with a bored tone. "I don't like it in the bum."

"Oh, no," I said, forcing an obviously fake laugh and turning back to look at her, with what I hoped was a cute smile, this time looking her straight in the eye. "We don't like it in the bum. We LOVE it in the bum!"

The cat-girl laughed, genuinely, I thought, although you never can tell with a cat. The two tourists glanced over at us and walked out of the shop in a hurry. It must've been something I said.

"That's good," she said. "It's good to know what you like."

I figured out that she had decided to make me an ally, rather than a rival. Cats and pigs aren't looking for the same things in life, and I had heard that cat/pig friendships weren't uncommon, although I hadn't had a cat friend at school. They always looked down on us pigs, although I think they preferred us to apes and dogs, especially dogs. You just had to remember that they're cats, and expect them to be catty from time to time.

"Where are you from?" She said, folding her arms and looking me up and down again.

"I'm from Nottingham," I said.

I'd worked out for myself, when talking to other kids on family holidays at Butlin's in Skegness, that there was no point in telling people where I was actually from, as nobody had heard of the place. What you tell people, when you're from some unknown backwater, is that you're from the nearest city.

"Oh, right," the cat-girl said, bored again. "Are you here visiting friends or something?"

"Yeah... I'm just here for the weekend," I said, affecting a similar world-weary tone.

Just then a group of German-or-Austrian-or-something tourists came in and started jabbering away enthusiastically in German or Austrian or something. I decided to leave, and explore Hamden Town a little more.

"See ya, then," I said, fluttering my fingers in a friendly wave before turning to head out.

"Bye," the cat-girl said, turning her attention to the Teutonic interlopers poking noisily around the store.

As I walked back out into the hubbub of Hamden High Street, I happened to glance over my shoulder and back at The Black Violet. There was a handwritten notice Blu-tacked to the inside of the window. 'HELP WANTED,' it said. I decided to call back before the place closed.

I walked past the The Black Violet again, later on that afternoon, after a meal of egg, chips, and beans in a cafe on what I would later learn was Pork Farm Road. I looked in the window and made out like I was checking out the rows of studded belts and band T-shirts that hung there, but I was really looking into the interior of the shop again. The cat-girl shop assistant was talking to another cat.

The second cat had long blonde hair and was wearing hippyish clothes, like Stevie Nicks, or someone impossibly lame like that. She was jittery and nervous, all hand wringing and no eye contact. Her yellow tail hung limp and motionless from a hole just below the waistband of her ankle-length purple skirt. The nervous cat-girl handed the shop cat a piece of paper and they chatted a little longer. The shop cat nodded and smiled vacantly. After an awkward goodbye, the new cat turned and headed out, glancing around nervously as she disappeared into the crowd on the high street. She smelled of fear, fags and fish. I saw the cat in the shop sigh, roll her green eyes and shake her head. She tore the sheet of paper in half, screwed it up and tossed it somewhere behind the counter, presumably into a bin. I looked at the sign hanging the other side of the glass door, made a mental note of the closing time of the shop, and went for another wander. I spent the rest of the afternoon trying to formulate a plan. If I asked about the job in The Black Violet and actually got it, how would I make that work? I'd need somewhere to stay in London. How on earth was I going to find a place? As I walked along the high street, I passed a shop selling super-expensive lingerie. A young rabbit-girl bounded out of the door as I was approaching, followed by a middle-aged ape in a suit who was weighed down with several shopping bags. The dynamic was obvious, even to my young eyes. Could I sleep my way into London? Find a boyfriend with a flat and use him for a place to stay? That was an option, I supposed, but I'd rather not have to pimp myself out to find somewhere to crash.

I just so happened, by design, to be walking by The Black Violet as the cat-girl was shutting up shop. It had gotten dark by then, and the light spilling out of the various shops and bars gave the whole scene a kind of cosy, festive feel. I always loved the darker months more than the summer, and still do. I think it's because autumn and winter are more romantic.

"Hello again," I said as I walked by. "Busy day?"

"Oh, it's you, is it?" the cat said, fastening a series of padlocks around the metal shutters she had pulled across the door and windows. "Yes. It was pretty busy. Saturdays always are... especially since that bitch Rachel fucked off back to wherever she came from. I've been short-staffed for a couple of weeks."

"Oh really?" I said. "I've shop experience."

"But you don't live around here, do you?" The cat-girl said over her shoulder as she secured the shop for the night.

"Well, I come down fairly often," I lied. "I reckon I could stop at my mate's if you want to try me out."

The cat locked the final padlock and straightened up with ballerina grace. She turned and looked at me.

"My name's Felina," she said, looking me up and down once more. "I'm spitting feathers here... Wanna go for a drink?"

I introduced myself and said OK, of course, and pretty soon we were standing in a smoke-filled pub on the corner of the high street called The Elephant Shed. The place was really busy. It was mainly full of skins and punks, and I spotted a couple of punky pig girls and a handful of skinhead dogs amongst the apes. The Jam's *Going Underground* was playing on the jukebox. I never liked The Jam, I couldn't stand their skinny ties and suits, it looked too much like the hated school uniform I had had to wear, but that's an all-right song, I suppose. I was surprised when a pig girl at the bar said hello to me. I had been taught by my provincial kin that Londoners were an unfriendly bunch, but that wasn't the experience I was having. I said hello to the pig, and complimented her spiky purple hair, which seemed to go over well.

It seemed that everyone in the place knew Felina, and she'd said hello to at least a dozen people before we even got to the bar. She was the only cat in the place, which I think she liked, but there were a couple of pale-faced gothic apes in there, and she nodded to them as we walked in. It was clear that she was some kind of face on the scene. Felina asked me what I wanted, bought us both drinks, and turned and scanned the bar.

"I'm not standing up. I've been on my fucking paws all day," she said, taking a delicate sip of her snakebite and black. "I know that guy sat over there by the jukebox. We can get a seat at his table."

"See ya later," I said to the purple-haired pig, and followed Felina's swaying tail, deeper into the smoke-filled bar.

We pushed our way through the throng and stopped by a small, circular table in the corner. There was a man, an ape, sat at the table by himself, nursing a pint of lager.

"Good evening, David," Felina said. "Do you think we could squeeze in at your table?"

The man looked up. He was around thirty, I'd have guessed, and appeared to be some kind of metaller. He was a skinny guy with bad skin. He had long, greasy hair and was wearing a Motörhead T-shirt and faded blue jeans. He smelled of Indian food and, for some reason, Tipp-Ex. I was surprised that the super cool goth cat-girl from the fashionable shop was friends with someone like that, but Dave had hidden talents, and Felina was a born networker. While she might've sometimes seemed superficial in her choice of friends, hanging out with the best-looking and best-dressed people on the scene, she also knew when someone was useful.

"Yeah... Grab that stool over there, no-one's sitting on it," he said, moving himself along the bench that ran along the back wall and squeezing into the corner. "And I reckon one of you can fit in here."

I grabbed the stool and sat down. Felina took the bench, squished in between Dave and a massive skinhead goat in a West Ham shirt who was sat at the next table with his noisy, meathead friends. UB40's *One in Ten* started playing on the jukebox, and all the skins joined in, singing as if they were at Upton Park cheering on The Hammers. I hate football, but thanks to my brother I know more about it than I want to.

"All right, love?" the goat shouted over the sound of his friends' boisterous singing as Felina sat down.

"No. Fuck off Kevin. Don't even try," Felina said, turning her back on the goat. "So, Dave... How're things in the photography business?"

"Good, thanks," the greasy metaller replied, relighting a cocktail-stick-thin rollup. "Got some new contacts for magazines in Europe. Maybe some things you'd be interested in."

"Really?" Felina said, removing a packet of fags from her handbag and offering me one, which I refused.

"Yeah... Denmark. They'll publish anything over there, and there's a real interest in domination at the moment, especially cat-girl stuff. The session we did the other week should be coming out any day now, I'll drop a copy into the shop. You working much?"

"I've got my regulars," Felina answered. "Just a couple of nights a week, but it adds to the pittance I earn at the shop."

"What about your friend?" Dave asked, nodding in my direction.

"Oh, Swinella?" Felina said, smiling over at me. "We've only just met, actually. You ever done any modelling, Swinella?"

And that's how I got my name. The truth is, I liked it from the start. I had guessed that Felina wasn't Felina's real name; that'd be too much of a coincidence, her parents calling her that and then her turning out to be a cat. A new name for my new life in London sounded about right, and Swinella was perfect. I hadn't done any modelling, of course, and I had no idea what Felina and Dave were talking about.

"Not really," I said.

"Well, I'm in here most nights," Dave said, exhaling a cloud of sickly-sweet smoke. "If you want to do some trial shots I won't charge you much, y'know... Put a bit of a portfolio together. You've got a good look."

"Now you hang on a minute there... I'm not going to let you take advantage of the poor girl," Felina said, raising her cigarette in her slender hand and pointing at Dave. "You'll not charge her anything. Swinella..." she said, turning to me and placing her hand on my arm. "I'm your manager now. Anyone wants to take pictures of you, they go through me."

I really didn't know what was happening, but I went with it."That's right," I said to Dave, haughtily. "Felina is my manager. Talk to her."

I had to leave quite early to get my train back to the Midlands, but not before Felina had offered me a trial shift at The Black Violet the following Wednesday. I said my goodbyes and hurried back to St Pancras, only just arriving in time to catch the last train home.

The next day I told my parents I had a job interview at a clothes shop in Nottingham the following Wednesday, that I'd have to take the day off from the newsagents, and that I'd be out all day.

I headed back to Hamden Town and to my trial shift at The Black Violet. Felina and I had a right laugh working together. We took the piss out of the customers constantly, criticising their poor fashion choices after they'd left the shop, belittling them to their faces when we thought we could get away with it. We were aloof, we were arrogant, and we saw it as our job to remind the tourists that they were just that, tourists, part-timers, filler tracks in the great album of life.

We listened to Siouxie, who we both loved, and drank about a million cups of black coffee; two sugars for me, none for Felina. I took my tea without sugar, but I'd always found coffee too bitter to drink without a couple of sugars.

When one of Felina's gothy cat-girl friends came in, a stunning dark-skinned redhead called Gatita, Felina introduced me by saying that I was the new girl at the shop, even though I was only a few hours into my trial shift, and we hadn't talked about my getting the job or not.

"I'm sooo glad you've found her," Gatita purred, looking me over with her gorgeous amber eyes and smiling a plump-lipped crooked smile. "She seems perfect."

After the shift had ended, we went for a drink at The Elephant Shed.

"So," Felina said. "Can you start tomorrow?"

"Er," I stumbled. "Well, I've got to sort things out at home. Can I start Monday?"

"Nope," Felina shook her head. "I'll give you tomorrow off, but you start Friday, or not at all. You'll be paid in cash at the end of the day. Take a day off and you'll not get paid. We don't do sick pay or holiday pay, but if you want to sign on the dole, that's your business. There's no contract, which means I can get rid of you whenever I feel like it."

"I've nowhere to stay, though," I confessed. "My friend that was living down here is moving to... Somewhere else, um... Tomorrow. They're moving, and I won't be able to crash there anymore, so, um... I came down on the train this morning, and I'm going back later."

"I assumed it was something like that" Felina said, laughing. "I saw that the second you walked in. You're so obviously fresh meat. You can stay at mine while you sort yourself out. I have a flatmate, but he'll be no bother. I've wanted rid of him for a while. I only let him move in as a favour to a friend of mine. The flat is owned by the same people who own The Black Violet, so your rent will come out of your wages. It's a pretty good set-up."

And that's how it happened. Looking back now, it seems amazing that everything fell into place so easily, but I've come to believe that if you're following your true path, then doors will just open. The universe conspires to make our dreams come true, we just have to get out of our own way and let it happen.

I headed back home and told my parents some bullshit story about how the manager at the shop in Nottingham had offered me a job in their London branch. I said that one of the girls who worked in the London store had a spare room in their flat that I could rent; it wasn't that far from the truth. My parents were surprisingly cool with it. I think they were a bit relieved, actually. I'd be out from under their feet, making my way in the world.

I packed my bags, taking only the essentials: clothes, makeup and my trusty rolling pin. I copied a few of my favourite records onto tape; I'd have to buy a cassette player when I got settled in London. Mum and Dad woke up early on Friday morning to see me off. It ended up being a bit emotional in the end. Mum cried, which surprised me, while Jason hovered nervously in the background. Dad pressed a ten-pound note into my hand at the door.

"Look after yourself, son," he said, realising his mistake as it came out of his mouth.

I let it go. It was a bit awkward, though. Working class people in those days never hugged or expressed themselves emotionally. They never talked about their feelings, unless it was in an outburst of anger, or if they were drunk. I don't think I ever hugged my dad, not ever. Mum gave me a peck on the cheek, and I walked away.

CHAPTER FOUR

I ARRIVE

"Sorry, Mike," Felina said to the skinny goth guy sat smoking and watching TV, as we walked into her third-floor flat on one of the streets branching off Porkway. "You're moving out. Swinella's moving in. She's having your room. I'll give you a week's grace while you sort yourself out with somewhere new. You can sleep on the sofa."

I was horrified. I didn't realise that Felina was going to kick someone out so I could have their room.

"Fucking hell, Felina," the boy protested. "Where am I meant to go?"

"That's not my problem," the cat said. "You knew it was only temporary. Swinella's working at the shop now. She needs somewhere to stay. That makes her my priority."

Mike stood up with a scowl, went out of the living room into what I presume was his bedroom, and slammed the door. I could still smell his annoyance after he'd left the room.

I looked around. The small flat consisted of a living room and neat, open-plan kitchen. The ceilings were high, and while the kitchen was windowless, the living room had two large windows overlooking the quiet street outside. There were two doors leading directly out of the living room, one of which Mike had just stormed through, which I correctly assumed led to the bedrooms. There was a third door at the end of a short corridor next to the kitchen, which I guessed led to the bathroom. The flat was clean, warm and super-cosy. It was actually more tasteful than I'd expected, more Byronesque than Halloween. Vintage furnishings in dark reds and purples, and a lot of black, of course. Crimson curtains with black nets on the windows. I should have known really; Felina was a stylish post-punk arty goth, not some tasteless pantomime-vampire goth from the provinces. The flat smelled of a comforting mix of cigarette smoke, fish, toast, coffee and red wine.

"That was fun." Felina smiled. "Tea?"

Mike came out of his room his room wearing a dyed black army jacket and a face like a smacked arse. He stomped out of the flat with a scowl. He came back an hour or so later and went back into his room without saying a word to either of us. Eventually he emerged, carrying a large, green, overstuffed army kit bag and a battered suitcase.

"I'm going to The Dev'. I'd rather sleep on their sofa than look at your cunt face for another minute," Mike said.

"Wonderful!" Felina declared, smiling. "Then it worked out fine for everyone. I'll see you in the pub. You can buy me a drink for putting up with you staring at my tail for the past three months. Bye!"

Mike shook his head and scowled, before walking out of the flat and slamming the door behind him.

"He's going to hate me now," I protested.

"So?" Felina shrugged.

"I don't like to be hated," I said.

"Get used to it... Learn to like it," Felina said. "Half of Hamden hates me. The other half either want to fuck me or be me. Some of them hate *and* want to fuck me. That's the kind of dynamic that means something in this life."

"Yes, but half of Hamden doesn't want to fuck me or be me!" I answered.

"Not yet," Felina said with a smirk. "But they will. Especially when you drop that extra stone you don't need to be carrying."

"I'm not fat!" I cried, looking down at myself.

"No, but you'll look better skinny," Felina said. "Most of you pigs are a bit curvy, so if you can slim down, you'll stand out. And standing out is what it's all about. You're tall, that's good. If your waist was four inches smaller and your heels four inches taller, you'd own this fucking town. We'll starve you, get you a new wardrobe of nice, tight-fitting clothes, and then you can have your pick of the guys, or girls, or whatever it is you're into. We'll get you someone with money, and then you can fleece them."

It was dawning on me that Felina actually was a cat. Like I said, I'd never had a cat-girl friend before, and I guess I expected her to be less catty but, in some twisted way, I kinda liked what she was saying. I wanted to own that fucking town; I knew that the very first second I'd arrived. I realised that Felina was taking over where Caroline had left off. She was going to be my teacher and guide for the next chapter of my life.

"So," I said. "You're skinny. What's your advice for losing weight?"

"Be a cat," she said with a laugh. "Or failing that... Skip breakfast, avoid bread. No solids between eight o'clock at night and noon. Stop taking sugar in your coffee... you can easily wean yourself off it. That's it."

"OK... that sounds easy enough," I said.

"You should start smoking."

"No."

"Yes."

"No."

"Why not? It's punk rock."

"How is it punk rock?" I argued. "My parents and grandparents smoke, and they're definitely not punk rock! It costs money and gives you cancer... Whoooo... punk rock!"

"It'll help you slim down, fatty." Felina said, fishing her fags out of her black snakeskin handbag. "And you'll never get cancer, trust me on that."

"No. I can slim down fine without smoking."

"Well... At least you've admitted you should lose some weight," Felina shrugged, lighting up. "I think I should have a look at you naked. Take off your clothes."

"What?!"

"Look, we're going to be sharing the flat," she said, taking a drag of her coffin-nail and exhaling an acrid cloud of blue poisonous smoke. "I'm obviously going to see you naked. Take off your clothes."

Felina was able to speak in a tone that was difficult to resist. I remembered our first little status struggle when we first met. Should I have stared her down and asserted myself? I'd already done that with the smoking thing, so maybe I should give a little. But, to be honest, I liked the idea of showing her my body. I'd always felt that I had exhibitionist tendencies, but that they'd been overshadowed by the mixed feelings I'd had about being a piglette. I wanted both to be seen and to hide away at the same time. It was very confusing. I took off my jumper and T-shirt. I sat straight-backed on the sofa in my black bra.

"Your tits are even smaller than I thought," Felina said, examining me with a detached air of professionalism, holding her cigarette high. "That's good. They'll age better... Well, they won't age at all. Do you really need the bra? Take it off."

I did as she said, but I realised that I didn't need to be coy about it. To the cat this was business. I slipped off my bra, squared my shoulders and looked Felina in the eye.

"Big nipples," Felina mumbled to herself, as if making an inventory. "Don't wear a bra any more, you don't need it."

"But I like to wear a bra," I protested. "It makes me feel, I dunno... More feminine."

"Those little, perky tits will look better without a bra," Felina stated. "Especially when your nipples get hard. The big tit obsession is a conspiracy perpetuated by heterosexual men who stupidly think that value is somehow connected to quantity, which is typical male reductive thinking. Big tits are for lumpenproletariat *Sun* readers. How many runway models have massive tits? None. Why? Because the fashion industry is run by homos. If fashion was run by straight men, it'd essentially be a never- ending issue of *Razzle*." (*Razzle* was a cheap porno mag that, for some reason, Felina was obsessed with.)

"Stand up," Felina commanded.

I stood up.

"Just take everything off," she snapped, impatiently, taking a long drag of her smouldering cancer-stick.

I slipped off my shoes, socks, tights and knickers. I stood with my hands on my hips and looked down at the cat on the sofa. My cheeks reddened and Felina's green eyes widened as she stared at my penis.

"I mean… Wow," she said. "That's the smallest dick I ever saw. You don't shave, do you? You pigs are hairless?"

"That's right," I said.

"I'm not jealous of much in this life," Felina said, shaking her head. "But I'm jealous of that. At least you won't leave the bath full of dirty stubble, like I do."

She moved her hand close to my crotch and spread her fingers, looking from her hand to my dicklette and back again.

"It's literally the same size as the last two bones of my little finger," she said. "And you've got no balls, right? Lift your dick out the way for me."

"Pigs have no balls," I said, gingerly taking hold of the end of my cock and lifting it up towards my abdomen. "Look."

"I like what you've got," she said approvingly. "It makes sense."

And with that last statement Felina pretty much summed up not only us pigs, but all bestiamorphs. We make sense. There's an undeniable rightness about the way that our bodies are in sync with our drives and desires. My dick wouldn't be the right tool for an ape-boy or a goat or a dog, but for me it was the perfect fit.

"And you still think I need to lose a stone?" I asked.

"Oh god, no," Felina said. "You don't need to do anything. But if you want to be your absolute peak self, then you should lose a stone at least, maybe two. It's war out there, and your body is your primary weapon. The truth is, you probably look better naked as you are, but in clothes you'll look better skinny. And as you'll be seen in clothes most of the time, that's what we have to make our priority.

I never really agreed with Felina's worldview. In fact, I don't even think she believed half the stuff she said herself, she just said it to be edgy or something. I didn't, and still don't, think that 'it's a war out there' but, as always, I decided to go with it and see where it led.

"Do you want a boyfriend? A girlfriend? What's your goal?" Felina asked. "Do you want romance, or just someone to fuck, or maybe someone to use, y'know, for money and presents."

"Are you asking me if I'm a whore?" I asked.

"No," Felina laughed, stubbing out her fag in an overfilled glass ashtray. "We're all whores here, I'm just trying to find out what kind of whore you are... What payment you require."

"I don't know," I admitted. "I think I'd like someone to do stuff with, like, go to the cinema and gigs and stuff, but if I'm honest, I do like, y'know, no-strings kind of sex. I've never had a boyfriend, but I've had sex a bunch of times."

After fucking Daniel and losing my virginity I'd had several one-night stands with random blokes. I'd go to Kock Schitty, a music venue in Nottingham that had club nights on as well as gigs, and pick up some guy who I thought might be a decent shag. Often they weren't a decent shag as a lot of the time they were too drunk to get it up, but at least it meant I'd have somewhere to crash after the club. Even if they couldn't get it up after a night on the piss, they'd usually have the hangover horn in the morning and I'd get a bit of something out of them. Strangely, I'd only ever fucked apes. Goats seemed more interested in ape-girls and rabbits, and I never really met a dog I fancied.

"If you want to earn a bit of money, and you've no problem with it, I might be able to get you some work," she said. "Look at this."

Felina reached over to a small table at the side of her chair, picked up a magazine, and tossed it over to where I sat on the sofa. I picked it up. It was a smallish, digest-sized magazine with a colour photograph on the cover. The title of the publication, *Pussy Power*, was written in red on the cover. The picture on the cover featured a cat-girl, not unlike Felina, but with blonde hair and blue eyes, fucking a masked guy with a large, prodigiously-veined, black strap-on. The cat-girl was staring at the camera open-mouthed and winking. She was heavily made up, with scarlet lips and dark metallic blue eyeshadow. She was dressed in a black leather corset and fishnet stockings.

"Turn to page twenty three," Felina commanded.

I did as she said, and there she was: Felina, dressed and made up in a similar fashion to the cat-girl on the cover, whipping a helpless ape-boy tied to some kind of wooden cross, like a giant 'X'. I flicked the pages. Felina's section was about ten pages long, and ended with her fucking her victim with a large flesh-coloured dildo. The final page showed the guy shooting his load all over himself. Felina was curling her lip in a sneer, one viciously-clawed hand holding the dildo, and the other grasping his throat.

"Wow," I said. "I had no idea you did… You do… This, um… Kind of thing. It's pretty amazing."

"Well, The Black Violet doesn't pay too well. Not well enough to keep me in the manner to which I've grown accustomed, anyway," she said. "I do it a few times a month. Not usually for magazines, I only do that now and again. No, usually I work with private clients, y'know? I've a small set of boys, regulars, and I see one or two of them a week. It keeps me in snakebite and shoes… And of course, the main reason to do it is that it's fun. A lot of fun."

"And is this, um… Is this kind of thing that you do with your… regulars?"

"No, mainly I do humiliation, foot worship and C.P.," she said. "Stuff like that… Y'know."

I didn't know.

"What's C.P.?" I asked.

"Corporal punishment," Felina replied. "Canes and whipping and stuff. Needle play. Cock and ball torture."

"Not so much anal then?" I asked, trying to come across all nonchalant.

"Not really," Felina laughed. "I sometimes do fisting and strap-on, and I know what I'm doing. It's more Gatita's thing, to be honest. Her and I sometimes do doubles. There's good money in sodomy, but you have to get a reputation for doing it, and doing it well. It takes time. Remember… The internet hasn't been invented yet, so you have to go through contact mags and meet people at private parties and stuff like that. If I was doing it full time, I'd get some tart cards out in the phone boxes around King's Cross and Soho, but that's always a bit random and chaotic, and most blokes who call are just piss-heads looking for an escort, either that or guys having a wank who're trying to blag a bit of free phone sex."

"The inter-what hasn't been invented yet?" I asked.

"Nothing," Felina said, looking down at the magazine. "Those pictures were taken by Dave. Remember? You met him when we went for that first drink at The Elephant."

"Oh, right, yeah," I said. "He was on about some Danish magazines or something. He said he might be able to get me work."

"Would you be into it?" Felina asked, with a raised eyebrow.

"I might be."

"Well, let me think it over," Felina said, a sly smile dancing across her flawless feline face.

We spent the rest of the night making small talk and watching crap on TV, but my eyes kept being drawn to the cover of the magazine that lay on the coffee table.

CHAPTER FIVE

GORDITA AND THE TRIFLE

Gordita was fat. I first saw her a few days after I'd started working at The Black Violet. She was sitting alone in the snug at the goth pub, The Devil's Shire Harms, pretty much filling the entirety of one of the two benches that faced each other across the chipped black table. She was fat and she was a pig. She was a fat pig. It was just after six on a chilly but clear evening in March, and Felina and I had headed out for a drink after shutting up shop. It was midweek, and the place was pretty quiet, just a dozen or so Goths nursing pints of snakebite and black while Echo And The Bunnymen's *The Cutter* played on the jukebox.

We walked to the bar and Felina introduced me to the bartender, a peroxide blonde gay boy called Wayne Mansfield. It turned out that Wayne's real name wasn't 'Mansfield'; that was just a nickname. Obviously, it referenced Jayne Mansfield, the Hollywood blonde who had been cursed by Anton Lavey and decapitated in a car crash while sucking some bloke's dick, but it was also a nod to Wayne's hometown of Mansfield, which happened to be just down the road from where I grew up. Wayne immediately began calling me 'duck' like a proper Nottinghamshire person, which really made me happy. Nobody had called me 'duck' since I moved down, and it was nice to hear.

After the introductions were made Felina ordered a snakebite and black for herself and a vodka-soda for me. According to Felina, vodka-soda was the lowest-calorie alcoholic beverage, so that's what I drank from there on.

"There's one of your people over there," Felina said, rolling her cat's eyes in the direction of the snug. "Go and say hello. You have to."

"I know," I said, sighing. "But she's so big and scary-looking. I'm nervous."

"I've told you before," Felina said, exasperated. "Whenever we see a fellow 'morph it's considered good manners to acknowledge them, and when we see one of our own kind, we always say hello. That is the law. And anyway... I know her she's... she's something."

As if to prove her point, at that moment a tall goat walked into the pub. He looked like a metaller, like most goats. Leather jacket, long grey hair, bullet belt and, of course, a goatee beard. He nodded to us as he walked over to join a pair of blonde tarty metaller ape girls sat in the far corner.

"Alright, girls?" He said gruffly as he passed.

"Evening," Felina said, nodding slightly.

I just smiled at him as he walked by. I was wary of goats back then, and still believed the lie that, if you gave one any attention at all, he'd then spend the rest of the night pestering you for sex, and you'd probably succumb to his pheromones.

"Go," Felina said, scowling at me.

I walked over to the fat pig girl's table. She smiled reassuringly as I came over.

"Hi," I nervously said. "I'm Swinella. I've just moved down here and, um... I thought that I'd, y'know... Come over? And say hello?"

The fat pig laughed, revealing shiny golden crowns on her lower canines, which I instantly thought was the coolest thing ever. Her jowls wobbled and her little piggy eyes twinkled with amusement at my obvious anxiety.

"New in town, eh?" She said with a smile and an accent I couldn't place, southern European, I thought, Spanish or Portuguese or something like that. "Your cat friend teaching you the ropes? That's good."

The hefty porcine raised her pint of Guinness to Felina, who returned the salute with her own half-pint glass of sickly-purple snakebite and black.

"I'm Gordita," the corpulent swine said. "Sit for a while, let's get to know each other... Us *porcas* gotta stick together, no?"

I glanced over at Felina, but she had started talking to some curly-haired ginger Goth boy and wasn't looking our way any more. I sat down.

Gordita must've weighed twenty stone, and she was not shy in showing it. She was wearing a black leather mini-skirt that barely covered anything. Her wide, pale pink belly hung over her waistband. The skirt just about covered her crotch, and not much else. Her impossibly meaty thighs were wrapped in wide fishnet tights, her dimpled skin pressing through the holes in the fabric like soft cheese being pushed through a string vest.

She had massive, jiggly round tits and wore a ripped black Alien Sex Fiend T-shirt, through which I could clearly see a red bra that more closely resembled scaffolding than it did underwear. She had dry, henna-orange Bettie Page hair, big silver rings on each of her chubby fingers, and a heavy silver septum ring in her snout. I noticed that she was wearing a silver pendant like Felina's, a septagram, and I guessed it must be a popular design. Her eyes were caked in mascara and eyeliner, her cheeks were rouged and her lips were pillar-box red. If I was being honest, and a mean cunt or a cat, I'd have said she looked a fucking mess, but the truth was, it worked. All of the elements, when viewed separately, were wrong, but when put together the overall look was a million kinds of right, and that was one hundred percent down to her attitude, her obvious no-fucks-to-give confidence, and I liked her already. She smelled of Estée Lauder's Youth Dew, all lavender, jasmine and patchouli. She had taken a shower before heading out and didn't smoke. I suppose adding fags to her weight would've been too much of a health risk, even for a don't-give-a-fuck swine like her.

"Well now," she said, flashing those golden tusks in an intimidating grin. "You must be the skinniest piglette I ever saw."

I didn't know what to say.

"It's ok, *porcita*, it's cool, we're good... I'm here for you," she laughed. "I'm just fucking with you. Tell me your name, at least."

"Oh, I'm sorry," I said. "I'm Swinella."

"Of course you are!" Gordita laughed. "And who else could you possibly be?"

"I like your teeth," I smiled. "They look really good."

"Why thank you, chica," Gordita said. "My *papito* got them for me. I'm meeting him here in a minute. I'll introduce you. He'll love you... He doesn't like skinny, but he'll love you, he's a cunt, I hate him. Have you been in London long? You sound like you're from up the north."

"I'm from the Midlands," I said. "I've only been in town a few days, actually. I'm working at The Black Violet."

"Ah, I never go in there," Gordita explained. "They only do clothes for skinny bitches, like you and your cat friend, there's nothing in there that fits a real woman. I'm only joking, *porcita*, when I call you bitches... but you are bitches, no?"

"Um... No?" I ventured. "Maybe... I..."

"Oh *porcita*, if you're not a bitch now, you'll be one soon, that's the nature of Hamden Town, but it's OK, we love it. Do you love it? We love it."

"I do love it... Everyone is so nice," I hazarded.

Gordita laughed, "Everyone is 'nice'? OK, maybe you're not a bitch... Yet."

"How long have you been here?" I asked. "Where did you come from, y'know, originally?"

"I've been here forever," Gordita answered, waving one of her bejewelled hands in the air. "I'll never leave now... I can't even remember where I come from, baby-girl. The outside world is not so important, really."

At that moment the door to the street swung open and a small, bespectacled man walked in. Gordita waved at him.

"Here I am, Papito, here!" she called, in a high pitched,

sugary voice, as if anyone could miss her. "Get me a pint of Guinness, Papito… and a bag of crisps, I'm starving here already! Two bags!"

The skinny little man nodded his head and headed to the bar.

"He pays for everything," Gordita said out of the corner of her mouth in a theatrical whisper that they probably heard in The Elephant Shed up the road. "You should get one. I can show you a magazine that has personal ads from men like him, but you'd have to get fat and fabulous like me. They like meat on a pig, pork, lots of fatty pork… These needle-dicked motherfuckers."

The man came over, his small, bespectacled eyes wandering across Gordita's ample curves with a mixture of wonder and desire.

"Shall I leave you two alone?" I asked, taking my handbag from the table.

"Oh no, *chica*," the corpulent hoggess said. "Stay a little longer. I think your cat friend doesn't miss you so much."

I looked over at the bar. Felina seemed fine chatting to the ginger goth boy. She was making extravagant gestures with her claws in the air in front of his face and enthusiastically describing something with a series of thrusting motions. He looked entranced, and more than a little fearful. The skinny little man squeezed in beside Gordita, even though it would have made more sense for him to sit next to me as she was almost filling the bench she was sat on.

"This," Gordita said, gesturing towards me with her extravagantly-ringed hand. "Is Swinella. She's new in town."

"Hello, Swinella," the man said, offering his hand.

I shook the man's hand and smiled. His grip was weak and his fingers cold to the touch. I try not to judge, but I thought he was a particularly disappointing specimen of manhood. When Gordita had spoken of her *papito* I had expected some king of huge alpha male, not a skinny little guy in a brown suit who could've be an accountant or something. It later turned out he actually was an accountant, for some firm in The City that paid exceptionally well. I guess, in his world, he was an alpha male.

"Nice to meet you, Swinella," he said in a whiny little voice. "I'm Nigel."

We made small talk for a bit. Gordita wolfed down her crisps and noisily gulped her Guinness.

"Oh, Papito," she declared upon draining her glass. "I'm still hungry. What shall we do?!"

"Well," Nigel said. "I've got more food back at my hotel, if you'd like to come over?"

"Oh yes, Papito," Gordita moaned, rubbing her big round belly with her pudgy beringed hands. "That sounds wonderful. Can I bring some friends?"

"If you like," the accountant smiled, clearly getting so excited that I thought for a second that his glasses were going to steam up.

"Will you join us?" Gordita said, smiling mischievously.

"Well, I'm out with Felina, really," I replied, but then I remembered that I was in Hamden Town to experience new things. "But fuck it… I see her every day. I'll tag along."

The three of us stood and gathered our things. I told Felina I was heading off with the obese pig and her *papito*. Felina grinned, baring her fangs, a wicked glint in her sea-green eyes, and told me to have a good time. As we were about to head out I was surprised when Gordita made a gesture to the goat boy who had come into the pub earlier. He stood, said goodbye to his bimbo metaller friends, and followed us out onto Bentish Town Road.

"I booked us a room at the Holiday Inn," Nigel explained. "It's just around the corner. Do we need to pick anything up on the way?"

"Get me some cans from the offy," the goat boy rudely said, before turning to me. "I'm Andrew."

"Swinella," I said.

The goat boy lit a fag and looked me up and down, nodding approvingly, a devilish twinkle in his amber goat's eyes. I could smell his musky goat pheromones, all lust and masculine desire, but I wasn't going to fall for it. I focused instead on the smell of Gordita's spicy Estée Lauder perfume.

"And you're coming with us?" He asked.

"It looks like it," I answered.

"Good. I like to have an audience. It makes me perform better. Maybe you'll even feel like joining in."

Joining in with what, I didn't know, but of course even naive me had an inkling as to what was about to go down at The Holiday Inn.

We called in the offy for Andrew's cans and made our way to the hotel. Nigel had obviously already checked in as he had the key with him. We followed him up to the room and he opened the door. The room was lit by a half dozen low wattage red lamps that I guessed Nigel had brought with him earlier. The dressing table was piled high with cakes and pastries, with a huge bowl of trifle standing in the middle, like a creamy citadel overlooking a sugary city.

"Oh Papito!" Gordita declared. "You shouldn't have!"

Gordita waddled over to the dressing table and picked up a cream bun, stuffing it messily into her maw and smearing cream all over her chops.

"Mmmmmm..." she moaned, caressing her expansive gut with her free hand.

Andrew sat himself down on a chair and cracked open a can of Hofmeister. He sat with his legs wide apart. His massive package was clearly defined beneath the tight black denim of his skinny jeans. I stood in a corner, not really knowing what to do.

"Do you want some cake?" Nigel asked me, grinning nervously and nodding.

"No thanks," I said. "I've eaten."

Nigel seemed a little crestfallen at my answer, and turned back to watch Gordita stuffing her face. The plus-size piglette had devoured two or three sticky cream cakes already. She turned to look at Nigel, fluttering her heavily mascaraed eyelashes.

"Oh Papito," she murmured through, red lips slick with cream. "I'm getting soooo hot, I think I might have to take off some clothes."

I got the impression I was watching a scene that the three of them had played out several times before: either that or they were working through some kind of preplanned script. The only unexpected, rogue element was probably my presence. I wandered over to where Andrew sat, bent over and picked up one of the warm cans of lager. Gordita and Nigel seemed unaware of my presence, but I noticed that Andrew's goat eyes were watching my every move and scanning my body from top to toe; his pheromones had increased slightly in their intensity. I pulled the chair from the dressing table, dragged it over to the wall and sat down, crossing my legs. I opened my can and tried to look casual. I focused on the smell of the lager and used it to block out the goat's powerful pheromones. Gordita had sat on the bed and removed her shredded T-shirt. She sat with her pudgy legs wide open and pushed another cake into her sticky, eager maw.

"Help me with my bra," she said, her voice muffled by a mouthful of cake.

The skinny accountant moved behind her and, with some difficulty, unhooked the back of the industrial strength undergarment. Gordita's huge melons swung free. I noticed that Andrew had unfastened his jeans and pulled out his cock. It was, of course, massive, a good ten inches, and thick. His pubes were abundant, grey and wiry. He began to casually slide his foreskin back and forth over the glistening pink head of his ample weapon. Nigel glanced over and saw that Andrew was ready for action.

"Are you satisfied, my love?" Nigel asked Gordita.

"You know I'm never satisfied, Papito," Gordita said, fluttering her eyelashes. "I'm soooo hungry, and I'm soooo thin, don't you think?"

"You could definitely do with putting on some weight," Nigel said, nodding, wide-eyed and eager. "Why don't you have some trifle?"

"Oh, Papito," Gordita moaned. "It's not just my mouth that needs stuffing."

Gordita rolled onto her back and began, with some difficulty, to peel down her leather mini-skirt, making low, seductive grunts as she did so. Nigel, like a true gent, stepped in and helped her, pulling off her skirt, followed by her wide fishnets, and then her black lace thong. I was surprised to see that Gordita was so fat that she had no visible penis. I knew that somewhere in the depths of her ample, hairless, pubic mound, a tiny, flaccid dick was hidden, but it was hidden very well indeed, like a tiny man sunk beneath the surface of a pool of fleshy pink quicksand.

"But what else needs stuffing?" Nigel said, stepping back from the bed and casting Gordita's clothes to one side.

"Aside from my mouth, I only have one hole that can be stuffed," Gordita said demurely. "You see, Nigel... I'm a pig... I'm a fat, sweaty hog, and pigs don't have cunts like nice, clean, normal girls. Pigs have to be fucked in the bum, that's the only way a pig can be fucked, in our shitty, piggy arseholes."

I was quite impressed by Gordita's commitment to the role she was playing. Hearing her talk like that turned me on slightly, and I felt my own puckered bumhole twitch a little as she continued.

"And I'm a big girl, Papito," she grunted. "I need a big, big cock to stuff my greedy pig-hole."

Right on cue, Andrew stood up and removed his jeans. Gordita rolled on her front and presented her haunches. She was so fat that when she got on all fours her big, pink belly rested on the bed. She placed her head on the bed, her face turned sideways towards Nigel, reached behind herself and, as best she could, pulled her massive arse cheeks apart with her fat sausage-like fingers. All of a sudden, she farted, high pitched, long and profound, like the final trumpet on the day of judgement.

Andrew shook his head and rolled his goat eyes, no doubt grateful that the two rocker girls he'd left in The Dev' couldn't see him now. I moved into the armchair that Andrew had vacated and made myself comfortable. The whole scene was ridiculous, but I was into it. If I'd been able to get an erection, I'm pretty sure I would've had one then; as it was, my nipples had grown hard beneath my bra and my bumhole was involuntarily clenching and unclenching. I lifted the can to my mouth and took a deep swallow of tepid lager.

"I wish I was fatter, Papito," Gordita said, looking over at the nerdish accountant as Andrew got into position behind her. "I want to be the fattest pig girl in the whole world!"

Nigel went over to the dressing table and picked up the trifle. He carried it over to the bed as if it were some holy sacrament, an offering to the goddess of chub. Gordita let go of her gigantic buttocks and placed her hands on the bed, pushing herself up on all fours and arching her back. Nigel placed the trifle between her meaty hands and stood back. Andrew grabbed her curly tail and pulled it upwards, causing Gordita's massive arse to rise slightly and present her pigussy. He gobbed on his fingers and rubbed the spit onto Gordita's rusty bullet hole, then he took his throbbing goat dick and pressed its glistening purple helmet onto her puckered portal. The goat took a deep breath in through his nose and plunged in. At the very same moment that Andrew rammed his rod into her waiting aris, Gordita plunged her snout into the bowl of trifle.

"Fuck my fucking shit pipe!" Gordita called out, between grunts and sloppy fuck farts, her face covered with trifle while Andrew rode her like she was a sweaty rodeo hippo. "Oh Daddy! The goat is fucking my fat shit-hole! Look, Daddy! Look!"

Nigel had fished his own unimpressive worm out of his brown suit trousers and was wanking like a chimp, red faced and focused. Andrew was pummelling Gordita's arsehole as if his goaty life depended on it. I really didn't know what to do with myself. Was I meant to join in? Or just watch? I just couldn't believe it. Gordita was farting and sweating and grunting, her face smeared in trifle, like the victim of a particularly vicious attack by the Phantom Flan Flinger. The bed looked like it was going to collapse any second. Jesus-fucking-Christ, I wouldn't have been surprised if the entire hotel had collapsed! Nigel moved over to Gordita's head, furiously wanking, like an ape possessed. The creamy hog scooped up a handful of trifle and smeared it on her rotund visage.

"LOOK PAPITO! LOOK DADDY!" she yelled. "MY ARSEHOLE IS GETTING CREAMPIED! OOOOOH DIOS... I'M GETTING CREAMPIED IN MY SHIT BASKET, PAPITO... THE DIRTY GOAT IS GOING TO CUM IN ME... FUCK, DADDY...

FUUUCK!!!"

Right on cue Andrew clenched his buttocks and let out a guttural bleat, obviously emptying his nutsack into the husky sow's shit-sock. The goat, his work finished, staggered away from the bed, wiped his cock with a hand towel, pulled up his pants and jeans, sat down heavily on the dressing table and closed his yellow eyes, shaking his head. At first, I thought he was disgusted with himself, but then I realised his body was shaking with quiet laughter. I suppose if you're going to do what he just did, then you'd better have a good sense of humour about it.

"I need a poo, Papito." Gordita moaned. "Bring me the bowl."

Nigel grabbed the ruined trifle and placed it on the floor at the foot of the bed. Gordita rolled onto her back, swung her dimpled legs over the edge of the bed, and stood unsteadily. She blinked, her eyes like two raisins in the cream smeared ruin of her face. She took a few steps, squatted over the bowl and began to push. A wet fart, like a choking bullfrog, escaped from her battered onion ring, followed by a stream of stringy white goat cum. Great ropes of thick, putrid ectoplasm fell out of her shit pipe and onto the remains of the trifle. Gordita pushed harder, and I thought for a second she might prolapse or follow through, but she merely deposited the last of Andrew's man-fat into the bowl. After all the commotion the room became eerily silent.

"Papito," Gordita whispered, breathing hard.

"Yes, baby," Nigel said, his primate wanking slowed to a rhythmic edging.

"I'm still hungry."

"Then you better finish that trifle," Nigel said, his hand beginning to speed up as he tugged away at his ineffective joystick.

Gordita gingerly lowered herself to the floor and began to noisily eat the cum riddled trifle with great gusto, swallowing huge mouthfuls of spunky, sherry-flavoured sponge and rancid cum-infused yellow custard. Nigel began to pant hard. He moved into position and dribbled a pathetic teardrop of watery jism onto Gordita's sweaty shoulder-blade, letting out something between a moan and a sob as he did so.

There was a moment's awkward silence as everyone looked around the destroyed hotel room. I knew I'd never look at a trifle in the same way. Andrew took a long drink of lager and belched.

"Well," he said, getting to his feet. "I better run back to The Dev'… Hopefully those two chicks are still there."

"Yeah… Erm… I should get back too. I don't want to leave Felina all on her lonesome," I said, standing up.

The goat and I smiled at Nigel and Gordita and made our way to the door.

"Come and hang out with us again, won't you?" Gordita called out, beaming at us from where she sat on the floor, her face caked in trifle and cum. "We had a lovely time!"

Andrew and I headed out of the hotel and walked back to The Dev' in silence. I looked through the window as we approached the pub and spotted Felina sitting at a table with Gatita. Andrew and I shared a knowing look as we walked into the pub. I went over to join the cats as he walked to the back of the pub to look for his girls.

"You weren't gone for very long at all," Felina said as I sat down. "Did you have a good time with your friends?"

"Well… I've got a tale to tell," I said. "But right now, I could really do with a drink."

CHAPTER SIX

CIRCUMCISION

"You should get circumcised," Felina said, one evening, when we were getting ready for a night out.

I was walking around the flat Pooh-Bearing after a shower (that's wearing a top, but no bottoms, for those not in the know, like Winnie the Pooh). I was wearing an old rip-off Seditionaries T-shirt, the one with the two cowboys standing face to face with their cocks almost touching, and a pair of furry pink slippers. I turned and faced her, putting my hands on my hips and thrusting my crotch out towards where she sat on the sofa.

"Do you think so?" I said, looking down at my tiny, impotent protuberance.

"Yeah," she replied, nodding sagely. "I think it'd look really cute. It'd be neater and, best of all, there'd be less of it. I think you should trim the rind off that bacon."

She was right, of course. If I had my foreskin cut off there would be less actual pork down there, and I could see what she meant about it looking neater. My foreskin was quite long and loose, like a tapir's nose.

"How do I arrange it, though?" I said.

"I don't know," Felina replied, furrowing her brow. "I suppose you ask your doctor to refer you or something?"

But I had a better idea than asking some ape doctor for help. I went into the Bestiamorph's Advice Centre in Soho and asked them. It was really nice to have a place like that to go. There was nothing like that where I grew up, but in London we did have a bit of community support. They were super-helpful and, after a short wait, a serious, bespectacled dog boy saw me, listened to what I had to say, and disappeared into the mysterious back room of the centre. He returned after a few minutes with the phone number of a clinic in West London.

"I need to take the afternoon off on Friday," I told Felina that evening.

"What?" she said, with cattish indignation. "I'll never get cover on such short notice! What are you doing? No, no, no… You'll have to work. We're getting a delivery that day. I need you. No."

"I'm booked in for my circumcision," I said.

"What?!" Felina immediately brightened and opened her cat eyes wide. "Really? Then of course you can have the afternoon off! Take the day off! Where are you getting it done? Who's doing it? How much does it cost? Show me your dicklette, I want to say goodbye! Can I come and watch? Damn… I have to work on Friday. That stupid pig-faced bitch I work with has already booked the day off!"

I answered all of Felina's questions and, when Friday arrived, I found myself standing outside of a rather plain six-floor Edwardian building in Hammerfist. There was a series of doorbells with the names of the businesses that were located in the building next to them. I found the clinic's bell and rang it.

"Yes?" A tinny voice answered from a speaker set in the wall.

"I have an appointment at two."

The door buzzed and I pushed it open. I found myself in a corridor with several doors leading off it. The circumcision clinic was on the first floor; door number five. I headed up the stairs, found the door, and knocked.

"Enter," a woman's deep voice said from the other side.

I walked through the door and into a waiting room, just like in a regular doctor's or a dentist's. A severe, middle-aged woman in an old-fashioned nurse's uniform sat behind a wide wooden desk and looked me up and down from behind her half-moon spectacles.

"I'm Swinella," I said. "Swinella Porksword. I have an appointment at two."

"Yes," the woman said, sternly. "Please take a seat and fill out your details."

The nurse handed me a sheet of paper on a clipboard, and a pen. I took a seat and filled out the form. It was basic information and only took a few minutes. I passed the nurse the clipboard after I had filled in the form and sat back down. I was feeling a little nervous and, to my surprise, a little excited, too. The nurse looked over my form briefly, then stood up and walked out of the waiting room. As she passed, I noticed that her waist beneath her tight, starched nurse's uniform was very small, maybe no more than twenty inches. She was wearing cream-coloured, round-toed patent-leather pumps with incredibly high heels. She smelt of Shalimar perfume, Silk Cut fags and Mellow Birds. She returned immediately and held the door open.

"The doctor will see you now."

I stood up and headed towards the door, smiling at the nurse as I passed. She did not return my smile, but merely looked me up and down with a slight smirk. I walked into the doctor's office. He was an older man, possibly in his sixties, or even early seventies. His grey hair was thinning and was combed into a wet-looking side parting. He wore a white doctor's coat over the top of a striped shirt and burgundy tie. He smelt of Brylcreem, piss and Rich Tea biscuits.

"Ah, Miss Porksword," he said, in what I assumed was a German accent. "Please to hang up your coat and take ein seat."

I placed my bag on the floor, hung my leather jacket on a hook by the door, and sat down, crossing my legs and holding my knee in both hands.

"So... You are here for a circumcision, yah? Very good," he said, looking over my form. "Now, it's a very simple pro-cee-dure. Everything on your paporworks looks to be in order. I just have to ask your reasons for seeking this pro-cee-dure here today, yah?"

"Well, as you can see, I'm a pig, although I prefer the term 'piglette', but pig is fine," I began, a little flustered; I had not expected to have to explain myself. "And we piglettes, as I'm sure you know, well, we have very little penises anyway, but that doesn't matter, um... So my friend Felina, she's a cat, by the way, we were talking one night and we thought that it might be good for me to get circumcised, and I thought it was a really good idea, I mean... I'm not using the thing anyway, so why not, y'know, trim it down a bit, make it neater, and so I rang up to make the appointment. You see, I don't actually use my penis, I mean, it's still sensitive, but I don't use it for, y'know... sex, or anything. Wayne Mansfield said I should just get the whole thing cut off, but I don't want that... I think he was joking anyway, but you never can tell with Wayne Mansfield. That's not his real name, I mean, Wayne is, but not Mansfield, he's just from Mansfield and his name is Wayne. Have you ever been to Mansfield? No, why would you? And, yeah, I just want it. I mean, I do really want it, because, at the end of the day... I think it'll, um... I think it'll look... cute?"

The doctor stared at me for a few moments.

"I'll just write 'personal' on the form," he finally said.

I nodded, glad the interrogation was over. The doctor pressed a button on his desk and I heard a faint buzz from the other side of the door. I heard the clicking of heels, and the nurse walked in and handed me a pale blue hospital gown.

"If you'll just follow me," she said, heading towards another door and opening it. "Just go in there and remove all of your clothing and put on the gown. It fastens at the back."

I did as the nurse suggested. There was a long mirror in the room where I'd been told to get changed, and I wondered why that was. Did they put it there so people could have a last look at their foreskins? So they could check themselves out in the blue medical robe? The funny thing is, I did take a last look at my foreskin. I pulled it back over my little, sensitive pink glans. I had no doubts I was doing the right thing. The idea of my clit being exposed all the time struck me as kind of perverse, and I liked it. To this day I still think it's weird that people do this to their babies without thinking, just because it's something they've been told to do. Like, what are you doing? You're cutting a bit of your child's dick off for literally no reason. I was getting it done because I wanted it, but no baby wants it. To me it's like piercing your baby's nipples or something. People are weird.

There was a knock on the door.

"We're ready for you now," I heard the nurse say.

I lay on the padded table. The doctor stood on my right side, the nurse on my left.

"Open your legs for me a little," the doctor said, moving an overhead lamp into position above my crotch.

"To be honest there isn't not much skin to take from here," he said, his dry, latex gloved hands pulling my dick around a little. "You see, if we take too much it makes the erections problematic."

"Well, that's not an issue for me," I said, slightly annoyed as I thought I'd already explained this. "I don't get them. I've never had them, so you can do what looks best."

I glanced at the nurse. She was staring at my little hairless pig-dick, wide eyed. I opened my legs a little wider and lifted my pelvis a little. I wanted her to have a good look. Maybe they'd never had a pig in here before? It was possible, I supposed. She turned her head slightly and surreptitiously took a look under my arse, obviously intrigued by my curly pink tail.

"Very gut," the doctor said. "I'll inject the anaesthetic now.

You are going to feel a couple of pricks, nothing serious. Then in a few minutes we will start the pro-cee-dure."

The doctor did as he said. The injections were not too bad, and I could feel my dicklette getting numb almost instantly. While we were waiting for the anaesthetic to take effect, the nurse and I chatted a lit bit. She asked where I worked and whatnot, just making small talk while I lay there exposed, all casual. I was completely relaxed and comfortable. I could tell that the austere nurse was warming to me now she'd seen me naked and vulnerable. I knew that I had piqued her curiosity in some way.

"How does that feel now?" the German doctor asked in his bierkeller accent, pinching my numb nub between his forefinger and thumb.

"I can feel you doing something," I said. "But just the tugging. I can't feel your fingers."

"Yah," he said, nodding. "It will be fine, I am sure of it. If you feel pain let me know, and I can inject again."

The nurse took something metallic from a trolley by the bed and handed it to the doctor. To my regret I didn't watch the procedure, and I can't actually remember if he used scissors or a scalpel. I watched the nurse, and the nurse watched the doctor. I wanted to hold her hand, but of course I didn't.

I had thought that the foreskin would come off in one piece, like a ring that could be dried out and worn on a finger, but he actually took it off in pieces. While I didn't watch the action, I did see the little scraps of bloody skin being placed in a stainless steel kidney dish off to one side.

"I think that that is enough," he said, after a few minutes. "Take a look, if you please…"

"Take more if you can," I replied, looking down at my traumatised butterbean. "Like I said… I don't get erections, so you can, um… make it as tight as you can."

"OK," the doctor said, nodding. "I can take a little more."

The nurse glanced over at me, smiling with her eyes briefly, before turning back to the job in hand. The doctor took a few more scraps of skin from me, and then the nurse handed him the suturing equipment.

"These stitches will dissolve in about a week," the doctor said. "Do not attempt to take them out yourself if they take longer."

The doctor finished stitching me up. I was circumcised now, and always would be. It was a strange feeling to have permanently changed, albeit slightly, the size and shape and appearance of my penis. I'd walked into the clinic with one penis, and I'd walk out with a different penis. How very odd! And I'd enjoyed the experience much more than I had expected. It had felt really good, lying there in front of two strangers while they messed around with my numb, impotent cocktail sausage. I clambered off the bed and stood up.

"Do you feel all right?" the nurse asked.

"Yes," I said. "I feel fine."

I headed back to the changing room, got dressed, said my goodbyes and left, leaving a small part of myself behind.

The night after my circumcision, I had a strange dream. I dreamt I was lying on a low bed on the floor of a Japanese room.

The blinds were drawn and it was bright sunshine outside. Somehow I knew I was in San Francisco, a place I've never been to and know next to nothing about. I was lying on my front, naked, and a man was sticking needles in my back. The needles were attached to a stick about a foot long, and every now and again the man would dip the needles in a little cup of ink, before sticking them into my skin and jabbing them back and forth. I couldn't see my back, but I knew that the man was poking in a huge picture of a snake that would eventually cover my entire back, and I knew that when he was finished, the snake would stay on my back forever. I told Felina about the dream as we sat in the living room drinking our coffees before work.

"What?" she said, with a bemused expression on her cat-girl face. "He was drawing a snake on you? With a needle?"

"Yes!" I replied. "Like, poking it in... and I knew that when he finished it, it wouldn't come off... ever."

"That's stupid," Felina said. "Your body would just heal it away or something... that'd never work."

"I know, but that's dreams, isn't it?" I said with a shrug. "I don't know what it means."

"Well... Dreams are just dreams, aren't they?" Felina said, standing up and grabbing her coat. "All it means is that you're weird. C'mon, let's go to work."

CHAPTER SEVEN

BAPHO

I had settled nicely into my life in Hamden Town. I was the happiest I'd ever been. My job at The Black Violet didn't pay well, but I was able to live pretty cheaply. I made most of my own clothes by customising things I'd buy from charity shops and from the army surplus place under the railway arches by Hamden Road station. I'd add a rip here and there, stick in a few safety pins, dangle some chains, sew on patches, put on a badge or two. I'd dye clothes, usually black of course, boiling them on the gas stove in our flat while Felina was at work. She didn't like the smell of the dying clothes bubbling away over the gas ring, but it worked out OK as she worked alone Tuesdays and Thursdays, so I could dye clothes on those days. I worked in the shop on my own on Mondays and Wednesdays, and we both worked Friday and Saturday. On Sundays everything was closed except pubs, which opened midday to two, and then again in the evening from seven to ten thirty. If you wanted a drink after that, there were illegal, late-night places hidden away on the edges of Hamden Town. I didn't like those late-night places, though. We'd sometimes go to them with Wayne after he'd finished at The Dev', but I always felt they were full of people who should've gone home a long time ago.

I discovered an ancient haberdashery, on Bentish Town Road, where I could buy all sorts of interesting buttons, and I'd replace the original buttons on most of the items of clothing I bought with shiny metallic or brightly-coloured plastic ones. Felina was impressed by my resourcefulness, and pretty soon my creations made their way into The Black Violet itself. Every time one of my custom pieces sold, I'd get a small commission from the shop, but the best of my creations I'd save for myself.

I soon found out that I wasn't the only one doing this. The hippies working on the market, often industrious little rabbit-girls, would make simple clothes, sarongs and stuff, with material they'd buy from Bangladeshi fabric shops in Brick Lane. They'd take plain white dresses, tie-dye them, and sell them to tourists for ten times the original price. I hated tie dye, both the process and the look of it, but I admired the hustle. The hippies would go on missions to India and return with boxes of contraband silver jewellery, if they returned at all.

In Hamden Town it seemed everyone had their hustle, their side gig. Guys would get girls to sneak little cassette recorders into gigs in their bras or pants, and then record the show, resulting in a booming business in bootlegged live albums, usually sold on tape, but sometimes pressed onto vinyl. Hardly anyone could afford the expensive, custom-made bondage wear that appeared in fashion magazines from time to time, but that didn't matter, we just improvised. We were expressing ourselves, and that was what was important.

I hung out with Felina most of the time, and we got on really well. Even though she was a prominent face on the scene, I soon worked out that she had very few actual friends. She would say hello to dozens of people drinking in The Elephant Shed or The Devil's Shire Harms, but she never wanted more than that, and we'd often sit by ourselves. She was very tight with Gatita and Wayne, and that was about it. Boys didn't seem to dare to try and chat Felina up, unless they were drunk or wanted to be dominated, or both. If they came on all submissive and started talking sheepishly about being punished, calling her *mistress* or *madam* or something like that, then she would hand them a card with a telephone number on it and tell them to call her agent, before politely asking them to leave us alone as we were having a private conversation. One evening in the pub, not long after my arrival, I asked her who her agent was.

"Oh, that?" She replied. "That's the phone number of a Turkish restaurant on Green Lanes. I don't know if they've sold much *Meze* because of me, but I'm pretty sure they're fed up with desperate guys ringing them and asking for a whipping."

"And nobody's ever pulled you up about it?" I asked.

"Nah… They're always tourists, aren't they? You never see them twice. Locals don't try it on with me."

My diet went well, and I lost the stone Felina had told me to, and a little more. She was right, I looked good skinny. I was also slowly being turned slightly Gothic by my cat friend, but I didn't mind. Felina had no time for the punk gigs that I wanted to go to at The Cardiff Castle, but I didn't mind going to goth gigs at The Dev', or at The Electric Ball Bag for bigger bands.

"Punk's gone shit though, hasn't it?" she said to me one time, when we were talking about gigs and bands and whatnot. "It used to be more creative, had more women involved, it used to be more queer, but now it's this whole bonehead Oi! movement. They're more skinhead than the skinheads. Look at Siouxsie and the Damned and the Cure. They were the better bands to come out of the punk scene, and they were really Goth bands all along. And don't get me started on that awful Two-tone thing. It's all lads and football and lumpen working-class bollocks. I hate the working class."

"You know I'm working-class, right?" I said. "If my mate Caroline from back home was here now, she'd give you a fucking kicking."

"Yeah? Well... Caroline isn't here now, is she? She never left that shit-hole town you came from, right? And why is that?"

I guess Felina had a point. By moving to *that London* I'd removed myself from my background, become separated from my roots. I could move back to my shit-hole small town at any point, but I couldn't really go back. The people there would think that I thought I was better than them, better than the place where I'd started out, and you know what? I was better than where I came from. The only good thing about a small town is that you hate it, and you have to leave. Being different in a small town (and I'm not just talking about being a bestiamorph here) was a death sentence. You might live to a ripe old age, you might think that you'd maintained your individuality, but your potential died on the vine. Wandering around wearing the T-shirt of a band you'd gotten into in your teens when you're middle-aged is not the act of rebellion, individuality and self-assertion you assume it is, but you don't notice, because any genuine spirit of individuality you once had is gone. You never beat the small town; eventually the small town beats you, a death of a thousand if, buts and maybes. I had decided that that wouldn't be my story, and I'd been lucky, very lucky, to land on my trotters the way I had. But you don't want to read about all that real world bollocks, do you? You want to find out what happened the first time I fucked a goat, right? OK, let's go.

It was a rainy April night when Felina and I found ourselves at a Hawkwind gig at The Electric Ball Bag. Neither of us were Hawkwind fans, but Felina knew the doorman and we blagged our way in for free, just to have something to do. Hawkwind were meant to have a good light-show, which we thought might be entertaining for a minute, and we could always leave if we got bored; it hadn't cost us anything, after all. The crowd was one of the most eclectic gatherings you could've imagined at that time. Hawkwind appealed to a cross section of hippies, metallers, goths and punks. The air was thick with the smell of weed and patchouli oil. Felina and I got ourselves drinks and stood at the back of the crowded hall, and it was there that I caught the eye of a tall, good-looking goat boy.

"That goat keeps looking at me," I said to Felina out of the side of my mouth.

"Of course he does, he's a goat," Felina nonchalantly replied. "And you're a girl."

"No. I mean he's looking at me specifically, not just at every girl in the place like they usually do."

Felina casually looked at the goat out of the corner of her eye for a minute.

"You're right," she finally admitted. "It looks like he's only goat eyes for you."

"Oh, god," I groaned. "But seriously... I've never been with one. What's it like?"

"This might be your chance to find out," Felina said. "He's coming over."

I glanced back towards where the goat had been standing, and Felina was right; he was heading our way. He was taller than average, which, being a relatively tall girl, was something I liked. He was quite muscular, in a wiry kind of way. Goats only grow facial hair on their chins, no moustaches or sideburns, and many of them go grey during puberty. This guy had the grey hair, shoulder-length and wavy, and kept his goatee trimmed fairly short, about an inch long. He was wearing a battered black leather biker jacket, blue jeans tucked into black motorcycle boots, and a white vest. It was a good look for a goat, and I thought he looked pretty fucking sexy. As he came closer, I could make out his yellow eyes with their horizontal rectangular pupils, and the tiny horns just below his hairline.

I always found the eyes of goats much more otherworldly than the eyes of cats, I guess because we encounter four-legged cats in real life more often than we do four-legged goats. It's weird to think that goats have a different field of vision to everyone else, that they see the world in wide-screen. Everything is more cinematic for them, which must be kind of cool. I sniffed the air as the goat boy approached.

As I've said, one of the features of our enhanced sense of smell is that we can focus in on one particular odour in a room full of different smells. In the same way that everyone can pick out a single face in a group of people, we can pick out one person's smell in a crowd. The approaching goat boy smelled clean, so that was good, but he also smelled goatish. I can always smell a goat's musky, aphrodisiac pheromones, when I encounter one; all pigs and dogs can. It works on everyone else's subconscious, but not on ours, as we're aware of it and we're not as easily manipulated by smells as everyone else. We can just choose to smell something else. It kind of smells like freshly-mown grass and Bovril. It's not unpleasant, actually. Perfumers have been trying to synthesise it for decades, with absolutely no success.

"All right, girls?" the goat said in a West Midland's accent, with a broad, impish grin, addressing us both, but only glancing at Felina for a second before looking back at me. "Having a good night?"

"So far," Felina said, crossing her arms, pouting, and looking the goat up and down with an expression of unconcealed disdain, her black tail snaking around her thigh in an agitated fashion.

"Yes," I quickly interjected with a smile. "How about yourself?"

"Not bad. I'm just here with a few mates, y'know," the goat said, ignoring my rude cat friend. "You like Hawkwind then?"

"You'd think so, wouldn't you?" Felina said, nudging between myself and the goat. "As we're at a Hawkwind gig.

"Oh, yeah, right," the goat said, looking down his hooked nose at the cat and shrugging slightly. "That makes sense."

"It does, yeah," Felina said. "But actually, no, we don't like Hawkwind. We got in for free because we know people... We're probably going to have one drink and leave."

"I like Hawkwind," I said, brightly. "I might stay."

"Do you want a drink?" The goat said. "I'm Bapho, by the way."

"Of course you are," Felina muttered under her breath.

"I'm Swinella, and this is Felina," I said. "I'll have a vodka and soda, if you're going to the bar. Felina's leaving though, so you don't have to get her owt."

"Well, as you're buying..." Felina said, scowling at me. "I'll have a snakebite and black, with ice."

"Why're you being a cunt to him?" I said to Felina as Bapho squeezed his way through the throng waiting to be served at the bar. "He seems nice."

"I can't help it," she said. "And anyway, he's only being nice because he wants to fuck you. He's a goat."

"Can't he be nice AND want to fuck me?" I asked. "I thought you were all sex-positive and stuff. You're prejudiced against goats."

"I'm just really frustrated right now. I need to hurt someone," Felina admitted. "I've not sunk my claws into anyone for ages. I want to make someone suffer... I'm fucking gagging!"

"There's at least a dozen blokes staring at you right now," I laughed. "Pick one."

Felina looked around and selected a face from the crowd. She pointed to an older hippyish ape guy in his late thirties or early forties, who had been glancing over at her since we arrived. Felina pointed to the floor directly in front of where she stood. The man came over, a cheesy grin on his stupid face.

"All right, love?" he said. "Fancy a pint?"

"Not with you," Felina said, waving him away with a clawed hand. "You can leave."

"Cunt," the man said, before shaking his head and skulking back to his friends.

"See… There's no one here for me," Felina said, sighing and rolling her eyes. "No respect. Any of them. I'm going to go to The Palais after this, at least there are real people there."

Hamden Palais was a club near Pornington Crescent tube station that played a lot of electronic, New-Romantic kind of stuff. Felina was right: she would be more likely to meet someone who shared her proclivities there.

"Come along if you like," Felina said. "Bring Goaty if you want."

"I think I might be busy," I said with a smile.

We walked back to the flat through the cold, spring rain, making small talk as we went. We headed into the building and up the stairs. I turned the key and opened the door. Felina always left a crimson and orange Tiffany lamp switched on when we went out at night. That meant we didn't have to turn on the harsh overhead light when we walked into the flat. Leaving the lamp on made coming home more welcoming, a soft transition from the cold dark outside to the cosy inside. Felina could operate in complete darkness really well, anyway, due to her cat night vision, so I suppose the lamp was left on for my benefit, which was nice. I'd seen Felina reading and doing her nails in almost complete darkness before, with just a single candle burning far away on the kitchen table. It was quite impressive.

I closed the door behind Bapho after he had walked through it. I didn't speak. There was nothing to say. We both knew what we were there to do. I removed my leather jacket and boots. Bapho did the same. I pointed to the sofa, turned and headed into the bathroom.

I had recently purchased an extra-long douching nozzle from the gay shop near the bridge, along with a few buttplugs of various sizes. The douching nozzle was like a foot-long length of black hose with a rounded tip, really good for a nice, deep clean.

I kept all of my anal equipment proudly displayed on the top of a chest of drawers in my bedroom, like an altar; I had nothing to hide. There was a pair of black candles in some nice brass candlesticks I'd found on a second-hand stall in the market on either side of the display, and a little nickel thurible I sometimes used for burning incense.

I undressed, cleaned out my pig-hole, dried myself and wrapped a fluffy pink towel around my body, under my armpits and over my boobs. I let the towel hang hitched up over the base of my tail at the back so Bapho would have a good view of my arse. I walked back into the living room and beckoned to the goat-boy. Bapho had removed his boots and leather jacket. He stood up. I headed into my bedroom, which thankfully I had tidied earlier that day, and he followed. I lit a few of the candles that stood in empty, wax-encrusted wine bottles around the room, as well as the two black candles on my little altar. Bapho sat on the edge of the double bed and looked around disinterestedly at my shrine to sodomy and my posters of Patti Smith, Nico and Siouxie Sioux. I dropped to my knees, my face level with his bulging crotch. He placed his hands on his thighs, opened his legs and looked down at me with his goat eyes, the flickering candlelight making his devilish face look even more satanic. I tried my best to look wide-eyed and innocent as I gazed up at him from my place on the floor. I stroked his legs, his muscles hard beneath his tight blue jeans. His enormous package began to twitch and grow as I undid his belt, button and flies. I tugged at his jeans and pulled them down to just above his knees. He was wearing white Y-fronts that were straining to contain his prodigious meat. The smell of his pheromones was almost overpowering, but in a good way, and my head spun from the effects of the heady scent.

    I pulled his underwear down and released the beast. His cock was huge, lying semi-erect in its nest of curly grey pubes. I placed my hands on my own kneeling thighs and gazed at it. I felt like I was having some kind of religious experience, and it only occurred to me there and then that this would be the first time a fellow bestiamorph had fucked me, an actual bestiamorph cock deep inside my soft, hairless, pink body. Back in the Midlands I'd only fucked apes. I cupped his balls in my hand and leaned forward, nuzzling his cock with my snout and inhaling his goaty musk. With my free hand I grasped his shaft. I rubbed my snout from his pubes to the tip of his cock, back and forth, breathing deeper and deeper. I licked the place where the taut skin of his dick met the loose skin of his sack, using my hand to pull his shaft into my face, squishing my piggy nose with the increasing hardness of his animal arousal. My heart began to pound, not in my chest, but inside my pelvis, behind my little limp dicklette and above my twitching piggy arse-cunt. I slipped out of the towel, letting it fall onto the floor behind me. Bapho smiled down at me as his cock rose to its full size and majesty. I leant back and admired the behemoth. As it reached the full extent of its arousal, the mighty leviathan curved back upon itself, like an enormous, veiny, beige banana, the tip almost touching his navel. His foreskin retracted as his dick blossomed, slipping away from his glistening purple glans effortlessly. He must've been close to a foot long and as thick as my rolling pin. I was momentarily grateful for all the times I'd stretched out my cunt with the trusty utensil that I'd stolen from home economics class so long ago.

    I kissed the underside of his cock and ran my tongue up his shaft, flicking his frenulum. I took hold of the goat's dick and gently pulled it down, away from his abdomen, and began to kiss the shiny purple helmet, staring up into those alien yellow eyes with their sideways rectangular pupils, the candlelight catching the tips of his little horns. I used my thumbs to gently open his half-inch long piss slit and sniffed it, wanting to smell the inside of that epic beast. He smelt like piss and cum and desire and truth. I looked up and saw myself reflected in his satanic, barnyard gaze. I had never felt more of a pig. I had a sudden sense of the history of our people, a vision of bestiamorphs in ancient times, living far away from the settlements of apes. Bapho was the primordial animal spirit, he was a satyr, he was Pan. He had seduced milkmaids in the olive groves of Arcadia, frolicked with nymphs, naiads and dryads. He was Bacchus and Satan and Dionysius and Cernunnos, The Horned God. And me? I was a skinny pink-haired pig girl from the arse-end of nowhere who really, really wanted to get her back door smashed in good and proper.

I had never wanted to be fucked as badly as this. I stood up and leaned over him where he sat, keeping a grip on the iron-hard goat dick in my hand, revelling in the contrast between my nudity and his semi-undressed state. I straddled him, his cock squished between us. We began to kiss, open mouthed and hungry. It was then that I learned that goats have much longer tongues than everyone else. Bapho's tongue darted between my teeth and slowly withdrew, only to immediately return. I really wanted him to tongue my arsehole. His hands stroked my shoulders and upper back with a surprising degree of tenderness, before moving onto my tiny tits and taking hold of both nipples, which immediately tightened, like wingnuts. I pulled away from his mouth and thrust my chest forward, silently encouraging him to work on my tits. He began to pull my teats a little harder. I bit my lower lip and nodded, wide eyed.

I'd spent so much time tugging my nipples to make myself cum that even a big, strong goat boy like Bapho wouldn't have been able to inflict actual pain on them, only degrees of pleasure. He pulled and pulled, rocking me back and forth while

I made small grunts of approval. The familiar pressure behind my limp dicklette and empty scrotum began to build, and I knew I was going to cum.

I began to moan and looked down between his hands. My little impotent dicklette was pressed up against his massive cock, and the contrast drove me wild. My recent circumcision was still a thing of wonder to me, the permanent exposure of my pink, baked bean-sized glans turned me on as I gazed downwards. A perfectly clear emission of slick pre-cum had leaked from the tip of my dicklette and created a gummy salve glueing our two radically different penises together, a harbinger of my coming orgasm. My knees began to shake and I began to breathe faster. I closed my eyes and leaned in to kiss Bapho. We snogged long and deep as he pulled and jerked my tits with rough enthusiasm. I felt myself crossing the event horizon of my climax, and a few seconds later I came, hard. Moaning and shuddering I fell forward and Bapho took my weight.

I came back to myself, and after several moments of heavy breathing in his embrace, I leaned back. I looked at him, every fibre of my being asking, demanding, to be fucked. Bapho looked at his hands. The tips of his fingers were wet with my white pig milk. I rolled off him onto the bed and opened my legs wide, reaching around and grabbing the backs of my thighs and tipping my pelvis upwards. Bapho slipped off his jeans and pants, pulled his vest over his head and clambered between my legs. I clenched and unclenched my arse-cunt in anticipation. I desperately grabbed the bottle of lube from my bedside cabinet and rubbed a squirt into my eager fuck hole. He took hold of my ankles and, hands-free, guided that massive, curved weapon into my fun-centre.

I moaned as his billiard-ball sized helmet parted my puckered arse lips and slipped into me. In the beginning he just worked the first three or four inches of his rock-hard baton in and out of me, massaging my P-spot in a very agreeable manner, but I wanted more immediately. I clasped my ankles around his arse, just below his furry bob tail, and gently but firmly pulled him closer. With a cock that size he was probably used to not being able to sink all the way in, but I was a good girl, and I'd put in the hours, and the fists, buttplugs and rolling pins, and I knew I could take him. I felt him go deeper, until he hit the bend where my rectum transitioned into my large intestine proper. His massive helmet stopped its exploration there for several slow thrusts, and just nuzzled up against the bend, pushing its way a little further each time, politely knocking on the door, as it were, and then he popped into me properly, the shaft following where the head led.

I looked at his devilish satyr face, and I was sure I saw an expression of impressed satisfaction as the full twelve inches of his throbbing mutton truncheon buried itself in my eager piglette gash. He began fucking me slow and deep, pulling himself out a few inches before thrusting back in with increasing vigour, making me gasp each time. I began to lose myself in the rhythmic bucking, the in and out, as Bapho gradually built up both speed and velocity. I started to grunt with each thrust, low and hard. I reached under his armpits and wrapped my arms around him, pulling him towards me, wanting to give him as much leverage as possible as he fucked and fucked and fucked my slippery, wet, wide-open pig-slut cunt. He bore down on me. His weight felt so good, pinning me to the bed, my thighs pressed against my smooth, sweaty body. He rode me, pounded me, gritting his teeth and shaking out his long grey hair as he did. I began to sweat. My head began to swim. I wasn't sure if I'd be able to cum again so soon after my nipplegasm, but I was having a great time finding out. Bapho began to pant, no longer sliding so far out of my slippery hole, more grinding than fucking. I moaned. He was so very deep, literally up to his nuts in my guts. I could feel him moving around behind the wall of my abdominal muscles, pulverising my innards with his satanic majesty.

I suddenly had a thought, a moment of clarity in the depths of my revery. I tapped his hands and he let go of my ankles. I straightened my legs a little, so they were no longer pressed against my body, and I placed my feet either side of where he knelt fucking me. I raised my head from the pillow and looked down. My abdomen was visibly bulging where his cock was delving away inside of me. A semi-sphere the size of a grapefruit appeared and disappeared beneath my skin with each thrust, my bellybutton sitting at the peak of the hump created by his deep penetration. I reached down and placed the palms of my hands over my navel and felt him moving inside me.

He slowed and returned to his longer, deeper thrusts. I looked up at him. He was watching the spectacle with the same sense of wonder as I was. He looked from my bulging belly and into my eyes without slowing or missing a beat. We held eye contact for a few deliciously slow thrusts, my hands cradling the bulge he was creating in my belly. Something profound was happening. I started tripping out.

We bestiamorphs can't get pregnant, as you know, but I started to feel like the bulge in my belly was our baby, that the bumping that I felt beneath my skin was somehow related to the kick of an unborn child. That was what we bestiamorphs bought into the world when we fucked, not a new person, but sexual ecstasy. We created life this way. Bapho and I were the parents, not of a child, but of an ecstatic experience. I wanted this moment to last forever. And, at that very moment, he shot his muck into me.

Bapho let out something halfway between a moan and a bleat, thrusting his hips and throwing back his horned head, his grey hair, damp with sweat, clinging to his puckish face as torrents of hot spunk flowed into me. He looked magnificent. I could feel him filling me up; there seemed to be pints of the fucking stuff. My body fell limp and I lay there, skywest and crooked, fucked and filled and fulfilled. Bapho slowly, very slowly, drew his fat cock out of me, followed by a cascade of satanic spunk. I inhaled deeply, savouring the beautiful odour of his cum, tinged with the meaty perfume of my brutalised arsehole. Bapho flopped onto the bed by my side and exhaled a long, drawn-out breath.

I thought for a moment I might cry, the experience had been so moving, so profound. I felt I'd transcended time and space for a moment during our fucking, that I'd hit upon something that had always been missing from my life. All my previous sexual encounters had led to this moment, this epiphany. I was a goat-fucking anal pig-slut. I was mythology. I was a pagan flame. I was divine. Together Bapho and I had created a moment of perfection that would reverberate through eternity.

My eyes started to tingle. I was going to cry, in gratitude and love.

And then he fucking ruined it.

"Well, that was a bit of all right," he said, sitting up. "But I've got to go and meet my mates. They're going to The Red Cap after Hawkwind, and there's a barmaid in there I've been meaning to fuck for a while."

Bapho jumped up from the bed and pulled on his clothes.

"I enjoyed that, Swinella, you're a good fuck you are," he said, nodding sagely. "That bit with the belly sticking out when I was fucking you? That was dead good. Reminded me of that scene in *Alien* with John Hurt. Fucking wicked."

"Yeah... Er..." I fumbled to find the words, blinking away the tears, the emotion draining out of me and leaving me cold. "It was... something. It was all right. I liked it."

"Anyway," he said, heading to the door. "I might see you around. I don't usually fuck the same girl twice, but I might have another go with you, if you're up for it sometime? If neither of us is busy, and we're both bored, y'know, no promises or anything."

"Yeah... Maybe," I said.

"Right, I'll see myself out," he said, with a broad, devilish grin. "Take it easy."

And that was that. I lay in the bed trying to make sense of my emotions, of what had just happened. What I had interpreted as a profound, divine moment, he thought was just another fuck. I pulled on my nightie, went to the toilet, and shat out the remainder of the goat's thick, gelatinous cum. I washed the smudged makeup off my face, cleaned my teeth, went back into my bedroom, changed the spunk-soaked sheet and climbed into bed.

I had just settled down and was about to go to sleep when I heard the front door open and close, followed shortly by a gentle knock at my bedroom door.

"Come in," I said.

Felina swung the door open and strode into the room.

"So he's gone then? Was it any good? The Palais was shit. Nobody interesting about."

"Yeah, he's gone," I said, glumly. "It was amazing. The best shag of my life. I saw through time and touched the godhead."

"Then why're you so miserable?"

"I don't know…" I said with a sniff, tears welling up in my eyes. "It was amazing and… and I thought…"

"You thought it meant something," Felina said, not unsympathetically, shaking her head. "You thought it meant the same to him as it did to you, but he just upped and left after he'd shot his muck… Probably to fuck someone else."

I nodded, hot tears running down my face. I looked up at Felina, chin down and bottom lip thrust out.

"My god, Swinella," she laughed. "You are fucking pretty when you cry. You should do it more often."

"Fuck you," I said, laughing through the tears.

"Do you want one of my special hot chocolates?"

I nodded miserably. Felina went out of the room, and I heard her filling the kettle, followed by the sound of her bedroom door opening and closing. She came back a few minutes later wearing the oversized black Cure T-shirt she slept in. She flicked on the radio and tuned it to some foreign radio station, French or Belgian or something. I'd heard her listening to it before, late at night, when she was chilling out in her room. The station played nothing but accordion-heavy Gallic jazz all night long, and the DJ's whispering voice was super relaxing, even more so because I didn't understand a word he was saying.

Felina left again, smoked a quick fag while she waited for the kettle to whistle, and came back a few minutes later carrying two steaming mugs of sweet-smelling hot chocolate. She placed the mugs on my cluttered bedside table and blew out all but one of the candles.

"Move over, then," she said, climbing into bed beside me.

"I can smell why you call it your special hot chocolate," I said, referring to the aroma of whiskey that accompanied the sweet milky-chocolate smell curling out of the two mugs.

"It's good for what ails ya," she said, with an uncharacteristically warm smile. "You might've got a bit emotional when Goaty left, but it's good to see you post-buggeration. You have a glow about you."

We chatted while we drank our boozy chocolate. Felina gave me an in-depth review of her night at The Palais; who was there, what they were wearing, what the DJ played and didn't play. I told her all about my time with Bapho. She agreed that it sounded amazing and that he was probably a bit of a tosser.

Eventually I grew too tired to stay awake, I rolled onto my side, turning my back on Felina. She turned the same way, slid one arm beneath me, into and through the space between my shoulder and neck, just below the pillow. Her other arm curled around my waist, her clawed hand cupping the soft curve of my belly, her fingernails gently caressing my soft pink skin through the thin cotton of my nightie. She nuzzled her face into my back and began to purr.

It felt so right, the candlelight, the soft white noise of the rain falling on the slate rooftops of Hamden Town, the French jazz, and, most of all, Felina's contented purring. Everything combined and sent me off to sleep almost immediately.

The next morning, I awoke alone. The cat had gone, and the sun was shining.

CHAPTER EIGHT

THE HOUSE OF THE WAXING MOON

"See them?" Felina said, gesturing towards a group of people at another table, with a slight nod of her head. "What do you think they are?"

We were sat in The Dev' after work, as usual. Spring was turning into summer, and the evening was warm and cloudless. It was a typical, moderately busy midweek night. Soft Cell's *Memorabilia* was playing on the pub juke box. Wayne Mansfield was working the bar, his peroxide head bobbing this way and that as he pulled pints, served spirits and mixers, took cash and handed out change. Early evenings, midweek, the pubs in Hamden were mainly full of people who worked or lived locally. I liked those times the best. It wasn't too crowded and there were always people about you knew, drinking and hanging out. I'd already said hello to a quiet and introverted pig girl called Popper I'd become acquaintances with, and Felina had said hello to the half-dozen cat girls drinking in the pub.

I casually looked across the smoke-filled bar in the direction Felina had indicated and took a sip of vodka soda. A couple of tables over, there was a crowd of five apes. They were fairly standard-looking Goth fare, as far as I could tell.

"I dunno," I said. "They just look like normal Goths to me."

"Look at their teeth," Felina said.

I surreptitiously kept one eye on the group. One of them laughed, a skinny guy, with a streak of white in his backcombed black hair. He was wearing a purple, crushed-velvet frock-coat, and I saw that his upper canines were long and pointed.

"Oh," I exclaimed. "His teeth are like yours!"

"They are fucking not like fucking mine, for fuck's sake," Felina said, indignant, before lowering her voice to a conspiratorial whisper. "They're vampires. Teeth like mine... The cheek of you!"

"Vampires?" I said, eyes widening. "For real?"

"No. They're humans pretending to be vampires, but they still call themselves vampires and drink each other's blood and whatnot. There aren't any real vampires in here right now, thankfully," Felina said, leaning back in her seat, "Ironically real vampires tend to stay away from The Dev'... too much silver. See those girls over there?" She made a slight nod towards another table. "Witches."

I looked over and saw a table of young women, their clothes and hair leaning towards the hippy end of the Goth spectrum. Silver moon earrings, bangles and hennaed hair. I sniffed and isolated their scent from the potpourri of odours that swirled around them. They smelled of patchouli oil, roll-ups, cider and unshaved armpits.

"And that table over by the door? Satanists."

I looked at the alleged Satanists and saw a mismatched couple, a handsome guy with a shaved head and eyeliner and a slightly pudgy, tired-looking woman with crimped black hair and an oversized silver nose ring.

"He uses her to procure girls new to the scene for their sex magick rituals," Felina said with a shrug. "I admire them, in a way."

Felina raised her glass to the Satanists. The boy Satanist raised his own glass, returning the salute. The girl Satanist looked away and scowled.

"Any more?" I asked.

"Not right now," Felina said, looking around the bar. "I can't see any demons, but they aren't human anyway, so they wouldn't really count. Now, what do all of the people have in common?"

"They're all apes," I said, having already noticed this. "None of them are 'morphs."

"That's right," Felina said. "So, my theory is that apes don't know who they are until they join some group or other to tell them who they are, whereas we know who we are. That's the main difference between us and them. We know who we are. That's why they like football and politics and all that shit... So they can feel like they belong to something bigger than themselves."

"But not every ape is in some little group like that," I said. "And a lot of 'morphs like football."

"No, but every little group like those over there is made up exclusively of apes. Wouldn't it make sense for goats to be satanists? For rabbits to be witches? For cats to be vampires? But we don't do it. Why? Because we don't need to. We know who we are."

"You're a goth," I said, leaning in and whispering loudly. "You've joined a group to tell you who you are. Look at your clothes and record collection."

"No, I'm not! I'm not a goth!" Felina protested. "I'm naturally this way. I'm not trying to be like them, they're all trying to be like me!"

"Well," I laughed. "I am a punk... and I love it. And Punk Rock did help me find out who I am. If I hadn't gotten into punk I wouldn't be sat here now. You don't know, you're from London. It's hard to work out your identity in a small, redneck town in the arse end of nowhere. Music and fashion are the only way to do it."

"If you say so," Felina said dismissively, fishing her cigarettes out of her handbag and lighting a smoke.

"So, what's the plan for tonight?" I asked, changing the subject.

"Well, I can't stay out too long. I've an appointment."

"Oh really? With who?"

"A client," Felina said. "Foot worship. Want to come along? I don't think he'll mind. I won't give him a choice."

Of course I wanted to come along.

We left the pub and headed home. When we got back to the flat Felina stuck Nina Katzen's *Nunsexmonkrock* on the record player and got to work. Nina Katzen was a cat-girl singer from Germany, and her albums sounded exactly like the kind of music a cat-girl from Germany would produce.

Felina removed her boots and socks and began sprucing up

her feet. She gave herself a pedicure, pumiced away any dry skin, and rubbed lotion into her ghostly pale paws. To her credit, Felina did have very pretty feet, which was astounding when you looked at her collection of toe-crushing, wickedly high-heeled boots and shoes.

Felina explained to me that it was very common for blokes to fetishise feet. Apparently, some foot worship guys wanted horrible, dirty feet, to smell and stuff, but Felina's guy was one of the ones who preferred clean and perfect feet. It was interesting to watch Felina prepare her feet. She popped a pair of pink foam toe separators between her toes, and became fully absorbed in the task, taking great care painting her toenails a bright, pillarbox red.

"I'm more in the mood for black toenails," she said, looking back and admiring her handiwork. "But you have to give them what they want. You should do yours while we're here."

My feet were in need of a bit of care, so I cleaned off the chipped remains of the pink nail varnish I'd been wearing for the past few weeks and applied a coat of metallic green.

"Where are you meeting him?" I asked.

"There's a place that rents out rooms for this kind of stuff in Eweston, near the station. It's called The House of The Waxing Moon. We can jump on the bus after our toes have dried, and we'll be there in no time. The appointment is at half past nine."After we had used Felina's hairdryer to dry our nail varnish, the cat-girl retreated to her room. She returned a few minutes later dressed in one of her signature looks, tight-fitting PVC trousers and a black, polo-necked jumper with her silver septagram pendant over the top. She pulled on a double-breasted military jacket, black of course, and placed a wide-brimmed bolero hat on top of her bobbed hair.

"I'm going down there in my boots," she said, sitting at the kitchen table and pulling on a pair of fresh white cotton socks, followed by her fourteen-hole patent leather Dr Martins. "I'll change my shoes when we get there."

Felina grabbed a pair of red, open-toe sling-backs with vertigo-inducing heels and a thin ankle strap and thrust them into a leather holdall, along with a riding crop. She stood up and headed towards the door.

"Let's go to work."

A silver sliver of moon hung above the tiled rooftops as Felina and I walked up to an anonymous red door in a row of brownish-yellow four-storey terrace houses, most of which seemed to be serving as cheap bed and breakfasts.

Felina rang the doorbell and we waited. Just as I was beginning to think that no one was going to answer I heard the sound of heavy footsteps approaching the door from inside the building. The door swung open to reveal a familiar face.

"Gordita!" I exclaimed.

"*Cerdita!*" the hefty ham called out, a gold toothed smile lighting up her pudgy pig face. "What the fuck are you doing here? Are you a whore now? That's good. You should be a whore. You can use the money to buy food. *Hola* Felina, you fucking bitch. Come in, come in."

"Good evening, Gordita," Felina said cooly as we walked in. "I have an appointment at half past."

"You're in room two," Gordita said as she moved her flabby porcine bulk to one side to allow us to enter the building. "Shit Boy has prepared the room, so you're all ready to go."

We followed her as she stomped down the hallway. She was wearing a pair of wedge-heeled strappy sandals, her pudgy pink feet pressed hard against the lime-green straps, like over-chewed bubblegum. Her ample behind was wrapped in a too-short hot-pink mini skirt, her colossal hips rolling with every step, her curly tail swinging from side to side.

"Nigel really likes you, Swinella... We should hang out," she said over her shoulder with machine-gun rapidity. "Of course, everything is shit right now, but everything is going to be fine, really, but shit right now, but fine, *chica*, don't worry... Nigel is a bum, a fucking bum, but you know, *chica*, I do love him, I mean, not really, but he has money, not enough, of course. How can there ever be enough money in this shitty world? And my trotters? *Dios*... these fucking shoes!'

The lights were red and low, the walls were painted dark grey and the floor was tiled in a black and white chessboard pattern. We passed a closed door, from behind which I could hear a sharp noise, like someone intermittently clapping their hands, accompanied by a muffled woman's voice and the low moans of a man.

"Nigel will take us for dinner, if you want?" Gordita said. "He's a fucking piece of shit bum loser, but he'll pay, *chica*, he'll pay for everything."

"She's on a diet," Felina said. "Nigel can buy her clothes if he wants to throw his money about."

"Oh, he won't do that," Gordita scowled at Felina, wrinkling her snout and shaking her head. "That's not his thing at all."

I couldn't help but recall how the last time I'd seen her Gordita had had her snout buried in a bowl of trifle while a goat's ten-inch cock slid in and out of her greased fun-tube. I loved the way the people I'd met in Hamden Town just took things like that in their stride, it was like being in some alternate reality devoid of shame. So often you'll hear regular people saying that sex is natural and nothing to be ashamed of, but they don't really mean it. In Hamden I'd met people who actually lived without shame or fear of judgement, and it was amazing. I felt it gave me *carte blanche* to explore my own sexuality, and that was an exhilarating thing. Gordita opened a door and Felina and I walked through.

"Have fun!" Gordita called, smiling and flashing her golden tusks at me as I walked past.

Felina closed the door behind us and I looked around, the sound of Gordita's stomping footsteps fading away as she walked down the hall. It was a large room with a high ceiling. It was garishly decked out like some kind of hyper-feminine fever dream. The mauve carpet was thick and slightly grubby. The floor length velvet curtains were flamingo pink. The bed was covered with a peach candlewick spread and strewn with cream-coloured fluffy pillows. There was a dressing table loaded with makeup, a couple of large mirrors facing each other on opposite walls, a clothes rail full of dresses, and a shoe rack containing lots of pairs of large sized high heel shoes. A group of severed mannequin heads sat on a long shelf, wearing a collection of wigs in a variety of colours and styles. It was like being inside a giant cake, but a cake that smelled of cheap perfume, cigarette smoke and stale cum. It was gross, but I quite liked it in some weird way.

"They mainly use this room for sissy play," Felina explained, looking around and waving her clawed hand in the direction of the wigs and dresses. "That's why there're these mirrors and clothes and whatnot. This hideous decor makes me want to cough up a hairball, but it'll do. We don't need much equipment for tonight, just my paws."

Felina switched on a couple of pink lamps and then turned off the bright, overhead light. She slipped a tape into a cassette player on a shelf and pressed play. The sound of The Velvet Underground's *Sunday Morning* began playing at a discrete volume.

"Just sit on the bed and keep quiet," she said. "Our boy won't mind you being here, he'll either get turned on by it or he'll forget that you're there... but he'll probably be into it."

I did as she said, taking off my shoes before hopping onto the bed. I crossed my legs and leaned back against the padded headboard. Felina pulled a heavy batwing chair, upholstered in fuchsia velvet, away from the wall and into the middle of the room, turning it to face the doorway. She took off her boots and socks, and hid them under the bed. She took the red stilettos out of her bag and pulled them on, wincing slightly.

"I've never broken these fucking things in," she said, scowling at her shoes. "I only use them for sessions with this boy, so I've hardly walked in them at all."

Felina took a yellow-striped bottle of Giorgio Beverly Hills out of her bag and sprayed a small amount onto her ankles, just above the shoes. The room filled with a floral odour underscored with tones of peach, orange blossom and ylang-ylang. Outside in the hallway I heard the sound of the front door closing, followed a few seconds later by a timid knock at the door. Felina tossed the perfume bottle onto the bed, sat in the chair and straightened her back. She crossed her legs, placed the riding crop across her lap, and took a deep breath.

"Enter," she said in a loud, commandeering voice.

The door opened slowly and a pudgy, boring-looking ape man, of average height with greying hair and a receding hairline, walked in. He was wearing a charcoal-coloured pinstriped suit, cream shirt and maroon tie. He smelt of the tube and nervous anticipation. The man quietly closed the door behind him and turned to face Felina.

"Good evening, Mistress," he said, with a slight bow. "I hope you are well?"

"Never mind that, Mr Doormat" Felina said, harshly, pointing at the man with her riding crop, hard-faced and mean. "Strip. Then get down on your knees."

The man immediately began removing his clothes and placing them on top of the dresser, hesitating and looking over at me when he got down to his white vest and blue and white striped boxers.

"Never mind her," Felina snapped. "Get the rest of your kit

off. You know the drill, doormat."

The man gingerly took off his vest and pants and dropped them to the floor. His cock was like a nervous prawn trying desperately to hide itself in the tangled undergrowth of his pubes.

"On your knees," Felina commanded. "And then you may approach me."

The man sunk to his knees and began crawling towards Felina. There was something profound, almost religious, about the whole scene. Felina uncrossed her legs and placed her feet side by side on the floor in front of the chair. The man stopped in front of her and placed his forehead on the carpet a few inches away from Felina's feet. Her porcelain-white, scarlet-nailed toes wiggled slightly through the gap in the red high heeled shoes. The man breathed heavily and shivered. Felina's feet were his goddess, and he was here to worship.

"You may lift your head and look at them," Felina said.

The man slowly lifted his forehead from the carpet and gazed in wonder at Felina's feet.

"May I touch them, Mistress?" the man said.

"You may touch the toes of my left foot with the tip of one index finger," Felina said. "And nothing more... For now."

The man reached out a shaking finger and gently stroked Felina's toes where they poked through the red patent leather of her shoes.

"Oh, fuck..." he moaned, shaking his head and closing his eyes. "Can I smell them, Mistress? Can I smell your toes?"

"You are permitted to smell them," Felina said. "But no

touching. I don't want your dirty nose coming into contact with my perfect little toes."

The man placed his nose an inch or two from Felina's toes and inhaled deeply. He went from one foot to the other, even though I'm sure they both smelled the same. He genuinely seemed to be in some kind of ecstatic state as he huffed Felina's perfumed paws.

"There's a good boy, there's a good Mr Doormat... You like that, don't you?" Felina said. "Now... On your back, Mr Doormat... we haven't got all night."

The man did as he was told, turning onto his back and lying with his arms stretched out at his side. Felina reached down, unbuckled both her shoes, and removed them. She placed her instep onto his face and he inhaled, moaning as he breathed out. I noticed that his little prawn was no longer trying to hide in his unruly bush. The pink crustacean had stood to attention, and was now twitching and jumping as if it was the recipient of an ongoing series of small electric shocks. Felina curled her lip in a disdainful sneer as she moved her feet and began kneading the man's pectorals with her crimson toes. He moaned in delight, lifting his head from the floor to watch the action as best he could.

"Mistress Swinella," Felina said, turning to me and winking. "Why don't you make yourself more comfortable? Take off your socks and swing those hams over the edge of the bed."

I did as Felina said, pulling off my white ankle socks and sitting on the edge of the bed, with my feet resting lightly on the greasy Axminster.

"Turn your head, Doormat," Felina said. "Look at her trotters. You like that, don't you?"

The man strained his neck to look at me.

"Yes, Mistress," he said. "Very much, Mistress. Thank you, Mistress."

"Would you like Mistress Swinella to come over here and give us a hand? Or give us a foot, I should say."

"Yes, Mistress," the man moaned.

Felina stamped hard on the man's chest with the soles of both of her feet, making a loud slapping noise.

"Well, Mr Doormat, you're not going to get two for the price of one," Felina called out. "Mistress Swinella... Wiggle those tootsies! Mr Doormat... Take a look at what she's got."

I did as Felina said, holding my feet out and wiggling my toes. The man's eyes widened in wonder.

"Now then... I'm sure that if you're prepared to throw another fifty quid on top of what we've agreed, then maybe I can persuade Mistress Swinella to come over here and help us out."

"Yes, Mistress," the man said without hesitation. "Thank you, Mistress."

"Yes what?" Felina demanded.

"Yes please, Mistress," Mr Doormat said. "Please and thank you, Mistress."

"Good boy," Felina said. "Mistress Swinella... Come on over here, my love."

I had no idea what was expected of me, but fifty quid was fifty quid. I stood up from the bed and walked over.

"Stand just there," Felina said, pointing to a spot on the floor at the side of the prostrate foot lover. "You can keep me stable while I go for a little walk."

I did as Felina said and held out my hand. The domineering cat-girl took my hand in her perfectly-manicured, wickedly clawed hand, placed her feet firmly on the man's chest and stood up. The man groaned. Felina began to slowly walk along the length of the doormat's torso, curling her toes from time to time and digging her toenails into his skin.

"You like that, don't you, Mr Doormat?" Felina laughed as she bounced on his abdomen.

Felina began to run her toes through Mr Doormat's tangled bush as his dick twitched to and fro with increased urgency. I could see why Mr Doormat was a client of Felina's. She only weighed about seven stone wet through. If it had been Gordita bouncing up and down on him, he'd have burst like an overripe pumpkin. Felina began to pull at Mr Doormat's anxious member with her surprisingly prehensile toes, and he moaned and wriggled on the floor like someone trying to wake up from a nightmare. Felina hopped off Mr Doormat with cat-like grace and landed softly in the space between his spasming legs.

"Now then, Mistress Swinella," she said to me. "Why don't you sit on the throne while I give this little foot slave a very special massage. Mr Doormat... If you ask nicely Mistress Swinella might let you touch her trotters."

I sat down on the velvet chair and placed my feet either side of Mr Doormat's sweaty, red face.

"Please, Mistress Swinella, may I please touch your feet?" The submissive whined. "Please and thank you."

"No," I said. "You may not."

Felina looked over from where she stood between Doormat's twitching legs with an annoyed look on her face. I have very ticklish feet, and I didn't want Mr Doormat touching them. But I knew I had to play along with the scene somehow. I had to earn my fifty quid.

"Firstly," I said in as stern a voice as I could manage. "You call my feet 'trotters' at all times. Secondly, you haven't earned the right to touch me, not yet. Thirdly, if you're a good boy, I'll place my trotters on your chest and wiggle my toes. Would you like that?"

"Oh yes please, Mistress Swinella," Mr Doormat said. "I promise I won't touch your beautiful trotters. Thank you."

"My title isn't 'Mistress'... You don't get to call me that, only other mistresses call me that," I said, slapping his shoulder hard with the sole of my right foot. "It's 'Princess'."

"Sorry, Princess Swinella," the man moaned. "It won't happen again."

Felina looked over at me and grinned. I got the impression she was slightly impressed by my performance, but only slightly, of course; cats are never impressed that much by anything. I placed my feet onto Mr Doormat's sparsely haired chest and began to dig my toes into his skin. He was very hot, it was like he was running a fever, which I suppose in a way he was; a foot-slave sex fever. I looked between his legs. Felina lifted one of her feet up to her own face and spat on the bottom of her toes. She was a very flexible girl, with perfect balance, like most cats. She gracefully placed her foot back down and onto Mr Doormat's twitching cock and began to wank him off, dexterously sliding her toes up and down his tremulous four-inch shaft. She began to move her foot faster, his skin slippy with her fishy cat spit. Mr Doormat moaned and groaned. I pressed my toenails into his chest as hard as I could, and then bounced my heels up and down, before returning to digging in my nails. I was getting into it, so I placed the soles of my feet either side of his head and began to squeeze and squish his stupid face. Felina was slightly tapping his balls with the back of her foot; she really was incredibly good at standing on one leg. Mr Doormat moaned and groaned and began to hyperventilate. His body tensed and he suddenly shot his mess all over his chest. I felt a splash on one of my toes and I knew that he'd managed to fire a little bit of his rancid baby-gravy onto my skin. I had a stranger's spunk on me. I'd obviously had one-night stands with strangers before, but this was very different. I didn't even know Mr Doormat's real name, but a globule of his watery semen, the size of a split lentil, was sitting on my big toe like an opalescent verruca. I kept calm. It'd wash off. It wasn't a big deal. It was only spunk. I'd had plenty of spunk in and on me, and I was pretty sure I'd be getting a lot more. Then I had an idea.

"You've cum on my trotter, you dirty boy!" I cried out. "You'd better lick it off. Now!"

"Yes, Princess Swinella. At once," Mr Doormat said, turning onto all fours and leaning towards my soiled foot.

"No fucking about here!" I said. "Do it quickly. No free nibbles. No lingering."

Mr Doormat did exactly as he was told and licked his sticky

emission off my toe.

"Good boy," Felina said with a high-pitched, sadistic laugh.

Mr Doormat cleaned himself down with a white hand-towel that Felina took from a rail by the door, and got dressed. I was surprised at how quickly both Mr Doormat and Felina switched back to everyday reality after such an intense scene. Mr Doormat reached into his pocket and pulled out his wallet. He took a bunch of notes out and placed them on the dressing table. Felina took the cash, removed two twenties and a ten and handed them back to the man.

"Here," she said. "These are Princess Swinella's. Place them on the bedside cabinet."

Mr. Doormat did as she said and put the notes on the bedside cabinet, close by where I sat, bowing to me slightly as he did so. I struggled not to say thank you, but I managed to stay stone-faced as he placed the money down.

After he had gone, Felina and I got our stuff together and walked out of the room. It was exactly half past ten. The hour had gone really fast. At times I thought Felina was rushing Mr. Doormat along too quickly, but everything had ended right on time. Felina handed a twenty to Gordita as she showed us out. Felina had told me, just before we left the sissy room, that we had to give twenty percent of our earnings to the house. I passed a ten to my fat sister in sodomy.

"Ah... So you ARE a whore," Gordita said, looking me up and down with an approving smile as she took the money. "I'm happy for you, *chica*... It's good to be a whore, and to know it and to love it, do you love it? We love it. It's everything, really.

Todo."

Gordita opened the front door and grinned her chubby golden grin.

"Bye now, *chicas*," the stout sow said as we walked out. "Don't be strangers. I see you in The Dev' on Friday, no? Nigel is meeting me there, the asshole, I love him, but not really!"

"So…" Felina said as we sat side by side on the deserted upper deck of the number twenty nine back to Hamden Town. "How does it feel getting paid to let a stranger shoot his muck on your foot?"

"Good," I said, thinking it over and nodding. "It felt pretty good. I might do it again… Should the opportunity arise."

"Oh really?" Felina said with a laugh. "Oh… and one more thing."

"Yeah?" I asked. "What?"

"Fucking, Princess?! Seriously?!"

We both fell about laughing as the bus lurched up The Lambstead Road and on towards Hamden Town.

CHAPTER NINE

NURSE ELAINE

It was a slow, rainy Wednesday afternoon. Felina had the day off and I was working in The Black Violet alone. I was sat on the stool behind the till, drinking black coffee from a chipped mug and reading one of Felina's Marquis De Sade paperbacks, and both the book and the day were taking an eternity to end. I was listening to a tape by an American band called Suicide on the cassette player, and that was helping the time to pass. I'd never heard of Suicide until Felina introduced me to them, but I think at that time their first album was my most played tape.

I was wearing a pair of high-waisted Daisy Dukes that I'd made myself by viciously butchering a pair of regular blue jeans, cutting the legs off and making a hole beneath the waistband for my tail. I had on fishnet, lime green tights, white bobby socks, my trusty Doc Martin Mary Janes, and an oversize pink V-necked jumper that I'd found in a charity shop for 50p. Felina hated my pink jumper. I had made holes in the wrists so I could stick my thumbs through when I was wearing it, and Felina used to mime that she was vomiting whenever she saw it. The look was topped off with my black beret. Makeup was minimal, but a blue lip elevated the whole package. I knew I looked shit-hot, regardless of what Felina thought about my jumper.

The door opened and I was surprised to see a familiar face. It was the nurse from the circumcision clinic. She was wearing a knee length black raincoat, American tan tights and a pair of open-toed patent leather shiny black stilettos, with bright red nail polish on her toes, just about visible through her naff old-woman tights. She smelt of her usual perfume; Shalimar, Benson's and Mellow Birds, but with an undercurrent of nervousness that hadn't been present at the clinic. At first, she seemed not to notice me, her attention being taken by the racks of hanging clothing.

"Can I help you?" I asked, standing up and walking over.

"Oh, it's you," the nurse said, turning to me with a smile. "I thought I remembered that you said you worked here. I was just passing... I thought I'd come in and take a look at all these, these... Freaky fashions."

'Freaky fashions?' I thought. Seriously?

"Oh," I said. "I guess they're not really to your taste?"

"You'd be surprised," she replied, raising her eyebrows conspiratorially. "I've been known to get a bit freaky myself."

The nurse undid her beige raincoat to reveal a short red leather dress with a wide black belt. It was clear that she was wearing a tight corset under the dress, so maybe she was right, maybe she did 'get a bit freaky'. I stared at her tiny waist, intrigued.

"Oh, you've noticed this?" The nurse said, placing her hands on her narrow midsection. "Yes, I've been tight-lacing for years... it's a fancy of my husband's."

"It looks nice," I said, stepping back and taking in her

hourglass figure. "What size is your waist?"

"I'm about eighteen inches right now," she said, with some degree of pride. "I have to wear the corset all the time, except when I'm in the bath. It's uncomfortable, but I like it, if you know what I mean? It makes me feel held, in some way."

"I guess so, but I like to feel relaxed," I said with a shrug. "I don't think it's for me."

"I like your earrings, Swinella," she said. "Don't you think that's a bit kinky? How many have you got?"

"Just twelve," I said; I had never thought of my earrings as kinky, though. "Six in each ear."

"I have a lot of piercings myself," the nurse said. "You just can't see them."

"Ok," I said. "Um… cool."

"But I'd like to show you," she said, fastening her coat and tying the belt around her tightly cinched midriff. "Would you like to grab a drink when you've finished? I have a few errands to run, but I can call back at closing time. It'll be my treat."

I agreed to go for a drink after work. The nurse introduced herself as Elaine, browsed the shop for a few more minutes, and left with a cheery 'see ya later, alligator'.

I had to admit, I was ever so slightly fascinated by this strange, middle-aged woman. I was curious as to why she wanted to take me out for a drink. I wouldn't have to wait long to find out.

The Mother Black Cap was almost empty, which wasn't surprising for six thirty on a Wednesday evening. The only gay bar in Hamden Town, The Mother Black Cap was named after a famous witch who had allegedly lived in Hamden Town hundreds of years ago. The Red Cap, the pub opposite the tube station that was popular with metallers, was named after her rival, Mother Red Cap. The Mother Black Cap had an upstairs bar with a beer garden out the back, and a downstairs venue at street level that held drag shows and club nights. The truth is, The Mother Black Cap was the nicest bar in Hamden, but the music wasn't always to my taste. Probably the best thing about the place was that tourists didn't generally go in there, and the small beer garden out the back was the best-kept secret in Hamden Town. I have always liked the darkness of Hamden, the stories of witches and all that, but there was a much more recent horror story connected with The Mother Black Cap. The previous year, serial killer Dennis Nilson had picked up one of his many victims in that very bar, but at least that victim had escaped. I had no idea what Nurse Elaine had planned for me, hopefully nothing quite as extreme as Nilson.

"How's the circumcision healing?" Nurse Elaine said as we took our seats. "All good, I hope?"

"Yes," I said. "It's fine, thanks."

"Do you like it?"

I did like it. I thought it was fantastic. Having the glans, the most sensitive part of the genitals, just exposed like that, all the time, just hanging out there, it was fucking weird, but I dug it.

"Yeah," I said. "I do like it."

I decided to start leaning into our increasingly intimate conversation, to see where all of this was going.

"And," I began, hesitating, coyly looking down my snout at my drink and answering in a conspiratorial whisper, "And, y'know what? I enjoyed having it done."

Nurse Elaine smiled and sat back in her seat.

"That's what I thought," she said, nodding. "I've not been circumcised, of course, but I've experienced something similar. Remember when I told you I have piercings, but that you can't see them?"

I nodded.

"Well, that's because they're down there," she whispered loudly, gesturing towards her crotch with her eyes. "Y'know... 'below the belt'. I've got quite a lot of piercings hidden away. When you lay down to get your little tinkle trimmed, I saw how you reacted. It was the same way I react when I get more metal put through my... Well, through my cunt, Swinella."

I have to admit it, I was thoroughly intrigued. I had to see what she had going on in her knickers.

"Does it hurt?" I asked, eyes widening; it was the only thing I could think to ask.

"It really does, Swinella," she said with a wistful half smile. "It really does, but you know what? I like it. It took me a long while to work it out, because I don't like it when it's happening, but when it's all healed, I like the fact that it hurt. That I went through it. It gives me some kind of power... Power over myself, I guess, but also over the world. Over everything," she laughed. "And that's what keeps me going back for more. It hurts when I stretch the holes too, when I put thicker rings in... But I really like the weight of the bigger jewellery."

"How many do you have?" I asked, genuinely intrigued.

"Oh, Swinella," she said, with a sly smile. "You'll have to count them for me... I just can't remember."

"I'd be happy to," I said.

"Well, I can't just get it out here."

"I think you probably could," I replied, looking around the almost empty bar, Donna Summer's *I Feel Love* playing quietly in the background, like some kind of essential cliché.

Elaine laughed and shook her head.

"I don't think so," she said. "Do you live around here?"

"I do," I smiled; I could see where this was heading.

"If you want we could, um... Go back to your place?" She leaned in, placed her hand on mine, squeezing it slightly. "We can grab a bottle of wine, and I can, um... I can show you what I have. You can show me how your circumcision is healing... If you want?"

I wanted.

I unlocked the door to the flat and walked in. Felina was curled up on the sofa reading yet another impenetrable French erotic paperback.

"Eh-up, Felina," I announced as I flounced into the living room. "This is Nurse Elaine, she's from the circumcision clinic. We just bumped into each other, and she's just popping by to see how I'm healing. Had a nice day off? Good. I just need a corkscrew, and we'll get out of your hair."

I grabbed the corkscrew and a couple of glasses and we headed to my room. I opened my bedroom door and flicked on the light. Nurse Elaine walked through the doorway and into the carefully curated squalor of my punk rock boudoir. I turned and looked out into the living room to see Felina gawping at me wide-eyed. I winked, stuck my tongue out, and closed the door with a click.

"I didn't know you had a flatmate," she said. "And such a beautiful one. And a cat to boot!"

"Please, take a seat," I said, taking a pile of clean washing off the battered armchair that stood in the corner and throwing it onto the floor. "Yeah, Felina's ace. We get on really well."

Nurse Elaine removed her raincoat, folded it and placed it onto the arm of the chair, and sat down. I liked the way she sat; her heels and corset gave her a really nice, straight-backed posture. She kept her legs together and placed her hands on her knees. I'm pretty sure it was the first time she'd been in a room like mine. The wine bottle candlesticks, scattered clothing and makeup, and the bootleg punk rock posters probably wouldn't have been her first choice for interior decor. I saw Elaine glance over at the collection of anal accoutrements scattered on top of my chest of drawers, my altar to the dark goddess of sodomy. It felt really good to have her see those sex toys, knowing that she knew where they'd been. I flipped the tape that was in the cassette player. It was Patti Smith's first album, *Horses*. I pressed play and turned the volume down. Soft piano chords played gently at a discreet level. Jesus had died for someone's sins, but he certainly hadn't died for mine.

I took off my leather, threw it in the corner, flopped onto the bed, all casual punk-rock style, and removed my Mary Janes. I opened the bottle of wine, filled the glasses, handed one to Elaine, and reclined on my bed. I felt as if some kind of power dynamic had done a complete reversal. When I'd been at the circumcision clinic, I had been firmly in Nurse Elaine's territory, now she was in mine, and I had the upper hand.

"Is this something you do often, Nurse Elaine?" I asked, sipping my red wine and looking her up down. "What would your husband say, if he knew you were here now, with me?"

"To be honest, Swinella," she replied, "He'd probably be jealous as all fuck."

"But jealous of what? We're just two acquaintances sharing a bottle of wine."

"He'd be jealous of this," Nurse Elaine said, getting to her feet.

Nurse Elaine reached up and under the hem of her short, scarlet dress and began to remove her knickers. I saw that her American Tan tights were actually old-fashioned stocking with suspenders. As she pulled her underwear down I heard a metallic rattle. She slid her black lace thong down over her slender knees, dropped it onto the floor and nimbly sidestepped it in her wickedly heeled stilettos. She smiled a naughty smile and wiggled her hips from side to side. I heard the metallic rattle again, louder this time.

"That's better," she said. "I don't like having them all cooped up in my panties, but if I don't wear underwear, I sound like the tin man when I walk."

I was so ready to see what was going on beneath that red dress. I sat up and placed my glass on the bedside table. I sat with my elbows on my knees, leaning forward to better see the presentation. Nurse Elaine took a step towards me and gingerly took hold of the hem of her sluttish red mini dress with her manicured fingertips. She began to slowly lift the dress. She was shaved, of course, but that wasn't the thing that made her cunt exceptional. She had been right, in a way; there were too many rings hanging through her cunt to know for sure how many piercings she had without counting. She held her dress up with one hand, and with the other hand she began to caress her extravagantly decorated genitalia. The rings were thick, maybe a quarter of an inch, and the weight of them pulled her lips down slightly. They were each fastened by some kind of steel ball. There were bigger rings through her thick outer labia, and smaller ones, in both gauge and diameter, through her inner lips. There were also a couple of rings up top, near her clit. They were, without question, one extremely perforated set of beef curtains.

"Do you like them?" she asked.

I nodded, wide-eyed and fascinated.

"It's quite amazing," I said, reaching out and taking hold of one of the bigger rings hanging through her middle-aged mutton shutters. "Can I pull it?"

"Sure, but not really hard," she said, beginning to breathe heavier.

I gave the ring a gentle tug, it felt pretty solid. Nurse Elaine closed her eyes and moaned. I let go of the ring and ran my fingers back and forth over the medley of steel hanging through her tender piss flaps. The metal jingled pleasingly. Nurse Elaine undid her belt, unzipped the back of the dress, let it fall and stepped out of it. Without the belt and dress covering it, her waist looked even smaller.

"Oh, this old thing?" Nurse Elaine said, stroking her black cotton corset and circling her waist with her long fingers. "Do you like it?"

One thing I've noticed about sex people, kinksters, pervs, whatever you want to call them, is that they always ask you if you like the object of their fetish. I think it turns them on to have that validation, like having their kink reinforced and reflected back at them. Of course, I was happy to play along.

"It's amazing," I said. "So very hot. Are those rings uncomfortable?"

"In a way," she turned and admired herself in my mirror. "But the thing is, Swinella, I like it. I like the metal through my cunt lips, the discomfort is always bringing me back to myself. I know at all times who and what I am, through the constant pressure my body is under. It's hard to explain, I don't know if you understand?"

I did understand. I realised that, in some way, this woman had achieved through manipulation and modification of her body that which had been forced upon me by nature. My snout and my tail were the permanent reminders of who and what I was. With Nurse Elaine, her tightly constricted waist, the metal hanging from her mutton shutters, the vertigo-inducing heels that I'm pretty sure she wore all the time, they were constantly bringing her attention back to her otherness, her sexual difference. Bestiamorphs like me, at the end of the day, were born freaks. Nurse Elaine was a freak of her own making, a self-constructed Frankenstein's monster.

"I may as well show you my tits," she said, unfastening her bra and slipping it off.

Her boobs were pretty big, and they sagged impressively when she removed her black lacy bra. Both of her nipples were pierced, large rings, as big as her outer labia jewellery. She tugged them and smiled.

"It's your turn now, Swinella," she said, hands on hips. "I've shown you my little secrets. Let's see how your winky is healing."

I stood up. Nurse Elaine took my place, sitting straight backed on the edge of the bed. I slipped off my skirt, pulled down my tights and knickers, and thrust my pelvis towards the nurse. She leaned forward and assumed an air of professionalism.

"Oh, it's healed really nicely," she said. "You were right to ask the doctor to trim off a little more. I was very pleased when you did that, and quite surprised when he did as you asked. You know, he wouldn't have done that for most people. I think it's because you're a... You know... You're a pig."

Her fingers were cool as she reached out and took hold of my dicklette. She began to explore. I could tell she was feeling for my balls as she squeezed and prodded my empty scrotum. She looked me in the eye, leaned in and took my cock in her mouth, reaching behind me with both of her hands, one hand resting on my arse cheek, the other groping for my tail. She began to slurp and suck at my resolutely flaccid cock. It felt all right, but it didn't do much for me. She grabbed my tail and began to move her hand back and forwards along its length, like she was wanking it off. I had to suppress a laugh. Neither of the things she was doing were particularly turning me on. It would be like taking a regular person and expecting them to be turned on if you stroked their elbow and sucked their knee. After a few minutes of effort she stopped and looked up at me.

"What's the matter, baby," she said, in a weirdly childish voice. "Don't I turn you on?"

"It's nice," I said. "My dick is sensitive… But not like a boy's. It's more like a third, less sensitive, nipple, and like I said at the clinic, it never gets hard. And my tail is not really an erogenous zone, to be honest. It feels OK though."

"Your dick is less sensitive than your nipples?" she said, with a note of disbelief in her voice.

"I really am your first pig, aren't I?" I said.

"You're my first bestiamorph," she confessed.

"You know I'm a bottom, right?" I asked. "We're all bottoms, us pigs. I'm probably like you. I don't have a top bone in my body. I've never had the slightest inclination to fuck anyone. I've never shot a load, I've never had a hard on, and I never will. This is what makes us pigs. Not this," I pointed at my snout. "Or this," I turned and wagged my tail in her face.

"I didn't know. I'm sorry," Nurse Elaine looked crestfallen. "I didn't know. I suppose you're like a gay man, really? Like the woman in a gay relationship? Martha, not Arthur… I feel a bit stupid."

"Yeah, I don't really think that's how gay men work either…

like one of them is 'the woman'. I'm pretty sure they're both men... That's kind of the point," I said. "But I still don't think you get it. I'm like you, really. What you saw, when I had my dicklette trimmed, was kinship. We're the same."

"So we're like sisters," she said, her eyes lighting up.

"I guess," I said, unconvinced that we were anything 'like sisters'.

"And we can be friends?"

"Sure," I said. "If you want. I like you. You're interesting."

"I have to get going soon." She said, looking at her wristwatch. "My husband will be wondering where I am. But can we sit a while first?"

I flipped the tape over and sat down on the bed next to Nurse Elaine.

"Can we get under the covers?" She asked. "I'm a bit cold."

I nodded and pulled back the duvet. Nurse Elaine kicked off her stilettos and slipped into the bed.

"I've been through a lot," she suddenly said, wriggling close and wrapping her arms around me.

"We all have," was all I could think of to say.

"Will you play with my foo-foo for a bit?" she said.

I reached down and took hold of a handful of metal and meat. I already knew she was going to be soaking wet before I touched her. I had smelled her arousal, the pungent aroma of her middle-aged fanny batter starting to bubble and flow. I began to gently pull at her plethora of piercings. I slid an exploratory finger between her saturated mutton shutters, past her rings and gently probed her opening. Nurse Elaine closed her eyes and moaned. I added a second finger and worked her wet gash. I kissed her cheek and wrapped my free arm around her shoulders. She snuggled in closer and let out another low moan. Now, I'm not a top, but I am possessed with a never-ending curiosity about other people's bodies and sexualities. I wasn't turned on but, in a way, I was getting aroused by my very disconnection with the act I was taking part in. I was into the fact that I wasn't into it, if that makes sense? I experimentally pushed a third finger into her. She had quite the gaping bucket, and I supposed she was no stranger to big toys and a bit of fisting. That was something I could relate to. A fourth finger and a thumb slipped in with relative ease, and all without any lube other than her natural goo-goo muck. She was quite the juicy milf. I pulled my hand out of her sopping wet wizard's sleeve and began to stroke and pull at her rings.

"Oh fuck, Swinella," she moaned. "I can't believe..."

"What can't you believe, Elaine?" I whispered, nuzzling my snout into her L'Oréal Elnett-smelling hair.

"I can't believe that you're doing this," she said. "That I'm being touched by a..."

"By a what?" I asked.

"By... by someone like you."

I easily located her clit, mentally thanking Gail for giving me a detailed description of her pussy over the phone some years previously, and began to move my fingertip in small circles over and around her sensitive little button. There wasn't a ring through her actual clit, but she had a couple through the hood. Other than the phone sex with Gail, this was the first time I'd been intimate with another woman. I varied the speed and pressure as I worked, following the ebbs and flows of her growing arousal as I did. Her scrap metal rattled as I got down to work. Nurse Elaine reached out and started fumbling for my tits beneath my jumper, but I pulled away and shook my head.

"No," I said. "You don't get to touch me until you're invited."

Nurse Elaine nodded, pulled her hand out from under my jumper, and began to work her own nipple instead, pulling on the thick ring and squeezing her soft and saggy tit.

I increased the pressure and began to bite her neck, gently pressing my snout into her soft skin. I grunted softly, just to give her the full porcine experience. Her breathing became more and more rapid, a small moan escaping on every exhalation. She was going to cum any moment. She moved in to kiss me on the mouth. I turned my head away and she pressed her face into my pink jumper in lieu of the snogging I knew she so desperately craved. I was convinced she was about to blow her top when, all of a sudden, the bedroom door flew open.

"Fucking hell, Swinella!" Felina cried out, standing in the doorway with her hands on her slender hips. "I can't believe you're fingering someone in that horrible charity-shop jumper!"

"Felina!" I barked. "Can we not have some privacy here?!"

"Yeah, well, whatever... Wayne's here," Felina said. "I was only coming in to ask you if you were going to be sociable or not!"

"Eh-up, Swinella." Wayne Mansfield called out, his peroxide blonde head appearing over Felina's shoulder. "Y'alright, duck?"

Nurse Elaine raised her head from my chest and looked from

the doorway to my face and back again. I began to slowly move my finger; the sound of rattling metal could be clearly heard from beneath the duvet.

"I'm all right, Wayne," I said, with a mischievous smile. "I'm just a bit busy."

I increased the speed and pressure, and Nurse Elaine's eyes grew wide; the sound of rattling metal increased. She let out a long sigh and buried her head in my chest once more, no doubt trying to hide from our uninvited guests, but making no effort to stop what I was doing to her.

"I think I'll go back to the living room," Wayne said. "I'm missing *Corrie* here."

I never would've thought that 'I'm missing *Corrie* here' would've been the cue for Nurse Elaine to orgasm, but at that exact moment she went into convulsions and came hard.

"Fuuuuuuuuuuck!!!" She cried. "Oh fuck, oh fuck, oh fuck."

She grabbed her tits with both hands and pulled her snatch away from my still working fingers, burying her face deeper into my chest. I let her overworked clit escape, but I cupped her sopping cunt in my hand and held on, flaps, rings and all.

"Oooooh... Mmmmm..." she moaned, eyes closed, body shivering.

Felina stared for a moment, her cat eyes wide, her face fixed in a horrified, but fascinated, grin.

"I'm going to watch the telly, now," she eventually said. "Erm... Thanks for the show."

Felina let out one of her high-pitched cackles and closed the bedroom door.

"I have to go," Nurse Elaine said, lifting her bright red face from the pillow. "My husband, I..."

She climbed unsteadily out of the bed and began to gather her things. I placed my hands behind my head and lay back, enjoying the sight of her putting on her dress and shoes. This was a new thing for me. Had I just topped someone? I felt powerful, and not necessarily in a way that was completely sexual. I had enjoyed myself, but I wasn't so much turned on as intrigued.

I saw Nurse Elaine out of the flat and closed the front door.

"What the fuck..." said Felina, staring at me, wide-eyed from the sofa, "just happened in your fucking room?!"

I sat down on the armchair between the windows and faced Felina and Wayne, who were both looking at me gone out. Wayne even leaned over and turned down our black and white portable TV so that he could hear my answer.

"That was the nurse from my circumcision," I said. "I just fingered her. She had a load of rings through her cunt, and a corset and...."

"You're a dyke," Wayne said in a loud whisper. "You like licking old pennies."

Wayne always said that cunts tasted like old pennies, which was strange, as he also claimed that the last time he had been anywhere near a minge was when he fell out of one. I don't know which gynaecological expert told him that cunts tasted like old pennies, but it was probably Felina.

"I dunno." I said, shrugging. "She just seemed... interesting."

"You like old women!" Felina said, laughing.

"She's not old, she's like forty or something," I protested.

"That's old," Wayne screeched. "She's twice as old as you! She's old enough to be your mother."

"Yeah? Well she's not old enough to be your mother, is she? You poisonous old queen!" I shouted, pointing at Wayne and scowling. "Mind, what are you? Twenty-seven or something? That'd make your mum thirteen when she shitted you out, so yeah, maybe she is the same age as your mum."

Everybody cracked up at that, including Wayne. I went and grabbed the remainder of the bottle of wine from my bedroom and we sat around talking for the rest of the evening, Wayne heading out on a booze run before the off licence closed. I told them all about the encounter and, even though they took the piss, I could tell they were intrigued by Nurse Elaine and what had passed between us. Wayne eventually left around half ten to meet some guy at The Mother Black Cap. Felina made one of her special hot chocolates and we settled down on the sofa. I'd checked the TV listings in the paper earlier that day. There was an old Hammer House of Horror film on at eleven, a lesbian vampire effort called *Lust For A Vampire*.

"It really doesn't get any better than this," I said, as Felina and I sat side by side on the sofa, sipping hot chocolate with our feet on the coffee table.

"No," said the cat, dropping her usual cynicism and leaning in to rest her head on my shoulder. "It really doesn't."

CHAPTER TEN

PLUGGED

Something Nurse Elaine had said kept popping back into my head. Something about her corset and the thick metal rings hanging through her meaty cunt lips. How the discomfort brought her back to herself, reminded her of who she was. I wanted something like that, but I wasn't about to get my junk pierced or start wearing a corset. There was something else I thought I might like to do, something more in keeping with my own preferences.

I decided to begin my experiments one Tuesday, on my day off. I headed out of my room after being woken up by Felina playing *Filth* by Swans while she was getting ready for work.

"Morning," I said, as I wandered out of my room, wearing a fluffy yellow dressing gown that I'd recently found on one of my charity shop expeditions.

"You know someone probably died in that piss-coloured dressing gown?" Felina said.

My catty flatmate was sat on the sofa, her legs curled beneath her as she did her face, her mirror balanced on the arm of the settee. A cup of black coffee sat steaming on the coffee table, a cigarette burning away in the coffin-shaped ashtray beside it.

"I don't care," I answered. "They always wash the stuff they get in before they sell it."

"I swear, Swinella," Felina said, looking up from the mirror and grinning at me, all irony and pointed teeth. "You turn more into a goth with each passing day, swanning in here in your dead woman's robe. Come to the dark side... We have better clothes and music."

"It's really warm," I said, shrugging. "Is there enough water in the kettle for me?"

Felina said she thought so. I walked into the kitchen and made myself a cup of black coffee, no sugar. It had taken me a while to wean myself off sugar, but I'd managed it. Now I looked forward to drinking my bitter black mug of despair each morning. The grim reductivity of instant coffee without either milk or sugar seemed nicely post-punk and utilitarian, industrial, even. You could never imagine Joy Division drinking cappuccinos.

"What you up to today?" Felina asked as she sipped her coffee. "Out to seduce more middle-aged nurses?"

"Nurse Elaine was a one-off," I said, taking my place on the old armchair, opposite where Felina sat on the sofa. "I mean, she is a one-off."

"She was special," Felina conceded, nodding. "For an ape."

"I'm just going to hang out at the flat," I said, blowing across the steaming surface of my sad coffee. "I'm gonna have a bath and tidy up a bit and stuff. Read. Do some clothes."

Why didn't I just tell Felina what I was planning on doing that day? Sometimes I liked to keep things to myself. Privacy is not the same as secrecy, and sometimes it's good to keep things private. I asked Wayne why some gay men still liked to go cottaging when there were so many gay bars now? Because they like the subterfuge, he said, the thrill of doing something in the shadows. I understood that. If I'd have told Felina what I was planning it would've taken away some of the fun of it, and she'd have probably mentioned it at some inopportune moment. I just couldn't be bothered with that. First things first; coffee number two. To this day I always drink three coffees every morning, in quick succession. This is my replacement for breakfast, which I have vowed never to eat again, what with my being a skinny bitch and everything.

"Well... I guess I better go and meet my public," Felina said, pulling on her boots and coat, shouldering her bag and heading over to the door. "Pop in and see me later, if you feel like it. I'll be bored for sure."

"Oh, I will," I said. "I'll come in after lunch or something."

Felina left. I drained my coffee and made another. I moved on over to the sofa and stretched out. I opened my dressing gown and relaxed. I was in the mood for a wank, and my nipples were asking for attention. I closed my eyes and began to pinch and pull my little pig tits. The familiar pressure began to build behind my dicklette. If I kept up my tugging for too long, I'd come, but I didn't want to. I wanted to stay turned on, so I spent a while just edging, playing with my tits until I almost came, and then letting go and taking a few deep breaths, letting the fire subside.

I knew the drill, knew what would happen if I kept it up. If my nipple-wank didn't end in an orgasm, then my body would start craving more intense sensations. It wasn't long before my arsehole started twitching for attention. I teased myself for a little while longer, ignoring my body's insistent demands to be filled and stretched. I felt a little rumble, a little clenching in my bowel, and I knew it was time to have a shit; my morning coffee was having its usual laxative effect. As I was about to douche this was an ideal state of affairs. I slipped out of my dressing gown, stood up and headed into my bedroom. I looked at the collection of sodomernalia on top of my chest of drawers. At that point my altar held three flesh-coloured buttplugs (one medium, one large, one XL), a douching bulb, a foot-long douching shower attachment (for depth play preparation, of course), a couple of bottles of poppers, a litre of lube, three veiny, flesh-coloured rubber cocks of differing lengths and girths, and my trusty rolling pin. It still pleased me to wake up of a morning and see my arsehole arsenal sitting out in the open. I grabbed the shower attachment and headed for the bathroom. Now, I wasn't planning on indulging in depth play, but I figured I should clean out as much faecal detritus as possible before commencing my new backdoor adventure. I parked myself on the bog and squeezed out a nice, satisfying turd, a good eight incher, followed by a couple of more stubborn mini nugglettes. I removed the shower head, replaced it with my nozzle, and got the water running as close to body temperature as I could.

My relationship with cleaning out my party zone was, and is, complicated and contradictory. Our flat in Hamden Town had no central heating or double glazing, of course, and so washing out your arsehole when the temperature outside was Baltic was a chore. Straddling the bathtub, shivering, my teeth chattering while I hosed out my slurry pit was not my idea of fun. But if it was warm and I was in the mood, then the douching could actually be a very enjoyable experience. Then there were those times when the poo was never ending; just when you thought everything was sparkly and brand-new you'd feel that familiar pressure in your rectum and have to pretty much start again. I eventually learned, and this took me a long time to figure out, that I should be avoiding insoluble fibre. If I had been eating a lot of insoluble fibre, bran flakes, wholemeal pasta or something, then my shit pipe would contain an endless supply of gritty pebbledash. I'd be there forever, hosing out the nutty silage that had accumulated in my tunnel of love. Not fun. Then there were the times when I thought I'd done a good job, only to find five minutes into the session that there was an unwelcome smear of bum gravy on my dildo/rolling pin/buttplug/lover's cock. For this reason, I was extra diligent when my buggery involved another person. When I was fucking myself, it was a pain to have some anal marmite turn up, the brown spectre at the backyard feast, but it was not a big deal to sort it out, clean the mess, re-douche and carry on. If a shitty, uninvited guest made an unexpected appearance when I was with another person, though, that was not cool. Sometimes I was jealous of people with vaginas, but not really. I felt that periods wouldn't have been my jam at all. I'd sometimes wonder what it would be like to be into scat, to love getting covered in shit, to wallow in the filth. Sometimes I'd even fantasise about being into turd play. I'd wank myself off while imagining being covered in shit and piss, and it was all right for a wank. I could get into it, but if I ever approached it in real life, I'd get turned off pretty quick. 'It doesn't taste the same as it smells,' a scat fan had said to me once, as if that made it better. But never say never, maybe one day I'd find myself being drawn down a shitty rabbit hole, maybe not. I'd just have to wait and see.

Anyway, as far as I recall, the cleaning out of my arse-cunt on that particular morning was without event. I wandered back into my bedroom, grabbed the medium and large buttplugs and the lube, and headed back to the living room. I spread a brown (of course) bath towel over the sofa. I stuck Felina's copy of *Pop-Eyes* by Danielle Dax on the record player and set myself down. I half lay, half sat on my left side so I could easily access my pink donut with my right hand. Whenever I'm setting out on a self-spelunking adventure, I always like to test the water with my fingers first. I pushed my tail out of the way, gave my rim a little tickle and slid my middle finger in. Of course, it went in easily enough, as did a second and third. There was no point in my beating around the bush. I took the medium-sized rubber buttplug, lubed her up, and slipped her in. There was a little bit of resistance, but not much. I sat back and relaxed, enjoying the feeling. I let the plug settle for a few minutes, and then I slipped her out again, holding her at the widest point to give my sphincter a good stretch. I pulled her out and pushed her in a few more times, to the accompaniment of a staccato of wet, slurpy micro-farts. If I'd have walked about with her inside me she'd have definitely slipped out, so it was time to let her big sister have a go. I placed the medium-sized buttplug on a paper towel on the coffee table and grabbed the large.

The bigger girl took a little more effort. She was a little bit bigger than my fist, but obviously more ergonomically suited to the task in hand. I relaxed and pushed open my hungry hole and pressed the slippery tip of the pink rubber plug into my arsehole. I began to fuck myself with the buttplug, getting her a little deeper each time, until she popped in. Once she was in, I let out a deep breath and relaxed. It felt good. I usually began to wank my tits whenever I used a plug, pulling and tugging my overly sensitive, but virtually indestructible, nipples while enjoying the deliciously satisfying feeling of being filled and stretched, but this time I held back.

I stood from the sofa, went into my bedroom, and got dressed. I put on knickers, a pair of fishnets, and then a pair of ripped black jeans. I don't actually like wearing trousers, but I thought they'd help with keeping everything held in place. I was wearing plenty of clothes over my arse, and everything felt pretty secure. I finished the look off with a white vest and my Denis The Menace jumper. I decided to spend a bit of time on my face, as it was my day off. I used a new foundation I'd recently bought from Boots, but not worn before. It was a couple of shades lighter than my usual foundation, and I thought it made me look pale and sensitive, like a poet. I did my eyes *à la* Siouxsie, in shades of green and yellow, with a heavy black winged eyeliner, and I topped it off with a very dark green lip. I thought I looked well good. I put on my Docs and my leather jacket, and headed out of the flat.

It felt good walking down the street with the plug in my arse. Of course, I'd gotten used to everyone I encountered knowing from the second they met me that I was a backdoor bandit, my snout making it as clear as if I'd had 'ANAL BABE' written on my forehead. But having that warm plug nestling comfortably in my rectummy as I bowled down Hamden High Street gave me an extra level of shit stabbee-ness that I really liked. My snout and tail told the world who and what I was, but my plug reminded me who I was.

As I approached The Black Violet I saw Susan walking towards me. Susan was a petite, dark-skinned Welsh pig-girl I'd spoken to several times in The Elephant Shed. Her parents had come over from Jamaica in the nineteen fifties and for some reason made their way to Cardiff. Susan was having none of that and, like myself, as soon as she was able, she'd made her way to Hamden Town. She was a super nice, gentle piglette who never had a bad word to say about anyone. She worked in Bulldog Boots, a boot and shoe shop round the back of the tube station. Her look leaned towards the skinhead end of punk; Fred Perry polo shirts and knee-high Docs, topped off with short, bleached blonde tightly-curled afro hair. She was known for letting groups of rough, working-class skinhead lads run a train on her eager arsehole whenever she got horny, which was usually for a few days a month around the full moon. The rest of the time she led a chaste life.

"All right, Susan?" I asked as we approached each other. "How's it hanging?"

"All good with me, Swinella," she said in her soft Welsh

brogue, a broad smile crossing her face. "How's you?"

"Yeah, really good," I said, smiling. "It's my day off, so I'm just having a bit of a wander."

Talking to someone in the street while being actively filled and stretched was a new experience for me, and I liked it. It crossed my mind, there and then, to tell Susan that I was plugged, what with her being a fellow porker and all-round anal warrior; it's not like she would've judged me, but I held back. My internal friend was my secret. Like Nurse Elaine's pussy rings, it worked best as a hidden, private part of myself, something just for me.

We chatted for a while, talking about gigs and stuff, but Susan was on her lunch break and had to head back to the boot shop. We said our goodbyes, and as we walked away from each other I glanced back at her and looked at her plump little bum bouncing along beneath her tartan skirt, her brown curly tail swinging to and fro as she wiggled her arse. And then it occurred to me; she was probably wearing something in her arse as well. Why on earth did I think I'd invented daytime buttplugging? Susan was a couple of years older than me and had lived in Hamden for a while, she was ahead of me in the piglette game of life. Probably loads of pigs are plugging all of the time, I suddenly thought, and I just never realised it.

After bumping into Susan I wandered into The Black Violet to say hello to Felina. It was near closing time and my beautiful cat flatmate was cashing up. I offered to lend a hand and got to work sweeping the shop and straightening the displays.

It was still light outside. The nights had drawn out and summer was finally here. I'd miss the winter, though. After my first year in Hamden, I realised that January and February, and October and November, were the best months of the year to live in Hamden Town. We were lousy with tourists in the spring and summer, and we got really busy over Christmas, but we had a couple of quiet months either side of December when Hamden belonged to us. I loved it when a thick autumnal mist settled over the streets during the cold, grey afternoons, giving the streetlights and shopfronts an ethereal, soft-focus look that I really felt in my heart. It always made me think of Jack the Ripper, and all those old horror films set in the Victorian London fog.

The door swung open and she walked in like she owned the place. She was tall, over six foot, and was wearing a black leather cap pushed up towards the back of her head. Her hair was long and silver-grey and hung down her back in a single plait. She wore leather gloves, and a long black coat that almost came down to the floor. I would've described her as handsome, rather than beautiful, but she was incredibly striking. Her olive skin was flawless, her neck slender, and she carried herself with an air of supreme confidence, but without a trace of arrogance. She had what people called 'poise': her back was straight, her shoulders back, her chin held high. She looked like she might have been a dancer in her youth. Her large eyes were deep and black beneath her silver eyebrows, and her full lips had a purplish hue. I had a hard time guessing her age, she was older than us, but 'timeless' would've been the only way I could've described her. She could've been anything between thirty five and sixty.

"Lily," Felina said, a tone of surprise in her voice. "I didn't know you were coming in today... You should've called."

"Do I have to make an appointment to see you now, Felina," the visitor said, bemused.

"N-no, Lily... I mean, I'd have, er..." Felina stumbled over her words, the first time I'd ever seen her flustered.

Lily smiled and began to remove the tight leather glove from her right hand, one finger at a time.

"Oh relax, Felina," she said, with a deep laugh. "I'm not here to see you. I'm here to meet the new pig."

The tall woman turned and looked over to where I stood between the clothes rails with the sweeping brush in my hands.

"Um... Hello," I said, stepping forward with a smile and holding out my hand. "I'm Swinella."

"Of course you are," Lily said, reaching out and shaking my hand gently, looking me in the eye.

I looked down at her hand. Her fingers were long and graceful and cool to the touch. Her nails were short and black and highly reflective. She held my hand as she gazed deep into my eyes, a wry half-smile on her perfect face. I felt my cheeks redden and blush as she studied me. I smiled for no reason and blinked, batting my long eyelashes. Lily eventually let go of my hand and turned to Felina.

"You were right, Felina," Lily said approvingly. "She is adorable. The question is... Do we want to keep her? And does she want to stay?"

"She likes it here. She fits in well. I think she'll stay. " Felina said, looking my way. "You will stay, won't you?"

Lily looked back over at me and raised an enquiring eyebrow, her head tilted to one side.

"Oh yes," I said, with a smile and a shrug. "I don't ever want to leave. I love it here. It's everything I ever wanted."

Lily nodded slowly, and looked me up and down.

"You look good. You bring something," she said, smiling benevolently. "Your energy is... useful."

Lily pulled on her glove and headed over to the door. Felina hurried from behind the counter and darted ahead of her, pulling the door open and smiling. For a second I thought she was going to bow.

"Thank you, Felina," Lily said, walking towards the open doorway.

"You're welcome," Felina said. "Please, drop by whenever you feel like it... We'd love to see you any time... Any time that suits you."

Lily stopped in the doorway and turned back to me, a wider, warmer smile softening her face.

"Keep wearing that buttplug while you're out and about," she said with a twinkle in her dark eye. "I like it. Nurse Elaine has been a good influence on you. You'll see her again, I think..."

And with that she was out the door and gone, out into the early summer evening. Felina closed the door behind her, took a deep breath and slowly exhaled. She closed her eyes and shook her head slightly.

"Who the fuck was that?" I asked.

Felina stared at me with her vertical slit pupils and shook her head.

"You wouldn't believe me if I told you," she said, "and what's this about a buttplug? Have you got one up you right now? And you didn't tell me? How long have you been doing that, you dirty little piglette?"

"Yeah, whatever... It's hardly a surprise, is it?" I said, annoyed that Felina knew about my casual daytime plugging. "Tell me about this Lily person."

"You'll find out soon enough," she said. "Come on... Let's finish up and go to the pub. I need a drink."

After the encounter with Lily, Felina and I headed to The Elephant's, and that's where I met Rasher and Bullseye for the first time. I spotted Bullseye first. It was a really nice evening, and shafts of sunlight were falling over the rooftops opposite, through the high windows and into the smoky barroom.

Some old rockabilly guy with a greying quiff was DJing in the corner. He was playing an endless set of identical records that all seemed determined to 'rock this town, rock it inside out'. It was easy music to like but, as far as I was concerned, it was impossible music to love.

I was sat with Felina at a table in the corner when he walked into the pub. He was short, as most dogs are. He had the turned-up nose, extended lower canines, bushy eyebrows and larger-than-average brown eyes that gave away his doggishness, but unlike the dogs I had known back home, he walked with a swagger, an arrogance, almost. He was a skinhead. His hair was cropped to almost nothing. He wore eighteen-hole oxblood steel toe cap boots, tight blue jeans that had been splashed with bleach to create a marbling pattern, and a blindingly white T-shirt. Red braces hung from his waistband and he was wearing a padded green bomber jacket decorated with patches. His fists were studded with sovereign rings and he wore thick gold chains around his wrists and neck. He was undoubtedly a geezer. Most surprising of all, to me, was his tail. Most dogs have a tail of at least a foot in length, but this boy's tail was just a stub of a couple of inches. It poked out of the hole below his waistband, a stunted protuberance covered in short brown fur.

"I fucking hate dogs," Felina said, seeing where I was looking.

"Why?" I asked. "I think he looks cool."

"I don't know why. There's just something about them," Felina replied. "And of course, you think he looks cool. You're a punk, and punks are skinhead-adjacent."

"Why is his tail so short, though?"

"He's had it docked," Felina said with a sneer. "Some stupid dogs are reclaiming fucking docking, believe it or not."

Before the bestiamorph equal rights movement of the early twentieth century, it was common practice to remove our tails after they had grown. Not only did they crop our tails, they filed our teeth and made cats and goats wear tinted glasses all the time, so nobody had to see their weirdly-shaped pupils. We didn't even get the right to vote until nineteen twenty eight. It was as if the main issue around the existence of bestiamorphs was how we made apes feel.

"I mean, can you believe it?" Felina said with distaste. "After centuries of apes cutting off our tails, we then start doing it to ourselves? And who do you think started that? Dogs, that's who."

"But I've seen you wearing sunglasses at night," I argued. "Didn't they make cats do that years ago?"

"That's different," Felina declared. "I'm a cat, and it's me that's doing it, so it's all good."

I burst out laughing, and after a moment Felina joined in.

"You twat!" I said. "Can you actually hear yourself?"

"Nobody wrote a song called *Cool for Dogs*," she said. "They should know their place."

"Fucking hell," I said. "You're an actual bestiaphobe! And you absolutely hate that song."

"Nobody wrote a song called *Love Dogs*, either. It's just dogs. I can't help it! Disliking dogs is as much a part of being a cat as loving getting fucked in the bumhole is part of being a pig. It's in my nature."

"You are terrible," I said. "He's not going to chase you up a tree."

"I'd like to see him fucking try," Felina said with a scowl.

"I'd pay money to see him try!" I said, laughing.

Just then, another skinhead boy walked in, and this one caught my attention even more than the dog standing at the bar. The second skinhead was a pig, a pig-boy.

"Look at that one," I said to Felina. "Don't make it obvious!"

Of course, Felina was as unsubtle as possible as she craned her neck and stared hard at the newcomer.

"Oh yeah," she said. "I've seen him around here before."

I had known that some pigs presented as boys, I'd even seen some around, but I'd never spoken to one, and actually I found them quite intimidating in some mysterious kind of way. The boy pig was dressed almost identically to his dog friend, apart from his boots, which were black, as were his braces. The pig boy accepted a pint of lager from his canine friend and the two of them leaned on the bar and scanned the room. The pig-boy's eyes rested on me, and he nodded a hello.

"Go and talk to him," Felina said, nudging me. "You know the law."

I walked over to the two bestiamorph skinheads, more than a little nervous.

"Hello," I said to the pig. "How's it going?"

"Oh, look at this," the dog said in a high pitched, whiny voice, looking down his upturned nose at me. "The blow-in piglette wants to say hello!"

"Shut up, Bullseye," the pig-boy said in a strong cockney accent. "Ignore her, she's just in bitch mode 'cos she ain't got none in ages. I'm Rasher."

"Swinella," I said, nodding. "Nice to meet you."

The dog had turned his back on us slightly and was staring out of the window with a bored look on his face.

"This rude cunt is Bullseye," Rasher said, nodding towards his friend.

Bullseye glanced back at me with an unpleasant half smile and then turned back to the window. The dog fished around in his bomber jacket and pulled out a packet of ten Benson's and a box of Swan Vestas. He offered a fag to Rasher, who took one, and then with a great show of reluctance offered me one.

"Er, no thanks," I said. "I don't smoke."

Bullseye raised his bushy dog eyebrows and put the pack back in his pocket. When I tell you that everyone smoked, you'd better believe it; everybody smoked, everywhere. I just didn't like it, which back then made me the anomaly. The two skins shared a match to light their smokes. Bullseye shook out the match, dropped it on the floor and returned to his vigil. The Elephant Shed was on a corner and had big windows, so it was actually quite a good spot for people watching, but I still found the dog unnecessarily rude.

"So, Swinella," Rasher said, exhaling a cloud of acrid blue smoke. "New in town?"

I gave Rasher a quick account of my recent move to Hamden, but, really, I just wanted to know all about his being a boy pig, what it was that made him a boy pig. All the pigs at my school were girls, what had made him express himself as male?

"Do you like Reggae?" Rasher asked.

"Yeah, it's all right," I lied.

We punks were all meant to like Reggae music because of The Clash, but I wasn't massively into The Clash, and I didn't get Reggae. I lied because I wanted Rasher to like me.

"Bullseye and me are going to a Blue Beat night at The Drogheda Castle later, you should come along," Rasher said. "But I'm guessing your cat friend isn't into that kind of thing?"

Bullseye tutted and rolled his big brown eyes.

"It's dead in 'ere, Rash'," Bullseye said. "There's nuffink going on and nobody here. Let's go to Mother's for a couple before the gig."

Bullseye stubbed out his fag in the dusty brown glass ashtray, drained his pint and walked out of the pub, his little tail bobbing along as he shimmied out the door, wiggling his arse.

"Don't take it too personally, love," Rasher smiled with a wink. "He can smell the cat on you, that's all. I'll see yer around."

And with that Rasher finished his drink and followed his friend through the door and out onto the street. I returned to Felina.

"I don't think that went so well." I said, confused. "The dog really took a dislike to me."

"Oh, this is too funny," Felina said with a smirk. "You're not used to people not liking you, are you? You do the adorable piglette thing so well that you just expect everyone to fall in love with you."

"Really?" I asked. "Am I that?"

"Don't you know that you're that?" Felina shook her head and raised her drawn-on pencil thin eyebrows.

"I just try to be nice," I said, crestfallen.

"Well, that dog is my favourite dog," she said. "I mean, that's not hard, because I don't actually like any dogs. He's really quite catty, the way he gave you the cold shoulder. I like him."

Wayne came in after finishing a day shift at The Dev' and we all got a bit pissed and had a right laugh. I almost forgot about the plug up my arse, and I almost forgot about my first meeting with Lily.

CHAPTER ELEVEN

LUCRETIA AND TARQUINIUS

It was a quiet evening in The Elephant Shed. Felina and I had popped in for a quick pint after work. *In A Rut* by The Ruts was playing in the background and there was a smattering of customers drinking and smoking scattered about the place in twos and threes, most of them people I recognised as working on the market or in nearby shops and hairdressers. I was drinking my usual vodka soda and Felina had a half of snakebite and black.

"Who's that?" I asked, gesturing over towards a solitary girl sat in the opposite corner of the pub, with what I hoped was a discreet nod of my head. "I've never seen her before."

The girl I was talking about was quite striking, and I was sure that if I'd been in the same space as her before I would've remembered. She was sat with one lean leg crossed over the other. She was tall, slim and had very long, super-straight and glossy black hair with a streak of silvery white on one side, like Lily Munster. Her incredible hair was combed into a sharp centre parting and hung either side of her ghostly-pale, but beautiful, face. She was what people would describe as 'willowy'. She was wearing a tight black dress and knee-high black boots with laces and chunky, flat soles. She was drinking a glass of red wine, reading an old leather-bound book and smoking. She seemed aloof, self-contained and mysterious.

"Oh," said Felina. "That's Lucretia. I know her. She's kind of weird. She's one of those demon girls."

"Demon girls?" I asked, surprised; when Felina had mentioned demons before, I'd assumed that she'd been joking.

"Yeah. She doesn't go out much. I don't think she works, either, she's got rich parents or something. I think she's from Israel… somewhere like that."

I was fascinated by this mysterious woman. There was something masculine about her energy, despite her being very beautiful and having her white face made up impeccably, with dark purple eyeshadow, heavy black eyeliner and mascara, and dark crimson lips, all topped off with delicately-curved eyebrows. Her nails were long and painted a light iridescent blue. I didn't think her chunky boots were responsible for her masculine vibe, it was something deeper than that.

"She comes in the shop sometimes, but not very often," Felina said. "I've chatted to her once or twice at Slimenight. I can introduce you, if you like? She's nice enough, for a demon."

"Oh, I don't know," I said, suddenly shy. "She doesn't seem to want to be disturbed."

"Don't be stupid," Felina said. "Come on."

Felina stood up, grabbed her leather jacket and, with catlike grace, sashayed across the almost empty pub with her tail swishing behind her, over to where Lucretia sat. I felt I had no choice but to follow. I picked up my handbag and my new black Harrington jacket (a recent acquisition from the army surplus shop) and followed.

"Hello, Lucretia," she said, smiling her cat-girl smile as we approached the table, flashing those perfect pointed little teeth. "My friend and I were just admiring your boots from across the room. Where'd you get them? If you don't mind me asking?"

"A friend bought them back from Berlin last year," Lucretia said in an unfamiliar accent, looking me up and down with a faint hint of amusement in her deep, brown eyes. "But I think you've seen them before, Felina."

"Maybe," Felina smiled. "May we join you?"

"Please do," Lucretia replied, after an awkward few seconds' hesitation.

We pulled up stools and sat down at Lucretia's table. The tall girl looked at me intently and slowly smiled. She smelt of Frankincense and fags, with an interesting, barely noticeable whiff of cock; I wondered if she had been fucked recently, but I couldn't smell any cum, just a slight odour of circumcised bell-end (yes, circumcised dicks smell different to foreskin-wearing helmets, something I had only recently learned myself, as prior to my own de-foreskination, I'd only encountered uncircumcised cocks. I'd caught the scent of circumcised cocks through men's clothes, of course, but I never knew why some cocks smelled different to others). Felina introduced me and Lucretia stared into my eyes.

"Tarquinius likes you," she said.

"I'm sorry?" I said blinking in confusion.

"Tarquinius is Lucretia's brother," Felina explained. "They're twins. Siamese twins."

"I... I don't understand," I said, looking from one girl to the other.

"I am two people in one," Lucretia said. "I carry my twin with me. He likes you."

I looked at Lucretia. If she had a Siamese twin, then that twin had to be very small, there were no unusual lumps or bumps to be seen under her tight-fitting black dress.

"Well," Felina suddenly announced. "I really must dye my hair tonight, any second now my roots are going to start showing and, as you know, that is an unforgivable sin in the circles I move in."

Felina stood, drained the remainder of her snakebite and black, and pulled on her leather jacket.

"See you later, Swinella," she said. "Bye, Lucretia."

And with those parting words she turned and stalked out of the pub, leaving me alone with the demon. I noticed through the window that she turned right at the door, the opposite direction to our flat. She was no doubt heading to The Dev' to blag a pint off Wayne Mansfield. Lucretia and I talked for a bit, her asking where I was from, how long I'd been in London, stuff like that.

"I wasn't going to stay much longer, actually," Lucretia said after about twenty minutes of superficial chit-chat. "I only stepped out for a bit of air and to buy some cigarettes. The music in here is not good... Too much punk and ska for my tastes. I was going to go in The Devil's Shire, but it was too busy in there for me."

"Oh, OK" I said. "Well... I can go home. *Blackadder's* on later."

"If you like, you can come back to my place for a tea. I drink mint tea. It's nice and it has no caffeine, so it won't keep you awake."

"If that's all right?" I said.

"I wouldn't have asked if it wasn't all right, Swinella."

Lucretia lived in a flat just round the corner, on a side street opposite Hamden Road Station. We headed up the stairs and walked into her home. It was surprisingly tasteful and colourful. Most Gothy types decorated their places in black and tried to create some kind of spooky graveyard aesthetic, but Lucretia's place was done out in dark purples, reds and oranges, and had a distinctly Middle Eastern vibe. It made me think of the Arabian Nights. There was a plethora of small, differently-coloured lamps positioned around the place, and they bathed the room in a diffused, rainbow light that gave everything an otherworldly, exotic appearance. The room smelt of cassia, a not-unpleasant blend of cinnamon and cloves. There was a pair of long, low sofas covered in patterned cushions and blankets, and, standing between the sofas, a heavy, dark wooden coffee table. A spread of tarot cards was placed out on the table. The floor was bare floorboards covered with Turkish rugs. There were lots of exotic-looking pot plants standing around on the floor, and on the windowsills and shelves. Lucretia had a lot of books similar to the one she'd been reading in the pub, old, leather-bound volumes stored in a couple of tall bookcases. It was very warm in her flat, super welcoming, and I felt comfortable straight away. Lucretia visibly relaxed when we walked into her domain.

"I like your place," I said, taking off my Harrington and

placing it on the arm of the sofa.

"Thanks," Lucretia smiled. "I'll make the tea. Make yourself at home."

I sat down on the comfortable sofa. Lucretia placed a record on the turntable and the familiar strains of *Cascade*, the opening track of Siouxie and The Banshees latest album, *A Kiss In The Dreamhouse*, began playing at a discreet volume. She wandered out of the room and into what I guessed was the kitchen. After a couple of minutes she returned with a pair of steaming terracotta cups. She placed them on the coffee table.

"Excuse me for a minute, won't you," she said, before disappearing into what I later learned was the bathroom.

I picked up my cup and inhaled. The mint tea smelled sweet and had an almost sedative-like aspect to its perfume. I felt myself relax a little more. I put the tea back on the table to cool and leaned back on the sofa, settling down further as I listened to the record play.

Lucretia returned after a couple of minutes. As she walked over to the sofa I noticed for the first time the bulge beneath her dress. She looked down at her crotch.

"Tarquinius has been cooped up in our underwear all day, so I had to free him," she said, sitting down on the opposite end of the sofa. "You don't mind?"

"No... No, it's fine, of course," I stammered. "It's your place."

"I'm guessing you've never met one of us demons before?" she said. "I'm also guessing that's why that naughty cat came over and introduced you to us."

"That's right," I answered. "I'm from a small town, I don't

think we have demons there."

"Maybe not," she languidly said, resting her elbow on her knee and leaning in conspiratorially. "So... What do you want to know?"

"Everything, I suppose," I said, trying not to look at the bulge in her dress.

"We are kind of as your friend said," Lucretia began. "We are like Siamese twins, but I have an almost entire body, and my little brother is nothing more than a penis and a pair or testicles. In my culture we were considered cursed for many thousands of years, just like you bestiamorphs, but we now see ourselves as blessed, as special. I am a woman, minus genitals, and my brother is a man... but only the genitals. This makes us more than humans in some way, but less in others. I will never be a mother. I will never know what it is to make love as a woman, but my brother and I complete each other in a manner that it is impossible for non-demons to understand. We are never alone, we talk to each other and we keep ourselves company. That's why we don't go out much. We are always together, and we're never lonely."

"That's fascinating," I said, genuinely intrigued. "Why don't people know about people like you?"

"Obviously, some people do know about us, but we're not talked about a great deal," she said. "We're still taboo, and we're a much smaller minority than you bestiamorphs. Even in a city the size of London, there are only a handful of us."

Lucretia leaned a little closer, and smiled an enigmatic smile.

"Would you like to meet him?" She said in a low voice, her

smile broadening.

I nodded.

"Tarquinius," she said in a gentle voice. "There's someone here who would like to say hello."

The bulge beneath her dress twitched a little and she smiled at it. She reached down and took hold of the hem and began to pull it up over her pale, slender thighs. The black dress slid over her pelvis, and she pulled it up as far as her abdomen. Tarquinius was a pretty big boy. The semi-erect penis was at least ten inches long in its current state, and I figured he still had a couple of inches to grow. He was circumcised high and tight, and was thick and veiny. He was completely shaven, or maybe naturally hairless, like myself, and his skin was a shade darker than Lucretia's alabaster tone. As I watched, the skin of his scrotum began to tighten and pull his large balls closer to her crotch.

"Swinella," Lucretia said, with more than a little pride. "Meet Tarquinius."

"Hello Tarquinius," I said, addressing the beautiful penis directly, feeling more than a little self-conscious and foolish. "It's lovely to meet you."

Lucretia cradled Tarquinius in her left hand and began to gently stroke him with her right hand, her long cobalt-blue fingernails gently grazing his delicate skin. The penis seemed relaxed despite his semi-erect condition, but also quite alert, twitching occasionally as his sister stroked him.

"That's better, isn't it?" Lucretia cooed. "Much better than being shut away in that tight, uncomfortable underwear."

She looked at me and smiled. I was becoming seriously aroused. I wanted Tarquinius inside me, and I was sure both he and Lucretia knew that.

"You see why we don't go out often?" She said. "We have everything we need when we're alone together. Well, almost everything... You see, Swinella, I myself am an asexual person. I have no genitals and no sexual urges at all, but my brother has needs. He likes to fuck from time to time. He is, after all, a penis."

I nodded sympathetically.

"I can see how that might be a challenge," I said.

"Do you like Tarquinius?" She asked.

"Yes," I replied. "He seems really lovely."

"Did you hear that, Tarquinius?" Lucretia said. "The nice pig-girl likes you!"

Tarquinius twitched in Lucretia's hand and began to swell, growing bigger and harder by the second. Obviously, it was clear where the evening was headed. I needed to clean myself out, to get my shit-hole presentable. I had my foot-long inch shower nozzle curled in the bottom of my handbag, as well as lube, poppers and my bulb douche. I liked to be prepared for whatever the day might throw at, or up, me. I'd need a proper good douching if I was going to accommodate the prodigious demon cock I saw rising before me.

"Do you mind if I use your bathroom," I said. "I... I might be a while, if that's ok?"

"Of course, Swinella," Lucretia smiled, lazily stroking the meaty baton lying in her lap. "Tarquinius and I will be waiting.

Take as long as you need. It's the door on the left, just after the kitchen."

I picked up my handbag and headed for the bathroom. I was excited; I had no idea what sex with Tarquinius would be like, but I was eager to find out. I closed the bathroom door behind me and removed my shoes, socks, fishnets and pale pink cotton knickers. I went through the familiar ritual and took my time, trying to do as thorough a job as possible. Lucretia's bathroom was as nice as her living room. She had numerous bars of exotically smelling soap that I'd never seen in shops, she'd lit candles when she had gone in there to release Tarquinius, and the ubiquitous pot plants gave everything a tropical feeling. It was probably the nicest place I'd ever rinsed out my arse hole.

After I had finished douching, I dried myself off and, as a final touch, squeezed some lube into my bum from a large plastic syringe I kept in my handbag for such occasions. I am nothing if not conscientious. I checked my makeup, fixed my slutty red lipstick, took off my red and black striped jumper and put my knickers back on. I walked back into the living room wearing nothing but my panties and my Velvet Underground T-shirt, the one with the big yellow banana on it.

Lucretia was reclining on the sofa stroking Tarquinius with both of her slender white hands. He had grown to his full size, at least twelve inches; his purple head glistened in the lamplight, the size and shape of a large hen's egg. A bottle of lube had magically appeared on the coffee table in front of where Lucretia sat.

"Do you mind if I watch?" Lucretia said. "I like to see

Tarquinius enjoying himself... He doesn't get out to play very often."

"Not at all," I said. "How do you guys usually do this?"

"You can do what you like with him," she said, letting go of the throbbing, veiny shaft, which had no difficulty standing upright on his own. "He's not too big?"

"No," I said, twitching my snout and grinning. "I can take him."

I walked over and joined them on the sofa, kneeling between Lucretia's open legs. I began to lick Tarquinius's shiny, throbbing helmet, flicking my tongue back and forth over the opening of his urethra. I inhaled deeply through my snout. Tarquinius had an undertone of spicy cinnamon beneath the musky smell of hungry cock, and I found it quite intoxicating. I took his lubed shaft in both my hands and began to slide them up and down his rigid pole. My small tits began to buzz and I remembered that I hadn't lactated in a while. I pulled off my T-shirt and exposed my hard pink nipples. A small white drop of milk appeared at the tip of each nipple as I threw my T-shirt over to the other side of the room.

"Oh," Lucretia said, surprised. "Look at that... You're leaking!"

"Yes," I said. "It sometimes happens when I'm really turned on."

"So you're really turned on?" Lucretia smiled. "Do you want him inside of you yet?"

"I do," I confessed, with a sound that was half laugh, half grunt. "I really do! I'm impatient and greedy... I am a pig, after all."

"Then climb on," Lucretia reached down and gently stroked my pink hair where I knelt between her slender milk-white thighs. "He's ready… He doesn't require much foreplay."

I straddled Lucretia and guided Tarquinius into my eager wet hole. I began to ride as Siouxie sang *Melt*, seductive and soft, in the background, the middle-eastern-sounding guitar suiting the mood perfectly. I rocked backwards and forwards, his huge girth filling me almost to the edge of my limit, to the very edge of my comfort zone. Twin streams of pig milk dribbled down my chest and I threw back my head and began to grunt softly with each thrust, my curly tail swinging up and down with each bounce, slapping the sofa on the downswing.

"Do you ever get hard?" Lucretia suddenly asked.

I opened my eyes to see that the raven-haired demon girl was looking at my tiny, flaccid cock. For the first time it properly hit me that I wasn't having sex with her at all, that she really was just an observer.

"Um… No," I said, trying to speak clearly through the growing ecstasy Tarquinius was creating, some twelve inches deep inside me. "I never have."

"Oh, I'm sorry," Lucretia said. "I didn't mean to take you out of the moment. Carry on, we can talk afterwards."

I thought about the situation for a second and decided I could give myself over to the deep fucking I was experiencing later on. Having a conversation with Lucretia while her brother was buried deep inside of me actually turned me on even more. I stopped moving my pelvis so much, slowing down to a gentle, almost imperceptible rocking.

"No, let's talk," I said, letting out a long breath. "It's good, I like it."

"OK," Lucretia said. "If you're sure?"

I nodded and pushed my hair out of my eyes.

"Your penis," she asked. "It doesn't work?"

"No," I reached down and gave the little fleshy appendage a tug. "It's a bit sensitive, but it doesn't get hard or cum or anything like that. It's more like a clit, really... actually, I'd say it's less sensitive than a clitoris. It's handy for pissing. I can piss standing up, like you."

Amazingly, this was the first time that I had realised that we were both girls with dicks. I had been focusing on our differences so much that I had overlooked our similarities. I straightened my thighs and slid Tarquinius almost all the way out before lowering myself back onto him. I didn't want him to feel neglected. He felt soooo fucking good, one of the best. So deep and hard, the rounded tip of his glans opening me up in all the right ways. I let out a satisfied grunt. Lucretia watched with a benign expression on her serene face.

"It means so much to me to see the two of you enjoying each other," she said. "I've never had a sexual feeling in my life, but I can see your joy, and it's a beautiful thing to behold."

"Can you feel it... like, can you feel what he feels?" I asked, resting with him deep inside of me for a moment and grinding my arse down onto her pelvis.

"Not really," she said. "I'm aware of Tarquinius, but to me he feels quite numb, like when you sleep on your arm and it goes dead… so your sliding up and down on him isn't particularly intense for me. What I do feel is his mood, his excitement, and that's giving me a lot of pleasure."

It was the strangest threesome I'd ever have, in fact, it wasn't really a threesome. I don't know what it was. A two and a halfsome, maybe? Even though the massive dick buried deep inside my stretched, wet, hungry pighole was attached to Lucretia, I knew she wasn't really a part of it. At that moment I really understood who and what they were.

"And what's the deal with your lactating?" Lucretia suddenly asked. "Do you do that all the time?"

I looked down at the rivulets of milk that were leaking out of my rock-hard nipples and over my pointy little pig tits.

"No, not at all… It only happens when I'm really turned on," I said between gasps. "Then it has to build up for a while. I won't lactate again for a bit after this. This is actually quite a lot of milk for me to produce. Do you want to try it?"

"Definitely!" Lucretia cried, laughing. "I've been waiting for you to ask."

I leaned forward and offered a nipple to the beautiful long-haired demon girl. She parted her crimson lips and took it in her mouth. I squeezed my petite boob and felt the hot liquid squirt out of my teat. Lucretia gulped it down. After a few seconds of contented suckling she let me go.

"It's really salty," she said. "I've never eaten pork, but it tastes like smoky bacon crisps… it's nice. More savoury than I expected, but not in a bad way."

"Well," I laughed. "I am a pig."

Lucretia drinking my milk did something to Tarquinius. He began twitching uncontrollably. He clearly wanted to cum in me. I threw my head back and began to grunt. I bounced and bounced, grinding my arse down onto the massive demon cock, wanting to take him as deep as possible, my tail flailing around behind me. I lifted myself a full six inches each time, the rock-hard, engorged cock filling me anew each time, stretching my pink bumhole, opening me up. I began to squeal like the piglette I was. I didn't care if the neighbours heard, and apparently neither did Lucretia. She just smiled and seemed to enjoy the show. I was going to come. I ground myself into Lucretia's crotch, trying to get Tarquinius as deep into me as was possible. Lucretia began rocking her pelvis in time to my bouncing bum, helping her little big brother get where he so desperately needed to go. I began to orgasm, my head spinning, and at that moment Tarquinius let forth a huge gush of hot cinnamon spice demon spunk. I felt the jets of cum penetrating even further into my body than his cock had; there seemed to be pints of the stuff! I squealed and squealed and squealed.

"FUCKING YES!" I cried. "FUCK OH FUCK OH FUCK!!!"

My body quivered and shook, and I collapsed on top of Lucretia, gasping for air. She kissed the top of my head and stroked my damp, sweaty shoulders. I began to cry uncontrollably, something that sometimes happens to me after a particularly epic orgasm.

"Did you enjoy that?" Lucretia asked, after my sobs had subsided a little.

"Yes, thank you," I murmured in a small voice, sniffing.

Eventually Tarquinius grew limp and soft inside of me and slowly slid out of my gaping cunt in a torrent of lube and cum.

"Would you look at that?" Lucretia said. "He's gone to sleep!"

"Typical man!" I said, sniffing away the tears.

I didn't really see much of Lucretia and Tarquinius after our first meeting. They preferred to stay at home rather than partake in the nightlife of Hamden Town, Lucretia reading her books and her cards and contentedly stroking Tarquinius while he lay half asleep in her lap. I really enjoyed fucking Tarquinius, but there were many more adventures to be had in Hamden town, and I was just beginning to find my feet. Lucretia would enter my life again, later that year, anyway, and in a manner that I never would have expected.

CHAPTER TWELVE

A PINT WITH RASHER

"I know what you've been dying to ask me," Rasher said moments after we'd taken our drinks over to a vacant table and sat down at a table in The Oxblood Arms, a relatively mainstream pub on the high street that catered to tourists and other boring types, Sham 69 playing tinny and quiet through the speakers on the walls.

The pub was dead, just us and the fruit machine in the corner playing itself. Rasher smelt of Lynx Spice, fags, boot polish and cockiness. He had no visible boobs and I found myself wondering if he'd just never grown them, or if he strapped them down somehow.

"And what's that?" I asked.

"Why do I dress like this? Why do I present as a boy?" he replied.

Well, Rasher had me sussed. I'd never met a boy pig before, although I'd seen some around the place, and I had been dying to talk to him about it ever since that first night in The Elephant Shed when Felina and I had spied Rasher and Bullseye at the bar.

I'd just popped out of the flat for a bit on my day off, when I bumped into him on the high street. It was a lovely, warm summer's afternoon. I was bare legged and wearing nothing but a ripped T-shirt, denim skirt, black tights, buttplug, white socks and boots. He was at a loose end as well, so we decided to grab a swift refresher.

"And?" I prompted.

"And what?" Rasher replied. "Where is it written that a pig should dress as a girl? I mean, we all started out as boys. I was just never attracted to all that girly shit you're wearing."

"Most pigs dress as girls," I said, shrugging. "That's all."

"So because most pigs dress as girls, all pigs should dress as girls?" Rasher laughed. "Why do you dye your hair and dress like that, Swinella? Most girls aren't punk, so why are you?"

"OK," I sighed. "People should dress as they like, of course, I know. I just think it's interesting. And you look great, you know. A skinhead pig-boy... It's brilliant, actually."

"Flattery will get you everywhere," Rasher smiled, taking a sip of foamy lager-top. "I just never had that moment, that feeling-like-a-girl moment that you had, but I probably got more trouble at school because of it. The other boys were always picking fights with me, but they left the girl pigs alone. I guess that's one of the reasons I became a skin. People are less inclined to mess with you when your head is shaved and you're wearing decent boots."

It never occurred to me that lads would be like that, but it made sense. I was a girl, so no threat. Rasher would've confused them and threatened their masculinity in a completely different way.

"And I love the skinhead life anyway, the music and the clothes and all that bollocks," Rasher said, with a sly grin. "And gay men love skinheads, so I get plenty of action... And the thing is, Swinella, poofs know their way around a bloke's arsehole way better than straight men do. The truth is... You're missing out by fucking straight men."

Five minutes into my drink with Rasher and I'd already had my eyes opened. Rasher lit a fag, leaned back in his seat and spread out, legs open wide and arms resting on the back of the bench he was sitting on.

"I don't only fuck men, for your information," I said, somewhat haughtily.

"Whatever..." Rasher said dismissively, wrinkling his snout. "Ever been fisted? I mean by someone other than yourself."

"No," I admitted. "Although I've often thought of it. I've been a bit scared of letting someone else do it... When I do it myself, I know what's going on, and I can ease up if I need to."

"You'll be fine if the other person knows what they're doing," he said with a cheeky wink and a drag on his fag.

"I guess I'll have to look for someone who 'knows their way around an arsehole', as you say," I said.

"You're talking to someone who knows his way around an arsehole," Rasher said. "I'll fist you any time you want, girl."

"But you don't fancy girls... Do you?"

"Not at all," Rasher laughed, shaking his shaven head. "I'm not asking you to be my fucking girlfriend! But I can fist you. We're both pigs... I'll do it for the community. I'll take one for the team, or give one for the team, I suppose. I've fisted blokes before, plenty of times, actually, even though I prefer catching to pitching... Sometimes there has to be a little give and take, y'know?"

My arsehole was twitching, my face had gotten hot, and I was sure my cheeks had flushed red. I was confused, though. I thought Rasher was super fucking hot. I'd have loved to have snogged him there and then, in the pub, but I knew that wasn't what was on the table. His approach was mechanical, masculine, I guess. He didn't fancy me, but he'd happily stick his trotter in my pooper for the general good of pigkind. I was turned on, flattered, disappointed, offended, all at the same time.

"I'm not offering romance," he said, as if reading my mind. "I'm just offering to open your mind, broaden your horizons, gape your dirty fucking pig cunt. One hog to another. It's up to you, take it or leave it."

"I'll take it," I said.

Rasher's gaff was on Bentish Town Road, so we wandered by The Elephant, down Hawley Crescent, turned left at The Dev', and were outside his place in no time at all. He led me through a door between an offy and a kebab shop, and up a flight of uncarpeted stairs. The flat he shared with Bullseye was pretty much what I expected. There were dogeared Reggae and Two-tone posters Blu-tacked to the walls, a black and white portable telly standing on a Newcastle Brown crate in the corner, an overflowing Skol ashtray that had obviously been stolen from a pub, and a load of Arsenal programmes scattered on a knackered coffee table that stood between a sofa and two armchairs that looked like they'd been salvaged from a skip. The place had an overwhelming aroma of fags, spunk, dirty socks, spunk and kebabs. And spunk (did I mention the spunk?). Rasher really was, one hundred percent, a boy. A lad. A right lemon squeezer.

"Nice place," I lied.

"Yeah, it's alright," Rasher said, unironically. "One of Bullseye's shag pieces pays the rent, some Turk from Turdpoke Lame. You get used to the smell from the kebab shop eventually... At least it's lamb and not pork. The bathroom's through there, go and rinse out ya shitter. My room's through there. Just undress from the waist down and come on in... I'll be waiting."

Rasher and Bullseye had the same foot long rubber shower attachment that I did, so I didn't have to get mine out of my haversack. I took off my Docs, socks, tights, knickers and skirt, popped out my buttplug, forced out a knobbly shit, turned on the taps, and squatted over the bath. I washed out my hole with lukewarm water and dried myself on a threadbare towel the colour of old chewing gum. As I stood there, half naked in the filthy bathroom, I suddenly realised that I was not into it at all. Was this how men fucked each other? All business, like changing a tyre or something? I decided to just go through with it, like I always did, just to get it over with. Rasher had been nice enough to offer to fist me, even though I was a girl, so I couldn't be rude and change my mind. I'd just get fisted, chalk it up, and head off home. I didn't have to enjoy it, I could look at it like going to the gym or something. A workout for my ring piece. No pain, no gain. And it'd be my first time with a fellow pig, probably my only time with a pig, when I thought about it.

Felina had insisted, shortly after I moved in, that I try every flavour of bestiamorph, and I'd agreed to give it a go. But we both admitted it'd be pretty difficult for me to fuck a pig. Felina called fucking all five bestiamorphs, plus an ape, the sexogram. I asked her if she'd done it and she just laughed in my face like, I was crazy for even asking.

Rasher's bedroom was, if anything, even more untidy than the living room. A shit-tip that stank of spunk (no surprises there), Lynx body spray, Vaseline (back to the old school) and minging socks. One of the walls was a collage of hardcore photos ripped from gay porno mags, the opposite wall was covered with Madness and Specials posters. The juxtaposition amused me: Terry Hall and Suggs gazing across the messy bedroom at a cornucopia of erect cocks and gaping arseholes.

"Lie on your back and open your legs," Rasher instructed, a businesslike expression on his face.

And they said romance was dead. I did as he said, none too happy about having to lie on top of his cum-rag sheets. Well, at least Felina would have a laugh when I told her about my escapades over tea that evening.

"Poppers," Rasher said, producing the familiar little brown bottle. "Don't bother with snorting it out the bottle, I'll pour some on a rag and you can huff away."

Rasher poured a sizeable amount of amyl onto a questionable looking rag (god only knows what it had been used for in the past, I think it might've started life as a handkerchief) and dropped the rag into a plastic bag.

"So we don't waste none," he said, passing me the bag. "Keep it sealed when you're not sniffing it."

I nodded. Rasher searched through the detritus of his bedroom for a minute, before pulling a greasy-looking pot of Vaseline out from under a pile of dirty laundry.

"Right," he said, pulling off the lid of the Vaseline. "Have a few good sniffs and I'll open you up like a tin of sardines."

Open me up like a tin of sardines? I felt pretty fucking sordid. Dirty sheets and gritty Vaseline was not my love language. Rasher began to grease up his trotter.

"Aren't you going to wear gloves or something?" I asked.

"Nah," he said. "I cut me nails last night and washed me hands this morning, so everything's cool."

Rasher took hold of my tail and pulled me towards him roughly.

"Poppers," he ordered.

I opened the bag, held it to my snout, and inhaled the headache-inducing perfume of the colon cavalier.

In just a few seconds everything changed, and everything made sense. Rasher's filthy flat, the potpourri of dirty laundry, kebab grease and cheap body spray. The porn stuck to the walls and the ubiquitous funk of rancid, stale jism. Rasher and Bullseye's flat wasn't a place lacking in style, as I had first thought. Squalor, filth, and dirt *was* the style. That was their aesthetic. That was what they liked: a dirty, seedy flat on The Bentish Town Road where they could indulge in their sexual escapades amongst the scattered debris of a carefree life lived for the moment. Rasher's rough fingers began to work their way into my soft, girlish hole with unsympathetic vigour, and I gasped and gave myself over.

"You filthy fucking faggot," Rasher snarled, pushing what I guessed were three fingers into me. "Dressing like a girl, pretending you're something soft and clean. We both know what you are behind all that grubby makeup, ya slag."

Rasher pumped harder and grunted, grabbed my tail with his free hand and pulled. He was rough, rougher than Bapho, rougher than any of the apes I'd fucked back home.

It was my first time being intimate with a fellow pig, and I saw that he knew my body, knew exactly how hard he could pull my tail without hurting me, knew his way around my arsehole, didn't waste time fucking around with my useless cock; It really does take one to know one. I huffed more poppers and my head spun. I felt filthy and, in that moment, I loved it. Rasher cleared his throat and spat onto my crotch, let go of my tail, and began pulling at my tiny, flaccid cock and empty scrotum. He slapped my scrotum hard. He knew I wasn't sensitive down there and that I could take it. I reached under my t-shirt and began squeezing my tits, pinching my buzzing nipples hard with shaking fingertips.

"Never mind your fucking udders," he said. "Do more poppers, I'm at the knuckles and you know you want the lot."

I did as he said, sniffing more poppers than I ever had before. My heart was racing and my body felt hot all over. There was a brief moment of discomfort, and then... POP! His knuckles had forced themselves all the way into me. His hand was inside me, my sphincter closing in on his wrist as he twisted his hand inside of my arse, moving backwards and forwards in small, rocking movements.

"Oh fuck!" I cried, my eyes watering, the crème de la crème of the Two-tone movement looking on in cool indifference from their place on the wall. Rasher was definitely a naughty boy from a nasty school. "Fucking ow, shit... Stop, don't stop, I mean! Fuck!"

I was being fisted, and by a fellow pig to boot. He didn't get very deep, I couldn't take him up to the elbow, which is how I'd always pictured it in my mind, but I'd never been fuller. Rasher pulled his hand almost all the way out of me, his knuckles on the edge of popping out, and then he plunged back in, and lights exploded behind my eyes. He repeated this move several times, punching my cunt with gusto, and I grunted and squealed with wild abandon. I don't know how, but suddenly I was on all fours and he was smacking my arse hard with his free hand, while his fisting hand turned and writhed inside of me like a bony battering ram. I buried my head in his filthy grey pillow and began to squeal and squeal and squeal.

"Fucking pig! Fucking pig! Fucking pig!" Rasher shouted between aggressive grunts. "You dirty fucking hog swine bitch slag!"

I was sure the neighbours would hear, but I didn't give a fuck, I wanted them to hear.

It hurt, but it hurt so good, just like Susan Cadogan said. I gasped, too tired to grunt or squeal, and gave myself over, dropping limp onto my stomach. Behind my useless cock and my vacant ball bag a familiar pressure began to build, a glowing red tension deep within my pelvis. My heart rate quickened, and

I began to breathe fast and hard and deep. It was going to happen, and he knew it. This was Rasher's turf, what had he said? 'Poofs know their way around a bloke's arsehole better than anyone else'? His hand moved, slid, turned and twisted, almost came all the way out of me, and then plunged back in. My heavy breathing turned to grunting, my grunting turned to squeals, and my squeals turned back into heavy, rapid gasps. The heat inside of me turned from red to orange to yellow to white and I exploded in a cataclysm of melted Vaseline, transparent pre-cum, busted arsehole and exhausted grunts. All tension had left my body, and I sank onto the dirty, unmade bed. I was a mess of goose-bumped, shivering pig-pink flesh, and I had a pounding, popper-induced headache. Rasher laughed.

"That all right for ya, Swinella?" He chortled.

I rolled onto my back and looked at him blinking and bleary-eyed.

"It was, erm..." I said. "It was... yeah."

"Well, I've got to go out in a minute. Sort yourself out."

And with that he sauntered out of the room, very full of himself, I thought. I heard the sound of laughter and talking coming from the living room. I clambered unsteadily to my feet and looked around. My skirt, kickers and tights were still in the bathroom. I thought about wrapping something around my waist, but the towel that hung on the radiator looked like it hadn't been washed since the seventies, so I just took a deep breath and walked through the door.

"Way-hey!" shouted Bullseye as I walked into the living room.

"Here she is! Our little fister sister! How's yer arse? No good for cracking walnuts, I'd say!"

"Unlike your busted face, Bullseye," I said, laughing.

I wandered home, my fun-centre squelching loose and moist under my knickers as I walked down Bentish Town Road. I'd definitely have to grab some aspirins from the chemists to take away the after-effects of Rasher's industrial-strength poppers.

I opened the door to our clean, cosy flat and walked on in. Bauhaus's *Stigmata Martyr* was playing on the living room record player, and Felina was making one of her favourite meals in the kitchen. A sandalwood-scented candle was burning in a saucer on the kitchen table, the smell of it mixing with the familiar scent of Felina's Yves Saint Laurent Opium perfume, the smell of a freshly-opened tin of mackerel adding to the welcoming aroma. A much better fragrance than the sordid stench of Rasher and Bullseye's filthy gaff.

"Good evening, flatmate," Felina said as I wandered into the kitchen. "How's it going?"

I sat at the pale blue Formica-topped kitchen table.

"I've just been fisted," I confessed, no point in beating about the bush.

"What?!" Felina cried, turning around and staring at me wide eyed, a piece of mackerel on Ryvita in her perfectly manicured hand. "By whom, exactly? Why didn't you ask me?! You know I've done fisting sessions before, I know what I'm doing. Who did it? Who fisted your slutty back door without my permission?

Who do I have to fall out with now?"

"It was Rasher," I confessed, with a nonchalant shrug. "At his place."

"Rasher? Rasher?!" Felina repeated, shaking her head in disbelief, her eyes wide. "Hmmm... Did you do anything else with him?"

"No," I said. "He's gay. He did it as a favour, one pig to another. He didn't even get undressed. It was very business-like. It was pretty good though."

"Not as good as if I'd have done it," Felina said, annoyed. "You only had to ask."

"I'd say he's an expert, to be honest," I said. "Poofs know their way around an arsehole."

"That's true," Felina conceded, nodding. "But so do I. I'm a pro."

"So's he."

"Then why don't you fuck off and move in with him?" she spat, sitting on the other kitchen chair in a dramatic huff.

"His place is a total shit-hole," I said. "And I like living with you. You smell nice."

"God, Swinella, you're such a crawly bumlick," Felina said, before daintily nibbling at the corner of her fishy cracker and letting out a sigh. "So, go on... Tell me all about it."

I recounted every detail of my fisting adventure on Bentish Town Road. Felina nodded sagely at some of the details, winced at my description of the disgusting flat, and laughed when I told her I had to parade though the living room bottomless in front of Bullseye. She finished her meal, washed the plate, and turned and looked at me with one of her sly, scheming expressions.

"But, y'know, pig-on-pig action. I bet there's money in that." she said, narrowing her cat's eyes in concentration. "I don't think I've ever seen boy pig and girl pig porn, not ever. Do you think Rasher might be into it?"

"Maybe... I'll have to ask him." I said. "Do you fancy going to the pictures? I don't feel like staying in or going to the pub."

We went to the cinema on Porkway and watched *The Hunger* with David Bowie, Catherine Deneuve and Susan Sarandon. It was kind of brilliant, although Felina insisted that real-life vampires were nothing like the ones in the film. I go and see it every year now.

CHAPTER THIRTEEN

FINCHLEY

"It's for you," Felina called through my bedroom door, one Tuesday evening after I had just got home from work.

I had heard the phone ring a few seconds earlier, followed by the muffled sound of Felina's voice as she picked it up and answered.

"Hello," I said into the receiver, wrapped in a fluffy brown towel, hair still damp from my recent shower.

"Swinella? Hi, how are you?" a tinny but familiar voice said. "It's Elaine. Nurse Elaine."

"Oh... hi," I said. "How's it going?"

"It's going well, baby," Nurse Elaine said, in what I imagine she thought was a seductive tone of voice, breathy and soft and slightly babyish. "I was just calling to see how you're doing... and to ask if you're free this Saturday evening?"

I hadn't seen Nurse Elaine since she'd visited my room, but I had hoped we'd meet again. I occasionally found myself idly thinking about her amazing pierced pussy and cinched waist during quiet periods when I was working in the shop, alone and daydreaming. I'd even bought myself to orgasm a couple of times whilst thinking about her, recalling our encounter as I fucked my greasy slack arsehole with hand or dildo: a composite scenario half memory and half fantasy.

"Well... I'm working Saturday, but I am free from seven." I said. "What are you thinking?"

"We're having a little *soirée* at our house, darling, and I'd like you to be there," Elaine said. "It's going to be one of *those* parties... Likeminded individuals, couples mainly, just a small gathering."

"One of those parties?" I asked. "One of what parties?"

"Oh, you know, dear... A party for enthusiasts, lifestyle people. People like us. They're all quite presentable, you know, all professional people. Clean... but dirty," Elaine let out a girlish giggle. "There will be fucking, but you don't have to do anything you don't want, just come along. Just watch, if that's what you want... I'd like you to watch me, y'know, and I want the gang to meet you."

I had to say yes, of course, my curiosity getting the better of me like it always did. I scribbled her address and phone number onto a scrap of paper and arranged to get there around half past eight. She lived in Finchley, which was only a short tube ride away. I'd have time to head home after work to get ready, and rinse out my arse-cunt... Just in case.

"I think I'm going to a wife swapping party or something on Saturday," I said to Felina after hanging up.

"Are we?" Felina asked. "Am I going to be your wife, or are you mine?"

"I said I'm going to a wife swapping party," I replied. "The invite was just for one... Sorry."

"You didn't even ask!" Felina protested. "I heard the whole

thing!"

"I didn't think you'd want to! It was Elaine... Nurse Elaine... You said she was old, you mocked me for fucking her! Why would I think you'd want to go to a party at her place?"

"Well," Felina said, crossing her arms and staring at the TV. "You could've asked me."

"I can call her back and ask if you can come, if you like?" I said, worried that I had offended my temperamental flatmate.

"Oh, I was never going to come anyway," Felina said, nonchalantly examining her claws and sighing. "But I like to be asked to things... just so I can turn them down. Anyway, I'm busy Saturday."

"Really?" I said, sitting down. "What're you doing?"

"I'm spending the evening here, alone. I'm going to enjoy having the place to myself for once," Felina said, staring at me and scowling. "Without my stupid pig flatmate using up all the oxygen in the room and annoying me."

"Good," I said, rolling my eyes. "I'm sure you'll have fun."

Felina let me head out as soon as we shut up shop so that I could get ready, offering to clean down and lock up on her own, which was nice of her. I rushed home, slipped out my buttplug, washed out my gravel pit, did my face, brushed my hair and tied it back into a tight ponytail. Felina had cut my fringe the night before to just the right length, just above my eyebrows, which I'd let Felina pluck when she cut my hair. She'd really gone to town on my brows, plucking them into thin inch long ticks with no curve to them. I had to draw the rest of eyebrow in myself when I got ready. It could be quite tricky to get them to match.

"I look like Spock!" I'd said when I looked in the mirror.

"Yes, but when you draw them in you'll have more freedom with the shape," Felina had said. "We should just get rid of them altogether. Like mine."

"No... I kind of like looking like Spock," I said, turning my head and examining myself from different angles. "I think these eyebrows are most logical."

I slipped on a black polo neck sweater that I'd borrowed from Felina, and a black leather mini skirt and fishnets. I put a string of pearls on over the top of the polo neck and switched my regular hoop earrings for a pair of large silver moons that hung from curved hooks. Felina had offered to lend me a pair of her stilettoed boots, but I'd never gotten used to wearing heels, so I went with my classic black Doc Martins. I pulled on my leather and was about to head out when the front door swung open.

"My, my, my..." Felina said as she walked into the flat. "Scrub up all right, don't you?"

Gatita followed Felina into the flat and looked me up and down, a crooked white fanged smile on her beautiful brown face.

"Fuckable," she said with a sharp nod, and my heart and sphincter skipped in simpatico.

"I bet that's not the only pearl necklace you'll end up wearing tonight," Felina said with a twinkle in her wicked green cats' eyes.

"I'll open the voddy," Gatita said, pulling a bottle of vodka out of her massive red leather handbag and sauntering into the kitchen, her slender hips rolling as she walked, her auburn tail swinging with each graceful step.

"You'll have a shot for the road," Felina said to me; it wasn't a question.

"Have you got it in?" Gatita said, walking back into the living room carrying three glasses and nodding towards my crotch with her eyebrows raised.

"No," I said. "Not right now. It's empty."

"Not for long," Felina said, raising her glass. "Cheers!"

The three of us downed the vodka. I nearly gagged, but managed to play it cool. I didn't want to look like a lightweight in front of the cats.

"Well... I better be off," I said. "See you later!"

"Bye, whore," Felina said, dismissing me with a wave of her claw.

"See ya later..." Gatita purred, with a wink of her amber eye.

I checked my pocket A to Z again on the train and got off at Finchley Central. The evening was warm and bright, and everyone on the tube seemed happy and relaxed. The house, a large semi-detached affair with a big front garden, was only a few minutes' walk from the tube station, and I found it easily enough. I was slightly early and, as I rang the doorbell, I felt a tingle of excitement. I was happy to see my older kinkster friend again, and I was intrigued to find out what her friends were like. I heard the sound of heels clicking along the hallway and the door swung open. Elaine beamed at me and stepped aside to let me enter, calling over her shoulder as she did.

"Paul! Paul! It's Swinella!"

"Oh, wonderful!" I heard a man's voice call from inside the house. "Bring her through!"

I walked into the bright light of the carpeted hallway and Elaine closed the door behind me.

"You look stunning," Elaine said, placing a hand on each of my shoulders, leaning in and giving me a kiss on the lips.

"So do you," I said, smiling and looking my host up and down.

Elaine was wearing a pink, see-through dressing gown with a faux fur trim, a white satin corset and peep-toe white stilettos. Her ample, middle-aged tits sagged slightly beneath the diaphanous material in a way that made my mouth water. Her heavyweight nipple rings were clearly visible through her gown, catching the light through the shimmering material. Elaine's hair was big, nothing like the severe ponytail she wore for work, more like Bonnie Tyler on a hen do, scrunched with L'Oriel mousse and diffused for maximum body. She'd obviously recently had highlights. She was wearing bright red lipstick, several shades lighter than her regular colour, heavy mascara and blue, pink and purple eyeshadow. It was all a bit *Reader's Wives Over 40*. It struck me that Elaine trying to look sexy was much less attractive than Elaine on a regular Wednesday afternoon. How disappointing!

"Hand me your jacket," Elaine said.

I did as she asked. She hung my leather on a row of hooks by the door and took me by the hand.

"Come," she said, raising her eyebrows and smiling.

As we walked along the tiled hallway Elaine's cunt rings rattled and her heels clicked in time. She sounded like the rhythm section of a German industrial band played through teeny-tiny speakers. We walked into the living room. Everything was shades of brown. Brown leather sofas, thick beige shag-pile carpet, wooden sideboard, patterned polyester curtains, damask flock wallpaper in cream and biscuit. Here in Finchley the world had clearly not turned day-glo. I was surprised and impressed to hear Blondie's *The Tide Is High* playing on the record player that sat on the sideboard. The room's only occupant was a man in his forties, sat on one of the sofas, wearing new-looking blue jeans, brown loafers, and a white shirt. The man's shirt was tucked into his jeans and open at the collar, revealing a thick gold chain. He smelled of Blue Stratos. The man stood and offered me his hand. I shook it. It was clammy.

"Delighted to meet you, er… Ha-ha-ha," Paul said. "My wife has told me a lot about you."

Paul looked me up and down and held onto my hand for an uncomfortably long amount of time.

"Please, take a seat, er… Ha-ha-ha" he said, staring at my nose and gesturing to the other sofa. "There's food on the table, vol-au-vents and Twiglets and stuff… but I'm sure you don't want to make a hog of yourself, er… Ha-ha-ha."

I had clearly made a terrible error.

"Now, Paul," Elaine said, waving a finger at her obvious cunt of a husband. "Be nice… Swinella is our guest."

"Yes, sorry, er… Ha-ha-ha!" Paul grinned, clearly anything but sorry. "Drink?"

"I'll have a Coke," I said coldly, fixing my gaze on the middle of his forehead.

"Nothing stronger? Er… Ha-ha-ha," Paul shrugged. "We've got some Babycham in the fridge."

"Just a Coke."

"Ok," Paul said, slightly crestfallen. "A Coke it is, er… Ha-ha-ha."

Paul headed out of the room. For some reason, when *The Tide Is High* ended it was not followed by *Angels On the Balcony*, which is the next track on Blondie's *Autoamerican* album, but by *Special Brew*, Bad Manner's paean to the overly strong, sickly-sweet Danish lager favoured by street drinkers, general ne'er-do-wells and, apparently, the Danish royal family.

"Don't mind Paul," Elaine said, sitting next me on the sofa and leaning close, her thigh pressed up against mine. "He's just nervous, he's never met anyone like you before. I'm sure you understand."

Oh, I understood all right. I always made a point of being as rude as possible to someone different to me when I met them for the first time, I mean, who wouldn't? Elaine slipped her arm around my shoulder and placed her other hand on my thigh, caressing me idly with her coral-pink fingernails.

"You look gorgeous tonight," she said coquettishly into my ear… too close, her breath hot and smelling of fags and cheap fizzy wine. "I can't wait to play with you later, baby."

Paul returned carrying three glasses. A champagne flute, no doubt containing the aforementioned Babycham, a tumbler of whiskey, and a glass of Coke. He handed the Coke to me and the champagne flute to Elaine, and sat down on the sofa opposite, legs open wide, shit-eating grin on his stupid tanned face. I smelt the Coke. It had vodka in it... not very much, but with my sense of smell it stood out like a foreskin at a naked bar mitzvah. I'm guessing Paul's plan was to gradually increase the amount of vodka in each Coke I drank, assuming I wouldn't notice: alcohol, the original date-rape drug. I placed the glass on the coffee table without touching it.

"So..." I said, looking around and raising my eyebrows. "It looks like I'm the only one here?"

"Oh," Elaine tried to explain. "We told the others the party was starting at nine... so that you'd have time to relax and meet Paul before everyone turned up."

"And who's everyone?" I asked.

"Just three other couples... Swingers, like the three of us," Paul said, leaning forward, elbows on knees. "Good people. Er... Ha-ha-ha. Dave has his own insurance firm, you know. Trevor is the manager of the largest office supply company in North London, and Mick is in finance in the city... Not sure what he does exactly, but it pays very well. He's got a Roller. Their wives are all very pretty... I mean, of course they are, er... Ha-ha-ha, otherwise we wouldn't invite them! Er... Ha-ha-ha. But I'm sure you'll hog all the attention tonight, er... Ha-ha-ha."

Special Brew ended and was followed, inexplicably, by the theme from the TV show *Minder*.

Paul sang along to the record and rocked in time to the music, raising his eyebrows and winking at me over his tumbler of Johnny Walker

"Well," I said, standing up and thinking on my feet. "I was going to tell you in advance, Elaine, but I can't stay... There's a gig in Hamden that I really have to go to. I didn't want to let you down, so I thought I'd pop in and say hello anyway, but I really must cut a dash."

"Oh no, Swinella," Elaine said, standing up with a crestfallen expression on her face. "But you haven't even touched your drink. Stay a little while longer, won't you?'

I backed around the sofa and towards the door.

"No, no..." I said. "I've got to go."

I headed for the door. Elaine followed me, her cunt rings rattling. Paul slouched back in his seat, shook his head and took an angry sip of his Scotch. I went into the hallway and grabbed my jacket from the hook.

"Don't go, honey," Elaine pleaded. "I wanted to see you again. Don't leave me."

"Elaaaine," Paul called from the living room. "I thought you said she was fun? I thought you said she was up for whatever?"

"Oh, do shut up, Paul," Elaine shouted back over her shoulder. "I'm dealing with this!"

I pulled on my jacket, opened the front door and stepped out onto the porch. Elaine followed me and gently pulled the door shut behind her with a soft click.

"Don't go, honey," she repeated. "Paul is just a little drunk. We had a few to loosen ourselves up before you came around."

The music in the living room suddenly leapt in volume. I'm Coming Out by Diana Ross randomly blaring out of the speakers. Elaine reached out and placed her hands on my upper arms and gripped hard.

"Stay... please," she murmured. "You're all I've got. You don't know..."

Her eyes looked up at me pleadingly, I thought for a second that she was going to cry. I pushed her against the wall of the porch and kissed her hard, my tongue sliding into her mouth. She went limp and kissed me back, making small animal noises. I breathed her in; Silk Cut, Babycham, hairspray and mousse, Opium by Yves Saint Laurent, all tinged with the scent of despair and desperation. It was a heady brew. I reached under her dressing gown and grabbed a handful of cunt and steel. She moaned. I thrust my tongue into her mouth and snogged her one last time, before letting go and pulling back.

"Now... Take your fucking ape hands off of me," I said, turning away and walking down the path towards the street.

"Swinella," she called after me. "Come back. After the gig, I mean... I'll be waiting."

I stopped at the garden gate and turned around.

"Oh, Elaine." I said pityingly, shaking my head. "There is no 'gig'... I just had to get out of... Out of whatever that was."

As I rode the tube back to Hamden, I felt myself filled with a strange mixture of pride, anger and disappointment. Disappointed because I had wanted Elaine's husband and friends to be how Elaine was but, in the end it had turned out that Elaine wasn't how Elaine was, or at least not how I had imagined her to be. I was proud of myself because I had sussed the situation immediately and extracted myself without hesitation. London had changed me, was changing me. I liked to think that I was always confident, and that I'd always stood up for myself, thanks in no small part to the tutoring I had received from Caroline back home, but I wasn't sure if the pre-Hamden Town version of myself would've handled that situation as well as I did.

When I got back to Hamden I turned left out of the tube station and walked towards Bentish Town. I had decided to walk by The Dev' and The Elephant, just to see if I could spot Felina through the window. If I did, I'd go in for a drink, and it turned out I was right to do so. Felina and Gatita were sat in The Dev' looking amazing, drinking snakebites and judging everyone. I went in, grabbed a drink from the bar, and, to much hilarity and repeating of details, told the two cats about the 'party'.

"Well," Felina said, shaking her pretty head. "I didn't want to say anything, but I didn't have high hopes for that particular engagement."

"No," I admitted, before draining my glass. "But I had to find out for myself, I suppose. I'm never leaving Hamden again. There's everything I need right here. I could've been with you two all along."

"Never?" asked Gatita with a raised eyebrow and a look of bemused curiosity. "Never leaving Hamden? Are you sure?"

"Yes," I nodded. "That's right. I just want to be here. Forever. With you."

"For ever?" Felina said. "Forever ever?"

"For eternity," I said, with a determined nod.

"Felina tells me you might be interested in doing some work," Gatita said changing the subject. "Some photographic work, y'know, with that nob-head Dave."

"I'm open to it," I said, a shiver of excitement running down my spine.

"I'd like to shoot with you," Gatita said with a mischievous smile on her plump purple lips. "If it's ok with Felina?"

"I've no problem with you shooting with Swinella," Felina said to Gatita with a slight shrug of her delicate shoulders. "I'm not her owner."

CHAPTER FOURTEEN

THE SUMMONING

"You look great," Felina said, tossing the magazine onto the coffee table. I picked it up and flicked back to my pages, and there I was, for all the world to see.

"Thanks," I said.

It was surreal seeing myself spread out in my complimentary copy of issue twenty three of *Fists of Fury: Bestiamorph Special*. Dave had popped into the shop earlier that day to drop the magazine off, and I had dutifully bought it home to show Felina, who had the day off. She'd been caning some guy at the house in Eweston. Usually, after a session with a client, Felina was in a nicely relaxed state of mind, but that evening she seemed agitated.

"Are you ok, cat-girl?" I asked.

Felina sighed and sipped her coffee.

"It's like with Rasher and the fisting... You keep having these milestones and I'm not there. I just thought, y'know... That your first session on camera would be with me."

"Really?" I said. "You should've said so... I would've loved that. But you told Gatita it was fine for her to shoot with me."

"It was fine, of course, it is fine... I'm not jealous, it's just..." Felina looked me in the eye, with a wry smile. "It's just... Seeing you there, all grown up, I don't know… It should've been me, that's all."

"It can be you," I said. "It'll be you next time."

"Next time won't be the first time," Felina said.

"It'll be the first time with you," I said. "And Gatita is your sister… Isn't that cool? And anyway, I wouldn't even be in Hamden if it wasn't for you. You were the first person I met here, my first friend. You gave me my first job. You have a lot of firsts. You'll always be my number one."

"Pass me the magazine," Felina sulkily said. "I want another look."

I walked across the living room and sat down next to Felina on the sofa, leaning in close and handing her the magazine. Felina flicked to my section and studied the photographs. The photo session had taken place in the function room of a pub on Pork Farm Road that I didn't know the name of. The two of us were pretending to be on a date. We had been told to dress as 'normal girls'. I was wearing a red dress, short and slutty, and red high heels that I borrowed from Gatita. I was wearing red lipstick with gross lipgloss, and blue mascara and eyeshadow. Gatita was in black; leather mini skirt and silky halter back, but she had toned down her make up and her auburn hair was scraped back into a tight dominatrix ponytail.

"You make good basic bitches," Felina said, contemplating the images. "You look so slutty."

Felina turned the page. Gatita and I had had to mime a scene where we went from getting off with each other to my being fisted in about six frames. It wasn't that difficult-

Frame one: Eye contact while drinking juice through a straw, legs crossed high, Gatita looking aggressively lustful and leaning in, myself looking coy.

Frame two: Leaning in for a kiss, eyes wide, Gatita's hand on my knee, my legs no longer crossed.

Frame three: Open mouth kiss, tongues for the camera, my eyes closed, Gatita's scarlet-clawed hand tugging at the hem of my dress.

Frame four: Hem of my dress lifted up, revealing my cocklette, Gatita's hand behind my head as she sneers into my slightly scared-looking face, eyes wide.

Frame five: My legs open wide, crotch lifted slightly, curly tail visible. Gatita leaning forward, the tips of her index and middle finger positioned on my hole.

Frame six: My head tossed back as I recline on the bench, Gatita inserting half of her hand into my wet hole.

Frame seven: Her hand all the way in me, just past the wrist, my head thrown back in ecstasy.

And that was it. First eye contact to fisting in seven quarter-page-size frames, if only real life were so simple. The rest of the piece was made up of shots of Gatita fisting me in various positions. On my knees on the pool table, bent over the bar, up against the fruit machine, leaning against the wall. I hadn't been fully turned on, although deep down I was really into the fact that I was able to do the photo shoot, to be so casual about everything; I obviously had a real thing about being blasé about sex. It was kind of like losing my virginity again. In fact, I had come to understand that 'losing' your virginity was a process. There are many milestones, not just that first time when you get fucked: there are multiple virginities, different virginities for different genders and sex acts, and different virginities for apes and the types of bestiamorphs. This makes sex, and life, much more fun and interesting. I'd lost my cat virginity and my on-camera virginity all at once. The completion of my sexogram came closer with each new encounter.

"Gatita has quite the talent for fisting with those claws, but not damaging the recipient," Felina said, nodding approvingly. "It's always easier with gloves on, but often these magazine people want to see skin on skin contact... They want you raw... Barebacked."

"Yes," I leaned in closer and looked over Felina's shoulder. "I was a bit worried before we started... I mean, those fucking nails are scary! But she kind of curls them in so they don't lacerate your guts... which is a bonus."

"It certainly is!" Felina laughed, relaxing a little bit and resting her head on my shoulder. "You look good though, I mean... you both do... It's good to see you wearing something different."

"Well, I'm not going to start dressing like a cheap slut to amuse you!" I said.

"But Swinella, dear... You already dress like a cheap slut," Felina said, sitting upright and looking me in the eye. "You are a cheap slut, so any clothes you wear are cheap slut clothes by definition."

"I don't present as a slut, though," I argued.

"You're a pig," Felina said condescendingly, gently tapping the end of my snout with the tip of her clawed index finger. "It doesn't matter what you wear, that snout says 'slut' to the world."

"Not all pigs are sluts," I said. "There are monogamous pigs."

"Maybe... But you're not one of them. You're a slut."

"Am I?" I said, I'd never thought about it that way before. "I always think of sluts as like, I dunno... Bimbos and stuff. *Razzle Dazzlers*, readers' wives. I thought I was just, y'know... Sexually open and free. Slut sounds like an insult."

"No, no, no..." Felina shook her head. "Slut is a compliment. You're a slut. You look like a slut... And it's brilliant. And... you're my slut."

"But you're not a slut? Just me?"

"I'm not a slut," Felina said with a shrug and a shake of her bobbed head. "I don't have it in me... I don't like people enough to be a slut. The truth is..."

"The truth is what?" I said, after a few moments of waiting for Felina to finish what she was about to say.

"Oh, never mind," she said, gracefully getting to her feet and stretching out her shoulders and spine with a satisfied meow.

"Do you want a cup of tea? *Top of The Pops* is on in a minute."

Felina was walking into the kitchen when the phone rang. She wandered over to where it sat on its own little shelf by the front door and picked up the receiver.

"Hello," she said, before falling silent for a minute. "Yes, of course. I'll tell her right away. Bye,"

My feline flatmate hung up the phone and turned to me with a serious expression on her face.

"That was Lily," she said. "She'd like you to go around to her house for tea tomorrow evening."

"Lily?" I said. "That weird woman with the silver hair who came in the shop? Why does she want me to go round for tea? How does she even have our number?"

"She's got everyone's number," Felina said. "You should go... She's actually very nice and she might have something for you. She kind of helps people out, people she likes."

"And has she helped you out?" I asked.

"We wouldn't be here, in this flat, working in The Black Violet, if it wasn't for Lily and her sister," Felina said. "You kind of have to go."

"What if I don't want to?" I said.

"Oh Swinella," Felina said with a reassuring grin. "You'll want to... You don't want to turn this down. It might be the offer of a lifetime."

It was a warm evening in early September. Felina told me to head off as soon as The Black Violet closed, that she'd lock up and see me at home later. The cat had given me a pensive once-over before I left, finally nodding her approval, hugging me and wishing me luck, all of which was very strange. She wasn't usually so serious, and she wasn't a hugger. When Felina wanted to express affection, she usually sneaked up on me when we were sat on the sofa watching TV. It was then she'd curl up and rest her head on my lap, purring contentedly while we watched some old film on BBC2.

The house was a large, ancient, tumbledown affair hidden down a winding side street that connected Pork Farm Road with Bentish Town Road. The door and window frames were painted a dusty matt black, the red bricks were stained with a sooty grey film, and the garden was a tangle of overgrown rose bushes. I opened the creaking gate and walked along the cobbled pathway towards the shadowy porch. The lead-panelled windows were dark, and nothing of the interior could be seen from the outside.

I knocked on the heavy wooden door. For a moment I thought no one was home, but then I heard the distant sound of a door opening and closing deep within the house, followed by the echoing tap of approaching footsteps that grew louder as they came closer. The handle turned and the door swung inwards.

I found myself face to face with a timid looking rabbit-girl. The girl was short and petite, as rabbits often are, and her blonde, almost white hair was held back with a black velvet Alice band, nicely framing her rosy-cheeked face. She was dressed in a vintage cream blouse with a black bow at the neck, and an ankle length black pleated skirt. She smelled like sandalwood and vanilla, and she had recently showered, washing her hair with Timotei shampoo. She wasn't wearing any makeup or jewellery at all. She didn't need to. Her skin was flawless, her large brown eyes were framed with luscious long, dark eyelashes, and her lips were a soft pink. Her upper lip, of course, was divided by a split, a philtrum, behind which her large incisor teeth were visible, and her ears were slightly pointed. I always thought that rabbittes' ears actually look more like pixie or Vulcan ears, not really like four-legged rabbit's ears at all, but I had to admit those little pointed elf ears were way cuter than if the rabbit-girls had actual floppy rabbit ears on top of their heads. She looked like she tasted of icing sugar.

"Hello," she said in a quiet voice, twitching her nose as she spoke, in that infuriatingly cute way that rabbit-girls do. "You must be Swinella?"

"That's right," I held out my hand. "I'm Swinella."

The rabbit-girl took my hand and shook it gently. Her hand was impossibly warm and soft; rabbits have a slightly higher body temperature than other people.

"I'm Chastity," she said, blushing slightly, nodding her head and blinking rapidly. "It's nice to meet you. Won't you come in?"

Chastity stood to one side and I entered the house. All was quiet within the building, the silence only broken by the slow, rhythmic ticking of a huge grandfather clock that stood in the hallway. The ceiling was high. and the floor was honeycomb-tiled in terracotta and black hexagons. All of the woodwork was painted black. The walls were painted a dark plum purple and the temperature was cool, a couple of degrees colder than the street outside.

"Mother is waiting for you in the drawing room," Chastity

said. "Can I take your coat?"

I handed my leather jacket to the earnest young rabbitte. She hung it on a hatstand at the foot of a wide staircase and turned and walked away. I followed her to the back of the house, which seemed to be much bigger on the inside than it had appeared to be from the outside. Chastity knocked lightly on a dark wooden door and waited.

"Come," a voice called out from the other side of the door.

The rabbit gently opened the door and gestured for me to follow. The room we entered was decorated as expected, cluttered Victoriana would've been the best way to describe the aesthetic. Lace and velvet, taxidermy, and bookshelves packed with old, dusty hardback books. A sepia-toned colour palette of black and browns, of soft greys and ivory.

Lily sat at a table wearing a black knitted shawl and a simple black dress, a black turban with an amethyst brooch framing her ageless face, her long silver hair tumbling down her back and over her shoulders. She was so composed and poised as she looked at the page of an ancient-looking book that lay open on the antique table in front of her. My head spun as I realised she didn't smell of anything. I hadn't noticed in the shop, but she was the first human being I'd ever encountered with absolutely no odour. I was freaked out, but tried to ignore it. She did not look up as we entered, but raised her right hand slightly, middle and forefingers extended like a blessing. Chastity placed her fingertips onto my forearm and looked up at me, smiling, showing those giant buck teeth and twitching her button nose. 'Wait', her large brown eyes said. After a few seconds Lily looked up and smiled.

"I simply cannot stop reading mid-paragraph," she said. "Please... won't you take a seat?"

Lily gently closed the book and gestured at a large, overstuffed chair by the large bay window that was littered with a half dozen plump, heavily embroidered cushions. I sat down. I tried to sit properly with my back straight and my knees together, one hand on top of the other on my lap. Lily closed her book, stood from the table, walked gracefully over to a chaise longue and sat down in a smooth, flowing movement. She kicked off a pair of green velvet ballet pumps and swung her legs up and under herself and propped herself up on her elbow. She was wearing red and black striped tights.

"I'm glad you came, Swinella," she said.

"Oh... I was glad you invited me," I said. "I always like meeting interesting people, that's why I moved down here."

"I meant I'm glad you came to Hamden Town," Lily smiled. "But I'm also glad you came for tea."

Chastity turned and left the room, closing the door gently behind her, presumably to prepare the aforementioned beverages.

"How are you finding it here in Hamden?" Lily asked, coupling an intense gaze with a warm smile.

"Oh, I love it," I said, truthfully. "It's everything I ever wanted. I feel so lucky to have found a job and a place so easily. Felina is amazing... Everyone else is as well, really, but Felina especially."

"Yes," Lily smiled. "She's a good cat-girl. She's been with us a long time."

"Are you the owner of The Black Violet?" I asked. "When I asked Felina about you, she was very... secretive. And that's not like her at all."

"My sister and I don't consider ourselves the owners of anything. We see ourselves more as gardeners. And Hamden Town is our garden," Lily explained in a calm, relaxing voice. "Your Felina probably has more than a few secrets you don't know about... All in good time, Swinella. All in good time."

I supposed Lily could've just been a rich weirdo, but that still wouldn't have explained Felina's deference. Cats don't respect wealth.

"How, though? If you don't mind me asking..." I said, trying to sound polite. "How is Hamden your garden... How do you mean?"

"We tend it," she smiled. "We look after it. We maintain its borders... Herbaceous and otherwise. We encourage its flowers to bloom. We'd like to help you to bloom, Swinella."

I didn't know what she was talking about. How could this woman help me 'bloom'? What did that even mean? Wasn't I already blooming? I was trying to be my most authentic self at all times. I was already saying yes to life.

"You're wondering how I can help you bloom, aren't you?" Lily said, with a slight nod and a knowing smile. "You're already doing a wonderful job. Do you ever think about what comes after Hamden?"

I never had. I was young, I guess I still am, but I just didn't really think beyond what I was getting up to that weekend; that evening, even. I just assumed everything was going to be all right. I'd found my place in the world. I'd just keep working at The Black Violet until something else came up. I guess I thought that one day I'd meet someone and settle down in some way, but I didn't really dwell on it.

"I'm just kind of living day-to-day," I finally said. "Isn't that what everyone my age does?"

"It's what a lot of people your age do," Lily agreed. "Wouldn't it be great if we could do that forever? Just live our lives for the moment?"

"Of course, that'd be perfect," I said. "But we all have to get older, I suppose."

"Do you have any questions, about life, Swinella?" Lily asked. "I mean... The meaning of life? Why we're here? Not questions for me, necessarily, I mean... Do you ever think about those things, philosophically speaking?"

Well, Lily certainly cut straight to the chase and didn't mess around with small talk. As I thought Lily's question over the door swung open, and Chastity walked in carrying a silver tray laden with a fine bone china tea set and a plate of red and white macaroons. She gently placed the tray onto an ornate occasional table draped in lace. The tea in the pot was Earl Grey, that undertone of bergamot was unmistakable, and there was a strong, citrusy odour coming from a plate of lemon slices.

"Milk and sugar?" Lily asked. "Or a slice of lemon, maybe?"

"Just a little milk," I answered.

Chastity poured a cup of tea for Lily, dropped in a slice of lemon with a pair of dainty silver tongues, and handed it over to her. She poured my tea, added a splash of milk, and passed me the cup and saucer. As she did so her large brown eyes widened and scanned me head to toe, a barely-noticeable smile fluttering across her soft pink lips and revealing her large rabbit teeth as she did so. The petite rabbitte handed a small plate to Lily, turned, picked up the plate of macaroons and held it out to her. Lily took three of the the sweet-smelling fancies.

"Macaroon?" Lily asked.

"Oh, go on then... I'll just take one," I answered with a smile. "I have to watch my weight."

Chastity handed me a plate and then held out the macaroons. I took one and said, 'Thank you'. The rabbitte turned and left the room, closing the door behind her with a barely audible click.

"She seems nice," I said.

"Oh... Chastity? She's wonderful," Lily said.

"I've never seen her around town," I said.

"No. She doesn't go out very much," Lily said, taking a bite of a macaroon. "She prefers to stay in."

"Does she live here with you?"

"She does. She's been with me since the beginning," Lily replied. "Now... Where were we? Oh, yes... What do you think life is, Swinella? Does it have a meaning? A purpose?"

"Um... I don't know," I admitted.

"What drives you?"

"Um... Well, y'know," I stammered. "Just... Enjoying life, I guess."

"Let me help you out a bit here, if I may," Lily said, leaning forward sightly. "You're driven by your desire. Desire is your compass. It will take you where you need to go. It bought you here, to Hamden Town... To my sitting room, and to me. Your desire is your true goddess. What is your desire? What do you want? Do not hesitate, Swinella."

"I want to be loved for who I am. I want to be seen, but I want to retreat from view when being seen becomes too much. I want to experience pleasure. I want to avoid pain. I want music and friends and dancing and to sleep well in a warm, comfortable bed and to watch old horror films at midnight on a black-and-white TV in a cosy flat in Hamden Town with my cat... With my best friend. I want to belong, y'know? I want to be far from the world and its problems, its wars and politics and all that stuff. I want to laugh... I want to cry as well, I suppose... to have a full range of ... um... Feelings," I was on a roll, for some reason I was finding it incredibly easy to open up to this woman. "I want to be home, not back home with my parents, but real home. Where I came from, wherever that was."

"Where you came from?" Lily asked, amused. "That's interesting. Where do you think you came from?"

"Somewhere like Hamden, where people are free to be themselves, where there's no judgement... I dunno. Where do bestiamorphs come from?"

"That's a good question. Where do your people come from?"

"A place where people are honest," I said, without thinking.

"When I asked what you desire, you described what you have," Lily glanced at my crotch. "Almost."

"All right," I said with a laugh. "I want to have sex. A lot. You know that, you know what I am."

"You're on the right track, Swinella," Lily said, with a gentle laugh. "Occasionally my sister and I get together with one or two close friends for an evening of conversation, a bite to eat and a glass or two of wine. Would you like to come along to one of our little get-togethers?"

"I think so," I said. "I made a decision a while back to never turn down invites from interesting people... Even though they sometimes don't go as expected."

"That's the attitude," Lily said, clicking her fingers, pointing at me and smiling. "I'll arrange things with my sister and you can come over for dinner in a few weeks' time. Does that sound good to you?"

"Can I bring Felina?" I asked. "I'm sure she'd love to come."

"I think we'll have a night away from Felina," Lily said. "If that's all right with you?"

"Oh... OK," I said.

"You'll understand it all soon enough, Swinella" Lily said. "More tea?"

Lily poured us both another cup and we had a long chat about my background. I found myself completely opening up to this strange, ageless, scentless woman who had entered my life so unexpectedly. I told her about my school days, about Caroline and Gail, even about Daniel, about my parents, my first sexual experiences, when I realised I was a pig, and how I dealt with that. I told her how I'd made my way to Hamden Town after seeing the newspaper article, and how it was the image of the punk rock piglette, in the photo accompanying the article, that had made me deicide to make that first trip to Hamden.

"I was hoping to meet her, actually," I said. "She was quite distinctive, but I've never seen her around."

"Maybe she left town," Lily said. "People do."

We talked for a little while longer. I tried to find out more about Lily, politely asking questions about her life and background, but she skilfully and politely dodged all of my enquiries. She did, however, know a lot about the history of Hamden Town, and she told me all about how my new home town had developed from a rural area, to a transport hub in the industrial revolution where roads and canals and railways converged, and into the thriving alternative Mecca it became, after the opening of its iconic market in the early seventies.

"It's been really nice getting to know you, Swinella, but I have to carry on with my studies," Lily finally said after I had been there for an hour or two. "Chastity will see you out."

Lily clapped her hands twice, loudly and in quick succession. The door opened and Chastity entered. I stood up. Lily didn't stand, but offered me her hand. I stepped up and shook it. Her hand was cool and her grip was firm, but gentle. She held on to my hand for longer than was normal, gazing intently into my eyes.

"I'm looking forward to seeing you again in a few week's time," she said, finally letting go of my hand. "I think my sister will like you."

"Thank you," I said. "I can't wait."

Lily stepped into her ballet flats, stood up and walked back to the table and her book. I glanced at Chastity, who nodded towards the door and turned and walked out. I followed. The rabbitte closed the sitting room door and walked away down the tiled hallway.

"I'm glad you came," Chastity said as she retrieved my jacket from the hatstand by the stairs. "You look nice. I want to get to know you."

Her rabbit pheromones were stronger now. After my experience with the goat, I was less confident of my abilities to resist the aphrodisiac qualities of goats' and rabbits' sex hormones.

"I'm glad I came too," I said. "Lily seems super interesting."

"Oh, Mother is that… and so much more," Chastity said, rapidly blinking and wriggling her ears. "But I'm more interested in you."

"Um, OK… That's nice," I said, not knowing how to deal with the situation. "We'll see each other again, soon, won't we? You'll be at the meeting?"

"Of course," Chastity said, leaning close and licking her full, pink, bifurcated upper-lip. "Do you want me?"

"Um… You're very nice." I said.

"Can I have a kiss?" the rabbit said, closing her eyes and moving closer, placing a warm hand on my chest.

She smelled so good, like flowers and meadows and warm, sunny days. Undertones of strawberry and elderflower, and beneath it all the fresh smell of her damp, pink cunt. I leaned in, placed my hand gently behind her neck and kissed her, mouth open. She tasted of peaches and cream, her tongue warm and sweet. She squeaked slightly, cute little noises as we snogged in the dark hallway. I inhaled deeply. Her pheromones were definitely having an effect on me. She reached under my jacket and began to fondle my tits. I pulled her closer.

"Chastity!" Lily's voice called out from behind the sitting room door. "Let Swinella go! She'll be back soon enough!"

The rabbit girl pulled away and looked up at me through blinking eyelashes, her cheeks flushed bright reddish-pink.

"I'm sorry… I couldn't…" she stammered, looking away. "You remind me of someone I miss."

"It's ok," I said, reaching out and opening the door, my head beginning to clear from the effects of her scent. "I'll be off."

I walked out and onto the cobblestone path.

"You taste really good," I said. "See you soon."

"Bye," Chastity said, all sad face and big, brown eyes.

"How was it?" Felina asked the second I walked through the door and into our cosy, candlelit home.

"It was nice," I said, slipping out of my leather and tossing it on the back of a chair. "We had tea… Earl Grey… And macaroons."

"Yes, I'm sure that was lovely," Felina said, shaking her head. "But what else?"

"Well… Lily invited me to dinner with her sister," I said.

"She did?" Felina said, her cat's eyes widening. "That's brilliant!"

"Is it? It's just a dinner invite, it's really nice of her, I guess…" I said.

"It's not just an invite to dinner," Felina said, sternly.

"It's not? What is it then?"

"I can't say, not yet," she said, with a broad grin on her perfect, heart-shaped face. "It's not my place, but I'm very happy for you."

I decided to let Felina be mysterious.

Later that evening Felina and I went out. A few pints in The Elephant's and The Dev', where we were joined by Gatita and Wayne Mansfield. After The Elephant's we headed to some midweek goth thing at Hamden Palais: skinny, pale, angular boys and girls dancing to skinny, pale, angular music. Felina and I were a little drunk when we arrived at the Palais, and we made our way straight to the dance floor, throwing dramatic shadows through the fog of a smoke machine that was being rhythmically shattered by the machine-gun flash of a bright white strobe light.

It was in those moments I felt really free, really alive. Moving my body to the thump of the drum machine on The Sisters of Mercy's *Temple of Love*, or swaying to the more ethereal, psychedelic tones of Siouxie's *Dear Prudence*. Felina, Gatita, Wayne and I would wander in and out of the fog, snake-hipped, dramatically waving our arms in time to the music.

We were ghosts lost in some nocturnal, romantic underworld. I wanted those nights to last forever, lost in music, caught in a trap. I felt almost weightless, free from past or present. Nothing but the night to live for. I could wax lyrical forever about the fleeting joys of youth, living in the moment with your friends, caught between childhood and adulthood, those few brief years of freedom from responsibility that feel like they'll never end, but of course, everything ends. If I could've stopped my life, hit pause and stayed there forever, I would've, in a heartbeat.

I watched Felina and Gatita as they danced, so graceful, so lithe, so self-contained. They were perfect. I could see why the ancient Egyptians worshipped them. They'd dance close, almost as if they were flirting with each other. Felina would turn her back on Gatita and shimmy her shoulders, while Gatita placed her hands on her own naked shoulders and rolled her hips forward, Felina's tail wrapping itself around Gatita's thigh for a second, before whipping away. Then they'd part for a while, dancing a few feet apart before snaking back towards each other. It was amazing to see, and people would dance nearby to watch the two cats gyrate out of the corners of their eyes.

"You could have anybody in this place tonight," I said to Felina as we took a break from dancing to have a drink, leaning on the bar and watching Wayne's histrionics as he flung himself around to Southern Death Cult's *Moya*.

"None of them deserve me," Felina said, haughtily, with a dismissive wave of her cigarette.

"There's loads of all-right looking people in here tonight," I said, looking around.

As if on cue a really fit, androgynous-looking boy with spiky peroxide hair and sensitive, kohled eyes wandered over and began talking to Felina. He smelled relatively clean, but obviously nervous.

"I've got to say..." he cautiously began.

"But have you got to?" Felina interrupted, holding her cigarette high and adopting her best ice-cold face. "I mean... You could always not."

The boy stopped in his tracks and hesitated, and to be fair to him he just nodded and wandered off.

"Why are you always like that any time someone talks to you?" I asked. "He was really fit. I would've."

"That's you," Felina said with a shrug. "You're a slut. Any attention is good attention to you."

"That's not fair!" I protested. "I have some discretion, and anyway... he *was* fit!"

"What are you two on about?" Gatita said, wandering back over from her visit to the ladies' room.

"Why does Felina never pull?" I said. "She's always getting chatted up, and always knocks them back."

"Well, she's not going to give her virginity away to some random bloke, is she?" Gatita said with a shrug. "Not after all this time... Oh, I love this song!"

The slow drum beat and bass intro to Specimen's *Kiss Kiss Bang Bang* had begun booming out of the nightclub's speakers, and Gatita immediately began sashaying towards the dance floor, arms raised, body writhing.

"You're a... You've never..." I was shocked. "But... I..."

"Oh do shut up, Swinella. It's different for cats. Don't make it a thing," Felina said. "Let's dance."

I didn't know what to say about the revelation that Felina was a virgin, so I didn't mention it. But it played on my mind. She was so sexually aware, so confident, but she'd never actually committed the basic act? I was baffled.

CHAPTER FIFTEEN

DOGGING

"You know," Felina said, one sunny Saturday morning before work in late September, as we were sat in a greasy spoon on Pork Farm Road. "You can always fuck a dog if you're desperate... I wouldn't judge you if you did."

"Who says I'm desperate?" I asked, offended. "I'm not desperate at all."

"Didn't you say you wanted to fuck the set?" Felina said, all offhand. "Remember? All of the 'morphs... The sexogram. You're taking your time getting around to doing it. You've been here, what? Eight months? Sort your life out!"

Two loud skinhead dogs had just finished their fry-ups, necked their mugs of tea, and left the cafe, initiating Felina's comment.

"The sexogram was your idea!" I said. "You want to live vicariously through my arsehole!"

The overweight Greek proprietor of the cafe raised his bushy eyebrows at the sound of my shrill protestations, before continuing to wipe the counter. I'm sure he'd seen and heard it all before.

"They pretty much do anything you tell them... or so I'm told," she said, looking after the hounds through the window as they walked away, hands stuffed into the pockets of their green bomber jackets.

"Yeah, I know," I said, popping a slice of fried mushroom slathered in HP sauce into my gob and swallowing. "That makes it less fun though, right?"

"Maybe, but sometimes when you're hungry you just want a Pot Noodle... Sometimes all you wanna do is get something hot inside you."

"Something hot with no nutritional value?"

"Well... Yes," Felina said, taking a sip from her steaming mug of black coffee. "And speaking of nutrition... Should you really be eating that plate of fried flotsam and jetsam? You don't want to get porky."

I looked at the po-faced cat-girl with what I hoped was a deeply offended expression on my face, but which I knew was betrayed by a smile I couldn't quite suppress.

"You know that's a hate crime, right?" I said. "You don't get to call us 'porky'. And anyway, I only have a fry up once in a blue moon... I'm allowed a treat now and then."

"You are. You're looking very svelte these days... I like it. And I can call you porky, you called me catty the other day."

"It's not the same, you tone-deaf bitch. Apes like cats. Being called cat-like is a compliment to an ape. Most apes eat four-legged pigs, and the ones that don't eat pigs don't eat them because they're 'dirty'... But they love cats. Not all 'morphs are created equal in the eyes of apes. When an ape calls another ape porky it's an insult. You think it's the same being a cat as being a pig? Nobody ever worshipped us. When you call me 'porky' you're using the language of the oppressor. You need to check your vocabulary."

"Wait a minute... you just called me a bitch! I'm calling the Canine Anti-defamation League!"

"You?!" I laughed. "You're calling the Canine Anti-defamation League? Don't make me piss. They'd run you out of town!"

"You should fuck Rasher's mate Bullseye."

"Bullseye's not into girls and he's one hundred percent a bottom," I said. "You know that."

"Neither is Rasher, but he still stuck his greasy trotter up your shit-funnel," Felina said. "And anyway, I thought you were versatile now. Didn't you kind of top that old woman with all the piercings in her twat?"

"What I did with Rasher was different. That was a pig thing... You wouldn't understand," I said, thinking it over. "And for the sexogram I feel I have to be the one getting fucked. I make the rules, and them's the rules."

"I suppose so," Felina conceded, rolling her eyes. "But c'mon... Fuck a dog... For me."

"For you? You don't even like dogs!"

"I don't dislike them really, it's just a game. When a four-legged dog chases a four-legged cat, they know they're not going to catch her, they just do it for fun. It's a cats and dogs thing... *You* wouldn't understand."

"Do you want to watch? Is that is? Do you want to watch me making the bestiamorph with two backs... With a dog?"

"Fuck off."

"Oh c'mon... You don't want to see some hairy, smelly dog

hanging out the back of me? Slobbering and wagging his tail?"

Felina mimed throwing up.

"What's that, catgirl? Got a hairball caught in your throat?" I decided to double down. "If you like... After the dog has finished fucking me, you can suck his Pedigree Chum-flavoured doggy cock snot out of my battered calamari. You'd like that, wouldn't you?"

"I'm going to the loo," Felina announced, standing up from the yellow Formica-topped table. "I won't be back... I'm going to kill myself. I simply cannot live with the image you've just planted in my fragile mind. Goodbye. Forever."

"I am going to fuck a dog," I announced when Felina returned from the lav'. "You wanted it, you're going to get it, and anyway... It's one of the last two of the menagerie for me. I've been intimate with cat, goat, pig and ape... There's only dog and rabbit left on the menu that I haven't tried, so I guess you're right... I have to fuck a dog, just for completion, if nothing else."

"I'm not going to watch," Felina said, wrinkling her nose. "And good luck trying to find a rabbit to top you."

"You're not invited to watch! I know cats don't have much of a sense of humour, but that was what everyone else calls 'a joke'," I said. "But you're right. I might have to bend the rules a bit when it comes to fucking a rabbit."

"Good. Although I do expect to hear all about it."

"Yes... I'll tell you all the gory details," I sighed, rolling my eyes. "As per usual."

"When? Have you picked one already?"

"Tonight. And no, I haven't 'picked one'… I'm not at Battersea Dog's Home. I'm going to find one at The Drogheda Castle. Want to come?"

"No. Go with Wayne. He's always gagging to go to The Drog' to perv over the skinhead boys. He'll be delighted, I'm sure. I'm going to stay in and paint my claws. I'll be in my room after ten, so you can have the living room to yourselves. You and the dog. The dog you're going to fuck. The dog that's going to stick its actual dog pizzle into your actual sweaty pork-pocket… Ugh."

"You'll be in your room with a glass to the wall, listening, massaging your pink jelly bean and wishing it was you giving the dog a bone."

"No, no… and no," Felina said, rolling her green cats' eyes and scrunching her perfect little nose into a grimace. "I'd rather die."

I believed her.

After our breakfast at the caff, we headed off to open the shop. During my lunch break I nipped into The Dev'. I knew that Wayne Mansfield was working a day shift, and I wanted to see him. The Dev' was almost empty. Wayne made me a cup of coffee and we began making plans for that evening.

I got myself dressed up for a night out on the pull. One of Felina's many theories was that we are drawn to whatever scene we find ourselves in because we want to fuck people in that scene. Goths are goths because they want to fuck goths, punks want to fuck punks, metalers want to fuck metalers, as if the different youth cultures were all kinks, fetishes masquerading as fashion and music. It was a pretty good theory, and when I argued that it was the music and the attitude that drew me to punk rock, Felina said that the sexual, fetishistic drive into a scene was subconscious, and afterwards our conscious minds used music and fashion as an excuse for why we were attracted to a certain subculture in the first place. This theory didn't apply to Felina herself of course.

Whether Felina was right or wrong about our drives, it was a fact that we tended to fuck and date within our own tribes. I was actually an anomaly in this regard, as I'd fuck anybody from any subculture if I fancied them, but as Felina had pointed out, I was, in fact, 'a slut'. With this in mind I dressed as close to skinhead as I could; oxblood Mary Janes, white ankle socks, bare legs, blue denim skirt from a charity shop (20p, bargain!) white vest (nipples are at their most visible through a white top with no print, it's the shadows) and a burgundy Harrington (found by Wayne Mansfield in The Dev' one night at closing time). I scraped my hair into a tight ponytail and brushed my fringe over my forehead. I wore minimum makeup, just mascara and eyeliner. I took the twelve silver hoops out of my ears and replaced them with gold studs. I checked myself in the mirror and thought I looked pretty damn good. Oi!

"I don't know why you've made so much effort," Felina said when I emerged from my room. "Like I said over breakfast, dogs will do whatever you tell them. You can turn up looking like shit and just pick one."

"That doesn't mean I want to go out looking like shit though, does it?"

"I suppose not," Felina conceded with a shrug of her slender shoulders. "Off you go then, I've got claws to maintain."

Felina was sat on the sofa with her nail varnishes and files spread out on the coffee table. Her feet were soaking in the blue plastic bowl we used for washing the dishes, and there was a towel and pumice stone on the sofa by her side. Joy Division's *Unknown Pleasures* was playing in the background on the record player. I did't really like Joy Division, I know it's not cool to say that because the singer topped himself, but they were just so dreary.

"Right," I said, heading for the door. "I'm meeting Wayne in The Dev' in a minute anyway."

"Try not to grunt too loud when you're getting fucked," Felina said with a tired sigh.

I rocked up to The Dev' at half past six. Wayne's shift was due to finish at seven, and he was in a buoyant mood, cracking jokes with the punters in the busy bar. I sat at the bar in the corner by the men's bogs and Wayne slid a glass of vodka and soda over the bar without my asking for it.

"What's on at The Drog' tonight anyway, duck?" I asked Wayne in a break between orders.

"I think it's some old school ska and reggae thing... Shouldn't be too offensive, and it's less likely to get all aggro than them bonehead Oi! Nights they sometimes have there."

"That's good," I said. "I can't be arsed with all that hyper-masculine bollocks. Should be a laid-back session... Do you think it'll be busy?"

"Should be," Wayne conceded. "Why do you want to go there anyway?"

I hadn't told Wayne that I was trawling for dog-seed. He would've gone all hysterical and made it his mission to find me a suitable fuck.

"Just for a change, y'know... And Felina's not into anything skinhead. She fucking hates Ska and Reggae," I said with a shrug. "But she said you sometimes like that kind of thing, so that's why I asked you."

"I'm not into the music, duck" Wayne said. "But them boys... With the shaved heads and boots, and them tight jeans and Ben Sherman's... Fuck me, it's a strong look!"

"It is," I conceded, nodding sagely.

Wayne knocked off at seven. He nipped upstairs to his room above the pub and came back down wearing a black bomber jacket over the top of a black Fred Perry polo shirt. He was wearing black skinny jeans with a wallet chain and black fourteen-hole Docs. He was dressed like a skinhead whose clothes had all been stolen and dyed black by a mischievous goth, I thought his blond mop of hair kind of let the look down though. We went round the corner and had a bag of chips, mushy peas on top for me, curry sauce for him, before taking a slow walk up Porkway and over to The Drogheda Castle.

Skinheads are surprisingly clean. The backroom of the small venue was awash with the smell of soap and shaving foam and cheap aftershave, all underscored by a powerful dose of testosterone. The bass-heavy sound system was pumping out a series of older Trojan Records tunes. As we walked in, about half a dozen skinhead girls were shuffling about in the middle of the small dance floor. Appropriately enough they were stepping in time to Symarip's *Skinhead Girl*, pints and fags in hands. The night was still early, and the music would probably take a turn towards more upbeat, contemporary music as the lager flowed and the dance floor filled, the booze helping the lads lose their inhibitions and edge their way onto the dance floor. Wayne and I made our way to the bar at the back of the room and ordered two pints of Skol. I had decided to commit to my role and eschew my vodka and soda for once, just to look the part. A quick scan of the room, which at this point was only about a quarter full, revealed no dogs in attendance, just a bunch of apes. I was the only 'morph in the venue, which felt weird, as that hardly ever happened in Hamden Town. Wayne leaned against the bar and tried to look tough, holding his fag between his thumb and forefinger as he inhaled, sucking his cheeks in hard, like a proper lad, and frowning for no particular reason, nodding his head in time to the music.

"Don't overdo it, duck," I whispered loudly over the music. "You don't want any potential trade to think you're a geezer."

"I know what I'm doing, duck," Wayne said, blowing smoke out of the corner of his mouth. "You just concentrate on finding a dog to fuck, Ya filthy swine."

"Oh... so you know why we're here, then?"

"Of course I do," Wayne laughed. "You're here as part of your ongoing mission to complete the set. You've been busy since you got here... Apes, goats, cats... I hear you even got it on with another pig."

"Well," I conceded. "I think it's important to try everything."

"I'm very proud of you... Not bad for a minger like you," Wayne said, raising his glass. "I'll drink to that."

I took a sip of foamy lager and scowled at Wayne, not sure if I was being slagged off or complimented. Just then, the door into the venue swung open and a pair of familiar faces sauntered in on time to the beat.

"Look who's here!" Bullseye called out as he and Rasher swaggered towards the bar. "It's your girlfriend... And that peroxide poof from The Dev'!"

"Fuck off, Bullshit," Rasher said, winking at me and giving Bullseye a dig on the shoulder with a fist heavy with sovereign rings, causing the dog to stumble and playact being seriously assaulted. "Swinella's part of my crew, she ain't my missus... you wouldn't understand. All right Wayne, how's the hospitality industry?"

"It's a living," Wayne said, trying to appear nonchalant. "How's tricks?"

"Still turning 'em," Rasher said with a wink. "No complaints so far. Swinella knows."

Rasher was wearing a white England football top, tight blue jeans and shiny black boots. Bullseye was wearing a red Fred Perry with white trim, Sta Press dogtooth check trousers, and oxblood brogues. They were both weighed down with chunky gold jewellery, and they smelt of salt and vinegar.

"Chips on the way in lads?" I asked. "Can't fault ya, we did the same."

"Gotta line the stomach before a night on the pop, girl," Rasher said. "You know the rules."

The pig and the dog got their drinks in and started bopping to the music, bouncing up and down to the beat. Some burly skin across the room shouted a greeting at the pair and they bowled off to socialise.

"Fuck me, duck," Wayne said. "That Bullseye's fucking fit, though. He's a fit bull terrier. He's not like any other of the dogs around here. I don't think he just does what people tell him like the rest of 'em."

I nodded. Bullseye and Rasher were stars, and they knew it. They were proper working-class queer from Somers Town; never in the closet, not scared of a punch up, loved their mums, football, lager, having a laugh. What I knew about Bullseye, something Rasher had told me, was that while he was all swagger outside, he was a total filth-bag submissive in bed. A bottomless pit and a pitiless Bottom; pimp in the streets, whore in the sheets.

"Remember back home?" I said. "All the dogs were such victims."

"I hung out with the dogs at my school, they were all right… Gay boys and dogs are natural friends at school… Like fat kids and asthmatics walking together at the back during cross country running," Wayne said. "But I never fancied any of 'em, not until I moved down here. London dogs are different, more confident."

"So…" I said. "You fancy dogs! That's why you were so eager to come here."

Wayne just sighed dramatically and drained his glass.

"Another pint, duck?" he said.

"Why not?"

The venue filled, the dance floor became crowded, the music increased in volume and tempo, and the lager took me into its fuzzy embrace. It was a warm night out there in Hamden; we were having an Indian summer, and The Drog' was heating up. All the ingredients on the skinhead reggae and ska scene were so right, the music, the clothes. Everyone was relaxed and smiling, just living in the moment. Lads and lasses were snogging in the darkened corners, people danced without inhibition or pretence. It was all just so real, which was why Felina hated it, I guess. In here a cat would just look stupid and up herself. All that pretence and affectedness wouldn't work here, this was proper, no bullshit, no messing.

I was bopping away to Gangsters by The Specials, when I turned around and saw a familiar snout. It was Susan, the Jamaican pig girl from Wales. She was dancing away, her blonde, cropped afro bouncing as she hopped from one foot to the other in time to the music, her curly tail swinging from left to right as she danced.

"Swinella!" she squealed. "What you doing here?! I fawt you was a goth?"

"A goth?" I laughed, shouting over the music. "No, I just live with one."

"Ya on the pull?" Susan asked, leaning into yell in my ear. "Who do ya fancy? I'll have a word. I know everybody here."

It really was that easy. Within two minutes Susan was over the other side of the room talking to a tall dog I'd spotted some time earlier. He was well built, with really muscular arms. He was wearing a tight-fitting white t-shirt and skinny black jeans tucked into shiny black boots with yellow laces that almost came up to his knees. Susan was stood on tip toes shouting into his ear and vaguely waving her fag in the direction of the dance floor. The big dog looked over, caught my eye, and smiled. I shyly smiled back, batting my eyelashes and trying to look demure. The dog drained his almost-full pint in one, put the glass on a table, and swaggered over, just as *Do The Rocksteady* by The Bodysnatchers started pumping out of the speakers.

"All right love," he growled into my ear. "I'm Toby."

He smelled clean and fresh, and a little bit doggy. I didn't think he was a smoker, and, judging by his breath, he'd probably only had a couple of pints. I got the impression he might've been into some kind of sport. He had the trademark big brown eyes, upturned nose, bushy eyebrows and oversized lower canine teeth typical of his people. His cropped hair was light blonde, with black spots the size of fifty pees spread evenly across his head. His long, graceful tail was also blonde with black spots, and was wagging slightly as he introduced himself.

"Swinella," I shouted back. "Nice to meet you."

We danced together for a few numbers, moving close from time to time. He was probably the fittest dog I'd ever seen and, as we danced, I started having weird fantasies about him being The One. The One! I'd never even thought of such a thing before, and I put it down to the fundamentally conservative, working-class nature of the skinhead scene. They were all about traditional family values and shit like that, football clubs and all that bollocks. Their whole thing was belonging to something, something clearly defined. Where're you from? Who do you support? Who do you know? Where did you go to school? All the stuff that I'd run away from, but they did it here in London, and most of them were actual locals, unlike on the other scenes. That kind of rigid sense of belonging helped explained why some skinheads were attracted to far-right politics and racism and all that bullshit, but in Hamden Town everything was much more inclusive and diverse. The skins in Hamden were proper, into Ska and Reggae and Northern Soul. Proper music for proper people.

By the end of the third or fourth song I'd managed to snap out of my domestic fantasies and started to see Toby for what he was. A dog I was about to fuck. I asked him if he fancied a walk (not spotting the subtle cynophobia until I'd asked the question, but he either let it go or didn't notice either), and he said yes.

Wayne was dancing with Rasher and Bullseye, no doubt revelling in being seen associating with the two coolest 'morph gay boys on the skinhead scene. I wandered over with Toby in tow, holding his hand, and said my goodbyes. Wayne, Rasher and Bullseye all simultaneously looked the tall dog over, and I could see they were impressed, although Bullseye made a face like a bulldog licking piss off a nettle; he was used to being the hottest dog in the room, and the truth was, Toby had him beat on all fronts. Toby was a good six inches taller (very tall for a dog), had a better physique, and worst of all, Toby was pleasant and relaxed, something that was completely out of reach for a poisonous bitch like Bullseye.

The street outside The Drogheda Castle was busy with people going to and from pubs and restaurants, and to the cinema that was just down the road. I suggested that we grab a couple of cans from the offy and head up to The Regent's Wood, a woodland park at the far end of Porkway on the edge of Hamden Town. The Wood was pretty big, about five hundred acres (I looked that up in a book in Hamden library, but I don't know what an acre is. Suffice to say it was a pretty big bit of woodland to find in the middle of a city), and had been used for hunting in the eighteen hundreds. Nowadays the forest was mainly frequented by four-legged dog walkers, and, as I was about to find out, people into a bit of public shagging.

The moon was almost full, and we saw several other couples and small groups of people hanging out drinking, smoking and talking in the woods. Toby told me he knew where there was a good spot where we could chill out and drink our cans and get to know one another. After a ten-minute walk through the trees, we stopped and sat down on the warm grass.

"You're not from London," Toby said, sitting down next to me, his strong thigh up against mine. "Where are you from? How long have you been here?"

I told him about how I had made my way down to London, about Felina and The Black Violet and everything. I missed out the details of my sexual adventures, but said that I was really enjoying my life in Hamden. But I hadn't come into the woods to talk, and I placed my hand on Toby's leg and smiled. He just sat there, looking at me with his big eyes and grinning stupidly. I wondered if I had misread the situation, but how could I? I began to stroke the bulge in his tight black jeans, and his cock stiffened beneath my probing fingers, but still he just sat there looking at me all expectant, but not making a move. And then I remembered what Felina had told me. Dogs like to be told what to do.

"Kiss me," I said.

Immediately Toby leant in and we began to make out. He was an excellent kisser, and he tasted good. I began to knead his cock and balls, squeezing and fondling his package while we snogged deep and long. I was fully into it when I realised he wasn't going to do anything else, he wasn't going to pull up my skirt or grope my tits, not until I told him to. It was weird, but I decided that I could get into it. I pulled myself away from his wet mouth.

"Suck my tits," I said, pulling off my white vest.

Toby obliged immediately and began to suck, lick and kiss my nipples, which began to tingle the moment he made contact. I'd not lactated for a while, so the dog was going to get a treat soon enough. He was very good at not prioritising one tit over the other, and he moved from left to right at just the right moment. Just when I thought I was going to start leaking from one rock-hard nipple he would disengage and start working on the other, it was a massive turn-on, infuriating in a way, but a very effective way of building the tension of my arousal. I realised that because I had said 'suck my tits', plural, he was giving them equal attention so as not to disobey the instruction. I put up with the switching between nipples for as long as I could but, at some point, I decided I wanted to give him a taste of me.

"Stay on that one," I said as he was teasing my left nipple with gentle nips, licks and kisses. "Suck harder."

Toby did as he was told, and soon enough my juice began to flow. He looked up at me questioningly with his big, brown eyes, but continued to suck. I stroked his Dalmatian-spotted head.

"That's a good boy," I said.

When I felt I was coming to the end of the limited supply of pig milk flowing from my left tit, I told him to switch nipples, and he did so without hesitation, sucking deep and long, and obviously relishing my warm, salty, bacon-flavoured milk. When my right boob was drained, I gently grabbed the back of his neck and pulled him towards me. We began to snog again. I could smell his arousal, and I'm sure he could smell mine. His cock had grown hard as a bone beneath his tight jeans and I wanted him in me, beneath the stars and the trees, as nature had intended. It was then I noticed the figures standing amongst the trees and bushes. I stopped kissing him and whispered in his ear.

"There's people," I said, slightly panicked. "In the the trees. Watching."

"I know," Toby said. "I heard them come over while I was... while I was sucking your tits. I thought you knew. I thought that was why you suggested coming here. There's always people looking to either put on or see a show in the forest."

I sniffed the air. They were all men, all apes, and I guessed there was about half a dozen of them standing in a wide circle around me and Toby. I didn't know how to react, but I supposed if Toby thought it was safe, then it was. He was a big dog and, if anyone got too close, I was sure he'd see them off. I held him close and began to run my hands up and down his back.

"Well," I said. "I suppose we ought to put on a show then."

I took hold of the bottom of his vest and pulled it up over his broad, muscular back. When he was topless I began to eat his face again, my snout squishing into his cute, upturned nose. I fumbled with his belt, button and fly as we snogged, eventually pulling his jeans and boxers down and releasing his eager, stiff cock. He was a good size, not as big as Tarquinius or Bapho, but those cocks were exceptional. Toby looked like he'd be a comfortable shag, and that's nice as well. I don't always need to be stretched asunder. I got up on my knees and undid my skirt, pulling it down as Toby, and the men in the trees, looked on. I made a show of it. I stood up, let my skirt fall to the ground, and stepped out of it. I was naked now, except for my socks and shoes. I turned and presented my rump to Toby, reaching behind myself and pulling my arse cheeks apart.

"Eat my arsehole," I said, in a loud voice so that the audience could hear. "Get that tongue right in there... I want you to be able to tell me what I had for dinner last night."

Toby leapt into action, and did not disappoint. He knelt behind me, his hands gripping the front of my thighs, and began to lick my hole with unbridled enthusiasm, his tongue probing deep into my piggy arse-cunt. He moved around quite a bit, licking my empty scrotum, running his tongue up my arse crack all the way to the base of my curly tail. I could hear him sniffling and snuffling with enthusiasm, and I'm sure our audience could as well. I couldn't see it, but I was confident that his black and white spotted tail was wagging ten to the dozen.

Toby wasn't the only one having a ball. Out in the darkness of the trees and bushes I could hear the sound of shuffling wrists, and smell the dank perfume of male arousal, unwashed cocks, sweaty arse-cracks and viscous precum. The audience were enjoying the show. Soon it was time to move onto the main event, to get that dog's bone up me.

"It's time." I announced.

Toby disengaged from my gash, stood up and stepped back. I dropped to my knees and gobbed on my fingers. I used the spit to lube up my gash, placed my forearms on the ground, hands on top of each other, my head on the back of my hands, and arched my back. Toby knelt behind me and slid in. It was an easy entry. My hole was so well used at this point that an average-sized cock could slip into me with minimum preparation. I liked it. It made me feel like myself, being loose and ready.

Felina was right. I was a slut, and I owned it. I had learnt to tighten my pigussy by clenching my sphincter, and I did so. I didn't want the dog to feel like he was throwing a cocktail sausage down Oxford Street. Toby began to thrust with great enthusiasm, like you'd expect a dog to. Dogs, whether two or four-legged, do everything with great enthusiasm, when you think about it, whether it's barking or chasing a ball or fucking your arse. They commit and they're eager to please. I guess that's why people like them so much. The smell of arousal and the sound of wanking grew in intensity as the spectators got more and more into it.

"Yeah," I heard a hoarse voice whisper to itself in the darkness. "Fuck her... Fuck her proper. Dirty fucking bitch."

"I'm not a bitch, I'm a sow!" I called out in the general direction of the voice. "I'm a dirty fucking sow!"

"Fucking hell," Toby said between clenched teeth, thrusting hard and grabbing my tail in both hands. "You're fucking amazing."

I began to grunt, louder than I would've normally. I was putting on a show. Toby joined in, growling in the back of his throat as he fucked me deep and hard, his hairy bollocks slapping loudly against my smooth, empty sack like a round of applause. At that point one of the shadows emerged from the trees and sidled over.

"I say mate," the man said, tugging his cock and breathing hard. "Do you mind if I have a go on 'er?"

Toby stopped fucking me, holding his throbbing meat deep inside me, gripping my tail hard and pulling me towards him.

"What do you reckon, love?" he said. "Do you want this stranger to fuck ya, or not?"

I pulled free of Toby, his slimy weapon slipping out of my arse like a newborn puppy. I knelt upright, pulled my damp, sweaty hair out of its ponytail and vigorously shook my head, shoulders back. I turned and lay on my back. I could just about make out the man's face in the pale moonlight. He was some average-looking ape in his mid-twenties. I might've been a slut, but I was out of his league.

"No," I said in as petulant a voice as I could muster. "But he can cum on my face while you're riding me... if he wants?"

Toby grabbed my ankles and threw himself back up me, growling and fucking me hard. I let out a piggish squeal and grabbed my tits. The man knelt by my head, and in no less than five seconds unloaded his stinking ape crotch-yoghurt all over my snout and open mouth. It smelt strong, like salmon paste and stilton, like the bloke hadn't shot his muck for a while

"Any more for any more?" I called out, savoury, backed-up baby gravy coagulating on my lips, chin and snout.

Before I knew it three more apes were kneeling in a semicircle around my head, fist-pumping their glistening moonlit shafts as if their lives depended on it. Toby concentrated on the job in hand, fucking me with strong but steady thrusts, hands gripping my ankles tight. One after another the anonymous men shot their greasy man-batter onto my upturned visage, and soon I lost count of how many blokes had dribbled, flung and leaked their greyish-white bollock bullion onto my eager piggy face, but I'd guess it was around eight or nine. I had to wipe the jism out of my eyes more than once, licking my fingers clean afterwards. I had so much spunk on my face that I'm sure I looked like Gordita with her trifle face-mask. Eventually they stopped coming, and cumming, retreating back to the shadows to watch the end of the show after they had contributed their share.

"Lick my face," I said to Toby, smiling my sweetest, most innocent smile and gazing into his big, brown eyes, blinking away the spunk that threatened to stick my eyelids together. "Lick me clean, and then you can cum inside me."

Toby did as instructed, bending forwards and eagerly licking the spunk of over half a dozen strangers off of my face. It felt really nice, and once he had cleaned most of the cum from my filthy pig slut coupon we began to make out, the gummy jizz of a bunch of strangers tacky on our skin, making our mouths stick together and peel apart as we kissed. Toby's thrusts began to speed up, faster and faster, until at last he threw his head back, clenched his buttocks and howled, his dog cum pumping into me like the arterial spurt from a severed jugular. When he had finished jerking and squirting, I steadied myself by putting my hand on his shoulder and clambered shakily to my feet, clenching my arsehole tight. I bent my knees, cupped my palm under my hole and relaxed. An impressive load of dog cum and bum jelly slithered out of my brutalised pig-cunt and into my palm. I lifted my hand to my face and snuffled the entire mess of it, inhaling deeply. I tipped the overflowing handful of slimy arse sludge into my mouth, grunting and savouring the meaty taste of Toby's cum as it slid down my throat. I scanned the trees, licking my lips, but the audience had gone. The show was over.

We got dressed and walked back into Hamden. I couldn't go back to the pub, my makeup and hair having been wrecked by the cum of a bunch of unwashed apes. I thought about inviting the dog-boy back to the flat for the night, but he'd done his job, and his place wasn't too far away. He could just go home.

I gave Toby one last kiss on the corner of Porkway and Hamden High Street, and headed home. I didn't ask for his number. I knew where to find him, and I knew he'd come if I called.

Felina, good to her word, was in bed when I got home. I had a quick shower, washed the cum out of my hair, and went to bed.

Ape, cat, pig, goat, and now dog. I'd had them all. You could even throw in a demon for good measure. There was only rabbit to add to the collection and I'd have had the full menagerie.

I wouldn't have to wait very long.

CHAPTER SIXTEEN

CHASTITY

It was a cold and rainy evening in Hamden Town in early October. The weather had taken a turn for the autumnal, and in a few short weeks the clocks would go back, bringing on the early evenings that I always looked forward to.

Felina and I had closed up the shop together, and she'd headed home while I nipped to the supermarket to grab some basics. We were going to have fish fingers, potato waffles and mushy peas for tea. Felina had gone home to turn on the electric fire, light some candles, stick some music on and boil the kettle for a cuppa. We'd worked out an entire after-work system. We'd take it in turns to either make the flat cosy or run to the shop. The person doing the shop run would decide what we'd have for tea that evening from a list of meals we both liked. We ate a lot of fish.

I walked into the flat, and was surprised to see that we had a visitor. Chastity, the rabbitte who lived with Lily, was sat on the edge of one of the armchairs, knees together. She was wearing an ankle-length red tartan skirt, a green, mutton-sleeved jumper with a high roll-neck, and her black and white brogues. She wore a rust-coloured beret, her hair poking out at the back in two short pigtails. Over the top of her green sweater she was wearing the same silver star-pointed pedant that both Felina and Gordita wore. I realised that I'd never seen Felina without her pendant, which was interesting as she was always changing up the rest of her jewellery. I made a mental note to ask Felina if it symbolised anything. Chastity smiled nervously at me as I entered. She smelled of marzipan and anxiety. She was the cutest thing imaginable.

"Well, look here," Felina said, gesturing over at Chastity from where she sat reclining on the sofa. "We've got a guest."

"Hello, Chastity," I said, dropping the shopping bag onto the kitchen table. "What brings you to this neck of the woods?"

"Well, I..." the rabbitte began. "I thought, I wanted..."

Chastity looked over at Felina.

"I just remembered," Felina said, springing to her feet with effortless grace. "I've got to go in my room and do... something, I suppose."

Felina picked up her steaming mug of tea from the coffee table and slinked out of the living room and into her bedroom, turning in the doorway and looking over her shoulder at me.

"I'll leave you kids alone for a bit," she said, closing the door behind her with a smirk. "We can have dinner later."

I made myself a cuppa and sat down on the sofa.

"So... Chastity," I began. "How's things? How's Lily?"

"Really good," Chastity said, holding her steaming mug of tea in both hands and blowing on the surface, her ears wiggling as she blew; cute as a button at all times. "Mother is wonderful, as always. She enjoyed your visit the other day."

"I enjoyed it too," I said. "Lily is very interesting, and the house is lovely. Do you enjoy living with her?"

"I do. I'm very lucky," the rabbit girl said with a little twitch of her button nose and a nod.

"What do you do? For work? And, y'know, fun?" I asked. "I've never seen you around Hamden. Do you not go out much? Do you work for Lily?"

"There's not really any point my going out, I can't do anything, you know... Anything, um, with anyone."

"I don't really understand," I said. "What do you mean you can't do anything?"

"I made a promise, when I came here, when I agreed to stay... here, in Hamden," she said. "It's my choice... A hundred percent."

"What kind of promise," I asked, taking a sip of tea. "To who?"

"To Mother," Chastity said, nodding and staring into the middle distance with those big, brown eyes. "Forever. But I still want to be touched... You know?"

"Not really," I admitted, shaking my head slightly.

"Can I show you something?" she asked, blinking rapidly. "Something personal?"

"Of course... We're a very open house here," I laughed. "We have to be."

Chastity slowly stood up from the armchair and exhaled loudly.

"I don't know if I'm allowed to do this," she said, her soft cheeks reddening. "But I suppose you're going to stay, so I'm going to assume it's alright."

Chastity took the hem of her long, pleated tartan skirt and lifted it up over her waist. She was wearing some kind of metal device, like a shiny dome that seemed to fit snugly around her crotch, curved to fit the shape of her pubic bone. Underneath the metal plate she was wearing a pair of thick, white cotton, calf-length bloomers, Victorian style. The rabbitte did a slow turn so that I could see her complicated undergarments from all angles. The top of the plate was secured by a wide strip of thick leather to a belt wrapped tightly around Chastity's waist, above her hipbones and tight, like a corset. Around the back a sturdy-looking leather thong ran snugly up her arse-crack and connected the rear of the plate to the belt. There was a small, but solid-looking, padlock fixed in the middle of the belt, just below the high waistband of the bloomers.

"Oh," I said, raising my eyebrows. "That's... different."

"Yes," she said.

Chastity sat back down on the chair, relaxing fully and leaning back. She kept her skirt hitched up over her waist and opened her knees wide, pointing that shiny metal plate at me. She seemed to have relaxed now she'd shown me her weird underwear.

"It's so I can't, y'know... Fuck," she said.

"I'd guessed that," I replied. "But why? Don't you rabbits love to fuck... Isn't that your thing?"

"That's the point," Chastity said with an ironic smile. "I love to fuck... But I can't... And the thing is... It feels soooooo good. And when I do fuck... When I'm allowed... it's amaaaaazing."

I could smell her arousal from across the room. Showing me

her chastity belt had turned her on. I have to admit that she had one of the nicest-smelling cunts my snout had ever had the pleasure of encountering.

"Did you come tonight just to show me that?" I asked. "I mean, I'm glad you did..."

"Can we go in your room?" the petite rabbit asked, wiggling her ears and glancing around the flat. "I'd feel more comfortable in there."

"Sure."

We decamped into my room. Chastity looked over at my altar to sodomy.

"I like these," she said, pointing to the collection of anal toys, lube and poppers that sat proudly on top of my chest of drawers, flanked by candles.

"Thanks," I said, sitting on the unmade bed.

"This is quite big," she said, pointing at the medium-sized buttplug. "Does it go in easily?"

"Oh Chastity," I laughed. "That's the small one!"

"Really?! Where's the big one?" she said, looking around the room.

"Where do you think? It's inside me," I said with a laugh. "I wear a plug most days."

"It's in you right now?" she said, looking at my pelvis as if she had X-ray vision and could see the plug through my clothes and flesh.

"Yeah... I'm like the opposite of you. I'm being penetrated right now."

"Wow... That's so cool. Can I see?"

"Um... I just have to go to the toilet," I said. "Give me a minute."

I had learnt the hard way that when wearing a buttplug all day, one should only remove said plug while sitting on the toilet. After my first full day at work with my arse filled I had come home, gone into my room, dropped my pants and pulled out the plug with wild abandon. This had resulted in a streak of watery shit being flung across my sheepskin rug and onto the wall. After a couple of other minor mishaps I had learnt to carry a freezer bag (to deposit the buttplug in if I decided to remove it and leave it out), a small bottle of lube (if I had to remove it and wanted to put it back in), some toilet paper (if I found myself using a public toilet that had run out of paper, which was most of them in Hamden Town, and had to clean the plug before bagging/reinsertion) and a spare set of knickers, just in case (it is what it is). I headed into the bathroom, removed my knickers, tights and socks, pulled up my skirt, slipped out the plug, cleaned it, did a super quick bulb douche and wipe, and headed back to my bedroom, leaving my knickers, tights and socks in a bundle in the corner of the bathroom.

"Now... where were we?" I said, shutting the door behind me. "Oh... I see you've made yourself more comfortable."

Chastity had taken my place on the bed and had removed all of her clothes, except the bloomers and chastity belt, of course. She sat perched on the edge of my bed and looked at me with huge, expectant eyes. Everything about her was soft and nice and perfect. Her porcelain skin looked like she'd been rolled in icing sugar, her nipples were like pale pink cherries on top of the perfect round of her surprisingly large but firm tits. Her feet were small and perfect. They were the nicest smelling feet I'd ever encountered, like line-dried Egyptian cotton sheets. Her toenails were painted a translucent, glittery pink. She was like a living marshmallow that you just wanted to gobble up.

"I hope you don't mind... Just because I can't fuck, doesn't mean I can't get naked... Well, almost naked."

"No... You look..." I said. "You look so nice."

"Can I see?" she said, excitedly.

I removed my skirt, turned, bent over, and opened my cheeks.

"Oh, that's wonderful!" Chastity exclaimed, leaning forwards on the bed and reaching out. "Can I touch it?"

"If you want."

I felt her hand give the plug a gentle push. Then she took hold of the base of the plug and gave it a wiggle.

"How does it feel?" she asked.

"It feels good," I said. "Do you want to pull it out?"

"Can I? That'd be amazing!"

"Do it," I said. "But do it slowly..."

Chastity began to pull on the plug. It was quite a tight fit, despite my wearing it most days, and there was some resistance. The actual plug was much wider than the stem that attached it to the base.

"Pull harder," I said, pushing slightly.

Chastity did as I said, and after a little more tugging the buttplug popped out of my arsehole, followed by a loud, single pop fart like an exclamation mark.

"Wow! It's a lot bigger than the other one!" she exclaimed,

holding the plug gingerly. "It's as big as my hand."

"Well... I get fisted quite a lot these days, so my cunt is quite loose. That plug is just the right size... For now." I said.

"Hahahaha... you call your bumhole your cunt, that's so funny," she laughed, adorably covering her mouth with her free hand.

"It is my cunt," I said. "Your cunt is not your vagina, is it? You don't call your cunt your vagina, it's a different thing. Vagina is a medical thing. A cunt is a hole you get fucked in, that's my definition."

"So if someone is getting throat-fucked does that make their mouth their cunt?"

"It might... It sounds good, doesn't it?" I said. "Mouth cunt... Face cunt... 'fuck me in the fucking face-cunt you fucking cunt faced cunt of a cunt' sounds pretty damn sexy to me!" We both pissed ourselves laughing at that one, and the mood in my room became even more relaxed. I pulled off my T-shirt and sat next to the rabbit on the bed.

"Your dick is so small," she said, cocking her head on one side and looking at my cocklette. "It's so cute... Can I touch it?"

"Use some lube," I replied; since my circumcision I had begun using lube whenever I stimulated my cock, it just felt better all greasy and wet.

I passed Chastity a bottle of lube from the altar, opened my legs wide and reclined on the bed, leaning back on the wall. Chastity dribbled some lube onto my bits and began to stroke and fondle my dick. She squeezed my empty scrotum, her nose twitching in concentration.

"It doesn't work, does it?" She asked, continuing to gently tug and squeeze my fleshy noodle.

"It's not meant to do anything... I piss out of it, so it does the one job it has." I said. "And it feels pleasant when someone plays with it."

The eager rabbitte was getting into it, and so was I. My dicklette is not as sensitive as my tits and I've actually never come through stimulation of my penis, as you know, but it's still a nice sensation. I stared at Chastity, her snow-white skin, fresh pink nipples and lips, shiny blonde hair and big, brown eyes. So gorgeous, and yet she was kept locked up. One of the most desirable people I'd ever seen, and she was denied her most natural form of self-expression and pleasure. I began to seriously wonder what kind of game Lily was playing with her, with all of us.

"Why are you locked up?" I asked as her oily fingertips gently wanked my flaccid nubbin.

"Let's move," she said. "I want to keep playing with you. Can we have some music on?"

I got off the bed and pressed play on the cassette player. The tape in the deck was *Sonic Youth*, the eponymously titled debut E.P. by a band from New York. Wayne had taped it for me from his imported vinyl copy. I thought it sounded brilliant, but I couldn't see them getting very far. I returned to the bed. Chastity had moved and we lay down, side by side, Chastity on my right side, propped on her elbow so she could continue stroking my limp cock.

"Why're you locked up?" I repeated.

"You know..." she began thoughtful. "I've just worked it out, here and now, with your useless dick in my hand. I'm locked up for the same reason that you're impotent. Think about it. Why are you pigs impotent?"

"Well, one of the stories I read is that we're the reincarnated souls of people who loved sodomy so much in their previous lives that they want it to be the only way they can have sex, like the only option. At all... Forever." I said, recalling some occult book that Felina had lent me a while back. "But, y'know... That's just a theory."

"Forever... I like the sound of that," Chastity said with a smile. "What is sex, Swinella?"

"It's sex," I said, inhaling the beautiful perfume of Chastity's glossy hair: Timotei and freshly mown grass. "What do you mean?"

"Really... Sex is a build-up and release of energy. Your useless, impotent cock means that your sexual energy can only be released in other ways." The rabbit smiled down at me where I lay at her side and twitched her nose and wiggled her ears in concentration. "Through your... Your 'cunt'. Your release is a different flavour to other people's... Not because it's anal, loads of people are into anal, not just pigs. But you pigs are the only ones who're pure anal, really... Others can choose to be pure anal, I guess, but you don't have any option, except for, um... Celibacy. So I think you're right... Your dick doesn't work for fucking, so sodomy is the only option... And you love it!"

"And how is that like your metal pants?"

"Well... I can't release my sexual energy whenever and

wherever I want. I can only do it when the belt is removed. So you and I are both limited in our options, limited in how we can express ourselves sexually. But those limitations add, rather than take away, from our experiences. We're like hyper-focused as opposed to diffused like most people."

The rabbit made an interesting point. She was much more insightful than I had at first given her credit for. I was guilty of thinking that cute meant dumb; I'd have to have a word with myself. I was beginning to think her innocent, naive demeanour was an act.

"I like what you're saying," I said, enjoying the sensation of her hand stimulating my soft pink dicklette. "The difference is that the belt is a choice you've made, my limitations are anatomical. And I don't think of myself as impotent... My dick was never meant for fucking."

I was enjoying the sexual tension generated by Chastity and I very much. The dynamic was super nice and strange. We were so far from being able to shag in any standard way, but the eroticism of our encounter was intense as fuck, and I'd always liked having conversations while being casually stimulated (as you might recall if you can remember the chat I had with Lucretia while Tarquinius was buried deep inside my poo-chute).

"I don't know if I chose the belt," Chastity said. "Part of my enjoying wearing it is believing that I had no choice but to wear it. It was done to me, and now I can't fuck, I can't follow my true nature. Do you know what that's like for a rabbit?"

The gorgeous smell of Chastity's fresh little rabbit cunt had grown stronger and stronger while we talked. The pheromones were so powerful it was making my head spin, and to think before my encounter with the goat after the Hawkwind gig I'd thought I was immune to their effect!

"You said you can only fuck when the belt is removed," I said, inhaling her scent, feeling its chemical influence warm my body and give everything I looked at a soft, rose-coloured tint. "When is that? How often?"

"I have it removed once a year," she said, leaning in and flicking my nipple with the tip of her little pink tongue. "You'll see…"

The second she started paying attention to my tit I was lost. I threw my head back and grunted softly as she began to gently nibble my nipple. I looked down at her cute rodent face; she looked like a hamster drinking out of one of those water bottles with the metal tube that they fix to the side of their cage. She began to suck harder and harder, pinching from time to time with her oversized incisors. She let go of my cock and slid her hand down between my arse cheeks, I spread my legs wide. 'Yes,' I was saying, 'go there'. She understood the assignment and began cautiously fingering my arsehole, still wet with lube from the plug that'd not long since removed. My tit began to tingle. I knew I was going to lactate, it'd been a few weeks since my dogging session with Toby, and my milk had had a chance to build up again. Chastity began to double down, sucking hard and deep at my electrified tit. She began to moan and took most of my tit in her eager mouth.

"You've cum!" She said, disengaging the nipple and looking

up at me. "You've cum in my mouth! You've done a nipple cum!"

I laughed. I hadn't cum, of course, I'd lactated, but I knew what she meant.

"Can I do the other?" she asked.

"I'd rather you did. I don't want to feel unbalanced. I'll be walking in circles all day if you only do one. But would you like to grab that dildo from over there?" I said, pointing over to the altar.

The cute little rabbit jumped up, her bobtail bouncing as she hopped across the room. She grabbed the dildo, flopped back onto the bed and leaned over and began to work my other teat, rapidly sucking and nibbling as before. I guided her hand downwards, the one holding the dildo.

"I need you to put it in me," I said.

I rolled onto my back and opened my thighs. Chastity knelt by my side on the bed. She expertly guided the tip of the dildo into my arsehole and began to slide the first two or three inches in and out of me. I let out a long sigh that ended in a grunting moan. The rabbit continued to gently fuck me with the dildo as she leaned in and started working my nipple with her teeth and tongue. She began sucking harder and harder, simultaneously pushing the dildo deeper and deeper into me. My nipple began to tingle and I knew I was going to squirt and cum, hopefully at the same time. Chastity slowed her dildoing hand down to a stop.

"Don't stop," I moaned. "I'm going to cum…"

"Oh no, you're not," the rabbitte said with a surprisingly evil grin. "If I can't cum, you can't cum."

The little tease began to suck my nipple once more. My head swam from the effect of her pheromones. I felt as if I might have an out-of-body experience. I stroked her back dreamily as I felt myself squirt into her mouth.

"I have to go," Chastity suddenly said, giving me a quick peck on the mouth. "Mother will be wondering where I am."

The rabbit climbed off the bed and began gathering her things.

"You're inside me now," she said, smiling knowingly, her hand resting on her abdomen. "Think about it tonight, when you're lying in bed and I'm back at Mother's. You're inside me. Your milk is a part of me."

Chastity got dressed. I slid the dildo out of my arse, stood up and slipped into my tatty yellow dressing gown.

"I really have to go," she said, leaning in and kissing me on the mouth, her sweet, warm tongue, still tasting of my bacon-flavoured milk, flicking into my mouth. "I want to stay... I really like you. I know you're with Felina, but I'm sure we'll become good friends. I'm going to see you again at the house anyway... I can't wait."

"I'm looking forward to it," I said, opening the bedroom door. "But I'm not with Felina..."

"Oh, I know you're not exclusive or anything," Chastity said, walking into the living room. "But you're in love, aren't you? And who wouldn't be in love with Felina? She's amazing... You're super lucky. I'm sure she's the best nesting partner. Anyway... Gotta run!"

And with that Chastity skipped to the door, turned, blew me a kiss, and headed out into the dark hallway, closing the door behind her.

She actually thought I was with Felina, that Felina and I were some kind of couple. How strange!

CHAPTER SEVENTEEN

A TABERNACLE OF WITCHES

It was a windswept and rainy November evening. I had my leather jacket fastened tight with the collar up. My tartan umbrella kept blowing inside out as I walked down the street towards Lily's house. It was around six o'clock and the streetlights had just turned on, their yellow luminescence bright against the cloudy black sky. I opened the gate, walked up the cobblestoned path and knocked on the door. Almost instantly the door swung open, and I was greeted by Chastity's beaming face, accompanied by the sweet smell of wildflowers and strawberries and cream.

"Swinella!" Chastity cried out in her cute little rabbit voice. "I'm so glad you're here! The ladies are waiting... Come in, come in."

I stepped into the hallway and gave my rodent friend a quick peck on the cheek. She was wearing a cream blouse, long sleeved and high collared, a biscuit-brown argyle cardigan with a white and brown diamond pattern, a belted knee-length dark olive green pencil skirt, seamed fishnet tights and smart brown brogues with yellow laces. A large black leather pouch hung from the belt at her waist. Her light blonde hair was held by a russet velvet Alice band. She was autumnal-toned, and looked as good as she smelt. Her large brown eyes scanned my face.

"How've you been, Chastity?" I asked as I slipped out of my leather jacket and hung it on the antique hatstand alongside two long black coats.

"Really good!" Chastity said, blushing and hopping slightly from foot to foot. "It was so nice seeing you at your place the other day, and seeing Felina... I don't really know her so well because she's in the... In the... The other... Thing... Um..."

"What other thing?" I asked, bemused.

"Oh, I really should't say," Chastity replied, blushing. "The Sisters are going to tell you everything tonight anyway... so, come on. Let's not keep them waiting."

I followed Chastity's bouncing bobtail down the hallway and towards the room where I had had tea with Lily on my previous visit. I heard the sound of laughter and women's voices coming from inside of the closed room. Chastity knocked on the door and opened it without waiting for an answer, standing to one side so that I could enter. The rabbit closed the door behind me, without entering the room herself.

I was momentarily overwhelmed by the smell of perfume and cosmetics, of incense and the scent of several vases of flowers of various types spread around the large, high-ceilinged room. There were three women sat around the room. Two of them I knew, the third I had never met. Lily was reclining on the chaise where she had sat during our chat on my previous visit, black cap atop her silver tresses. She was wearing a black knitted shawl over a dark, plum-coloured long-sleeved velvet dress and black woollen tights. Her green ballet flats lay on the floor by the chaise.

Sitting opposite Lily, I was pleased and surprised to see Lucretia. Lucretia smiled at me and raised a glass of red wine. She was sat with her legs crossed, her long-fingered white hand resting lightly on her knee. Her black hair, with its streak of white, hung either side of her face, and she looked stunning, with heavily made-up, dark, smoky eyes and a deep, wine-red lip. She was wearing a pair of high-waisted pleated black palazzo pants and a cropped black woollen jumper with short puffy sleeves that ended just above her elbows. Her feet were bare and her toenails painted a high-gloss black.

The third woman, the one I didn't know, sat in the large overstuffed armchair by the bay window regarding me with an expression of bemused curiosity.

"Ah, here's our guest of honour," Lily announced as I entered. "Swinella, welcome to our little gathering. I know I needn't introduce you to Lucretia, but this is my sister, Eva."

Lily waved a theatrical hand at the woman in the armchair. I walked over and shook Eva's outstretched hand. She looked to be slightly younger than Lily by a few years, and was a curvier, darker version of her sister, with a healthy, olive complexion. She had an abundance of wavy, nut-brown hair pouring out from beneath a red baker boy cap, not unlike the black fiddler's hat that her sister often wore. Eva was wearing a long black skirt and a thick dark green knitted jumper that looked really warm and comfortable. She had enormous boobs, and for some reason I just wanted to climb into her lap and snuggle, which was a weird feeling to have upon first meeting someone. Her fingernails were short and sea green, and her hand, weighed down with an impressive collection of chunky silver rings and bracelets, was super soft, gentle but strong. As we shook hands she seemed to be scrutinising me with her large, mischievously-glinting hazel eyes. Like her sister, Eva seemed to be totally devoid of any kind of scent.

"We meet at last," she said, mysteriously. "I've heard a lot about you, Swinella."

"Er…" I laughed nervously, glancing over at Lily and Lucretia. "All good, I hope?"

"Very good," Eva said with a knowing smile.

"Please, Swinella," Lily said. "Have a drink and make yourself comfortable."

Lily took a bottle from an occasional table by her chaise, poured out a glass of red wine, and reached over and handed it to me. I took it, thanked her and took a sip. The wine was very good, super fruity, like drinking jam. I sat down on the opposite end of the sofa that Lucretia was sitting on. I crossed my ankles and tried to relax. The three women looked at me. No one spoke for what seemed a very long time, but was probably only a few seconds.

"How's Tarquinius?" I asked Lucretia, wanting to break the silence.

"Oh, he's good, but he's sleeping right now," Lucretia said, glancing down at her crotch. "It's just us girls tonight."

"How are you finding Hamden, lovely," Eva said. "Do you like it here?"

"Oh, I love it," I said, smiling over at Lily's sister. "It's everything I ever wanted, really. I'm having the best time ever. It's as if the whole place was just... I don't know... As if it was made for me."

"Or as if you were made for it?" Eva said, with a tilt of her head and a raised eyebrow.

"Well, yes," I said, laughing. "Isn't that the same thing?"

"Maybe," she said, nodding. "Maybe you were just made for each other."

"Yeah," I said, nodding. "Maybe we were. I've really enjoyed meeting so many cool people, like Lucretia... and Tarquinius."

"And we loved meeting you, Swinella," Lucretia said with a knowing smile, letting her graceful fingertips fall onto my thigh for a moment. "Especially Tarquinius."

Everyone laughed at the implication, but not maliciously. I felt my cheeks blush, but I knew that everyone here knew what I got up to. I began to wonder if that was why I'd been invited over. Maybe this trio of witches wanted to fuck me or something? Lots of people did, but that definitely wasn't the vibe I was getting.

"Last time you visited me I asked you what you were going to do after Hamden, and you said you hadn't thought about it," Lily said. "Have you thought about it since then?"

"I have a bit," I said. "But to be honest, I can't imagine anything after Hamden. I guess I'll just stay here for as long as I can. Forever."

"What do you mean by 'forever'?" Eva asked, staring at me intently over the rim of her wine glass before taking a sip.

"Well... Until I get too old to stay, or until I die or something,"

I replied with a nervous laugh. "Isn't that what forever means? Until you die?"

"Not to us," Lucretia said, growing strangely serious. "To us forever means literally that. Forever... For eternity... World without end."

"How would you feel if we told you that you could stay in Hamden forever-ever... Never grow old, never leave?" Eva asked. "Never die."

"Well, I'd assume you were pulling my leg or something," I answered. "Things like that just aren't possible. Even if you could stay young and live forever, eventually the sun would burn itself out, or civilisation would collapse... There'd probably be a nuclear war or something. Forever isn't possible."

"She's a smart girl," Lily said, glancing over at her hazel-eyed brunette sister, before turning back to me. "Forever isn't possible, not in linear time but, if time ran in a circle, it could go on forever, no? Like a circular train track as opposed to one with a beginning and an end."

"Oh, yeah." I said, figuring this to be some kind of philosophical conversation now. "But time is... linear, right? It goes from the big bang until the end of the universe or something."

"Just indulge me for a moment," Eva said, raising a finger. "And imagine that you could step out of linear time... Time with a beginning and an end, and into circular time, like a loop, a circle. Then forever could exist. Maybe the loop could be fed by the energy coming into it from linear time. Think of a circular train track running off of a straight train track, taking its power from it. So long as the switching mechanism was kept in the right place, a train could come up the straight track, go into the circle and stay there forever. Round and around."

"I suppose time could go on forever if it was in a loop," I said, struggling with the concept. "But it isn't."

Lucretia placed her glass on a table by the sofa, leant over and placed her cool hand on top of my own, staring into my eyes.

"For us," she said, seriously. "Time is a circle. The three of us, and a few other people here in Hamden, relive nineteen eighty three over and over. We are in a time loop, a year-long loop, and we'd like you to join us. We'd like your train to pull off the straight line and onto the circle."

"You're joking!" I said, laughing and looking from one face to another. "Are you trying to make me look stupid? It's not possible."

None of the women joined in with my laughter, and I suddenly felt very uncomfortable. Why were they messing with me like this? I had thought that they were nice. Was this going to be like the evening in Finchley with Nurse Elaine and her stupid husband?

"I know it's a lot to take in, but my sister and I have been here since the beginning," Eva said, in a kind voice. "Lucretia and Tarquinius were amongst the first to join us, and over the years we've added over two dozen other individuals to our little family. And now we'd like to add you."

"What do you want from me, though?" I asked. "Why are you asking me to join you?"

"Let me explain," Eva said. "Every New Year's Eve we

perform a ritual. This ritual preserves the time loop, reinvigorates it and strengthens its borders. Initially the time loop was a little smaller, but as we've added more people into our family our territory has grown. The current boundaries of the time loop are Eweston Road to the south, York Way to the east, Pork Road into Wellington Road into Finchley Road to the west and to the north, a bunch of side streets running east to west south of Lambstead Heath."

"Wait," I said, head spinning. "So... What happens on New Year's Eve? You've lost me."

"Within the boundaries my sister just described," Lily said. "There are two covens of witches. We are witches, Swinella, which I guess you've already figured out... We know you're a bright girl. One coven, The Black Coven is headed by myself, the other, The Red Coven, by Eva. On the last day of the year, we perform a ritual. This ritual keeps the members of the covens within the time loop. When we wake up on New Year's Day, we find ourselves facing January the first nineteen eighty three, not January the first nineteen eighty four. And we get to live nineteen eighty three all over again. Forever."

"OK..." I said, thinking. "Right... Um... I don't know what to say."

This all sounded ridiculous to me, unreal, but my life from day one had had a ridiculous, unreal quality to it. If I could accept that there were demons in the world, why not witches? And if there were witches, why wouldn't they live forever in a time loop in Hamden Town? I mean, it was just as likely as anything else.

"I know," Lucretia said, squeezing my hand reassuringly. "It's a lot to take in."

"But we can always get back to that," Lily said with a broad smile. "Are you hungry? I've made one of my winter soups... I like to cook. Chastity should have everything ready in the dining room. We can take our wine."

The three ladies rose gracefully to their feet, and I followed them out of the door, wine in hand. We headed down the corridor to the back of the house, through another pair of double doors, and into a large dining room with a long, heavy wooden table that could've easily seated a dozen people. The room was decorated in the same Victorian style as the living room, of course, all lace and velvet, dark woodwork and flowers. Heavy moss-green embroidered curtains hung either side of a pair of patio doors. The rain had intensified since I'd arrived and was lashing down. There was a light out in the garden, and through the leaded windows of the patio doors I could see enormous rose bushes. Their flowers had gone for the season, but a few leaves were stubbornly hanging in there, despite the coming of winter and the cold weather.

A cosy fire was burning away in an ornate black iron fireplace, and a number of cream-coloured candles were flickering away here and there. Four places were set at the table, two on either side. Lily and Eva sat at one side of the table, Lucretia at the other. I sat next to Lucretia and gazed out onto the rainswept garden.

"I always look forward to winter," Lily said, smiling and gazing out of the doors. "Soup season, open fires, dark evenings... what's not to love?"

"Yes," I said, looking away from the garden and into her serene face. "And it's good for wearing lots of clothes... Cosy jumpers and whatnot. Nights in with the cat and late-night horror movies, drinking hot chocolate."

"What would you like to know about what we just told you?" Lily said, gazing into my eyes, a benign smile on her beautiful olive-skinned face. "You must have a lot of questions?"

"I can't really wrap my head about it, to be honest, and, I'm sorry, but I still kinda think you're messing with me," I said, looking from the black-eyed to the hazel-eyed witch. "I don't know where to start."

"Just ask the first thing that comes into your head, dear," Eva said.

"OK... Assuming that everything you've told me is true," I said, hesitatingly. "How come you don't meet yourself on New Year's Day."

"Good question," Eva said with an approving nod. "The simple answer is that it's impossible for two versions of you to inhabit the same timeline. So you're the only you in that particular timeline, the you in that timeline travelled back to New Year's Day, you're in the loop. That's the only you."

"I don't understand," I said, shaking my head slightly. "On New Year's Day this year I was at my parents', so wouldn't I be there as well as in Hamden? If I accepted what you're saying and entered this 'loop'. Could I call myself on the phone?"

"Reality is a self-regulating system," Lily said. "It's a lot more malleable than you think. In the timeline you'll have entered when you hop into the loop, you'll have moved down to London last year, in nineteen eighty two, something like that. The truth is, there are infinite timelines, and infinity is impossible to comprehend, but all things are possible. Try and think of the loop as a spiral if that helps."

That didn't help.

"But I didn't move down in eighty two," I said, confused. "I moved down this year."

"The thing is, love," Lucretia said. "You won't understand, you can't understand. Only Lily and Eva understand. I've been here for a very long time, and I don't understand."

"It doesn't make sense," I said.

"No," Lucretia conceded. "It doesn't… And that's kind of the point. Magic doesn't make sense… That's what makes it magic. That's literally how it works. Making sense is for science, not magic."

"Put it another way," Lily said. "Can you drive?"

"No," I replied.

"But you've been driven somewhere in a car?"

"Of course," I said.

"Of course you have," Lily said. "You can't drive, but you still got to your destination. You trusted that the driver knew what they were doing, and you got where you needed to go. Think of the time loop like that. My sister and I are in the driving seat… all you have to do is enjoy the ride."

"So I just have to trust you?" I asked. "That's all?"

"There's a little bit more than that. You will have a few obligations. Nothing comes for free," Eva answered, leaning back and smiling her warm, mystifying smile. "Do you trust us?"

The thing is, I did trust them. I mean, I wanted to trust them, so maybe I was being a victim of my own wishful thinking, but there was something about them, some ancient power. I could feel it. I knew they weren't lying.

At that point Chastity came into the room wheeling an antique hostess trolley. On top of the trolley there was a large silver soup tureen, and on the shelf beneath the tureen a stack of soup plates and a basket of bread rolls. Chastity placed a soup plate in front of each of us. Lily first, then Eva, Lucretia and me. She placed the basket of bread in the middle of the table and proceeded to serve us a couple of ladles of thick, steaming hot soup each, in the same order that the plates were placed in front of us. As she served me my soup, Chastity winked at me and smiled.

"Any more wine?" the rabbit asked.

"Go ahead, Swinella," Lily said, resting her elbows on the table, interlacing her slender fingers and resting her chin on her interlocked fingers. "You probably need it."

I nodded. Chastity uncorked a dusty bottle and filled everyone's glass, before walking out of the dining room and closing the doors behind her.

"So... If I'm to believe what you said," I began. "Then I'll take part in your ritual on New Year's Eve, and the next day I'll wake up, and it'll be New Year's Day this year, the one that's already gone?"

"Yes," Eva said.

"And then what?"

"Then you get to spend the year in Hamden, doing what you like to do," Lily said. "Fucking a lot, I suppose... That's your thing, isn't it? Going out dancing with your friends, gigs... All the stuff you love. Cosy nights in with your cat drinking hot chocolate and watching horror films, like you said."

"And I won't get old?"

"No," Eva said. "The time loop preserves you. Loopers are actually physically a year younger on New Year's Day than they were on New Year's Eve. So you'll never get old or tired, you'll be rejuvenated every time the wheel turns back."

"OK... Won't reliving the same year over and over get boring?" I asked.

"Not if you don't let it," Lucretia said. "And don't mistake living forever as having a perfect, eternal memory. Think of something you did this year."

"Er... I went to see Hawkwind at The Electric Ball Bag," I said. "And I hooked up with a goat boy after. It was a good night."

"Ok, well, you can go and see Hawkwind next year on that same date, it'll be repeated. You can hook up with that same goat again, if you want," Lucretia explained. "But if that gets boring, just give it a few years and you'll forget all the details, and then you can go again, and it'll be just like the first time. Same with books and going to the cinema, tv shows, plays... Everything. If you met someone in a pub this year, some tourist or something, and you took them home and fucked them, then that person will be in the same pub on that date every turning, and you can fuck them again, or skip a year if you're a bit bored of them. The only exceptions to this rule are people like ourselves, loop people, turning people, loopers. We aren't always in the same place at the same time every year, because we have the option of being where we want, as it's not our first time living that year, but literally millions of tourists visit Hamden in a year, so you'll always have new people to meet. It's the same year, the same events, the same weather, even, but you can choose what to do and what not to do. Avoid something for enough years and you'll forget everything about it. If you want to go and see Hawkwind next turning, I'll come with you. I don't remember ever going to that gig, but I know I must have... Some other nineteen eighty three, decades ago."

"And while you can't leave the borders of the time loop," Eva added. "You can get things bought in from the outside. If there's a book you want to read, the library can order it for you. If there's a record you want, the record store can order it in for you. If there are people you want to see, you can always talk to them on the phone, and you can invite them to Hamden for a visit. Of course, you can't tell them about us, and you can't cross the border. We don't have many rules, but the ones we have are cast iron."

"So you can phone your parents whenever you want," Eva said. "And from your perspective, they'll never die. They won't grow or move on, either. They'll keep telling you the same thing, but they'll always be there, living the same year again and again, over and over."

"But I can't cross... Where did you say? York Way or Eweston Road, and those other streets you mentioned?"

"That's right," Lily said. "But there's plenty to do within our borders... You've got all of those venues and pubs and nightclubs, the cinemas and the theatre, the comedy club. There's The Regent's Wood, Rosebud Hill Park, Belsize cemetery for when you're feeling all gothic, and, like Lucretia said, there are people coming in from the outside all the time... You know, to talk to and make love with and whatnot. Your memories will have completely faded out after about a hundred turning, but there's plenty here to keep you amused for a hundred years."

"Hang on," I said, the penny dropping. "That's why Felina never leaves Hamden! She's one of you..."

"That's right," Lily said. "Felina has been with us for some time. She pushed for your admittance to our little family. She really likes you... She loves you."

"But again, why me?" I said. "Out of everyone you could've made this offer to."

"Because... Like I said earlier, you were made for Hamden Town, and Hamden Town was made for you," Eva replied. "But there is something in it for us, of course... Other than the fact that we like you and we want you around."

"Our... Ritual, the one we perform on the last day of every year," Lily said. "Involves the harnessing of certain energies... Sexual energies, actually. Our covens are made up of people who each bring a different type of sexual energy to the mix."

"It's like this soup," Lily said, stirring the steaming bowl with her spoon. "It needs just the right balance of ingredients, of vegetables and herbs and spices, just the right amount of salt and pepper and stock, to work. Not too much of this... Not too little of that. It needs to be cooked for the right amount of time, and allowed to cool a little before eating."

"Why nineteen eighty three?" I asked. "Why not nineteen eighty two? or nineteen eighty four?"

"It just seemed right," Lily said. "And you hit upon something earlier... what if there's a nuclear war? We'd lose everything. All it would take is for the wrong psycho to get in charge of the USA or the Soviet Union, and we're done. All of us. Oh, and my sister was quite enamoured by that Mr. Orwell, the one who used to live just off Bentish Town Road and write those books, weren't you Eva?"

"Oh yes... I really liked him," Eva said. "He used to come over for tea. So clever, but kind of miserable with it."

"So," Lily said. "What do you think?"

What did I think? Were they crazy? Were they playing a game with me? Or were they sincere? Forever, in Hamden Town? To spend eternity living the life I'd grown to love, with the people I'd also grown to love. I could dance and fuck and hang out with Felina forever, never grow old, never die. Our little flat. Us. Forever. It was too much. It was all too much.

The four of us ate our delicious soup in silence. I had a lot to think about. It all seemed too good to be true. It couldn't be true, but deep down I'd always known there was something strange, something magical, about my life. Since moving to Hamden I had felt as if someone, somewhere, was writing the story of my life, as a kind of magical spell. When I thought about it too much, I started to freak out, but when I relaxed and let it flow everything made sense.

"How was your soup?" Lily asked as I placed the silver soup spoon down onto the empty plate.

"Really nice," I answered, taking a sip of wine.

I was really full. I'd only eaten a bowl of soup and a bread roll, but I felt like I'd eaten an entire meal.

"Would you like to see the temple, before dessert," Eva said.

"There's a temple?" I asked.

"Of course," Eva replied with a smile. "A ritual needs a ritual space. It's not far away... It's beneath the house, actually."

"Oh... well, of course I'd like to see it," I answered.

"Chastity!" Lily called out in a loud voice accompanied by two swift claps.

The double doors swung open and the irrepressible rabbit skipped into the dining room with a grin on her lovely little face.

"Chastity... Can you show Swinella the temple," Eva said.

I thought the rabbitte was going to start hopping up and down, she seemed so pleased.

"Of course I can," Chastity said with unbridled enthusiasm, making small fists and shaking them in front of her chest in excitement. "Come on Swinella, let's go!"

"Go with your sister," Eva said. "Us old crones will wait here."

I followed Chastity out of the dining room and into the corridor. Chastity closed the double doors and turned to me.

"This is so exciting," she said. "I'm so glad it's me that gets to show you the temple for the first time. Come on."

The excitable rabbitte turned and walked away, a spring in her step, her bobtail bouncing as she walked. We headed down a dark corridor, past indistinct paintings and tapestries; we turned first this way, and then that, and I couldn't help but think again that the house seemed to be much bigger on the inside than it appeared to be on the outside.

"You'll never get bored here," Chastity said as she led me through the house, as if she knew what we'd been discussing in the dining room; then I remembered that rabbits have super hearing and realised that, of course, she would've heard everything. "There's always things to do. When you're initiated, we can see more of each other, if Mother allows it, which I'm sure she will... She's very nice."

"How long have you been here," I asked.

"Oh, a very, very long time," Chastity said, turning to face me and twitching her button nose. "Definitely over a hundred turnings. I'm a rassophore, that's what we call people who've been here over a hundred years. When you join you'll be a novice, until you forget everything from your before-times. I can't remember anything before I entered the loop. Imagine forgetting all the negative stuff that happened to you before you came here, even the small things, like that time you called your teacher 'Mum' at school. It just takes time."

Chastity stopped when we came to a huge, heavy wooden door with shiny iron rivets. She reached into the pouch that hung at her belt and pulled out a large iron key.

"This is it," she said, slipping the key into the lock and turning it.

The door swung open smoothly and silently. Chastity turned to face a long, ornate sideboard that ran along the wall opposite the door, and opened a drawer. She took out a box of matches and proceeded to light some candles in a large, silver candelabra that stood on the sideboard.

"So we can see. Shame we don't have cat eyes," she said, lifting the candelabra in both hands with some difficulty. "There's no electricity down there. Follow me."

Chastity headed through the doorway and I followed her as instructed. The air on the other side of the door was cool, slightly stale, and smelled of sandstone and incense. The steps were wide, smooth and shallow, easy to walk down. As we descended the stairs curved slightly to the right, and I was surprised by how deep underground they went. We seemed to be descending for a very long time. I'd assumed that the temple would be one floor below the ground, like a regular cellar, but we just went deeper and deeper. I was beginning to think we'd never get to the bottom, when Chastity said to watch my step, and we stepped out into a massive open chamber.

"I'll light some more candles," Chastity said. "You wait here."

The rabbit walked around the outer wall, lighting candles as she went. The candles were atop free-standing wrought-iron candelabra, spaced maybe six feet apart. Gradually the chamber was revealed, and I stood there staring, wide-eyed and open-mouthed.

The space that Chastity was in the process of illuminating was huge: a perfectly circular room some fifty feet wide, with a high, black domed ceiling. The wall (a circular room has only one wall, which is obvious when you think about it, but looks wrong when you write it down) was made of large, rough-hewn, grey stone bricks. The floor was made from highly-polished black marble and had a massive white seven-pointed star with two concentric circles inlaid in it, like the silver pendants I'd seen some of my friends wearing, its points nearly reaching the wall. Against the wall opposite, situated at the end of one of the star's points, there was an impressively-carved throne made of dark wood. At each of the ends of the other six points there were large double beds. They had simple frames, made out of the same wood as the chair. The beds had no blankets or pillows or duvets or anything, just a red silk sheet covering each mattress.

"This is The Black Temple," Chastity said, once all the candles were lit. "This is where we do our ritual. Mother will sit on the big chair... She rings the bell and does the chanting and stuff."

"It's... Very nice." I said, looking around. "Impressive."

"Yes," Chastity said, nodding in agreement. "I get to keep it clean... That's one of my privileges. Eva has a place like this under her house, but the ceiling is red. It's called The Red Temple, of course. I've never been in it, though... I'm not one of her children."

"But you are one of Lily's children. Am I one of Lily's children?" I asked. "You've allowed me to see the temple."

"Oh, of course you are!" Chastity said, bouncing over. "You always have been! You're my sister and this is your home. Isn't it wonderful?!"

"I don't know," I said, shaking my head slightly. "I'm confused."

"Why?"

"It seems too good to be true."

"Don't fight it, Swinella," Chastity said, growing serious.

"Sometimes things are just good, truth has nothing to do with it."

"How did you come to be here?" I asked.

"Oh, Swinella... That's another story for another book," Chastity replied. "What do you think this is? Hamden Town and The Black Temple, and all the people you've met?"

"I don't know," I shrugged. "It's just... It's just a really cool place."

"Swinella..." Chastity said in a low voice, scanning my face with her big black eyes. "This is Heaven. Not some stupid Christian heaven where you just sit on a cloud playing a harp or something, singing the praises of a jealous god. This is our heaven... A heaven of endless sex and music and friendship and joy... and love and magic. Maybe you don't have to die to get to Heaven, maybe you can just slide in... Provided you use the right kind of lube."

"I don't know what to do or think," I said, baffled. "I don't know what to say."

"Say yes... say yes to Heaven," Chastity said, taking my hand and gazing up into my eyes with an earnest expression on her pretty face, her dark, liquid eyes overflowing with sincerity. "Say yes to me."

I just stood there staring at the cute rabbit, with her big brown eyes, her split upper lip, buck teeth, pixie ears and her twitching button nose, as she held my hand and smiled. Time seemed to stand still. I was being offered everything I'd ever wanted, and I was finding it hard to take. Why couldn't I just accept it? Why was I looking for a problem? I closed my eyes and breathed deep. The odour of incense and the wax of the candles filled my snout, accompanied by the summer meadow perfume of Chastity and the smell of her fresh, pink pussy locked away in its steel cage. I opened my eyes, took a deep breath and looked around.

"Yes," I said.

"How was your meeting with The Sisters?" Felina asked as I walked into our flat.

"It was good... Really good." I said. "They, um... They told me everything, I think."

I dropped my handbag and hung my jacket on the back of a chair, wandered into the living room and flopped down onto the armchair.

"How long have you been here?" I asked. "In the loop, not in the flat."

"I don't know. I'm a rassophore," Felina said. "I can't remember arriving, so definitely over a hundred turns... Maybe thousands. You understand that I couldn't tell you?"

"Yeah. I get it... And you've never thought about leaving, stepping over the boundary and seeing what nineteen eighty four has to offer?"

"Not once," Felina said. "Whatever is out there could never be as good as what's in here. You only have to look at the news to see that. And I'd only end up old and dying, and then what?"

She was right.

"So... You're happy to live with me, here... Forever?" I asked.

"I am... why wouldn't I be? You're cute and you're tidy and

you're quiet, we give each other space... And best of all, you're funny... You get up to hilarious shenanigans, you do know that, right? With all your dogs and old women and stuff. I'd rather live here with you than with anyone else."

"OK, OK..." I finally said, nodding. "This is it. Forever. I'm going to spend eternity living in Hamden Town with you, working at The Black Violet... And getting fucked up the arse by an endless parade of goats and dogs and apes, as well as being fisted by all and sundry. I'm Swinella Porksword. Newest member of the black coven. Comedy porcine anal slut. Is that it?"

"Yes, that's it. That's you. That's your happily ever after... and I'm Felina Peggingsworth. Icon," she said, with a broad, Cheshire Cat grin. "Do you want a cup of tea?"

"Sure, why not?" I replied with a shrug. "Wait a minute... your last name is Peggingsworth?!"

CHAPTER EIGHTEEN

THE SEASON TO BE JOLLY

The festive season crept up on us, and The Black Violet got busier and busier as Christmas approached. I was invited back to Lily's house in mid-December for my initiation into her coven.

Chastity answered the front door and silently led me through the house. When we arrived at the door to the temple, she told me to remove my clothes. I did as she said and, when I had undressed, the uncharacteristically sombre rabbitte unlocked the door, opened it and gestured for me to go down, quietly closing the door behind me as I descended the warm stone steps.

Lily was standing in the centre of the star facing the doorway at the foot of the stairs. She was dressed in a simple long black robe. It was the first time I'd seen her without her hat, and her handsome face and silver hair stood out in the candlelit gloom of the temple. She was wearing the silver septagram pendant that so many of my friends wore, which I now knew marked them out as coven members. Incense smoke curled from the thuribles that hung from hooks evenly spaced along the wall between the candelabras.

She beckoned to me. I walked over and stood before her,

naked as the day I was born. Lily reached out towards my right hand and I obediently lifted it for her to take a hold of. She turned my hand palm upwards and took ahold of my thumb. Lily raised her other hand and I saw that she held a long silver needle. She smiled at me and pricked my thumb. There was no pain. A second after the pinprick a bead of crimson blood appeared on thumb. Lily leaned forward and licked away the blood with a swift nod of her head. She then stood upright, took one of my hands in each of her own, looked into my eyes, and began to chant in a strange, deep voice, in a language that I didn't recognise.

The chant lasted a few minutes, rising and falling in pitch and volume in a strange, discordant sing-song way. It seemed to repeat certain phrases at regular intervals. My head began to spin slightly, but not in a bad way. I felt almost euphoric. Lily stopped chanting. She let my hands go and they fell to my sides, then she produced a silver chain from somewhere within her robe and held it up. Hanging from the chain was a familiar silver pendant: the seven-pointed star with two concentric circles. I dipped my head forwards and Lily placed the chain over my head and around my neck. I straightened up. Lily leaned in and kissed my forehead. She took a deep breath and hugged me. I felt amazing. Suddenly I was overwhelmed with the most intense blend of contradictory emotions. I began to cry, hot tears filling my eyes as I buried my face in Mother's soft black robe. Lily gently let me go and took a step back, smiling at me with a hand on each of my shoulders.

"Welcome home," she said.

After my initiation Mother taught me a short prayer and showed me how to visualise the septagram, closing my eyes and picturing it floating just in front of my forehead, breathing in through my nose and out through my mouth. She told me that I should recite the prayer silently inside my head and visualise the star whenever I had sex, not the whole time I was fucking, of course, but at least once during the exchange. This would send a bit of sexual energy over to her, which she would use to keep the loop going between turnings.

After that we went upstairs. I got dressed and we had tea, and she outlined what would happen in the temple on New Year's Eve.

Me and Felina shut up shop early on Christmas Eve, headed down to The Dev' and got pissed, before stumbling back home and collapsing into bed. Wayne Mansfield and Gatita came around for Christmas dinner and we had roast salmon and watched *Diamonds Are Forever* on telly. Both of them complimented my new silver star pendant that I was now wearing proudly over my clothes and gave me a hug, even the usually cynical Wayne seemed quite emotional and sincere. I now knew that Felina, Wayne, Gatita, Chastity and Gordita were members of one of the covens. I wondered if I had met any other coven members thus far?

The two cats and Wayne had watched the same movie every Christmas Day for ever and knew every single word to the script. Apparently it was shown on a bank holiday in the springtime and they watched it then, as well, it was one of their little traditions. We were quite drunk when it came on and it was hilarious seeing Wayne recite all of Sean Connery's lines as the actor delivered them, while Felina played Tiffany Case, and Gatita played Miss Moneypenny and a bunch of other minor characters.

The shop was closed from Christmas Eve until the third of January. I spent most of the time off whoring myself out to anyone who wanted me. My sex drive seemed be at an all-time high. I just could not get enough, and of course I remembered to visualise the star and recite the prayer in my head the way Mother had shown me.

I was the only girl at a party at Rasher and Bullseye's horrible flat. Rasher and Bullseye were more or less naked at the party. Rasher wore a very tight cropped white vest that flattened his chest, so that's why I hadn't spotted his boobs beneath his t-shirt. Bullseye was stark bollock naked. It was the first time I'd seen either of them without the skinhead uniforms on, and I was surprised and pleased to see that they both wore silver stars around their necks. Rasher and Bullseye's friends had more or less turned me inside out. Me, Rasher and Bullseye had all embraced our assigned roles as sloppy pass-around party bottoms, and had been vigorously fucked and fisted by all and sundry. It was a lot of fun, despite being more than a little sordid. My head was throbbing for two days from all the poppers, and my arsehole looked and felt like the exit wound from a shotgun blast, but it was an awesome evening.

I gave Toby the dog a call and had him ride me in my bedroom one grey afternoon. I found him a little bit boring, to be honest, what with the always-needing-to-be-told what to do thing. He was much more fun to fuck when we had an audience, but the weather was too grim to have him sodomise me in Regent's Wood. I made a mental note to hook up with him in the summer. One good thing about that shag was that I was able to visualise the star and recite the prayer for most of the encounter, mainly because the sex was so boring. I had started to try and figure out who was in a coven, who lived in the loop. It was quite easy to suss out if someone was a looper, even without seeing their septagram, and Toby was clearly in linear time, but he'd always be around for me if I needed him. To think I almost fell for him that night in The Drog'. It made me laugh to look back; you can never love a civilian.

I got banged by a couple of goats I met at The Red Cap, and impressed them (and myself) by just how much hammer my arse-cunt could take. They both complimented me afterwards, telling me that it made a nice change to be able to ram their massive cocks all the way into a girl's guts without having to 'fuck about being all gentle and shit'. When they spit-roasted me I realised that I just had to get rid of my gag reflex. I wanted to be able to take massive cock orally just as proficiently as I could anally. That was going to be my project for the new year. I was going to learn to deep-throat properly, like a real pigslut, and I was going to need plenty of practice. Fun times ahead!

Felina and I did a shoot with Dave at The House of The Waxing Moon, just a few days after the party at Rasher and Bullseye's place, a couple of days before New Year's Eve.

This is the first time you've shot together, isn't it?" Dave said.

"Yeah," Felina answered. "We've done a few in-person sessions for a couple of my boys, but nothing on camera."

"That's cool," Dave said, winding on the film in his camera. "Should be fun. Swinella did a good job, that one time I shot her and Gatita in that pub."

The room we were in was at the back of the house in Eweston and was decorated in the style of a medieval dungeon, all heavy wood and wrought-iron furniture, stocks and manacles and a big 'X' shaped cross up against the wall. There were racks and racks of floggers, canes and riding crops, as well as a selection of leather masks and restraints. In the middle of the room a heavy-duty leather sling was hanging from the ceiling by a huge, industrial winch connected to four thick iron chains, one attached to each corner of the sling. This was where I was going to be spending most of the photo session.

I was actually quite concerned. My arsehole had been like a clown's pocket for the past couple of days. A big hairy ape boy skinhead at Rasher's party, with massive hands and a unibrow, had been particularly eager to punch fist me until I came multiple times, my body sticky with precum and pig milk.

When it was time to douche, I basically just reached up inside myself and pulled out a couple of turds by hand, and that was without any warming up, straight off the bat, as it were. I used my extra-long douching nozzle and did a very thorough job, right up inside me. We couldn't have any uninvited bum gravy or chocolate raisins turning up in the middle of a photoshoot.

I wandered naked out of the shower room where I'd just rinsed out my funcentre and clambered into the sling. Felina helped me get my trotters through the two loops of leather that hung from the front two chains, and I took hold of the other two chains that hung either side of my head.

"I'm ready when you are," Dave said.

Felina pulled my tail out from under me, all business-like, and turned to the photographer.

"Do you want milk?" she asked. "She's a bit dry in that department, I'm afraid."

I had told Felina earlier that day that I had lactated so heavily at the party that I might not be able to deliver any Frazzle-flavoured jus.

"It's not everyone's cup of tea, anyway," Dave said. "No pun intended. Just start with a bit of random humiliation, face to face. Snarls from you, Felina, a bit a fear from Swinella."

"Ok, that's easy enough," Felina said.

"But no talking, just facial expressions," Dave said. "Oh, and Swinella... Do you mind if Felina gobs in your mouth?"

"Of course not," I said. "What're friends for?"

Felina bought her beautiful face close to mine and snarled, curling her lip and baring her teeth. Dave snapped away. I tried to look scared. It was easy enough. Porn is like a parody of sex: you can't really overact in it, the more ridiculous you look, the more the viewer gets turned on. Felina and I were like cartoon versions of ourselves, and we really enjoyed chewing the scenery and camping it up to the max, it was very funny. I looked into her eyes and opened my mouth.

To my surprise Felina began to cough and snort. She wasn't just going to spit nicely into my mouth, she was attempting to cough up some eldritch slime beast from the depths of her nicotine-ravaged lungs. I was about to receive a payload of olive green lung butter directly into my mouth. I opened wider. Felina leaned over me and began to dribble the putrid phlegm from between her lips. It was like she was vomiting a terminally ill jellyfish directly out of her body and into mine. For a moment I felt like a baby bird, but I was totally not into it. I was so not into it that I was completely into it, as an act of total degradation. Felina reached up. She placed one latex gloved hand on the top of my head and grabbed my chin roughly with the other, holding my mouth open. She let the phlegm beast fall from her lips. It landed directly into my mouth, like a tumourous oyster. It was fucking disgusting, and I loved it. I made a big show of drooling some of the rancid blob down my chin. I parted my lips so that the phlegm hung between them in tiny ropes of gelatinous filth. The camera flashed and Felina stepped out of shot.

"You can spit it out, if you want," she said.

I looked her in the eye, winked, swallowed and opened my empty mouth.

"Fucking hell," Dave muttered under his breath as he took more pictures. "Ugh! Sorry, but ugh!"

Felina grabbed the Trex from the top of a stool that she had placed nearby before shooting started and greased up her hand and forearm. I opened my legs and relaxed my arsehole. She reached out and placed her fingertips on my hole, and with minimum force, popped into my shitter. A shocked expression crossed her face, and she pulled her hand all the way out, and in, and out, and in, and out. She rotated her wrist and pushed.

"Girl," she said in a low voice. "What the fuck... This is the loosest arse-cunt I've ever come across... How are your insides not all over the floor?"

"I've been kinda busy," I said.

"No fucking shit," Felina exclaimed.

"Oh definitely not," I said. "I reached up earlier and pulled it all out."

Felina fisted my busted pigussy and Dave got a bunch of shots. Felina pulled out.

"I reckon I can get both hands in," she said. "Shall we try?"

"Do whatever you want," I said with a grin. "That's what I'm here for."

"Yes," said Dave enthusiastically. "Try it... We can charge double. Double for double."

Felina stood upright and held her hand together in a prayer position in front of her chest. Dave snapped away. She closed her eyes for a couple of shots, and then opened them wide and looked up to the heavens. She lowered her hands and leaned forward, placing her middle fingertips on my busted gash, her hands still pressed together as if she was praying.

I took a deep breath and looked into her bright green cat's eyes. I nodded slightly, and I saw the flicker of a smile pass across her face. 'Take me to church' I repeated over and over in my head as her praying hands slid into me. I let my head fall backwards, damp strands of pink hair sticking to my clammy shoulders, and shut my eyes, the light of the camera like distant fireworks, flashing pink through my closed eyelids.

Felina stretched me out further and deeper than I'd ever gone before. I was more open even than when the burly skinhead had punch-fisted me into oblivion at Rasher's gaff. I was there, I was there, in the place I had been looking for from the moment my snout and tail had started to appear. My desire had led me there, like a guiding star, to this moment of transcendence. 'We don't have to die to go to Heaven' Chastity had said, and she was right; we just had to use enough lube. And then it appeared in my mind's eye, the silver star with its seven points, turning and shining against the backdrop of the camera's flash. The prayer Lily had taught me when she carried out my initiation began to play in my head on a loop as Felina opened me up wider and deeper, deeper and wider. For a moment I thought Felina had started reciting the prayer along with my mind, but then I realised it was the sound of my own voice, I was mumbling the prayer over and over in a distant, dreamlike state.

"Sisters red and black... I give myself to thee," I heard myself whispering as Felina's gloved hands slid in and out of my sopping wet ruined arse-cunt. "Hold me and guide me and teach me to be free. Sisters black and red... everything I do, is an expression of my devotion... and of my love for you."

And love them I did. They weren't even in the room with me and Felina and Dave, but they were everywhere in Hamden Town, at all times, and it was The Sisters who were fucking me: Felina was just their instrument, an extension of their will. I had never surrendered myself so fully. The fisting I was receiving was my baptism, my wedding and my funeral all rolled into one. 'This is it,' I thought.

And then I stopped thinking.

"It was fucking amazing," Felina said later that evening as we sat in The Dev' with Wayne and Gatita. "I had both hands right up her."

The Satanists at the next table were leaning in and listening to Felina's enthusiastic recounting of our session that afternoon, but I didn't care. Let them hear it. Let the whole world hear.

"I was basically washing my hands in her arsehole, like this," Felina rubbed her hands together. "And she was fucking loving it! She was making those cute little grunts that she does... And then she starts mumbling the prayer, right there, in front of Dave. He must've wondered what the fuck was going on."

Everybody laughed. I blushed a little and shrugged. It was against the rules to speak the prayer out loud in front of a non-coven member, but apparently I'd mumbled it more or less incoherently. Felina said it wasn't a problem, but I shouldn't do it again.

"I am what I am," I said.

"Ya fucking are, duck, there's no denying that... You are pure fucking filth," Wayne said, shaking his head before lowering his voice to a conspiratorial whisper. "I almost wish I was in The Black Coven, just to see you in action... not that I'm able to pay attention to what's going on around me when the ritual is happening."

"We must do another shoot together in the new year," Gatita purred, placing one of her immaculately-clawed, delicate brown hands on my arm and looking over at Felina. "The three of us... If you want to, that is?"

"We'll have to see if our anal superstar wants to," Felina said, smiling over at me and winking.

"Of course I want to," I said. "We should probably practice quite a lot as well, y'know, for the shoot... Just so everything is perfect. I think I'll need a lot of practice."

But before there would be any other shoots, or any practicing for any other shoots, there'd be New Year's Eve, the meetings of the red and black covens, the ritual and the turning.

CHAPTER NINETEEN

THE RITUAL

The twelve members of the Black Coven met on the evening of New Years Eve, nineteen eighty three, at Lily's house, at around seven o'clock. The Red Coven met at Eva's place in Rosebud Hill.

Felina and I had spent the day at home in a kind of heightened sense of excitement. We tried watching telly, and reading. We both had baths that lasted over an hour. We went for a walk around Regent's Wood, but it was bloody freezing, and we didn't stay out for long. There was frost on the ground and the thick, grey clouds overhead were threatening snow. It had already snowed several times since early December, which I really liked, although it never stayed for more than a few days.

Neither of us felt like eating, but we managed to cook and eat some beans on toast anyway. We knew that we'd need our strength for the long night ahead. We weren't allowed to drink before the ritual, so we couldn't even have a few beverages to help the time pass.

"I want a mohawk," I said as we sat around after lunch.

"A mohawk?!" Felina said. "Why?"

"For a change. I'll probably grow it back in the new year," I said. "And it'll give us something to do."

"What kind?" Felina asked.

"Just a short one... An inch or two, maybe with a little rat's tail at the back," I said. "There's some gel in the bathroom, I can spike it up. I think it'll look cool."

"Hmmm... Well..." Felina said, squinting at me through half-closed cat eyes. "You do have the face for it... I think it might look alright. Go and grab the scissors and clippers."

It is a well-known fact that any house wherein reside members of the punk and/or goth fraternity will, by default, contain some electric hair clippers, and our flat was no exception. Felina was a pretty good hairdresser, for an amateur. She cut her own fringe whenever it needed a trim, only ever visiting a hairdresser when she needed the back and sides chopping into shape. She also bleached and cut Wayne Mansfield's hair, and had trimmed Gatita's split ends on more than one occasion.

I sat topless on a chair in the kitchen and Felina examined my head from all angles.

"I think two inches wide, by about one and a half long," she said. "We can gel it into something like a short, dykey fin. Your roots are showing through a bit... We shoulda got them sorted before tonight, really, but I think with the mohawk a bit of darker hair near the scalp will add to the overall look, rather than make it look cheap and nasty... Although we both know that cheap and nasty is kind of your wheelhouse."

Felina was right. I'd been a bit slack with regards to my trademark pink hair. I'd been too busy shagging to stay on top of it.

"You've been too busy shagging to stay on top of it," Felina said, plugging in the clippers.

"If I were a celibate virgin like you, then I'd have time to primp and preen like you do," I said. "As it is I've got work to do... For Mother."

"Oh, listen to you!" Felina said. "You were only initiated five minutes ago and now you think you know it all. I'll have you know I do my bit for the team. What do you think all of those photo sessions and trips to the house in Eweston are for? It's all for The Sisters, it's all for the time-loop and the turning. I'm not the only virgin in the covens, I'll have you know... And we bring just as much to the mix as you slags do. Now... Sit down, shut up and keep still."

The catgirl stuck Specimen on the turntable and got to work, shaving the sides of my head into a narrow mohawk, and then trimming what hair was left down to the required length. I quickly showered after she had decided she was happy with the result (a shower and a bath in the same day? Some dirty punk I was), and then Felina used some L'Oréal Studio Line gel and hairspray, that Wayne had left behind, to sculpt my hair into a dynamic fin.

I checked myself in the mirror. I thought my new hair looked pretty good, and I was very happy with the result. I sneered at myself.

"Bloody hell!" Felina said. "It's nearly five. I've only got two hours to get ready... Let's go. You look amazing, brilliant, good call. Even though we'll be taking everything off when we get there, we've got to look the best we've ever looked when we arrive, it's the most important night of the year, after all."

Two hours was more than enough time to get ready, Felina could do a full face and put together a stunning look in about five minutes. She had had decades of practice, after all.

I was undecided on what to wear. I'd been thinking about the ritual in exactly the opposite way to Felina. As I was going to get naked almost immediately after arriving, I didn't think it really mattered what I wore. I was wrong, of course. The first bite is with the eye, and I wanted my fellow coven members to want me, especially as it was my debut. I went into my room and rummaged around in my wardrobe and chest of drawers, throwing potential items of clothing onto the bed.

In the end I went with a fairly typical Swinella look. I pulled a pair of lime green fishnets, that Felina hated, over the top of some thick black tights. I put on my best, cleanest pair of black knickers, and then a pair of thick black hiking socks over the tights. I had my black denim mini skirt washed and ironed, so that went on, followed by a faded black Seditionaries 'PERV' T-shirt that I'd chopped the arms off and shredded the back with horizontal slashes that looked really cool. I put on a bit more makeup than usual, going for a heavier, more dramatic smoky eye that Felina had taught me to do, and a bright red lip. I plucked my remaining eyebrow hairs away to nothing. With my new, harsher haircut and my eyebrowless face, I looked pretty intense, and anyone at the ritual would hopefully be quite surprised by the transformation. I didn't know if I was going to stick with my new look in the new (old?) year, but I was getting a kick out of it at that moment.

I walked back into the living room and knocked on Felina's bedroom door.

"Who is it?" her voice called out from behind the door.

"Who do you think it is?" I answered. "It's the police. Open up, we know you're in there."

"Enter."

Felina was sat, in the almost-dark doing her makeup. It was always weird to me, even after all that time, to find her functioning perfectly well in darkness. She had her bedroom curtains open, and the weak light from the streetlights reflected on the heavy snow clouds that hung above the blue tiled rooftops was enough for her cat's eyes to be able to do things that I'd need the big light on to do.

"Will I do?" I asked, performing a quick spin so she could see me from all angles.

"You'll do. I like the eyebrows," she said with a nod, snapping shut the compact she held in her hand. "I'll be out in a minute."

I closed the door and went back into the living room. I was actually a little anxious. I didn't know what to expect at the ritual. I only knew that there would be twelve participants, plus Mother, in attendance. I'd asked Felina if there'd be anyone I knew in the Black Coven, other than Chastity, but she'd remained tight-lipped and told me it was forbidden to speak of until after my first ritual, that I'd find out soon enough, and afterwards she'd tell me exactly who was in the Red Coven as well.

Felina finally emerged from her chamber. She looked stunning, of course. It was harder for her to raise her game, as her game was raised all of the time, but of course she was able to elevate her look for the occasion.

She was wearing a short, silk LBD, sheer black stockings, the tops of which were just visible peeking out from under her dress, and a pair of knee-high, black patent leather laced boots with a chunky sole and four-inch heel. Her makeup was flawless, of course. She was holding what appeared to be a dead animal in her hands. The dead animal had white fur with grey tips. It looked impossibly soft and gorgeous.

"What's that?" I asked pointing at the fur in her hands. "Is that real fur?"

"Of course it is," Felina said. "Why would I want any of that synthetic, fake crap? It's real fur, and it cost a fortune. It's so warm I can only wear it on the coldest of days."

Felina placed a smaller piece of fur on the sideboard and swung the coat around her shoulders with impossible grace, her slim arms slipping through the sleeves as she did so. She picked up the smaller piece of fur, which I couldn't help but think of as the coat's baby, walked to the mirror by the bathroom door, and carefully pulled it onto her head. It was a hat, obviously, like a fluffy pillbox or something. She looked so good that I could've died right there, but I had to challenge her about the fur.

"Isn't it, like, wrong to wear fur?" I asked. "People say it's cruel and stuff."

"But I love fur," Felina said, taking hold of the collar of the coat, closing her eyes and smiling and making a cute little snuggling motion with her lithe body.

"You love fur?" I said. "What about the animals? Don't you

love them?"

"Oh Swinella... How long have we lived together now? I'm a cat... I want furs from animals that have died in pain in cruel metal traps, alone and scared in the darkness. I want those furs to have been carried hundreds of miles across the Siberian tundra by rough, alcoholic fur trappers who have never felt love," she said, laughter like the tinkling of tiny bells, hands on hips, relishing a monologue that I'm sure she'd preformed countless times before. "I want my leather to come from bullfights, ideally from bulls that have killed a matador and then in turn had a sword thrust through their black hearts. I want expensive whalebone corsets. It takes a whale a long time to die, a very long time, and I want the sea around it to boil and turn red before it succumbs to the inevitable. I want my waist cinched by the agony of a dying leviathan, its power and strength destroyed by my desire... My desire to reduce my waist by just a few inches. I want diamonds from mines where men suffer under terrible conditions for very little pay. I want pearls from the most dangerous waters, where pearl fishermen regularly drown, pulled away by a vicious undertow, their bodies never found, their families distraught. I want fabric from dark, satanic mills. I want silkworms boiled by the million, regardless of what the voice of Buddha says. I want to be clothed and adorned in pain and fear and suffering. I am, after all is said and done, a fucking cat."

"Blimey," I said. "It's a good job you lot only make up one percent of the population, otherwise we'd be fucked."

The funny thing was, no matter how cruel Felina really was,

how heartless, I still loved her. That, dear reader, is the power of the cat.

It was snowing when we left the flat; large, soft flakes falling from the cloudy night sky, as if the stars themselves were descending to earth. Hamden was already packed with pissheads, part-timers out to make the best of the worst night of the year. We wound our way through the crowds and the noise, slipping like ghosts between the throngs of merrymakers. I had never felt more detached from the people around me. They were nothing more than scenery, really; they'd never know what we knew.

I was wearing my fourteen-hole boots, fingerless gloves and buttplug. I had my leather jacket fastened tight against the chilly December evening. Felina linked her arm through mine as we huddled together beneath my tartan umbrella. We weaved our way through the raucous party people, down the high street towards the canal, past the tenebrous market, and away from the crowd. We passed The Roundhaus and stopped on the corner of Pork Farm Road and Regent's Wood Road. Felina was turning left, towards Rosebud Hill and Eva's house, while I was going to continue down Pork Farm Road, towards Bellzend Graveyard and Lily's house.

I wished that Felina was in my coven, that we would be present at the same ritual, but she was Eva's daughter, not Lily's. We'd not see each other until we got home the next day. We hugged for a moment, bathed in the sodium glow of a yellow streetlight, large fluffy snowflakes sticking to Felina's fur. She smelt of Poison and fags and long dead foxes. She smelt of a future and past that were one and the same.

I wanted to stay in that moment forever, but the wheel of time kept turning and eventually we let each other go. Felina brushed the snow from her coat.

"See you a year ago," she said with a smile.

"See you tomorrow," I replied.

Felina turned and began trudging through the crispy snow towards Eva's house.

"Hey!" I shouted as she walked away.

The cat-girl stopped, turned around and looked at me. She'd never looked better, standing there in the falling snow, her perfect heart-shaped face framed by her black bobbed hair and the white fur. She simply radiated cat; beauty and grace personified. I knew why the ancients worshipped her. I worshipped her.

"I love you!" I called out.

"I know!" she yelled back with an ice-cold, glacial laugh, before turning and slinking into the dark shadows of the snowy side-street.

Chastity answered the door in a state of excitement so great that I thought she might explode.

"Swinella!" she cried, hugging me tight and bouncing up and down. "Come in, come in... Tonight's the night!"

I shook out my snowy umbrella and placed my leather on a chair by the foot of the stairs: the antique coat stand was already full to capacity. The house was really warm, and it felt good to be there after the freezing street. I could hear voices from down the corridor, and for a moment I grew nervous at the prospect of meeting so many new people.

"There's nothing to be afraid of," Chastity said, as if reading my mind. "Everyone's super nice."

The excitable little rabbit held out her hand and I took it, warm and soft, and walked down the corridor towards the sitting room.

Chastity opened the door without knocking, and I was greeted by the sounds and smells of a dozen people. I could smell the anticipation and sexual excitement in the air.

"And look who's here," Lily, who was standing talking to a tall, Asian ape girl, called out. "It's our newest sister, Swinella."

I looked around the room and smiled in what I hoped was a friendly way as the guests fell silent and stared at me. I was relieved to spot a couple of familiar faces in the room. Gordita's golden smile flashed from where she sat on the overstuffed armchair by the window, and Gatita, who was standing talking to a beautiful dark-skinned ape boy with a shaved head, winked at me and smiled her crooked smile. Bullseye was talking animatedly with a pair of goats by the fireplace, and even that tough-acting hound dog gave me a nod and a grin.

Mother broke away from the ape she was talking to and glided over to where I stood with Chastity by the door. She was wearing the same long black robe she had worn for my initiation, her head uncovered. She kissed me on both cheeks, put her arm around me and turned to the room.

"Now... Some of us can remember our first ritual... how

intimidating it can be to meet everyone for the first time," Mother said in a loud voice, looking from face to face. "So, with that in mind, Swinella and I are going to sit over here while you talk amongst yourselves. Chastity will bring you over one by one, to say hello to our new piglet."

Mother gently led me to an empty sofa set back against one of the walls next to an overburdened bookshelf. The other guests resumed their conversations, and I relaxed. Mother floated down onto the sofa. I sat next to her.

"How are you feeling?" she asked, placing a reassuring hand on my knee. "I like your hair... You look really beautiful."

"Thank you, Mother," I said, the first time I had called her that to her face. "I feel a bit nervous... But excited as well."

"Nervousness and excitement are the same emotion," Mother said. "Just looked at from different angles. Everything will be wonderful. You're here now. You're with us."

"I know," I said, looking into her dark eyes and feeling the love.

I perched on the edge of the sofa as, one by one, the guests, my fellow coven members, were brought over by Chastity to introduce themselves.

The two goats were called Dion and Will. Along with Bullseye there was another skinhead dog called Rolf, a burly blonde boy with a radiant smile and warm dark blue eyes. The second rabbit, a chubby little black girl with two big afro pigtails and a shy demeanour, was called Zekia. The tall Asian girl, who Mother was talking to when I arrived, was Jinlian. She was dressed in a dark orange evening dress, and had waist-length shiny black hair and friendly sparkling eyes. I liked her immediately. The dark-skinned, bald ape boy's name was Aurora. He was wearing a simple white shirt made of raw, unbleached cotton and a pair of light blue linen trousers. He looked like he'd just stepped off a beach somewhere in the south of France. The second cat, a stunning albino draped in pearls and dressed in a simple black t-shirt dress, was called Katsith. She had long white hair and mismatched eyes, one yellow and one blue.

Everyone was super nice, shaking my hand or kissing me on the cheek as they introduced themselves. Last of all Chastity brought over Gordita, Bullseye and Gatita.

"As you already know this motley crew," Mother said. "I instructed Chastity to bring them over together."

"Alright, spakka?" Bullseye said to me with a sneer, then, turning to Mother and nodding at me with a sideways tilt of his shaved head. "She's all right this one, I've seen her in action… very committed. Cunt like the Blackwell tunnel."

"Um… Thanks?" I said.

"Oh *Cerdita*," Gordita began, leaning in, taking me in her massive arms, and hugging me hard. "But you know Bullseye is right… You're a filthy sow, we love you, you fucking skinny whore slut."

Once Gordita had heaved her bulk out of the way, Gatita leaned in and kissed me on both cheeks.

"You look wonderful," she said, looking me up and down. "I love the new hair and eyebrows… So cute, so cute… I hope Mother picks me to begin with you."

"Well now," Mother said. "Now you know everyone, I believe it's time to head down to the temple."

Mother clapped her hands three times, and everyone began removing their clothes, folding them up, and placing them on whatever surface happened to be nearby. I followed suit, peeling off my hiking socks and tights, pulling down my knickers, and taking off my jumper and T-shirt. It felt good to be naked, and everyone in the room looked much better with their clothes off, stripped down to nothing but their silver septagrams. The goats were already hard, of course, satyrs that they were, and I was pleasantly surprised to see that Jinlian had a beautiful-looking cock hidden away under her panties.

Within a couple of minutes everyone was naked, everyone except for the two cats and Chastity. The cats had removed their clothes and replaced them with impressively sized strap-on cocks, and Chastity needed a little help to finish getting undressed. The little rabbit bounced over to Mother, still wearing her bloomers and metal crotch shield. Mother took a silver key from the table by her side and undid the padlock at the front of the belt. The belt came away and Chastity pulled down her bloomers. The smell of her cunt, her arousal and her rabbit pheromones hit me like a freight train, making my head spin and my eyes water. I glanced over at Bullseye and Gordita, looking for a reaction from my olfactorily-enhanced friends.

"Fucking hell," the dog whispered. "Gets me every turn, that does…"

Gordita was, for once, speechless. She simply took a deep breath, in through her snout, and closed her eyes.

Chastity looked over at me and bared her buck teeth, her nose twitching. I nodded. I understood.

The twelve members of the coven followed Mother through the house. Mother paused briefly to take a large golden goblet from the sideboard opposite the doorway, before leading us down the stone steps and into the temple.

Candles and incense were lit, and the chamber was warm. Mother walked into the centre of the star, and turned to face us with a benevolent smile across her timeless face. The rest of us spread out along the wall by the foot of the stairs. I had been briefed about what would happen next. One by one Mother would call out the names of the six bottoms in our coven, who for the purpose of the ritual were called *chalices*. The chalices would step forward, take a sip from the golden goblet that Mother was holding, and take their place on their allotted bed, filling the beds up anti-clockwise from the one to the immediate right of Mother's throne all the way around to the one on her left.

Mother would sit on her throne and ring a large brass handbell when the time was right, and the tops, referred to as *swords*, would all move anti-clockwise to the next mattress. None of us knew who we'd be fucking first, but over the course of the ritual all the chalices would get fucked by all of the swords.

"Swinella," Mother called out.

To my surprise I was going to be first, fucked right next to Mother's throne. I stepped forwards and bowed to Mother. She held out the golden goblet and I took a good mouthful of the potion, as instructed. It tasted like pear drops. I clambered onto the bed and sat on my knees, watching the ritual unfold before me.

Mother continued calling out the names of the chalices; Zekia, Aurora, Gordita, Bullseye, Chastity. I watched them take their places on their respective beds. I closed my eyes for a moment, breathed deep and tried to relax.

After the chalices, Mother called out the names of the swords. I was excited to see who'd be fucking my greedy little pig-hole first.

"Jinlian," Mother began.

So it was the long-haired ape girl who'd be riding my pig cunt first, followed by Dion, Rolf, Katsith, Will, and finally Gatita. Rather than Gatita being my first fuck of the ritual, she would be the last, which was also cool. Maybe it was because Gatita and I had already fucked? I don't know, but I'm sure nothing that Mother does is without reason. She would've wanted Gatita and I to be each other's last coupling for the energy we'd release when the turning happened. Gatita's strap-on would be the cock that would be up me when midnight came around. We'd be seeing in the new year together.

Mother walked over to the throne, placed the empty goblet on the floor, picked up the bell, and sat down. She began to chant in that same strange language she'd used at my initiation, her voice suddenly grown deep and loud and strangely resonant, as if someone had turned on a mic with a reverb unit. After a few minutes the chanting stopped and the bell rang.

I leaned forward on the bed, still on my knees, and pulled my cheeks apart and arched my back slightly. I was surprised to feel what could only be a tongue slip into my pussy and begin exploring my hole, kissing and licking, cool fingers grasping my flaccid dicklette and soft, empty sac. All around me I could hear the sounds of fucking. Soft moans and the slap of skin on skin. I could pick out Bullseye demanding to be fucked hard, Gordita's grunts and Chastity's high-pitched squeaks. But I was there to give of myself, not to listen to the others. Jinlian stopped frenching my well-used gash and grasped my hips, guiding her cock towards my arsehole. She slid into me easily. Her cock was super comfortable, but I didn't want to be too loose, so I began to rhythmically clench and unclench my cunt. We soon settled into a rhythm. And then I felt the effects of the potion taking hold.

I had forgotten that Mother had told me that the potion had psychotropic properties but, all of a sudden, I felt my perception shift into something more surreal than everyday reality. It felt like I'd crossed over into a dream without falling asleep, or that I'd just woken up from a dream. It's difficult to describe what happened to me, as we don't have much in the way of language to describe things that are beyond our everyday experiences, but I will try.

The first thing that struck me, as Jinlian slipped her gorgeous cock in and out of my sensitive, well-used hole, was that the temple was somehow very far away from any other point in space or time, that it could have been out in deep space, or on the bottom of the ocean, an incredible distance away from the nearest source of light or heat. It felt as if we'd slipped out of reality altogether into our own tiny, separate universe. Jinlian slowly pulled out of me and leaned back. I understood and turned around, lying on my back with my feet in the air, hands grasping the backs of my knees. Jinlian took hold of her dick and used the end to slap my useless cock and balls a few times. She leaned in and began to kiss me on the mouth, her long tongue sweet and wet and tasting vaguely of my arsehole, her hands resting on my shoulders as she bore down on me. Everything was becoming increasingly soft-focus, warm and fuzzy.

The walls seemed to be closing in and moving away at the same time, but strange as it was, I felt no anxiety or fear. This was my life now. I had crossed over into the weirdness some time ago. Really, as a bestiamorph, I had been born to the weirdness. It was my birthright, and my home.

Jinlian's snakelike hips began to gyrate as we made out, and from time to time I felt the tip of her beautiful cock bump up against my arsehole. I knew she was waiting for the right moment to slip back into me, and I wanted her. I wanted her so bad. I wanted that serpentine, mysterious feminine energy inside of me. From the moment Jinlian had disrobed in the drawing room, when I had first glanced her dick, I had known it was a female cock, not a male penis on a female body, as was the case with Lucretia and Tarquinius, but a woman's cock, like mine, but active. A cock that belonged entirely to the feminine principle. There was nothing of the masculine in her slender, delicate penis, just pure goddess love and energy; Venus as a penis.

Jinlian stopped kissing me and leant back, simultaneously entering me. I closed my eyes, and a rose-gold and scarlet fractal appeared behind my eyelids, an endless tunnel of kaleidoscopic light and colour. I was aware of the bed beneath me, of the sounds and smells of the temple, but they were far away now. Most of my awareness was taken by the warm glow created by the tip of Jinlian's cock gently massaging my P-spot. Pink starbursts exploded behind my eyes, obliterating the rose-gold fractal. I opened my eyes to find that the temple had grown darker, but somehow had become more illuminated at the same time. It was as if the candle flames had shrunk in intensity, but everything else had begun to glow with its own, internal light. One type of light had been replaced by another. Shadows became deeper and the flames of the candles seemed to have become illuminated globes. I wanted Jinlian inside me forever. And then the bell rang.

Jinlian slowly removed her dick from my cunt, smiled, blew me a kiss, and moved away to the next bed. Mother shouted a few short words in the strange language, and rang the bell again. I looked to my right and saw Dion walking past the front of Mother's throne, towards my bed. His muscular chest was already glistening with sweat, his great curved prick was wet with Chastity's cunt juice, and it smelled amazing. He grinned a puckish grin as he took his place between my legs.

I held up my hand, indicating that he should wait a moment before fucking me. I sat up, my head suddenly clear, and grabbed his dick. I bought it up to my snout and sniffed. The combination of pent-up, recently released rabbit fanny batter and goat arousal was almost too much. I could smell colour. He was so red, like fire, like blood, pure Martian masculine energy, hot and destructive, but accompanied by the fading odour of Chastity's cunt, baby pink and soft, the most comfortable colour in the world, so sweet, so delicate, and yet so immeasurably strong. I sniffed his monstrous cock for a few seconds more, before bouncing onto my back and swinging my legs into the air.

"Fuck me, Satan," I said through gritted teeth, my words sounding distant, the pitch quivering in some weird way. "Fuck me good, goat boy."

Dion didn't need telling twice. He didn't throw himself up me with wild abandon straight away, he at least had the decency to check out how accommodating my shit-pipe was, slowly inserting the entire length of his pizzle before commencing to fuck me. Hard. Fucking Dion was like fucking a mountain, granite cock and marble muscles, eyes like shards of yellow flint boring into my own. I threw my head back and grunted. Somewhere, a thousand miles away, I heard the howl of a wolf and the hiss of a lynx, the grunting of a wild boar and the squeaking of hares, and the sounds of bodies falling together and apart. The smell of animal arousal was almost visible in the temple, filling the air like the twisting clouds of incense smoke floating up and out of the thuribles. I placed my hands under my arse and tipped my pelvis forwards. I wanted Dion as deep inside me as was possible. I wanted him to know that I could take more. I wanted him to know that he wasn't all that, he wasn't that big. I wanted him to know that he wasn't anything that I couldn't handle.

"Fuck me... Fuck me... Fuck me..." I repeated like a mantra through gritted teeth, my voice echoing around my spinning head.

The goat growled and shook out his long grey hair. He was giving me everything he had. He was the unstoppable force, but I was the immovable object. I could see his aura, a halo of crimson flame. In a brief moment of clarity, as his pneumatic-drill hips pounded his massive fucking dick in and out of my indestructible fuck tunnel, I wondered if he was going to cum. And then the bell rang.

Rolf the dog bounded over with unbridled enthusiasm; like his predecessor he stank of Chastity's overflowing gash-goulash. I lay on my back, spread my legs wide as I could and looked the dog in the face.

"Eat my clit-dick, lick my arse," I said, before settling back like a queen.

The dog dropped to his knees and began to obediently lick my limp cocklette and soft scrotum, slurping and slobbering with wild, canine abandon.

"Don't forget the arse," I said.

Rolf switched his attention from my pink acorn to my arsehole, licking hard and deep. It was pretty good, and he definitely knew what he was doing. He might've been doing it for centuries, as far as I knew. I twisted my neck and looked around the room. Mother was sat on her throne, her lips chanting silently while her half-closed eyelids scanned the room, moving from bed to bed. All around me I could hear the low voices and moans, gasped commands and encouragements, and the fleshy, moist symphony of skin on skin, the wet, sucking sound of bodies merging. The head-spinning smell of goat and rabbit, cunt and arsehole, cock and sweat, filled the air.

"Fuck my fucking hole, you fucking skinny cat bitch," I heard Gordita say between asthmatic gasps, followed almost immediately by a series of deep, appreciative grunts.

"You like that, you fat fucking cunt?" Gatita replied with a low growl. "You fucking fat fucking fuck fat. I'll fucking ruin you, you fucking pink blob of shit."

I burst out laughing. Gatita and Gordita were the double act for which no-one waited, but for which the whole world craved. I needed to see.

"Get off me," I said to Rolf. "Ride me from behind, like a good dog... Deep and steady."

I got onto my knees, sending my head whirling, and presented my rump. Rolf took hold of my tail, pulled it up, and slid in. He started to fuck me, deep and steady, as requested.

I looked around the temple. My head still spun from the effects of the potion, and from the potpourri of pheromones, lube, and bodily sap. Everything was slightly blurred and glowing, the movement of bodies leaving trails in the air. The circular wall around the chamber looked like trees, and the domed ceiling like the vault of heaven.

As I had figured out from their voices, Gatita was fucking Gordita hard. The corpulent hoggess was bent over the end of her bed, feet wide apart, chubby, beringed hands pulling her dimpled flanks asunder to give the waif-like cat girl access to her pork rind shit cunt. I glanced over at the bed next to mine. Dion was hammering the fuck out of Zekia's rabbit pussy hole. She was spread out like a starfish, squeaking as he rammed his curved slab of mutton into her fresh rodential paper-cut cunt. For some reason I chose to isolate the smell of Dion's sweaty arse-crack. I'm not proud of it. I blame the potion.

On the next bed along, Jinlian was getting her lovely cock noshed by Aurora. This was the first time I'd seen two apes getting it on. It was a bit strange to me, actually. Like a meal with no seasoning, even though they were both beautiful. Aurora's bald head was bobbing up and down with clockwork efficiency. Jinlian's long, slender cock must've been a good nine inches, and the whole thing was deep in Aurora's throat. I envied his lack of gag reflex. I couldn't see his crotch, so I had a quick sniff, and was surprised to smell boy cunt. The odour was definitely pussy, but with a musky, masculine undertone, like Marmite.

Rolf was doing an efficient doglike job of fucking my back door, but Dion was a hard act to follow. I was into it, but if the ritual was an album, then he'd have been a filler. I was about to continue taking in the sights and smells of the temple when the bell rang.

The effects of the potion were coming in waves now. There were short periods, sometime lasting for minutes at a time, when I felt completely normal, only to realise that I was actually a long way from everyday reality. I think I was kind of getting used to being in an altered state of consciousness. And then I started to realise that I'd been here before.

Rolf had pulled his pizzle out of my pussy, smiled, and bounded away to fuck Zekia, and it was as Katsith was clambering onto my bed that I got the first wave of déjà vu. The albino cat-girl was managing to smile down at me in a way that was both comforting and menacing at the same time, like a really good horror movie that you've seen before. Her long white hair and yellow and blue eyes were so strange, and yet so alluring. She was naked but for her strap-on harness, her silver septagram and an abundance of pearls, necklaces, earrings and bracelets. I found myself wondering why I had never met her before the ritual, and then I knew, I really knew, that somehow I had met her, not only that, I'd been fucked by her, in the temple, at the ritual. For the first time a slight wave of panic passed through me, as if someone had walked over my grave. I shuddered. I had been there before, definitely, I'd just forgotten all about it until that moment. My heart rate began to rise, and for a moment I thought I might spill over into panic, but then I remembered something Lucretia had told me one night at her flat. 'If you ever get a feeling of *déjà vu*,' she'd said. 'Just relax, and remember... you're on the right track. That's what *déjà vu* means. It's reality giving you a little heads-up. Concentrate on whatever you're doing and it will pass, but acknowledge it... You're in the right place.'

I had been there before, because I'd always been there. Time is eternal. And, right now, an impossibly beautiful cat was greasing up her massive strap-on, slick with my rabbit friend's fragrant twat-aioli. A gorgeous, ice-cold smile passed across her ghostly face as she rolled her serpentine shoulders, raised her delicate chin and puffed out her perfect tits, nipples so pale as to be almost invisible against the glowing, alabaster of her skin. She looked demonic, transcendent, and my hot pig portal was ready to receive her infernal attention.

Katsith grabbed my ankles in her claws, inch-long black nails catching the candlelight and leaving illuminated trails in the air as she moved. She eased the first four inches of her cock into me, and then slowly back, almost all of the way out of me, before sliding back in, not too deep, just four or five inches, slow and steady. It was such a tease, but I didn't care, I just wanted to look at her, to take her in visually. I wanted to know her, I wanted to know everything about her. I began to worship her, for real, as an actual avatar of the goddess, and I'm sure she saw the adoration in my eyes. Everyone else, all the other bestiamorphs and apes, they can't compare to a cat. They're so much better than us, and so much worse: all we can do is bask in their glory. Katsith began to ever so slightly increase both the depth and the speed of her penetration, her white marble face impassive. She might've been a demon goddess from another dimension, but she was fucking me, she was serving me. The divine feminine feline was fucking my slutty slag sow cunt. I didn't own her the way I'd owned Daniel a year ago in my childhood bedroom, but she was still mine. I isolated the scent of the pussy cat's pussy. It smelled sweet, like fudge, really expensive fudge from Fortnum and Mason or somewhere like that, and its odour was a deep, plum colour. She began to pound me harder, deeper, harder, hitting me right on the P spot. A teardrop of perfectly clear precum emerged from the end of my tiny cocklette, dribbling onto my belly in a bright, glittering trail as she rode me harder and harder. She bared her little pointed teeth and meowed, shaking her white mane and wrinkling her little button nose, fixing me with her heterochromic gaze.

Suddenly the sounds of fucking that were all around me increased in volume. It was as if the sound had been turned down while I'd had my experience of déjà vu, and then someone had turned it up again, but much louder than before. Rabbit squeaks and Gordita's porcine grunts, the creak of a bed, the slurp of a cock leaving a hole, the repeated, ubiquitous machine-gun slap of skin on skin on skin. I was in the jungle, and the lion did not sleep.

I didn't want Katsith to stop, ever. She had increased and decreased her depth and speed several times, sometimes deep and slow, then shallow and fast, then deep and fast. It was a very considerate, nuanced fuck, not like the dog at all, who had fucked me like he was chasing a stick. I closed my eyes. The seven-pointed star appeared unsummoned in my mind's eye against a backdrop of ultraviolet flames. My heavy breathing had acquired a metallic quality, like I was a Cyberman or something. I felt really hot, but really good. My tits and cock were vibrating. I felt as if some invisible force was pressing me down onto the bed, and if that force disappeared I'd float up to the domed ceiling of the smoky, candlelit temple. I grabbed my star pendent and squeezed, its points digging into my hand. Then the bell rang.

I was so sloppy, fucked into a state of gape. I was wide-eyed and curly-tailed, skywest and crooked. I flipped myself over and presented. I couldn't remember who was fucking me next, I couldn't remember much of anything, so I decided to try and work it out from the way they fucked me.

My arse cheeks were suddenly pulled apart by rough, strong hands, and a massive curved cock slid into me without meeting any resistance. It was Will, the second goat, and he meant business, no messing around. He began to pound my hole with extreme prejudice, no subtlety at all. I suddenly became very vocal, my low grunts turning into high pitched squeals within a matter of seconds. I lost myself. I knew I was being the loudest person in the room, and I really didn't care. I heard the sound of squealing from across the room. Gordita had joined me in vocalising her pleasure in the loudest way possible. I started to sweat, the perspiration feeling cold on the freshly-shaved sides of my head. Will fucked me and fucked me and soon I was lost in a never-ending loop of insertion and withdrawal. I felt so right at that moment. I was part of something, a vital cog in a vital machine. I knew my place; on my knees getting fucked for Lily, for Eva, for the Goddess, for Hamden Town, for all of my family in The Black Temple, and in The Red Temple. I was the eternal hermaphrodite, androgyne whore, triple outcast. Pig. Woman. Queer. I was an immaculate misconception, the lie that told the truth. For a while I lost myself in the fantasy of not liking being fucked. I told myself that I was only doing it for others, for the good of the coven, that I didn't want ten inches of slick, throbbing goat cock brutally ramming in and out of my beautifully-stretched piglette gash. 'I hate this,' I thought to myself as Will relentlessly pounded my hole, like a never-ending avalanche. 'I'm a good girl... I'm doing this for him... For everyone else... I don't want this... This primal beast, with his massive hot cock and his horns and tail, I don't want him stretching and fucking me, not in front of all these people. I'm such a slut, I'm such a cheap fucking slag... I'm a cheap slag... I'm a hole for other people to get sick in... I'm a pig whore slut, and... and... and I fucking love it! I fucking love it so much... I was born for this, slag slut whore cunt pig filth anal cunt fuckfuckfuck!'

I knew I was about to come. The goat had got me there. I was gonna disappear into sexual oblivion, and what with the effects of the potion, I wasn't sure that I'd ever come back. I felt as if my coming orgasm might destroy the world.

And then the bell rang.

Will withdrew, gave my quivering arse a friendly slap of appreciation, and fucked off around the star to service Zekia's fragrant little rabbit mimsy. I looked to my left and saw Gatita walking past Mother's chair and towards my bed. She was glowing with her own sparkling light, she was lit from within. Her brown skin was slick with sweat. Her long red hair was tied back in a plait, with loose strands plastered to her gorgeous face. Her strap-on was wet with the smell of every kind of cunt and arsehole. She didn't climb between my legs and fuck me straight away, instead she lay on the bed beside me and kissed my forehead.

"I'm so glad you're here," she said, her voice echoing and vibrating as she showered my burning hot face with little cool kisses. "We all are."

I looked into her amber eyes. Her vertically slit pupils were dilated to the point of being almost circular. I kissed her on the mouth, and she returned the kiss with tongue and a sultry purr, while all around us the coven fucked us into eternity. We kissed, deep and long and wet and true. I wrapped my arms around her and pulled her close.

"I..." I said, pulling away from her face and gazing into her eyes. "I..."

"I know, I know. I feel it. Let's look," Gatita said with a mischievous grin on her glowing face. "C'mon."

Gatita helped me to my shaking knees. We kneeled side by side and hand in hand on the sweat-soaked crimson silk sheet and looked around the temple. I looked to our right and saw Will, still rank with the smell of me, fucking Zekia in the arse. It had never even occurred to me that the non-pigs might appreciate a bit of back door action. I'd foolishly thought sodomy was 'our thing' exclusively. Zekia was on all fours, back arched, bobtail swinging with each thrust of Will's hips. I could smell her arsehole and her cunt, steaming with lust and submission, little cries escaping from her throat with each battering swing of the pendulum.

On the next bed along I saw Aurora straddling Katsith, pinning the albino cat-girl to the bed and bouncing up and down on her strap-on with wild abandon, his eyes closed. As I watched the pretty bald boy raised his arms, grabbed the back of his own head, and began to cry out rhythmically as he ground down onto the indefatigable rubber cock. I focused my sense for smell on his smooth armpits and inhaled, the musk of his arousal was particularly strong in his underarms, and I loved to taste it; so primal, so rich, so vital.

On the next bed along Rolf the dog was fucking Gordita. The corpulent sow was the most unresponsive of the participants at the ritual at that moment. She was lying on the edge of the bed, her feet firmly planted on the floor, while the enthusiastic dog fucked her, his hands holding onto her pudgy hips for dear life. As we looked over Gordita tipped her head back, blinked her eyes open and stared at us through dilated pupils. Her porcine face broke into a broad grin and she proceeded to stick her tongue out at me and Gatita, before laughing, closing her piggy little eyes, and relaxing back into her fucking. She was such a fully-realised, unapologetic fat pig. I loved her then, and now, and always.

I looked over at the next bed and, through the swirling clouds of incense, I was treated to the sight of hot goat and dog boy-on-boy action. Dion was fucking Bullseye, his hands wrapped around the skinhead dog's throat, choking him as he fucked him, Bullseye's legs wrapped around the goat's lower back. Bullseye liked it rough, the rougher the better, and I was glad I knew that about him, their fucking was so intense. Dion slapped Bullseye around the face, not too hard, but harder than I'd have liked, and Bullseye egged him on, spitting at the goat and baring his teeth. It was all too masc' for me, but I knew they were both loving it. I found myself wondering if they ever hooked up outside of the ritual chamber, or if they saved it for New Year's Eve. I could always ask them, we were family now, after all.

And then it was Chastity. Dear, sweet Chastity. I looked over at the final bed, the one immediately to the left of Mother's throne.

The softly-spoken rabbitte was giving it her all. She was straddling Jinlian, who lay beneath her on the bed with her hands behind her head, a dreamy smile on her perfect face. Chastity was glowing. Her face was radiant, celestial, divine. Her eyes were closed. She was gripping her tits and biting her lower lip with her oversized rodent teeth as she rocked her hips in small, rapid movements. She was moving so fast that her pelvis was a blur (although that could've been an effect of the potion). Every so often she would let out a high-pitched squeak and wrinkle her cute little nose. She was soaked in sweat, not all of it her own, and I could smell that she'd produced a huge amount of both types of female ejaculate. I could smell the fructose and ammonia from across the chamber. Jinlian's smooth, snakelike body was wet with Chastity's free-flowing cunt juice, her hair was damp with sweat, and I'm sure she was enjoying taking it easy while the rabbit did all of the work. As we watched Chastity stopped squeezing her boobs and reached down between her legs, rapidly rubbing her clit in small circles. She began to moan, low and deep, her manically bouncing crotch slowing down to a slow grind. Suddenly she hopped off Jinlian's cock and thrust her cunt towards her face. Jinlian grabbed Chastity's arse in both hands, raised her head from the bed and opened her mouth. Chastity threw her head back and screamed. A geyser of hot, salty fluid exploded from her sweet, wet cunt, spraying into Jinlian's face. Jinlian pulled Chastity towards her and clamped her mouth onto her cunt and began to lick and kiss the still erupting rabbit girl's battered twat. Jinlian suddenly threw Chastity onto her back, clambered between her legs, grabbed her ankles and pulled her legs apart into a wide split. Jinlian dived in, throwing her slender cock into the rabbit's sacred space, her face still dripping with Chastity's fragrant elixir.

I glanced over at Mother. She was staring at Gatita and I with a bemused frown on her face. I suddenly remembered that the cat and I were meant to be participants, not spectators. I looked at Gatita and she looked at me and grinned. I felt as if we were two naughty schoolgirls who had just been caught bunking off. I quickly got off my knees and on my back. Gatita grabbed my tail and pulled me into position. She sneered at me, raised her hand, and curled her vicious claws into a fist. I threw my arms out to the sides and prepared myself to receive the sacrament.

Her fist met with some resistance at first. Even though I'd already been fucked by five cocks of varying sizes, none of them had had the girth of Gatita's hand. I relaxed and pushed and she slid in. I could hear music, though none was playing in the temple. The various sounds coming from my friends on the other beds seemed to coalesce into a pattern. The rhythmic thump of the bed to my left where Will was pounding Zekia became a bass drum, her high-pitched squeaks some kind of organ stab, insistent like the infectious offbeat of an urgent ska tune. Katsith was fucking Aurora from behind, her thighs slapping the ape-boy's bum cheeks like a snare. Bullseye growled, Gordita grunted, Chastity squeaked, Rolf howled, Dion bleated, all accompanied by the rattle, wallop and crack of a half dozen beds bouncing and buckling beneath the combined force of our fucking.

Gatita slid her arm deeper into me, past the bend, deeper into my body and soul. I couldn't feel the bed beneath me anymore. I couldn't remember how I had gotten there, I knew nothing, not even my own name. She must've gone past the elbow, must've been in me up to her bicep. I moaned, my voice sounding distant and metallic. The rose-gold fractal appeared behind my eyes once more, with the seven-pointed silver star spinning in the foreground. I began to recite the prayer, but I kept getting lost and mixing the words up. I couldn't really feel my body anymore, did she have two hands in me now? Or was it her strap-on? How had I gotten there? Just a small-town piglette adrift in an uncaring world. How had I found myself in 'that London', lying on a bed in a temple in Hamden Town, being fisted and fucked by a selection of the most delectable creatures on the face of the earth? I should go back to the beginning. I should go back. To the beginning.

CHAPTER TWENTY

NINETEEN EIGHTY THREE

Everything became a blur. The last thing I remembered was Gatita fisting me. As far as I could recall I'd fallen asleep with her hand inside of me. If anything happened after that I couldn't remember it. I'd woken up lying on the bed in the temple. The candles had almost burned out, and everyone had left. Everyone except for Bullseye who I saw blinking and stretching on his bed as I sat up and looked around.

"Fucking hell," the dog said, grinning at me. "How was it for you?"

I couldn't really answer. I didn't have the words.

"It was," I began, shaking my head. "It was... Something."

"I get ya," Bullseye said with a guttural laugh like Sid James. "It's a bit much the first time. To be honest... It's a bit much every time."

We clambered off our beds and stumbled naked upstairs. Everyone was in the drawing room drinking coffee, either dressed or getting dressed, chatting quietly or lost in their own thoughts. The room stank of sex and fatigue. I put on my clothes, downed a coffee, and quickly worked out that everyone really wanted to leave, to go home, to shower, to sleep and process.

When the last of us was dressed, and we'd all downed our drinks, we trooped to the front door. Everyone had to hug and kiss everyone else, so that took forever in the crowded hallway. As we filed out Mother hugged us all and kissed us on the forehead. I was the last to leave. Mother held me longer than the others, their voices fading as they headed off into the bright, cold morning.

"Welcome home, Swinella," Mother said after kissing me on the forehead. "Happy old year."

Tears welled up in my eyes as I looked into Mother's shining, benevolent face. I didn't know what to say, I couldn't have spoken even if I did.

"Don't say anything," Mother said, reading my mind. "We can have a long talk, sometime soon. You're always welcome here."

I stepped out onto the cobbled pathway and turned to face the door. Mother and Chastity both waved at me, Chastity beaming all over her cute, well-fucked rabbit face. I waved, turned and headed off homewards, back to my cat and our little flat.

The new old year had begun. On the second of January I started to get a bit of cabin fever and decided to go for a walk. The Black Violet would be reopening the following morning and it'd be back to business as usual. The weather was nice and bright, cold but sunny, a couple of inches of soft snow turning Hamden Town into a Christmas card. I asked Felina if she wanted a wander, but she said no, she'd rather curl up on the sofa and take a nap. I spiked up my mohawk (I'd already decided to grow it out in the new year, but I wanted to rock it for a bit longer), pulled on my leather jacket, and headed out of the door.

Hamden Town was quiet. Things were returning to normal after the Christmas and New Year festivities, but the tourists had yet to return. The sunlight was far too much for my piggy eyes. I reached into my jacket pocket and pulled out the vintage sunglasses that Felina had given me last (this?) summer, the ones with the pale pink frames, and slipped them on. When I'd left the flat I had intended to take a stroll in The Regent's Wood, but for some reason I'd changed my mind and headed down the high street. I smiled as I passed The Black Violet, its shutters locked and bolted, its interior dark and shadowy. I was looking forward to getting back in there, back to life, back to reality. I wandered aimlessly towards the market.

As I was crossing the bridge over the stagnant canal I spotted two young punk girls heading my way from the opposite side of the bridge. We were on a collision course to meet in the middle. When the girls clocked me they started whispering to each other, and as we came closer one of them smiled at me and began to speak in a northern accent.

"Excuse me, um..." she began nervously, fidgeting with the strap of her handbag. "Do you, er, live around here?"

"I do," I said with what I hoped was a reassuring smile. "Are you lost?'

"Well... No, not really," the braver of the two girls continued while her friend hovered in the background." "We just wondered where there was to, y'know, go... And hang out and stuff? A lot of places are shut, aren't they? We wanted to go to The Black Violet and The Silver Moonbeam and them shops. We don't have them shops where we live. It's shit there. We're just down visiting my sister, she lives down here."

I was filling them in about Hamden Town, relishing my role as punk rock elder, explaining that everything would be pretty much back to normal the next day, when a man's voice called out from behind us.

"Excuse me girls," the voice said in a cockney accent. "I don't suppose you'd let me take your picture, would ya? You look really good, proper trendy, y'know... It's for a newspaper, you'll be famous."

I turned to see a young guy in a cheap grey suit and overcoat holding an expensive-looking camera. The two girls stood either side of me and we struck a pose. I did my best Sid Vicious sneer and stuck two fingers up at the photographer as he clicked away. The photographer thanked us and walked away. I continued talking to the two girls for a while. I told them to go into Soho, it'd probably be a bit more interesting for them than Hamden was right then. They asked me if I wanted to come to Soho with them. I smiled and told them I never left Hamden Town, they laughed, like I was joking. I told them to be careful in Soho, and to pop into The Black Violet the following day. They thanked me and headed off, clearly happy to have had a chat with a genuine resident Hamden Town punk rock piglette.

I grabbed some milk and headed home. I'd gotten a bit cold and I wanted to have a cup of tea in the warm.

I walked into the flat and into the kitchen, dropping my leather onto the back of a chair and tossing my sunglasses onto the table. The Cure was playing on the record player, candles were lit, the flat was warm and cosy. Felina came out of her bedroom dressed in her black silk pyjamas, wrapped her slender arms around me and hugged me from behind while I was filling the kettle. She rested her head on my back and began to softly purr. I drew a deep breath.

"Well... I'm home," I said.

Gloria Sync is an author and full time chaos witch. She resides in the hinterland between Sherwood Forest and the Nine Ladies. She is a distant relative of the last person in England to have been publicly beheaded with an axe. *Swinella* is her first novel.

Dirty Sexy Words was set up by Zak Jane Kier, who runs Dirty Sexy Words mobile book shop, which can also be found online at www.dirtysexywords.com.

For more information on bestiamorphs and Hamden Town visit www.hamdentown.com

Katsith, the second Hamden Town Tale, will be published in 2025.